A Kendall O'Dell Mystery

THE DEVIL'S CRADLE

SYLVIA NOBEL

Nite Owl Books

Phoenix,
Arizona

ADDITIONAL TITLES IN
SYLVIA NOBEL'S AWARD-WINNNG
KENDALL O'DELL MYSTERY SERIES

#1 Deadly Sanctuary
#3 Dark Moon Crossing
#4 Seeds of Vengeance
#5 Forbidden Entry
#6 Benevolent Evil

Also by this author
Chasing Rayna
A Scent of Jasmine

Published by
Nite Owl Books
Phoenix, Arizona

VISIT OUR WEBSITE:
WWW.NITEOWLBOOKS.COM
TO PREVIEW THE FIRST CHAPTER
OF EACH BOOK, UPDATES
ON BOOK SIGNINGS /APPEARANCES
OR NEW RELEASES BY THIS AUTHOR

Acknowledgments

The author wished to acknowledge the invaluable
assistance of the following people:

John Pintek, former Cochise County Sheriff
Scott Lewis, Mining Engineer
Mark Hay, Geohydrologist
Al Hirales, Copper Queen Mine, Bisbee, AZ
John & Dell Gammon, Gleeson, AZ
Harold Perlman, Pharmacist
Gayle Nobel
Kelly Scott-Olson, ATG Productions
Tim Gorey, Geologist
Leisha

Phoenix, Arizona

For information, contact Nite Owl Books
11801 N. Tatum Blvd #143
Phoenix, AZ 85028
602-618-0724
E-mail: beverlyniteowlbooks@gmail.com
www.niteowlbooks.com

ISBN 9780966110586

Cover Design by
Christy A. Moeller, *ATG Productions, LLC.*
www.atgproductions.com

Library of Congress Control Number: 99-0705536

To

My loving family and supportive friends

&

In Memory of Max

There it was again. That feeling. Gnawing at my insides. Disturbing my train of thought. Hard as I tried, I couldn't shake the growing sense of agitation.

Wedged behind my desk in the small newspaper office, the phone jammed against my ear, I fidgeted in the chair and stared longingly out the smudged window at the cottonwood trees tossing in the sultry August wind that swept across the desert floor every afternoon. In the distance, mountains of hazy purple, crowned with thunderheads taunting the promise of rain, beckoned to me.

Massaging the ache in my neck, I tried to refocus my attention to the matter at hand. The disembodied voice droning on and on at the other end of the line was beginning to tax my patience.

I sighed inwardly. Might as well give the feeling a name. Restlessness. I was restless and bored. And trapped. I wondered, not for the first time, if I hadn't made another one of my colossal blunders of judgement. I seemed to do well in the mistake department.

"Ah hem!" I tuned out the prattling in my ear and glanced at the doorway. Our receptionist, Ginger King, was planted there for the second time since lunch. The look of suppressed excitement on her freckled face, combined with hand gestures that rivaled a navy signalman, left little doubt that she intended to capture my attention this time.

"It's your brother, Patrick, calling from Pittsburgh again," she called in a loud whisper, "and I don't think he's gonna take no for an answer this time."

I cupped my hand over the receiver. "Ask him if I can call him back. Markham Bainbridge is on the line and he's mad as a wet hen." I paused. "Make that a rooster."

She grinned at my little joke, but remained firm. "You can't. He's fixin' to catch a plane right shortly and says he's got something real important to tell ya."

My heart jolted. Uh oh. The rush of anxiety must have shown on my face because she took a quick step forward. "Now, dumplin', don't wet your drawers or nothin'," she soothed. "Your family's all hunky-dory, but he told me he's got a heap o' news that'll make your day and then some."

My innate curiosity got the best of me. I pressed my hand tighter on the mouthpiece. "Tell him to hang on."

She flashed a hundred-watt grin and gave me an enthusiastic thumbs-up before turning to leave.

Laughter gathered in my throat. Ginger was such a delight. Quirky. Bubbly. Always upbeat. What would I do without her?

"Miss O'Dell, are you listening to me?" Mr. Bainbridge's testy voice crackled in my ear.

"Ahhh, yes, yes, I heard you," I fibbed, straining to remember what he'd said last. "We're extremely sorry for the misstatement attributed to you and there will be a retraction in Saturday's paper."

"Page one?" he goaded.

"Page one. And sorry again for the mix up." Before he could utter another syllable, I punched the blinking button. "Patrick? This had better be good."

"Keep your shirt on, Sis," he chuckled. "How's it going? You settling into your new duties okay?"

"I guess. Being an editor is certainly no picnic. No wait, it's a headache and a half."

His laugh was sympathetic. "You sound just like Dad. He always said reporting in the field was a lot more fun than pushing papers and dealing with all the other crap. But listen, I've come across a story you may find interesting," he announced, a reflective note entering his voice. "You in the market for a scoop?"

"Are you kidding?" I swiped the list of problem calls away and grabbed my notepad. In the background, I could hear the din of airport noise as I waited for him to begin.

"I'll make this short and sweet, because we're boarding pretty soon. Okay, here's what I know. Margie's second cousin has a girlfriend at her college and her name is..." He paused as if he were reading something. "Angela. Yeah, Angela Martin. Anyway, this girl's mother passed away last March and she's been living kind of hand-to-mouth working nights and going to school and then, whammo, out of the blue she gets this really weird letter last week from some doctor she's never heard of from out there in Arizona."

I tightened the grip on my pen. "Explain really weird."

"You're gonna love this," he said, raising his voice over the clamor. "The guy claims he knew her mother, Rita, a long time ago and that Angela isn't really Angela."

"You lost me."

"This doctor—Orcutt's his name—claims her mom gave her a fake identity."

"Interesting. Why?"

"Angela says she doesn't have a clue, and she's also been under the impression her father died when she was a little kid. Well, guess what? He actually just passed away a couple of weeks ago and here's the corker. She's the sole heiress to some old mining town out there."

"A town?"

"Yeah. A whole town."

"Well, that might be no big deal. There are a lot of played-out mines in this state. Are you talking about a ghost town?"

"No, no. The doctor lives there and apparently mining engineers have discovered a huge new vein of gold. Angela could end up being a very rich young woman."

"Now this is starting to get good. Tell me more." I scribbled furiously as he fed me additional information.

When he was finished, I blew out a low whistle. "Pat, this is great stuff. But, why are you torturing me with this gem? I can't do it justice from here. The story ought to be covered by someone there in Pittsburgh."

"But, Kendall, the girl is coming out your way."

"Here? To Arizona?"

"Yeah, silly. Why do you think I called you?"

A spark of anticipation warmed me. "Well, why didn't you say so? When?"

"The beginning of next week, I think."

"That soon?" My mind began to work feverishly.

"Yeah. Margie's helping her book a flight into Tucson."

"Why Tucson?"

"She's supposed to see her mother's lawyer there. Angela said Dr. Orcutt was going to phone her later this week with more details. Oh, listen, Margie told her you'd arrange to have someone meet her at the airport and kind of show her the ropes. Was that okay?"

That was so like my sister-in-law to forge ahead without bothering to check with the parties involved. "Not really. Tucson is a four-hour drive from here and I'm pretty short-handed right now...but I'll tell you what, if you fly her into Phoenix, I'll do my best to meet her plane. After that, I don't know. Is she renting a car?"

"Oops. I forgot to tell you something important. This girl is an epileptic so, she's not allowed to drive. Listen, Sis," he said in a distracted tone. "I have to go now."

"Wait, wait, wait. Just one more thing. Is this girl in agreement? I mean, before I go out on a limb, how do I know she'll consent to let me write this story?"

"You don't. I'm just passing along the information Margie gave me," he said cheerfully. "I guess it will be up to you to convince her."

"You're such a dear," I replied dryly. "How long will she be staying?"

"Don't know that either. I'll call you Sunday when I get back from Atlanta."

By the time I'd thanked him and cradled the phone, my spirits were going through the roof. For the first time in weeks my doldrums completely vanished.

Re-reading the notes, my thoughts leapfrogged over each other until the barest glimmer of an idea began to form. It was illogical. It was unrealistic. But as the concept grew in scope, so did the list of obstacles confronting me.

I jumped up and paced the cluttered room, lamenting my decision to take the reins as editor of the *Castle Valley Sun.* It had seemed like a great idea seven weeks ago, but the naked truth was, it wasn't fun. And every fiber of my being screamed out for me to get back to what I liked best—investigative reporting. I loved it, I needed it and I could feel clear down to my bone marrow that this was going to be one hell of a good story. The solution was simple enough, I thought, slumping behind the desk once more. All I had to do was find someone to take my place in six days.

The cracked-vinyl chair gave a protesting squeak when I swung around to stare dejectedly out the window as if somehow I expected to find the answer to my dilemma amid the shimmering heat waves rising from the asphalt parking lot.

"Flapdoodle," I complained aloud, borrowing Ginger's favorite phrase. "Double flapdoodle!"

"Double Flapdoodle?" inquired a voice behind me. "Now that sounds mighty serious."

Startled, I looked around to see Tally slouching in the doorway. Before I could answer, he strode in, his boots clicking smartly against the bare concrete floor still awaiting new carpet. He turned the wooden chair in front of my desk around and straddled it. As always, his nearness made my pulse rate pick up considerably.

"You look like you're carrying the weight of the world on those pretty shoulders. What's up, boss?" He laid his hand out and I slid mine into it.

"Oh...this and that. And quit calling me boss," I chided with mock severity.

He grinned and pushed his Stetson away from his forehead. "Anything I can do?"

For a moment, I said nothing, just rejoiced in the feel of his fingers closing around my own and the look of genuine affection emanating from his dark eyes.

I'd fallen in love with this quiet, easy-going man the first time I'd laid eyes on him. He'd demonstrated admirably that his feelings were mutual, but even so, we'd come to the conclusion independently that since we'd only known each other barely three months, and each had less-than-successful marriages behind us, it would be unwise to rush things even though Ginger was already working up a list of caterers and busily compiling a guest file.

"Come on, Kendall," he persisted, giving my hand a gentle squeeze. "I can tell something's bugging you."

I sighed deeply. "Oh, Tally, I've got myself boxed into a corner and I don't know how to get myself out."

Traces of a smile brushed his mouth. "Now why do I find that hard to believe?"

I knew he was teasing, but his breeziness exacerbated my already souring mood. I pulled my hand away. "Easy for you to say. You're not stuck in this...this dull, gray jail cell ten hours a day," I retorted, gesturing impatiently at the pictureless, posterless walls, bared in preparation for painters who'd yet to make an appearance.

"Well now," he said, tipping his hat back far enough to reveal a few dark curls, "correct me if I'm wrong, but I could have sworn I heard you say something about looking forward to a nice, cozy desk job. Something...mmmmm...a bit more sedate than your last assignment. Something about having a job description that didn't include the words..." he paused, looking pensive, then raised one hand to stretch invisible words in the air, "possible life-threatening situations may be included..."

I made a face at him. "Okay. Okay. So I was

wrong. Sitting around here is giving me a colossal case of cabin fever." I smacked my palm on the desk for emphasis and Tally just grinned at me, seemingly unaffected by my theatrics.

"This doesn't have anything to do with the phone call from your brother, does it?" he asked quietly.

I stared at him. "How did you know about that?" His bland expression and small shrug said it all. "Oh. Ginger, of course. What was I thinking?" As much as I adored my fun-loving friend, her insatiable penchant for gossip drove me to distraction.

"So," he continued, "I'll consider that a yes and ask you again, what's wrong?"

I pointed to my notes. "I'm bursting to follow up on this." As I excitedly reiterated Patrick's story, he seemed only mildly attentive and when I'd finished he said, "Well, it sounds kind of interesting, but nothing to get all riled up about."

"*Kind* of interesting?" I leaped to my feet once again. "Don't you see what an incredible human interest story this is? Think about it. Here's a young woman who has spent her whole life believing she's someone else. Why did her mother lie to her? Why was she never told that her father was alive all this time? Up until she received notice a few weeks ago, that is," I added, my mind creating wondrous possibilities as I paced from one end of the room to another. Suddenly, I pulled up short. "Where is this place, Morgan's Folly?"

Tally rubbed his chin, frowning in thought. "I think it's down near Bisbee. Not far from the Mexican border." He looked around the room. "Tugg used to keep a topographical map in here. Where is it?"

I crossed the room and rummaged around behind

one of the scarred bookcases piled high with past issues of the *Sun*. "Here it is," I said at length, pulling it out along with a half dozen enormous dust bunnies.

Tally blew off the layer of grime and laid the map flat on the desk. "Morgan's Folly," he said, tapping the paper with his forefinger. "And now that you mention it, I remember reading something about it last spring, right around the time you started here." He stared into space a few seconds, looking hopeful, then blank. "Sorry," he said, shaking his head. "I can't think of what it was right now, but it'll come to me."

"It doesn't matter anyway," I said with a disheartened sigh. "There's no way I can get away to do this story. Even entertaining the possibility is an exercise in futility."

"Why?"

I fixed him with a look of incredulity. "Who's going to take my place? Jim? He's the only full time reporter we've got until I can fill the vacancy. And so far, I haven't had much luck. Even with the new capital, the new equipment coming and," I brandished my hand about, "this old place finally getting a facelift, applicants haven't been exactly stampeding in the door."

"I thought we had an ad running in the Phoenix paper."

"We do, but only a handful of people have even called. All I can figure is that experienced reporters don't want to work for some dinky tabloid that only publishes twice a week. And let's face it, Castle Valley isn't exactly a Mecca of hot breaking news topics."

He edged me a wry grin. "Oh, I think you've already proven that theory wrong."

Remembering the excitement and danger of my first,

and what proved to be my last really compelling assignment, gave me a momentary rush. "It was pretty exciting, huh?" I glanced at the cast still encasing his injured arm and then we exchanged a solemn look as the memory of that stormy day in June hung between us.

"Come here," he growled, drawing me close to his lean body. Snuggling happily against his soft cotton shirt, I wrapped my arms around his waist. My lips found his automatically and for a few minutes the irritations of the day faded into insignificance.

"Mmmmm," I murmured, nuzzling his neck, breathing in the masculine, outdoorsy scent of him. "Why don't you come over to the house tonight for dinner and then we can watch the moonrise over Castle Rock."

"Best invitation I've had all day," he replied huskily, dipping his head to extract another kiss from me, his hands gently massaging my back and neck. When we finally drew apart, his sensuous lips broke into that crooked grin I loved so much. "Feel better?"

"Yeah. I guess."

My half-hearted response snuffed out the fiery glow in his eyes. He dropped his arms to his side. "So, what are you saying? That nothing is going to make you happy unless you and only you get to follow up on this story?"

He was right. Perhaps I was overreacting, but the yearning inside me was so strong, it was almost a physical pain. I looked away. "There's no point in discussing it further. We don't have enough support staff, so there's not a chance in hell I could do it anyway. And that's that." I knew I sounded like a petulant child, but I couldn't seem to stop myself.

He grasped my shoulders hard. "You're about as subtle as a loaded freight train. Listen, you know I'd help you out if I could, but if you'll recall, *you* assigned me to cover the Cardinal's training camp in Flagstaff next week. And after that, you know I was planning to go down to San Pedro and buy that stallion I told you about."

"Thanks for depressing me further." At the look of displeasure clouding his face, I regretted my words instantly. When? When would I ever learn to keep my big mouth shut?

He gave me a long, level stare. Unlike me, he seemed to be mentally counting to ten before speaking. "What's wrong with giving Morton Tuggs a call? He and Mary got home from their cruise last week."

I shot him a look of disbelief, remembering Tugg's final words before he'd left. 'Can't do it anymore, Kendall,' he'd said to me. 'The damn job's too short on fun and too long on stress.' "Tugg? What makes you think he'd be willing to sub for me?"

"How long will it take you to get the story?"

"I'm not sure. A week, maybe. And who knows, this girl may not want a nosy reporter delving into her private family history."

"Call him."

"Even if he did agree, I'd never get past Mary," I reminded him ungraciously.

Tally tossed me one of his inscrutable looks and strode towards the door, calling back over his shoulder "Your mulishness will always be one of your most endearing qualities."

I watched him walk away feeling more than a little remorse. Well, that was priceless. Not only had I ruined the romantic moment, I'd solved nothing. If we were still on for this evening, I'd make it a point to make my apology memorable for him.

My despondent mood worsened when Harry announced that the old press we'd been nursing along until the new one arrived had stopped dead in the middle of the print run. Then, Jim called in to say his car had broken down so he couldn't get to the council meeting and Lupe went home sick.

Sure, I thought glumly, Tugg would be champing at the bit to come back to all these problems. The dream of getting the story wilted and died.

It was closing in on seven o'clock before I wearily shouldered my purse and headed for the front door. I had my hand on the knob when an unseen force seemed to grab hold of me. I stood perfectly still for a minute and then as if in a trance, I retraced my steps to the reception desk and picked up the phone. My mouth was powder dry when the female voice answered. "Mary?" I managed to croak. "This is Kendall O'Dell. Would Tugg happen to be around?"

People never ceased to amaze me, I decided as I sat sipping a glass of fragrant sun tea in Mary's tidy kitchen the following afternoon while waiting for Tugg. Having come there fully cognizant of the woman's propensity for zealously safeguarding her husband's health and welfare, combined with her notorious reputation for pretty much directing every aspect of the man's life, I expected her to take after me with a broom when I tentatively floated the idea of Tugg temporarily re-assuming his duties as editor. Instead, she dropped her dishcloth and rushed at me, mouth agape, eyes bulging, and crushed me to her generous bosom in a breath-robbing embrace.

"You're an absolute lifesaver," she squealed before abruptly lowering her voice to a fierce whisper. "He's driving me crazy. Stomach ulcers or no, if he doesn't get busy on something soon and get out of this house for a while..." she paused before concluding ominously, "there may be bloodshed."

Underneath her bravado, I knew what she meant.

Tugg, a big bear of a man, crusty and likable, fit perfectly into the category of workaholic. Life as an invalid would never suit him and I had the feeling he'd rather die with his boots on.

Appearing tanned and rested, Tugg greeted me with enthusiasm and then, with a flushed and anxious Mary urging him on, he readily agreed to my request. Would he be able to fill in for a minimum of one week, possibly two? Absolutely, they both chimed in at once and as I drove away their beaming faces mirrored relief and gratitude.

Elated, I finished out the rest of the week, packed my bags and headed for Sky Harbor Airport in Phoenix by seven o'clock Monday morning. As Castle Valley receded behind me, I had to admit to myself that as much as I'd grown to love this dusty little town, it had become my prison. One I'd created for myself albeit, but a prison nonetheless.

My only regret was leaving Tally. Last night, he'd been particularly attentive and again this morning, after likening me to a falcon being freed, he had reluctantly sent me on my way. I could still taste the remains of his urgent, deliciously prolonged kiss that had left my ears ringing and a heat rushing through my veins that rivaled the air temperature.

A master at hiding his true emotions, Tally had worn an expression of tolerant benevolence as he settled me behind the wheel of my car. But when I looked up at him after starting the engine, a wary glint had entered his eyes.

"Think you can stay out of trouble this time?"

I flashed him an impish grin. "Now what fun would that be?"

"I mean it, Kendall."

Hoping to allay his fears, I'd reminded him again

that this assignment bore no resemblance to my previous one. This one was safe. Purely a human interest story. What possible danger could there be?

Content with my decision, I watched the cactus and rock-strewn landscape gradually give way to the vast expanse of asphalt and concrete that transformed Phoenix into a sizzling griddle each summer. I joined the mass of humanity choking the freeway system and crawled my way to the airport.

It was much later than I'd planned by the time I reached the garage and began the quest for an empty space. After circling endlessly, I was fuming aloud as I sped toward the outdoor parking on the roof.

As I searched anew, my mind replayed yesterday's phone call from Patrick. After giving me the flight number and a brief description of the girl, my sister-in-law, Margie, picked up the extension and filled in some more blanks.

According to her, Angela was still in a complete state of shock over the strange turn of events and even more mystified following Dr. Orcutt's telephone call on Friday informing her that the attorney in Tucson was holding a confidential letter from her mother. He'd told her it was vitally important that she read it before coming to Morgan's Folly.

"Angela had other questions but he refused to answer them on the phone," Margie continued in a gossipy tone. "Don't you think that's odd? None of us can figure out why the man is being so secretive about everything. I'm wondering now if we advised her correctly. We might be sending her out there on some wild goose chase."

My anxious heart thumped harder. "You're sure she's really going through with this?"

"Unless she changes her mind at the last minute,

that's the plan," Patrick broke in. "The poor kid's never flown before and she's scared half to death about that, too."

That floored me. I didn't know anyone who hadn't been on a plane at least once and decided that this young woman must lead a very sheltered life.

I told them that I'd decided to handle the story personally and to tell Angela or whatever her name was, I'd be available to drive her to Tucson, Morgan's Folly, or anywhere else she needed to go.

"Do me a favor, would you?" Margie added. "Go easy on her, Kendall. Emotionally, she's pretty fragile."

"Well, I was planning to shut her in a small room with a really bright light and grill her with questions." When I was met with complete silence, I added hastily, "Just kidding, Margie."

"Oh, good," continued my humorless sister-in-law. "She's a darling girl, but kind of...different."

"Don't worry," I'd replied before hanging up, "I'll be gentle."

So now, as I parked the car and hurried across the scalding pavement to the elevator, I hoped I'd be able to put this girl at ease enough to confide in me. Uptight people were generally pretty close-mouthed.

Inside the terminal, I checked flight information on the monitors. Crap. Angela's plane had landed fifteen minutes earlier. It seemed to take hours to get through the congested security area and I was glad that I'd opted for sneakers as I broke into a lope. Dodging the ebb and flow of two-way foot traffic, I finally decided that my attempt to hurry was as useless as trying to swim in a riptide. And, as fate would have it, her flight was at the very furthest gate.

The crowd thinned as I reached the far end of the terminal and I picked up my pace again, thinking that perhaps Margie was right. Anxious as I was to learn Angela's story, I'd best not come on like gangbusters if this girl proved to be as shy and withdrawn as she'd been described.

Short of breath, I pounded down the carpeted hallway, which had suddenly become as noiseless as a hotel corridor on a Christmas morning. I rounded the corner to the waiting area only to feel my heart sink into my shoes. Rows of empty plastic chairs gaped back at me.

I turned in a slow circle, peering in all directions, examining each person who happened by. No one matched the picture I'd formed in my mind of a frail, young woman with dark hair. Where could she have gone so quickly? I wasn't *that* late.

Shading my eyes, I squinted through the massive panes of glass out onto the shimmering tarmac where a giant blue and gold jet sat parked. People on carts scurried back and forth while maintenance crews swarmed around the aircraft, prepping for the next flight.

I cursed my fate. This was hardly the best way to begin what might prove to be a tenuous relationship at best with the young stranger. And since I'd already failed the simple test of showing up on time to meet her flight, she just might tell me to take a flying leap and give the story to someone else. And who could blame her?

Mentally kicking myself, I turned to retrace my steps. She must have gone to baggage claim. Where else could she possibly be?

"Oh, miss? Wait a minute!"

I swiveled around to see a blonde woman clad in a blue and gold flight attendant's uniform, running towards me. "Are you Kendall O'Dell?" she gasped, closing the gap between us.

"Yes, but..."

She assessed the obvious question in my eyes and waved a small piece of paper in the air. "It says here to look for a tall redhead wearing a green T-shirt, so I guessed that had to be you."

A small knot of consternation formed in my stomach. "Where did you get that?"

"One of our passengers had some kind of a seizure. We found this note in her hand. Can you come with me?"

"Of course." I fell into step with her. "Where is she?"

"Still on the plane. Her medic-alert bracelet identifies her as epileptic. Do you have any experience with this sort of thing."

"I'm afraid not." I followed her up the jet-way wondering what I was getting into. It was ironic that I'd gone to the trouble of picking up two books before leaving Castle Valley. One detailed the history of mining in southern Arizona, and I'd read most of that. The second was a book on epilepsy and unfortunately, it was now residing unread at the bottom of my suitcase. All I could remember from various magazine articles was that seizures were usually categorized as either grand mal or petit mal. The latter would be preferable, I thought grimly.

A tall gray-haired man who appeared to be the pilot and several other flight attendants looked around expectantly as we approached the rear of the airliner. Their collective expressions conveyed a mixture of concern and relief. I hoped I appeared more confident than I felt as the small crowd parted to reveal a young woman with short-cropped brown hair slumped in the aisle seat.

Recalling Patrick's description, there was little doubt in my mind that this was Angela Martin. As I knelt next to her, noting her pale, almost translucent complexion, I wished I'd taken the time to read the book.

"We've sent for the paramedics," announced the pilot, "and we'll be boarding passengers as soon as we refuel." He sounded impatient.

As if she'd heard him, the girl stirred slightly and I noticed an almost imperceptible flicker of her eyelids. Seconds later I was staring into glassy brown eyes. "Angela?" I began in a gentle tone, "I'm Kendall O'Dell. Are you all right? Is there anything we should do?"

She appeared disoriented and slightly fearful as her gaze roamed over the sea of faces bending towards her. She swallowed hard and self-consciously wiped the thin stream of saliva seeping from one corner of her mouth. "No, no," she said faintly, sitting up straight and taking a few deep breaths. "I'm...I'm fine now. I'm terribly sorry for inconveniencing..."

"That's quite all right, dear," said one of the flight attendants, patting her gently on one shoulder. "We're just glad you're...awake."

"Would you like a drink of water or something?" I asked.

"Yes, thank you."

I made eye contact with the woman who'd chased me down and she gave me a quick nod before heading to the plane's galley.

Satisfied that the crisis was over, the pilot hurried to cancel the paramedics and the group began to disperse. At Angela's direction, I located her carry-on luggage a few rows forward and after she'd drunk the water and thanked the attendants once more, we made our way into the terminal.

Judging by the pinched expression on her face, and

sensing it was important that I not dwell on what had happened to her on the plane, I bit back the questions I was dying to ask.

While we threaded our way through the burgeoning crowd, she appeared confused, dazed, spacey even, like a small child lost at an amusement park. Patrick had mentioned that she was eight years my junior, but even at twenty she somehow struck me as much younger.

Even though we'd been delayed at least a half an hour, apparently so had the luggage. People were three rows deep at the baggage claim by the time we arrived and the air rumbled with a vociferous chorus of complaints.

Another ten minutes passed before it was announced that the problem had finally been repaired and a cheer erupted as the first bag tumbled down the metal chute.

"It's about time," I sighed, turning to Angela. "You'd think that they'd..." My voice trailed off when I noticed her strange expression. Goggle-eyed, she stared as various pieces of luggage slid down and began their journey around the carousel. When the same bags began to pass for the fourth time, I broke the silence between us.

"What exactly are we looking for?"

She turned puzzled eyes on me. "What?"

"What do your suitcases look like?"

"Oh. They're light blue with red trim." Her obvious chagrin triggered the faintest flush to appear on her high cheekbones. The small dots of color made the rest of her skin look ghostly white, bluish almost. Was she going to have another seizure?

I pointed to the benches beneath the windows near the exit. "Why don't you go sit down over there. I'll get your things."

"I'm sorry," she mumbled, pressing a hand to her

forehead. "It's just that I was so nervous about flying and I'm kind of... fuzzy after I have one of my...spells."

"No problem." I wished she'd stop apologizing for something she obviously had no control over. After snagging her two bags from the carousel, I motioned towards the door. Being a relative newcomer myself, I sympathized with her reaction of pure shock when the suffocating wall of heat slammed into us.

She stopped dead in her tracks. "It feels like a thousand degrees out here! How do you stand it?"

"With great difficulty. I've been burning up since I got here last April but it's much worse now because of the high humidity. Welcome to Arizona's rainy season which is called the monsoon."

"I can hardly breathe."

I punched the elevator button. "Don't worry, it's supposed to be a little cooler where we're headed."

"I hope so."

By the time we reached my car, her steps were faltering and her beet-red face glistened with perspiration. As I loaded the luggage into the trunk, I said with a smile, "People who've been here awhile keep assuring me that eventually one does get accustomed to this."

She cast me a look of sincere doubt when I opened the passenger door and a blast of hot air poured out. "Sorry about that," I said with an apologetic shrug. "I couldn't find a space inside the garage."

Gunning the engine, I dialed the air-conditioner to high and headed for the freeway that would take us south to Tucson. "Do you have the address of the attorney you're supposed to see?" I asked, glancing in her direction. "What time are you expected?"

She fumbled in her purse. "I told his secretary what

time I'd get in and she said anytime after one was okay."

I glanced at the clock. It was a two hour drive and if we added another hour for lunch that would be just about right. "All right. Just sit back, relax and enjoy the scenery."

She gave me a faint nod, leaned her head back and closed her eyes.

It seemed to take forever to get beyond the sprawling suburbs and strip shopping centers but, as the Phoenix skyline diminished behind us and we cruised into the open desert once more, a heady feeling of freedom gripped me. I was looking forward with great relish to visiting a portion of this fascinating state I'd never seen before, not to mention the anticipation of tackling the new assignment.

We'd passed several towns with interesting names like Sacaton and Casa Grande before I heard her stirring beside me. "Miss O'Dell?"

"Please call me Kendall."

"Okay. Um...thank you for...everything. I haven't had an attack like that for a long time. Stress can cause them and with everything that's happened..."

"I understand."

She grew silent again but I knew something was wrong because of the way she was gnawing at her fingernails. "Please don't think I'm being ungrateful," she suddenly blurted out, "but I'm having a real hard time dealing with all this and to be honest, I don't know how long, or even if I'm going to stay here at all. But, if I do," she added, a note of conviction entering her voice, "I'm not sure I want anything printed in your newspaper."

My heart skipped and I slid a glance at her. The thought of losing this juicy story before I even got it was simply unacceptable. Patrick said it was up to me to convince her, so I'd better get cracking.

"I know how you feel," I began, choosing my words with care. "Sharing private family matters can be difficult so we'll just play everything by ear for starters. Later on, if you decide to allow me an exclusive on this, I give you my word that nothing will be printed without your say so. Plus that, I may be able to help you over some rough spots if you'll let me."

She said nothing, but appeared to be thinking it over. I charged ahead. "Look, maybe you'd feel more comfortable if you knew a little more about me. What did Margie tell you?"

"Just that you're divorced, you moved here from Philadelphia last spring because of asthma and that you're a reporter."

I rolled my eyes. Leave it to Margie to come up with such a brief, insipid biography. "Well, I like to think I have just a bit more depth than that."

"She also said if you got too pushy and pried too much, I was to send you packing."

The flare of irritation heated my face. My sister-in-law was a real prize. "I prefer to think of it as perseverance. It's true that I've been accused of being hotheaded at times, and true that patience sometimes eludes me, but I have a good sense of humor, I bathe regularly and," I said, tossing her an impish grin, "I'm a very good listener."

Dividing my attention between her and the road, I felt a surge of elation when I was rewarded with the faintest flicker of a smile. "What did Margie and Patrick tell you about me?"

I repeated the information my brother had given me. "He also told me you actually talked to Dr. Orcutt and that he wasn't very forthcoming with you."

"That's for sure. When I first got his letter, I thought it was some kind of a sick joke. And then, when he called, well...he sounded like maybe he was uncomfortable talking to me."

"What did he tell you?"

"First, I asked him why I should believe any of it and then I got this creepy chill when he started telling me personal stuff about my mother."

"What kind of stuff?"

"He described what she looked like. He told me her maiden name and he knew the exact day that she died. Things like that. But the really weird part was that he knew all about me. I mean, here's this stranger on the phone calling me from someplace I never even knew existed and telling me I now own it. It still doesn't seem real. But the hardest part..." she faltered, swallowing hard, "is finding out that my mother *lied* to me all these years. Why would she do that?"

I glanced at her stricken face, but decided not to speculate until I had more facts. "Perhaps the letter will help explain things."

"I hope so. Right now, I feel like my whole life has been one huge question mark."

"What do you mean?"

"A thousand things. Like...why we moved around so often, or why our phone number was always unlisted, or why we got our mail at a Post Office box? I always felt like we were on the run from something. You know, like we were in the Witness Protection Program, or something. I used to imagine all kinds of crazy stuff."

"Did you ever ask about your father?"

"Sure. Lots of times. But she never wanted to talk about the past. And whenever I'd bring him up, she'd get this weird look on her face. Then she'd get real moody and sad. Sometimes, I'd find her sitting alone crying, and then I'd feel awful. So," she said, exhaling a deep sigh, "after a while, I just quit asking. But, she did other strange things too."

"Like what?"

"I don't know, tons of things now that I think about it. You know, I didn't even know my illness was called epilepsy until after she died!"

"You're kidding."

"No. She acted like...I don't know, like she was ashamed of it or something. She told me it was just fainting spells and to never, ever talk about it with anyone."

"Didn't she take you to a doctor?"

"Oh, sure, I had a bunch of brain tests. EEG's they're called, and I take medicine, but the doctor didn't give it a name either. It was just 'my condition' and," her voice held a touch of resentment when she added, "I thought I had some horrible disease, like leprosy."

I frowned in disbelief. "That seems rather cruel."

"I guess, in a way, but then my mom fussed over me a lot of the time too. I always thought she was just being overprotective, but now...I don't know."

I edged another look at her. She seemed to be ruminating more to herself than confessing to me. But I was glad that she now felt confident enough to confide in me, so I offered no further opinion.

For a while then we rode in silence, both occupied with our private thoughts until I heard her murmur, "The landscape here seems strange. Dry and lonesome looking."

She was squinting across a particularly barren stretch of sparsely foliated sand toward a row of jagged mountains on the horizon which, according to the map I'd studied earlier, were aptly named the Sawtooth Range.

I knew what she meant, I thought, adjusting my sunglasses against the glare. Having also grown up among dense green forests and friendly rolling hills, my first impression of Arizona had struck me as a forbidding composite of cactus and rock and sunlight so harsh, at times it seemed to burn the color from the sky.

"I know you said it's the rainy season, but it sure doesn't look like it ever rains," she remarked, watching a dust devil spiral past. I couldn't help smiling to myself. I'd uttered those exact words myself less than four months ago.

"By the way," she said, yawning, "Dr. Orcutt's nurse called late last night to give me a message from him. He suggested that after my meeting in Tucson, it would be much easier if we take the shortcut. She told me we'll save about an hour's driving time and can probably be there by dinner time."

"I wasn't aware there was a shortcut."

She rummaged around in her purse again and extracted a scrap of paper. "We're supposed to take the old road. State route 181."

"I wonder why Dr. Orcutt didn't call and tell you this himself?"

"Who knows? Maybe he was busy delivering a baby or something."

"Okay, I'll check the map when we stop for gas."

We cruised past an eye-catching rock formation called Picacho Peak and reached Tucson before noon. The downtown district appeared to be much smaller than Phoenix, boasting an assortment of mid-size office buildings and only a few high-rises. One in particular stood tall against the desert terrain like a gleaming block of blue ice. Once we pulled off the freeway onto the side streets, the graceful pueblo-style homes showed off the distinct Spanish influence. I was impressed with the clear, smog-free air and stunning beauty of the Santa Catalina and Santa Rita Mountains, which rose majestically in the distance. We had lunch and gassed up the car before driving to the address Angela read to me. When I pulled into the parking area of the coral adobe-walled office building, she seemed visibly nervous as she actively chewed on one thumbnail.

Once inside, I accompanied her along a plant-studded hallway until we reached a door that read: Clarence Hutton Attorney-at-Law.

"I need to check in with my office," I said, tapping my watch. "But I'll go in if you like."

She seemed to be weighing my offer then all at once she squared her jaw. "That's okay, Kendall. I think I need to do this alone."

Bravo! I cheered to myself. Underneath her timorous demeanor ran a semblance of backbone. "Okay. I'm going to find a phone then I'll wait for you over there." I gestured towards two armchairs flanking the elevator.

Back in the lobby, I waited a few minutes for an elderly woman to finish her conversation, then punched in all the necessary numbers from my calling card. After a few rings I heard Ginger's cheery voice. "Castle Valley Sun."

I chatted with her a few minutes and then asked to speak to Tugg. "Sure thing, sugar pie, but before I connect you, I thought you'd like to know that Tally's already pining away for you."

"What makes you say that?"

"Because he told me to be sure 'n tell him the very second you called 'cuz he needs to yak at you a spell."

I laughed at her colorful Texas dialect and told her I'd be tickled pink. A thrill of delight raced through me just knowing I'd get to speak to him one more time today.

After answering several office-related questions for Tugg, I felt more and more positive that I'd made the right decision. Judging from the lilt in his voice, he sounded happy to be ensconced in the spot I'd just liberated myself from. With a promise to phone him tomorrow, we said our good-byes and he transferred me to Tally's extension.

"Hey there," came his pleasant baritone over the line. "How's it going?"

"Okay so far. We're still in Tucson and I don't have much to report yet. So, what's up? You miss me?"

"Yeah, I miss you," he replied gruffly, "but that's not why I wanted to talk to you."

I tried my best to sound coquettish. "And here I was hoping that it was."

"You remember that article on Morgan's Folly I was telling you about?"

"Yeah."

"Well, I found it."

Did I detect a somber edge to his words? "And?"

"How about I read it to you."

"Okay."

For a few seconds there was nothing but the sound of paper crinkling in my ear before he said, "Here goes. Thursday night, May 3rd, sixty-four year old Grady Morgan, owner and operator of the once-prosperous Morgan Mining Company, sustained serious head injuries resulting from a fall from the second story balcony of his home. The examining physician called to the scene confirmed that alcohol could have been a factor.

Mr. Morgan was rushed by ambulance to the hospital in Bisbee twenty miles away and from there was flown to St. Joseph's Hospital in Phoenix where he is listed in critical condition.

Morgan's housekeeper, Marta Nuñez, claimed that she heard shouts and witnessed what appeared to be the figure of a woman fleeing the scene. Deputy Sheriff Clark Brewster stated, "As a result of initial investigations by sheriff's detectives, there is no evidence at this time to indicate that Mr. Morgan's fall was anything other than accidental."

As I stood there silently digesting all the data, his voice turned ominous. "I think the operative words are 'at this time,' don't you?"

The same three words that apparently disturbed him lit a fire in me. "Sounds intriguing."

"Keeping in mind that Grady Morgan died since this was written, it is possible the focus of the investigation may have changed by now so your cock-sure assessment that this story holds no danger may not be correct after all."

There was no mistaking the uneasiness in his tone, but I was undeterred. "Tally, I can't back out now."

"I'm not suggesting that, Kendall, but I hope you'll be on your guard. I'd like to have every luscious inch of you back in one piece."

I warmed to his obvious concern. "I'll be careful, and you be careful too. As far as I'm concerned, you could be in more danger from Mexican bandits down there than I could ever be."

He chuckled. "Okay, we're even. So long for now, beautiful boss lady."

Was I lucky or what? "Bye yourself, handsome cowboy."

I sighed happily and was poised to hang up when I heard Ginger in the background demanding to speak to me.

"Hey, girlfriend," she said, coming on the line again.

"Y'all been listening to the radio?"

"No. Why?"

"There's one humdinger of a storm blowing in. The weatherman says it's the tail end of one of them big `ol tropical storms so you better watch your butt."

I turned to the wide picture window. Sure enough, massive clouds with billowing cauliflower tops pushed skyward over the southeastern horizon like great white cathedrals. It looked like the normal afternoon buildup of clouds, but a tiny shudder of apprehension raced through me. "Thanks, Ginger. I'm sure we'll be there long before anything major develops."

I hadn't planned to talk for twenty minutes and hoped Angela hadn't been waiting too long as I retraced my steps towards the lawyer's office. When I didn't see her, I settled into one of the chairs with a magazine, thinking that her meeting must have entailed more than just picking up a letter.

Moments later I heard what sounded like a muffled sob. Mystified, I turned to look behind me, seeing nothing but a few potted plants in a dimly lit corridor leading to an exit. When I heard the sound again, I rose to investigate.

My breath caught when I spied Angela hunched on the floor beside a leafy rubber plant, her knees pulled tightly to her chest, a wad of papers clutched in one hand. She rocked back and forth as silent tears streamed down her face.

Had she suffered another seizure? My initial shock dissolved into concern as I knelt in front of her. "Angela, what's wrong?"

The eyes that met mine were deep, dark pools of misery. "Angela doesn't exist," she whimpered. "She never existed. And neither do I."

At first she was inconsolable, alternating between sobs, bursts of hysterical laughter, and babbling almost incoherently about her father, and her birthday not being in April after all. I finally got her settled down and escorted her into the ladies room. While she was splashing water on her tear-streaked face, I began to read over some of the papers she'd pressed into my hand.

The first bundle contained various personal papers belonging to her mother, a birth certificate, a record of her baptism, and her marriage license. I set them aside and suppressed a gasp of shock as I began to scan Angela's birth certificate. She was right. Her recorded month of birth was October and the year listed would mean she was not twenty, but twenty-one. Before I could finish studying the document, she said in a hushed voice, "Read the letter."

For a few seconds, I stared at her grief-stricken face, then put the birth certificate aside and unfolded the next sheet of paper.

MY DARLING AUDREY,

I CAN CALL YOU THAT AT LONG LAST, FOR YOU KNOW NOW THAT THIS IS YOUR GIVEN NAME. I WILL BE GONE WHEN YOU READ THIS AND I PRAY THAT ONE DAY YOU WILL BE ABLE TO FIND IT IN YOUR HEART TO FORGIVE ME. YOU WILL NEVER KNOW THE AGONY I HAVE SUFFERED WONDERING IF I MADE THE RIGHT DECISION TO RUN AWAY WITH YOU EIGHTEEN YEARS AGO, AND THAT EVERYTHING I HAVE DONE SINCE WAS TO PROTECT YOUR BEST INTERESTS.

I NEVER PLANNED TO TELL YOU ABOUT YOUR FATHER, GRADY MORGAN. HE WAS AN EVIL MAN AND I HAVE ALWAYS FELT THAT YOU WOULD BE BETTER OFF NEVER KNOWING THAT HE EXISTED. BUT THINGS HAVE CHANGED NOW AND I MUST MAKE MY PEACE WITH GOD. BECAUSE OF THAT LONG-AGO DECISION, I HAVE NOTHING OF VALUE TO LEAVE YOU AND IT SEEMS WRONG TO DEPRIVE YOU OF YOUR RIGHTFUL INHERITANCE AND ALL THAT COMES WITH IT.

DR. MILES ORCUTT HAS BEEN A DEAR AND TRUSTED FRIEND. HE WILL GIVE YOU GOOD ADVICE. HE HAS ALWAYS KEPT HIS PROMISES TO ME AND HAS GIVEN ME HIS WORD THAT YOU WILL NOT BE CONTACTED UNTIL YOUR FATHER'S DEATH.

IN CLOSING, IT IS MY FERVENT HOPE THAT YOU WILL UNDERSTAND THAT I LOVE YOU WITH ALL MY HEART, AND THAT MY SOLE PURPOSE WAS TO KEEP US BOTH FROM HARM'S WAY. THERE IS SO MUCH THAT MUST REMAIN UNSAID

AND MY DYING WISH IS FOR YOU TO HAVE A HAPPY LIFE. BUT FOR YOUR OWN PEACE OF MIND, REMEMBER, MY DARLING, THAT THE SECRETS OF THE DEAD ARE BEST BURIED WITH THEM.

It was signed your loving mother, RITA BARNES MORGAN, and dated a few months prior to her death.

A multitude of emotions churned inside me when I raised my head to meet Angela's—or Audrey's as I now must think of her—red-rimmed eyes in the bathroom mirror. I tried to fathom how she must feel at this moment. I couldn't.

For lack of anything else, I said, "Do you want to go someplace and have a cup of coffee or something?"

"No," she said shakily, folding her arms across her chest. "I don't want to be out in public again. I've already made a spectacle of myself once today."

Her shoulders slumped in defeat, she presented a truly pathetic picture. But, even in her distraught state, I thought about what an arresting face she had—perfect rosebud-shaped lips, a small slightly upturned nose and the most striking set of eyes I'd ever seen. Cavernous, and chocolate brown in color, they were crowned with a magnificent set of dark, thick brows that presented a stark contrast to her ashen, yet flawless skin.

There seemed little I could say in the way of consolation so, operating entirely on instinct I slipped an arm around her shoulders. There were no appropriate words to cushion the devastating blow she'd just received, so I figured a dose of good old-fashioned comfort was about all I could furnish at the moment.

She managed a brief smile and leaned into me for an instant, eyes closed. I experienced a sudden rush of empathy, feeling as though somehow I'd stepped out of my reporter's role and into that of guardian. "We can talk when you're ready," I offered gently. "Shall we go?"

She nodded, folded the papers into her purse and started towards the door. "I need to take my medicine," she informed me as we stepped into the hallway.

At the water fountain, I watched her fumble with pills and felt a sudden stab of guilt. "Are you sure you want to go through with this?"

She raised solemn eyes to me. "I have to now."

"I'm curious about something," I said to her as we headed outside to the car. "Why did your mother choose to have her affairs handled by a lawyer in Tucson instead of closer to home?"

She shrugged. "Mr. Hutton said he'd known my mother since high school and that she trusted him to keep her secret."

"I'm wondering why Dr. Orcutt contacted you first. Was Mr. Hutton aware of your mother's medical condition?"

Grimacing from the heat, she sank into the passenger seat and fumbled with the seat belt before answering. "He said he had written instructions from her not to release these papers to me until he'd received formal notice of my father's death. Dr. Orcutt sent him a copy of the death certificate along with a note telling him that he planned to contact me."

"I see. It seems your mother was very methodical," I said, maneuvering the car into traffic. "She apparently thought of everything."

Back on the main highway once more, Audrey sat huddled against the passenger door facing the window, her legs tucked beneath her. Her body language clearly conveyed her desire to be left alone, so I kept my own counsel, sensing that one single question directed at her now would only cause her to withdraw further. I sighed inwardly. This was going to be no easy assignment.

The information in the letter from her mother had piqued my curiosity to no end—especially the part about the secrets of the dead being buried with them. Talk about melodramatic. But, that statement combined with the other carefully veiled sentences reaffirmed my belief that this was going to be one hell of a story when we got to the bottom of all the whys and wherefores.

I set the cruise control at seventy-five and let my mind drift. For a time, I raced with a Southern Pacific freight train until it picked up speed and vanished into the spectacular panorama now unfolding before me—endless miles of Sonoran desert dotted with yucca and cholla and dressed out with stately stands of saguaro cactus stretching away into the distance to meld with majestic mountain ranges.

An hour later, feeling recharged with the sheer exhilaration of being on the open road, I swung off the freeway and headed south again. The two-lane highway began a gentle climb that gradually transformed the prickly landscape into golden grasslands blanketed with clumps of mesquite and greasewood.

Rounding the crest of a hill, I felt a mild twinge of uneasiness at the scene ahead. Thunderheads that only hours ago had been snowy plumes, were gathering into an ominous curtain of charcoal gray streaked periodically with jagged forks of lightning.

The clouds seemed to grow blacker with each passing moment and my nervousness increased. I slid a quick look at Audrey. Apparently asleep, her head lolled gently with the rocking motion of the car. No point in worrying her. She'd been through enough turmoil today.

Having personally been at the mercy of a violent summer storm not that long ago, I viewed them with equal parts of fascination and dismay. I switched on the radio, keeping the volume low, and roamed through the channels hoping to catch a weather report. It was obvious we were getting closer to the Mexican border because I had trouble finding a station where the announcer spoke something other than Spanish.

After a time, Audrey stirred, yawned, and said out-of-the-blue, "You've got the prettiest red hair I've ever seen."

"Well, thank you."

"I always wanted to wear mine long and curly like that, but Mom always cut it short." She paused and I could feel her eyes on me. "I'll bet you have a boyfriend, don't you?"

Okay, I thought. She wants to chitchat. Talk about something mundane and safe. Probably anything to avoid the painful topic that had to be tearing her up inside.

"Yep," I answered with a wide smile. "Tally writes the sports section at the newspaper."

"Tally? That's a strange name."

I laughed. "It's a nickname. His name is really Bradley Talverson and he owns and operates the Starfire, which just happens to be one of the biggest cattle ranches in the state."

"Hmmm. So he's rich. And is he also tall, dark and handsome?" Her words had a wistful edge.

"As a matter of fact, he is."

She sat in silence a few seconds and then said, "So, if he's so rich, why is he working at your newspaper?"

"It's a rather long story, but let's just say it takes his mind off the problems of running a ranch. And how about you? Do you have a boyfriend?"

"Once. For about two weeks. Until I had one of my seizures. Then he took off like a scalded dog."

"I'm sorry to hear that."

"It hurt a lot at first, but I'm used to people getting grossed out. One day I asked my friend Robin to tell me what I look like when I'm...you know, and she said it's really kind of awful so I guess I don't blame him. And by the way, promise me you won't tell anyone about my epilepsy."

I tossed her a skeptical look. "That medic alert bracelet is kind of a dead giveaway, wouldn't you say?"

She fingered it thoughtfully for a moment. "It's only to let people know if I happen to have a seizure in public. But I don't just march up and tell people because...well, they treat me funny," she said, her tone ripe with melancholy. "So, please say you won't tell."

A little voice inside warned me that might not be wise, but I reluctantly agreed.

"And listen. If I should happen to have one in front of you, don't panic. I'm not going to die. I'm not going to swallow my tongue. And for heaven's sake, please don't call the fire department like they did once when I was in grade school."

"So...I should do...nothing?"

"Most of the time. Except if I might, you know, crack my head on something sharp. Lately, I've been having them in my sleep, but if I'm awake, I usually have some warning."

"Like how?" I asked, navigating the car against the growing force of the wind. I didn't want to say anything to frighten her, but the darkening sky was worrisome, especially since I was totally unfamiliar with the road situation up ahead.

"That's kind of hard to explain," she went on, nervously twirling the bracelet on her wrist. "Sometimes there's what the doctors call an aura. It's a really weird feeling that just comes over you. It's like...well, you can hear, see and smell when a seizure is coming. When that happens, I have time to sit down or lie down on the floor. But most of the time I get caught by surprise and it's more like being hit over the head with a hammer."

"I see," I answered, not really paying close attention to her as I searched for the landmark that would signal our turn onto the shortcut. The gas station attendant I'd questioned in Tucson had confirmed that it would take us over the Dragoon Mountains, bypassing Tombstone and Bisbee. He'd also said it would clip at least twenty-five miles off our trip and that sounded pretty good to me at that particular moment.

When the late afternoon sun vanished behind a cloud, Audrey finally sat up and took notice. "Well, what do you know," she marveled, gawking out the window. "Looks like we're going to have a shower."

"A shower might be a bit of an understatement, I'm afraid. These summer storms can sometimes pack quite a punch."

"Well, is it safe to keep going? I mean, should we stop?" she asked in a faint voice, nibbling again at her thumbnail.

I tried to sound confident. "I don't think there's anything to worry about. The whole thing could easily blow away without a drop, but the sooner we get to Morgan's Folly the better."

If I hadn't been looking for the burned-out ranch house flanked by a tattered wind mill, I'd have never seen the old road angling off to the left, almost hidden from sight between chest-high weeds and ragged pinions bordering the main highway. I braked and turned sharply, my eyes following the narrow band of asphalt that snaked across a flat valley and disappeared into squat foothills beyond.

We headed east, away from the path of the oncoming storm and I immediately felt better. There were even a few patches of blue sky showing. "By the way," I began, filling the lull in conversation, "did Dr. Orcutt give you any instructions on what we're supposed to do when we arrive?"

"Oh, I forgot to tell you. The last thing he said before hanging up was that I should go directly to his place. He said it was right near the clinic on...I think it was Quarry Street. I have the directions here," she said, scooping up her purse. She pulled out a piece of paper and stared at it, her brows knitted in a pensive frown.

"What is it?" I asked, dividing my attention between her and the road.

"He also said something else that was...well, sort of strange, I thought."

"What?"

"He said it was very important that I not talk to anyone else in town before talking to him. Why do you suppose he'd say that?"

I shook my head. "I don't know. Perhaps he's got information that will help smooth the way for you. Most likely somebody's been running things until now and..." Her sudden giggle surprised me. "What?"

"I was just thinking of my mother. She used to say life is what happens to you while you're making other plans and I sure never planned to be...what?" She hunched her shoulders. "Mayor or something?"

"It will be interesting to find out."

The narrow road didn't look very well traveled, but it was in reasonably good condition as it meandered through odd cone-shaped mounds that changed in color from cinnamon to deep vermilion as cloud shadows passed over them. We'd gone about four or five miles when it suddenly occurred to me that there'd been no other traffic since leaving the main highway. But no sooner had the thought materialized than I noticed a white pick-up pull out of a side road a couple of hundred yards ahead of us and accelerate around the corner.

The road narrowed even further into a series of challenging switchbacks and became more rutted as we wound over mountainous terrain that offered heart-stopping views before plunging into deep canyons. I spotted the white truck ahead of us every now and then, but with that exception, there were no other vehicles.

"We need to stop," Audrey announced suddenly. "I feel sick."

I took my eyes off the road long enough to notice her greenish complexion, then quickly searched for a safe place to pull over. As soon as I stopped, she got out and ran to the side of the road where she fell to her knees and began to retch.

I expelled a weary sigh and shut off the engine. Poor kid. Apparently, the unending switchbacks had made her carsick. Maybe the shortcut hadn't been such a great idea after all. But it seemed foolish to turn back at this point.

I left her alone for a few minutes and studied the map again. The exit to Morgan's Folly was only a mile ahead, but the remaining three would be on a dirt road. That didn't appeal to me one bit. Add bumps to another curving road and she might be sick the rest of the trip, I thought grimly, pushing open the car door. Not to mention the fact that it was getting late and I was beat.

A sudden blast of wind took me by surprise. I looked up and my heart faltered. The sky above looked positively menacing. Uh oh! Our twists and turns had taken us right back into the path of the storm. If it was already raining in the mountains ahead of us...

Thunder rumbled ominously so I hurried over to where Audrey now sat, her forehead resting on her knees. Not wanting to alarm her, I did my best to sound unruffled. "Audrey, are you okay?"

"I think so."

"If you're up to it, we probably ought to get going." I hoped she wouldn't suffer the consequences of losing her medication.

Her eyes were full of wonder when she raised her head. "Audrey," she repeated, in a half-whisper. "Audrey Morgan. It sounds so...weird to hear you call me that. And look at this." She swept her hand in a wide arc. "I was born right here in these mountains. Can you believe it? And my father lived here and died here...and I don't even remember him."

"Did Dr. Orcutt tell you how he died?"

She shook her head. "No. Just that he'd been in the hospital for a long time."

I could tell by her wide-eyed look that she didn't know what I knew about Grady Morgan's questionable death. I wrestled with the idea of sharing the information mentioned in the newspaper article with her, but decided against it. I'd verify it with the sheriff's department first.

Still closed in her own thoughts, Audrey seemed oblivious to the thunder echoing around us and to the moan of the rising wind.

I offered my hand to her. "We've got to go. It's only a few miles further."

The first drops of rain splattered on us and she blinked in puzzlement, seeming to finally notice that we were about to get drenched. "Mmmm. That smells good," she said, allowing me to haul her to her feet. "And it's so much cooler. This is really heaven."

I hated to tell her that it would be anything but that in a few minutes, but I didn't have to. When we reached the crest of the ridge, the gravity of the situation came home to her. "My God," she gasped, staring in horror. "That looks like a tornado!"

The adrenaline rush doubled my heart rate. It may not have been an actual tornado, but the funnel-like cloud descending from the inky sky looked menacing enough to make me grip the wheel and say a silent prayer as hail began to clatter against the windshield and careen off the hood.

"There's the turn-off," she shouted, pointing to the dirt road coming up on our left.

Wrenching the wheel, I accelerated through an open gate past a weather worn sign reading: MORGAN'S FOLLY pop. 200. A second larger sign nearby, lay face down along the shoulder.

I drove as fast as I dared, bouncing over the washboard surface, dodging potholes and rocks, accompanied by the deafening racket of hailstones driven straight at us by a horizontal wind.

Unfortunately, my goal of reaching our destination

before the deluge was thwarted when a blinding curtain of rain joined the hail. It came down so hard and fast, the wipers were rendered almost useless. Savage bolts of lightning struck so close the pungent smell of ozone permeated the air.

"Can you even see?" Audrey called over the rolling thunder.

I squinted through the foggy windshield. "Sort of."

The defroster helped a little, but as the glass cleared slightly, I didn't like what I saw. To call this thin ledge cut in the side of the mountain a road, was charitable at best. I suspected that even in good weather it was not much better.

My stomach curled into a hard knot as miniature waterfalls cascaded down the sheer cliffs onto the road that was swiftly becoming a slick, muddy river. Pebbles and stones showered down, pinging off the roof and punching dents in my hood.

"What's that?" Audrey cried, pointing to a dark shape looming ahead.

I slowed to a stop and stared with dismay through the swishing wipers at what looked like the remains of an old rusted drainpipe. How the hell had it gotten in the middle of the road?

"Do you think we have enough room to drive around it?" Audrey asked.

"Good question." I nudged the car forward, not relishing the idea of having to get out and slop around in the mud trying to move the thing, if that was even possible. "Looks like there might be just enough room to squeeze around it."

I maneuvered the wheel with care and rolled down the window so I could monitor my progress. Rain pelting my face, we inched by. It was close. One false move and my tires would have been shredded on the jagged edges of the corrugated metal pipe.

I exhaled a long breath when we cleared the obstacle. But my relief was short-lived. Cold horror washed over me when, not ten yards in front of us, a huge boulder crashed down and rolled across the road, disappearing over the edge of the embankment.

"Did you see that?" Audrey screeched, pressing one hand to her heart. "We could have been killed!"

I shuddered to think how right she was, but my options at that point were as narrow as the road. Even if I could somehow manage a miracle and turn us around, without four-wheel drive our chances of negotiating what was now a flowing quagmire seemed remote.

I drove on, my entire being focused squarely on the road that was quickly deteriorating into little more than a mud track. Downshifting, I slowed, easing the car into a hairpin turn. And then, all at once, we began to slide towards the edge of the ridge.

Everything that followed seemed to be in ultra-slow motion—my ineffectual hands trying desperately to turn the wheel, my leaden foot pressing non-responsive brakes. And it didn't help my level of concentration to have Audrey beside me, screaming like a banshee.

Staving off the surge of panic, I finally remembered to steer into the skid. The next few feet were crucial. We drifted so close to the precipice the rain-lashed treetops were visible in the ravine below. My heart seemed to have stopped temporarily and by the time I regained control and pulled back to the other side, the wave of relief left me weak and shaking.

"I think we should stop and wait till this passes over," Audrey squawked, her voice edged with hysteria as we headed downhill.

"Can't."

"What do you mean we *can't?*"

"Flashfloods. We've got to get out of this canyon pronto." My anxiety escalated once more as we approached the base of the slope and I slowed to assess our situation. The rain had diminished slightly, and for the moment, only a few inches of water tumbled over the smooth stones in the creek bed. But my recent personal experience had taught me how swiftly these normally dry washes could burgeon into raging white-water rapids.

We dare not stay here. The whole canyon could flood in a matter of seconds. Poised to make a run for it up the other side, my spirits sank when I noticed the fallen tree. Slashed in half and blackened by lightning, it lay stretched across the road. Now what? I cursed softly under my breath and tried to fight off a feeling of helplessness while I peered through the tangled overhang of branches. A spark of hope flared when I spotted the misty outlines of several houses perched against the ruddy hillside ahead.

"What are we going to do?" Audrey asked in a small voice.

"I hate to say it, but we're going to have to walk the rest of the way."

She gave a disheartened sigh and stared dejectedly at her long skirt and low-heeled pumps. "I'm not really dressed for hiking."

"Me neither. But we have no choice." I revved the car and splashed across the creek, parking on the incline a few feet from the charred tree. I hated to leave our luggage in the car, but it would be impossible for us to carry it very far in such wretched conditions.

More than a little irate about our predicament, I

pondered why Dr. Orcutt would even suggest such a hazardous route as we trudged up the hill with only our purses in tow.

Within minutes our clothing was soaked and it was no easy task negotiating the uneven ground, at times, ankle deep with mud. Sloshing through the muck, I marveled that I was actually cold, although it must have been at least seventy degrees. It was hard to believe that just a few hours ago we'd been baking in the desert heat.

"I'm so sorry about all this," Audrey whimpered as we struggled over the rise, slipping and sliding, holding on to each other to stay upright. "We should have stayed on the main road. If I hadn't been sick and held us up..."

"It's not your fault," I panted back. "I should have known better than to attempt a road like this in such a storm."

"I feel terrible about your car. It's all dented and scratched. I promise I'll pay for the damage."

"Let's worry about that later."

The rain had slowed to a drizzle when we finally stumbled onto level ground. Each laboring for breath, we got our first look at Audrey's inheritance—and it provoked complete silence.

To our right, the carcass of an ancient pick-up truck, rusted beyond belief, rested on its side in front of several ramshackle structures that must have once passed as houses. Trash and discarded appliances littered weed-choked yards.

An old railroad trestle, blackened by time and soot, spanned the deep, rocky gorge to our left and what remained of the tracks disappeared around an enormous pile of mine tailings.

Morgan's Folly, appearing deserted and cheerless in

the deepening twilight, lay wedged between steep slopes where tumbledown houses clung at precarious angles above the roofs of dilapidated buildings. There wasn't a light on anywhere and it gave the eerie impression that we'd stumbled onto a deserted western movie set.

I'm not exactly sure what I'd been expecting, but it wasn't this. And apparently, neither was Audrey. Her stunned expression spoke volumes. "It looks like a ghost town. Are you *positive* this is the right place?"

I shrugged. "That's what the sign said."

"No," she said with a definitive shake of her head. "You must be wrong. Don't tell me I came three thousand miles for...for this?"

"Well..."I began, attempting to put a positive spin on things, "it is sort of...quaint."

She turned horrified eyes on me. "Quaint? It's a shit hole!"

"Shit hole will do," I concurred quietly, convinced that my story was about to go up in smoke, but not blaming her one bit for her outburst.

As I watched her standing there, staring hollow-eyed at the dismal little town, I wondered if this was to be the end of our journey. Would she cut and run?

"I know one thing for sure," she said softly. "Whoever named this place certainly got it right. Morgan's Folly. Folly means mistake, doesn't it?"

"Yeah."

"I can't believe it. This *dump* is my birthright? My father's legacy to me? What a great joke!" Her shrill laugh was laced with bitterness.

I waited patiently until her laughter trailed off and forced a bright note into my voice. "As long as we're here why don't we try getting directions to Dr. Orcutt's house?

And let's not jump to conclusions. I have a feeling there may be more to this place than meets the eye or your mother wouldn't have made arrangements for you to be contacted."

"Are you nuts? I'm not staying here. I'd rather go back home and keep working nights at the storage locker. Let's go get the car and you can drive me back to Tucson right now."

"Audrey, it's almost eight o'clock. I'm tired. I'm hungry. And I need to visit the little girl's room very soon. Besides that, we're stuck here until we can get someone to move that tree out of the way. So, come on."

There had to be someone around somewhere. After all, the sign had proclaimed that 200 people lived here. But where were they?

We tramped the last few hundred yards until we connected with what could loosely be described as pavement. It was hard to tell because there were as many potholes as remaining chunks of concrete.

The main street sidewalks were pathetic—pitted and crumbling. All was silent except for our soggy footsteps and the splatter of rainwater dripping from mangled gutters and flowing darkly down the sides of once proud brick buildings. On closer inspection, it was gratifying to see that some of the structures we'd viewed from a distance that appeared ready for the wrecking ball were still functional and housed a few small businesses.

I wasn't sure which way to go when the unexpected squeak of a door opening nearby made us stop in our tracks and stare at the heavy-set man stepping from the Muleskinner Saloon as if he were an apparition.

He looked equally surprised and gawked at us for a few seconds before doffing a battered ball cap and mumbling, "Evening," as he held the door open for us. We returned the greeting and then watched him amble away into the gray mist.

"Thank goodness," Audrey sighed, her face reflecting relief at the comforting murmur of voices from within. "I was beginning to think we were the only people here."

I hesitated. It was not my normal habit to frequent bars in strange towns, but it appeared to be the only business open. I led the way inside.

There probably weren't more than two dozen patrons scattered about the lofty room. Four men wearing checked shirts, blue jeans and boots straddled bar stools while the remainder huddled around groupings of tables. The harsh light beaming from several kerosene lamps, intermingled with flickering candlelight, gave the place an atmosphere of bygone days.

It seemed oddly quiet for a bar, but was predictably stuffy with the stale odor of beer and tobacco smoke. My sudden sneeze brought the low rumble of conversation to an abrupt halt and every head swiveled in our direction.

I'm sure we must have presented a curious picture standing there, our matted hair dripping water onto the scarred wooden floor, our mud-caked clothing molded wetly against our bodies. Audrey flushed and self-consciously crossed her arms.

"You ladies been out for a little stroll in the rain?" one raunchy-looking guy at the bar finally inquired, his beady eyes fixed appreciatively on my wet T-shirt. I cringed inwardly, positive my nipples were poking out a mile through the thin material.

"Not intentionally," I said, wishing he'd look somewhere else. He didn't.

"You gals lost then?" boomed a voice from an open doorway behind the long mahogany bar.

"Well, yes...and no," I answered slowly, transfixed by the man's striking appearance. Tall and barrel-chested, he wore his snow-white hair shoulder length and his ruddy face was accented by an equally white handlebar mustache. I decided that if it was his goal in life to emulate an 1890's gunfighter, he'd done an admirable job.

"Ha!" snorted another patron, smacking his hand on the bar. "You saying you two actually come here on purpose? Or'd you get blowed in by the storm like one of them pelicans from the Gulf?"

That elicited loud guffaws from his barstool-buddies and a few people at the surrounding tables. It was heartening to know that our unexpected arrival had apparently added a little spice to what must have been an otherwise dull evening.

"I guess you could say a little of both," I said sweetly, mustering a wry smile. "We are here to see someone, but got stranded on the road."

The imposing man I assumed was the owner set the pitcher of beer he was holding onto the bar and stared questioningly at our muddy shoes. "What road?"

I thumbed over my shoulder. "Back there. A tree fell over and blocked the way in."

He shook his head in amazement and came around the end of the bar, walking toward us with a distinct limp. "Are you telling me you gals came in over the Boneyard?"

"What?"

"Boneyard Pass," he repeated, jerking his head in the direction we'd just come from. "So...you been out four-wheeling or something?"

"No. I'm driving a Volvo."

The man astride the first barstool, who was still having a visual love affair with my T-shirt, tipped back his low-slung western hat and blew out a long whistle. "Sonuvabitch. You ladies was real brave to tackle that road in a storm."

"Or real stupid," came the sarcastic comment from one of the tables in the far corner. "What's the matter? Can't you read?"

That brought another round of snickering and I turned to stare into the semi-darkness at my inquisitor. His angular face was barely visible in the dim candlelight. "Probably better than you," I snapped back, then turned to the group. "Somebody want to tell me what the joke is?"

"Didn't you see the sign?" the bartender interjected. "That road's been closed for two months."

Shocked into silence, my mind flashed back to the sign we'd seen laying face down in the dirt as we raced by. I had blamed it on the wind, but now I was having second thoughts.

Audrey, who'd been quiet the whole time, spoke up. "We didn't see any sign and we're not stupid. Come on, Kendall, let's go." Her lips were pinched in a straight line and those magnificent brows of hers had plunged into an angry V.

"Well, now, hold your horses there," the white-haired man said gruffly, firing a glare of warning around the room. "I'm sure nobody here means any offense. Ain't that right?"

Sheepish nods and a chorus of muffled apologies seemed to validate the group's respect for him. Turning his attention back to us, he bestowed a smile on Audrey that would have melted an iceberg. "Just to show you how friendly we can be how about I offer you gals a drink? On the house, of course."

His gracious words apparently mollified Audrey somewhat. "A cup of hot coffee or tea would be nice," she said warily. "And maybe you could tell us where we could get something to eat?"

"If you mean supper, I'm afraid not. The Huddle Cafe is the only eatin' place open 'round here nowadays and they're closed on Mondays. But, I'll tell you what. If you'll give me a few minutes I'd be happy to see what I can rustle up."

We were hardly in a position to refuse and gladly accepted his offer of coffee. Audrey wanted sugar, I ordered mine with a shot of Jack Daniel's.

Our generous benefactor introduced himself as Whitey Flanigan, owner and operator of the Muleskinner Saloon. Of course, I thought wryly, Whitey would have to be his name. What else?

Audrey's name was on the tip of my tongue when I remembered Dr. Orcutt's warning that she should refrain from talking to anyone before him, so I shot her a quick wink and introduced her only as Angela. She read the message in my eyes and gave him a tight-lipped smile.

When I told him who I was, his eyes lit with pleasure. "O'Dell, huh? A fine Irish name if ever there was one. Almost as fine as Flanigan."

Having established an immediate kinship, I was given a candle to find my way down a long, dark hallway to the ladies room and had to laugh at myself as I tried to repair the damage to my make-up and wind-blown hair in the wavering light.

So, the kerosene lamps weren't for effect after all. The power was out. I don't know why it hadn't dawned on me sooner. Because it was now dark, I hoped we'd be able to persuade someone to give us a ride back to my car for the luggage and then to the doctor's house. Besides food, a hot bath and change of clothing were foremost in my mind.

Audrey was next and after we'd each made ourselves as presentable as possible, Whitey served us a combination plate consisting of beer nuts, potato chips and popcorn. Audrey looked slightly nonplussed, but I was so hungry, I didn't care. Things were looking considerably brighter following the second cup of the abundantly laced coffee.

"How was everything?" Whitey inquired, clearing away the empty plates.

I exhaled a contented sigh. "Delicious. Thank you so much."

"Always my pleasure to help out two lovely ladies," he said giving us a courtly nod, and again, I couldn't help but visualize him posing in a faded brown sepia print. "So, you said you're here to visit someone..." He let the sentence hang, so Audrey filled in the blank with, "Oh, yes. We're supposed to see a Dr. Miles Orcutt. I wonder if you could give us directions?"

Her innocent question generated a collective gasp followed by a profound silence so complete you could have dropped a feather and heard it.

Whitey picked up our centerpiece and held the candle close to Audrey's face. "Well, I'll be go to hell," he breathed. "You must be the Morgan girl. By gum, you're the spittin' image of the ol' devil himself."

Everyone was standing now, staring at Audrey, their faces reflecting a mixture of curiosity and disbelief. But one particular couple caught my eye.

The thin-faced man I'd squared off with earlier, and a blonde woman with a height advantage of perhaps five inches, emerged from the gloom and purposefully pushed their way towards our table. The woman lurched to a halt and thrust her face into the candlelight. Audrey's instinctive recoil was understandable. Besides a blast of boozy breath, the wavering shadows highlighted the blonde's overly made-up features and emphasized her eyes, which had narrowed into thin slits of glittering malice.

"I don't know what you and Doc Orcutt think you're up to, but don't think for one lousy minute you're gonna get away with this, girlie," she slurred, punctuating each word with unsteady stabs of her finger. "An' another thing. If you know what's good for you, you'll go an' crawl back into the grave where you belong."

Audrey swallowed fearfully. "What do you mean?"

The woman blinked and opened her mouth to answer, but before she could, the man stepped in front of her. The expression on his face was nothing short of deadly. "Young woman, let me be blunt. If you intend to play this game, you'd better have yourself a carload of proof and one *hell* of a good lawyer because we all know damn well that Rita and Audrey Morgan have been dead for fifteen years."

In response to the man's bombastic remark, an expectant buzz rippled through the small gathering while Audrey sat frozen in open-mouthed astonishment as the couple finished their tirade and stomped away.

Scarlet lips curled in fury, the woman turned to hurl a final insult over her shoulder before flouncing after the man. At least she attempted to flounce. Apparently she was above the legal limit for walking and couldn't quite manage it. Instead, she stumbled into a chair, knocked it to the floor and would have fallen had her companion not swung around and grabbed her waist.

The drama heightened further when the lights chose that exact moment to flicker on. Everyone blinked like barn owls and the room suddenly rang with the rowdy words of a country western song blaring from an ancient jukebox.

Having lost the comparative anonymity of darkness,

the slender man looked a lot less formidable; however, he drew himself up to his full height in an effort to maintain some measure of decorum while he fought to keep the woman upright. After gaining control of the lurching female, he cast a final, defiant glare at Audrey before he half-dragged, half-carried his companion, out the door.

In the electrifying silence that prevailed in the wake of their dramatic exit, the full impact of the pair's remarks hit home and my stomach tingled with anticipation. This story might prove to be even better than I'd imagined.

But a quick glimpse at Audrey's face tempered my elation. Her eyes looked glassy and unfocused, so I figured shock coupled with information overload and jet lag were taking their toll. I stood and placed a comforting hand on her shoulder while making eye contact again with Whitey Flanigan who looked truly imposing in the overhead light. "Such a charming couple," I remarked dryly. "What on earth was *that* all about?

"The gentleman," he answered, turning to Audrey with a sheepish grin, "is your cousin, Haston Pickrell."

She rose unsteadily to her feet. "My cousin? Who was that *awful* woman with him?"

He chuckled. "Ah, yes. That lovely lady is the inimitable Jesse. His wife."

All semblance of color left her face. "What...what did they mean about my mother and me being dead?"

"That's what everyone thought."

One of the cowboys chimed in, "We all seen it in the paper. Back when we had one. Anyways, the article said you and your ma died in a car wreck in, oh, I dunno, somewheres like Oklahoma or Ohio."

I frowned at the group. "If you thought Audrey was dead, why did you act like you were expecting her?"

Whitey shrugged. "Jesse's been real busy spreading rumors all over town. She been telling everyone that Doc Orcutt cooked up a scheme with some hired imposter who was gonna show up and try to steal what rightfully belongs to them."

Audrey looked like she'd been slapped. "Why would she say such a thing?"

"Well now, little lady, you've got to realize that up until this very moment your cousin Haston was the heir apparent. You dropping in out of the blue so to speak has pretty much upset the whole damn apple cart." Whitey puffed out his chest and glanced around to make sure his captive audience was listening attentively.

"You'd best watch out for Jesse," called out one heavy-set man from atop his barstool. "Her Royal Highness is likely to hate your guts for dethroning her." His wheezy guffaw ignited loud laughter among the gathering.

"Dethroning her?" Audrey asked in a strained voice.

Whitey took center stage again. "Yep. You should have seen the two of them. Why, your old dad hadn't been gone two minutes and they were busy hauling their stuff up to the big house. Jesse's nose is all out of joint because now she's gonna have to move out. But that ain't the whole of it," he continued almost without taking a breath. "Most likely they're scared shitless...oops, I mean half to death that you're gonna act like your pa and try to stop the mine from re-opening."

Audrey collapsed into her chair. "I don't understand any of this."

I was hanging on every word and aching to hear more, but the look of bewilderment on Audrey's face concerned me. She looked positively shell-shocked. "Well, listen, you guys," I cut in, "we sure appreciate everything, but Miss Morgan's had a pretty rough day. Could someone give us a lift to the doctor's place?"

There were quite a few enthusiastic volunteers, including my biggest fan from the bar who was practically drooling at the chance, but thankfully Whitey shouted them all down and offered his services. After enlisting the aid of a friend to watch things until his return, he escorted us outside.

His eyes were brimming over with curiosity as he helped us into his jeep, but the look of distress on Audrey's face seemed to discourage him from probing further.

During the entire trip back down the rutted road to retrieve our luggage, she sat behind us in total silence, looking vague. I wondered if it was just her withdrawn nature, or a symptom of her epilepsy that enabled her to lose herself completely in another world. She was awake, but seemingly not quite with us.

The ride was rough and uncomfortable, but it sure beat walking. Arriving at the blackened tree, Whitey whistled in surprise. "Whew! You're damn lucky it didn't fall *on* you."

"Actually, we came pretty close to getting flattened with a sizable boulder further back," I informed him, pointing to the top of the hill.

He shook his head solemnly. "I'm not surprised. The Boneyard got washed out pretty bad back in June. I thought that gate was shut tight and locked."

It was on the tip of my tongue to mention why we'd taken that route, but he'd already slid to the ground and was busy dragging a broken limb aside. I left Audrey sitting in the back and followed him to my car. Unlocking the trunk, I asked, "Why is it called Boneyard Pass?"

"Happened about a hundred years ago," he said with

a grunt, pulling out the first suitcase. "Couple of fellas were hauling a freight wagon full of supplies when something spooked the mule team and the whole shebang tumbled over the edge."

"That's horrible. Did anyone survive?"

"Nope. All dead. Including the mules. They buried the men where they lay, but left them poor critters out there rotting in the sun till there was nothing left but a pile of bones."

Considering how close we'd come to repeating history this afternoon, I was almost sorry I'd asked.

When we'd completed our task and Whitey restarted the engine, I took a last look around. My poor little car looked awfully forlorn stranded there alone in the dark valley.

"I'll get hold of a few of the boys in the morning and we'll get her out for you," he volunteered, apparently noticing my concern.

Bucking and rocking back up the hill, I listened to Whitey chat amiably about himself. He'd worked the coal mines of West Virginia as a young man and migrated west to work for the Morgan Mining Company in the early fifties. He'd been employed first as a lowly mucker before moving up the ranks to operate a jackleg drill. That's where he'd been working a header in a drift when he'd gotten slabbed when a rock crashed down on him from the back injuring his leg so badly he'd been relegated to an office job.

"Whoa, hold on," I interjected with a laugh, noting the mischievous gleam in his eyes. "You may as well be speaking in a foreign language. You're going to have to interpret this mining terminology for me."

With the patience of a schoolteacher, he explained that mucking meant hauling out waste rock and that he'd been injured when a loose boulder fell from the ceiling of the tunnel while he'd been drilling the rock face. "Pushing papers don't get your adrenaline running like working down in the hole," he said, downshifting the jeep as the grade grew steeper, "but it was mighty damn good of old Jeb to keep me on."

"And who's old Jeb."

"Jeb Morgan was Grady's pa. He was still running the show even though he was well into his nineties." He blew out a nostalgic sigh. "And a more hootin', hollerin' place you never did see. Yes, siree, if the mine hadn't closed...let's see, it's been almost four years ago, I'd still be working there instead of selling suds to the handful of poor souls still hanging on here by their fingernails."

"Why *did* it close?" I inquired, holding tight to the handle above my door, trying to keep my teeth from clacking together as we bounded to the top of the hill.

He gave me a calculating glance. "That depends on who you talk to."

I raised a brow. "Meaning what?"

"Some say it was a simple combination of bad management plus the price of copper being in the toilet. Others swear it was because them damned bureaucrats from the EPA started breathing down our necks."

"What prompted that?"

He huffed out an impatient breath. "I'll tell you what it was. A bunch of them noisy environmentalists, blathering about pollution and kicking up a fuss about endangered birds and such, come storming into town demanding restrictions on this and regulations on that. Why it would have cost so darn much to appease them that Grady would've had to hock what there was left just to keep the mine open. After a couple a years of wrangling, he told 'em all to go to hell and shut her down."

"And that killed off the town," I mused softly.

"Just about. Businesses started to close right and left so pretty soon most of the younger folks with kids moved away. The schools closed up, most all the churches, and we only got one place left to even buy food. Hell, since the drug store packed it in last year, you have to drive clear over to Bisbee to get a damn prescription filled."

I shook my head in sympathy. "What a shame. Guess you're lucky you've still got a doctor here."

"That's for sure. But the doc's getting a bit long in the tooth. I wouldn't be surprised if he pulls in his shingle and retires pretty soon. Yep," he went on, his voice turning wistful, "we all thought things were as bad as they were gonna get when little by little, them hippie types started moving in for keeps. I mean to tell you, there's been a heap of scrapping amongst them and the regular town folk this past year so..." he paused, thumbing behind us, "I guess the future of what's going to happen to this place is gonna depend on this little lady."

Audrey hadn't said word one since we'd left the saloon, so I turned around to judge her reaction to Whitey's statement. She was staring dully out the window as if none of it mattered. I had a feeling it did, but she was too overwhelmed with everything to bother with any response. I decided then that it might be best to wait and hear Dr. Orcutt's version. I was well aware of how facts could get skewered in the rumor mills of small towns.

My second approach to Morgan's Folly wasn't quite so depressing now that a few lights gleamed from within the homes bordering the narrow winding streets and winked down at us from the steep hillsides.

Succumbing to the weariness invading my bones, I

rested my head against the window frame and let the rain-washed air blow in on my face. With the storm clouds now retreating beyond the distant mountains, brilliant patches of stars appeared to reclaim the night sky.

"Here we are," Whitey announced, pulling up in front of a two-story house flanked by towering cypress trees. The shadowy outlines of tall chimneys were back-lit in eerie amber light from one lone street lamp perched on the road above. "You gals want me to bring the bags inside?"

"No, no, we can manage from here," I said, breathing a sigh of relief as I pushed the door open and slid to the ground. "You've done enough. Thanks so much for all your help." About all I could think of at that moment was food, a hot bath, and sleep.

He left our luggage on the walkway leading up to the porch and favored me with a broad grin. "See you, Irish."

I returned a smile. "Same to you." It was nice to know our common ancestry had established an immediate bond between us and because of his unique position as bartender and 'head honcho of gossip central', no doubt his knowledge of this little town and its inhabitants would prove exceedingly valuable. The amiable expression on his face clouded slightly when he looked at Audrey. "Good luck to you, young lady. You're gonna need it." With that, he turned, climbed into the jeep and waved a friendly farewell.

Audrey watched wistfully as he roared out of sight. "I wish he was my cousin instead of Haston."

"Me too," I said absently, noting with dismay that except for the dull yellow glow of the porch light, the house was dark. It was only a little after ten, but it could have been midnight. Other than the faint yelping of coyotes somewhere in the distance and the steady hum of crickets, there was absolute dead silence.

"You're sure he's expecting us."

"I told his nurse last night we'd be coming. Why?"

I motioned toward the house. "It doesn't look like anyone is awake."

As she stood gawking, impatience bubbled up inside me. It had been an extraordinarily long day, I was dog-tired and I'd about had it. "Well, it looks as though she neglected to tell him," I grumbled, leaning down to pick up my bags, "but I guess that will be his problem."

"What are you going to do?"

I started up the steps. "Go to bed."

"Wait," she squealed, running after me. "Maybe we'd better go to a motel."

I stopped and turned. "Did you see anything even remotely resembling a motel?"

"No."

"Precisely."

Marching across the porch, I dropped the bags unceremoniously at my feet and parked a finger on the bell. It was inexcusable, but I felt a fiendish glee listening to it reverberate throughout the house. I knew myself well enough to know that fatigue was eroding my already short temper.

No sooner had I lifted my finger than a downstairs light flashed on. There were footsteps, the lock snapped, the door cracked open, and a wary female voice demanded, "Yes?"

"Mrs. Orcutt?" I inquired.

"Who are you?"

"My name is Kendall O'Dell and this is Audrey

Morgan. I believe you're expecting us and I apologize for being so late. We were unavoidably delayed." It would have been nice to add, 'because of your husband's rotten advice,' but I restrained myself.

My little speech was followed by one of the longest silences in history, and the wonderfully long hot bath I'd been envisioning began to fade away. What was the matter with her? "Mrs. Orcutt?"

"Ah, yes. Please come in." She swung the door open and stood aside, tightening the belt on her flowered robe as we dragged our luggage into the entry hall. When she snapped on a brighter overhead light, I could see her more clearly.

And she could see us more clearly too.

Brushing a wisp of graying brown hair from her gaunt face, her guarded expression switched first to disbelief, then to distaste as she surveyed our disheveled appearance. No doubt we looked like two female mud wrestlers, and I got the impression that she wished she'd hosed us down before inviting us into her home.

"Sorry about the mess," I said, trying to keep my mud-caked shoes on the braided throw rug and off the spotless white tile floor that led around the corner into a large kitchen. "My car got stuck on the road and we had to walk into town. Mr. Flanigan was kind enough to drive us here."

She frowned. "How do you know Whitey?"

"Well, we don't really. We just sort of stumbled onto the Muleskinner and...."

"We're very sorry we woke you," Audrey chimed in, sounding like a guilty child. "We tried to phone, but the lines are out."

It was then the woman's gaze fastened fully on

Audrey and there was subtle change behind her deep-set eyes. "So," she said at length, "you're Rita's girl."

Audrey looked gratified. I'm sure after having suffered the mortification of being labeled an imposter the woman's words of affirmation must have sounded reassuring. "Did you know her?"

"Of course," she replied. "Your mother was my husband's nurse."

Audrey's mouth sagged open. "His nurse?"

"She never told you she worked for him?"

In an almost inaudible voice, she answered, "She never told me she was a nurse."

A profusion of emotions flitted across Mrs. Orcutt's stoic face before she responded. "Well, it appears that I'm not the only one who's been kept in the dark all these years." Her remark was meant to sound breezy but her words were punctuated with unmistakable resentment.

Both women's disclosures were astonishing and I was eager to hear more, but also relieved when she added, "Miles won't be able to talk with you until tomorrow since he's already gone to bed." Her dismissive tone discouraged further conversation as she turned on her heel and swept into the kitchen.

Following her request that we leave our shoes on the rug, she asked if we were hungry and then directed us upstairs to the guestroom. Because we had to share a bathroom I wasn't able to linger in the tub as long as I would have liked. But it was just as well since I was anxious to get to the tray of sandwiches she'd prepared and left on the dresser before retiring a second time.

While Audrey showered, I alternately ate and jotted down everything I considered pertinent to the story. Even though the events of this unbelievably long day had already uncovered some remarkable findings, it appeared that the key to this puzzle lay with Dr. Orcutt.

And as much as I yearned to be a part of it, simple propriety dictated that I not interject myself in what promised to be a revealing, and most likely, emotional encounter. I'd have to be content with whatever Audrey chose to share with me afterwards.

I shoved my notebook aside when she emerged from the bathroom in a cloud of steam. Wrapped demurely in a pink ankle-length nightshirt, she looked more child-like than ever sitting cross-legged on the opposite bed pensively munching a sandwich.

"You gonna be okay?" I asked, watching her sober expression.

"I guess. I mean, it was good to get the mud off but I'm...I'm so confused about everything. I don't know what to think. I don't know how to feel. I keep telling myself this is all just a bad dream and I'm going to wake up and everything will be like it was before."

"You've had a lot to absorb in one day."

"Tell me about it. Let's see," she said, laying the sandwich down and counting her fingers. "I have a different name, a different age, I own a worthless tumbledown town in the middle of nowhere, I have a cousin who hates me and, oh yes," she added in a trembling voice, "his wife hates me too. And I can tell Mrs. Orcutt hates me..." Tears glistening in her eyes, she pressed her fingertips to her lips. "I don't know if I can stand to hear anymore."

Feeling rather helpless, I rose and sat next to her, slipping my arm around her shoulders for the second time that day. Her heart-rending sobs were so pitiful I was moved to the brink of tears myself.

It was unfortunate. She seemed to be one of the

true innocents of the world doomed to shoulder an incredibly heavy burden created by the actions of others. And she appeared to possess a scant supply of stamina. I wondered again about my own motives. Perhaps digging up the past was not the best course of action for Audrey Morgan.

When her weeping began to subside, I rose, pressed a wad of tissues into her hand, and then moved to the window. For a few minutes, I stood staring glumly at the stars glimmering above the dark outline of hills before turning back to her.

"Thank you, Kendall," she hiccuped, blowing her nose. "You've been so kind to me..." Pausing, she blinked back fresh tears and I feared she was going to break down again. "You're just as nice as your brother said you'd be."

I folded my arms and leaned back against the windowsill. "Listen, Audrey, I'll be the first to admit that I've got my heart set on doing this story, but if you want to forget this whole thing, it's fine by me."

She dabbed her eyes. "I don't know what to do."

I moved to my bed and pulled back the covers. "Why don't you sleep on it, things always look different in the morning."

She nodded and lay down with her face to the wall. I shut the light out and listened to the whir of the window air conditioner and finally to Audrey's soft snoring.

Exhaustion pressed me to the mattress like a lead blanket, but I was so keyed up my eyelids refused to stay closed as the day's events careened around inside my head.

A lot of things were bothering me. Especially the fact that Dr. Orcutt would deliberately direct us down a hazardous road like Boneyard Pass. I tensed again, remembering the giant boulder tumbling into the road. That had been way too close for comfort. Envisioning the section of rusted pipe in the road triggered another thought. What happened to the white pick-up truck that had been ahead of us? Had the driver continued on the road to Bisbee or turned onto the shortcut? And if that were so, where had the truck gone?

I turned over and plumped the pillow. From just the little I'd learned so far, Tally's suspicion that Grady Morgan's death might be something other than accidental was not all that farfetched. There appeared to be several warring factions at work, but try as I might I couldn't understand why Grady Morgan had opposed re-opening the mine. Wouldn't that have made good economic sense for him as well as everyone else?

I squeezed my eyes shut and tried to clear my mind. There was no point in driving myself nuts with questions when I had so few details. Some of the answers would most likely come tomorrow and so far everything boomeranged back to Dr. Orcutt.

Why was he so closely tied to the Morgan family? Why had he been the only living soul in town who knew that Rita and her daughter weren't really dead? Learning that Audrey's mother had been his nurse at least established a connection between them, but why had they maintained contact for eighteen years? He'd carried out Rita's final wish to contact Audrey about her inheritance, but he'd apparently done so reluctantly. Why? Passages from the letter written by Audrey's mother swam before my eyes. What were the other promises he'd sworn to keep?

A sudden thought struck me. I rose, quietly picked up Audrey's purse from the night stand and tiptoed into the bathroom, closing the door behind me and snapping on the light.

The repetitious hammering annoyed me because I couldn't figure out where it was coming from. Struggling to raise eyelids that felt as if someone had come in the night and weighed them down with anchors, I suddenly realized what it was. Someone was knocking at the bedroom door. "Yes?" I called out in a sleep-clogged voice, sitting up on the side of the bed.

The door edged open as Audrey stirred and Mrs. Orcutt stuck her head in. "Miss Morgan, if you want to talk to the doctor this morning you'll have to catch him before he starts seeing patients at the clinic." Her clipped voice held no trace of warmth.

"What time is it?" Audrey asked.

"Eight o'clock." She began to withdraw, but stopped, adding the aside, "Oh, Miss Morgan, I hope you won't find it necessary to involve my husband in any problems that may occur concerning this situation. He has not been well recently and has been advised to avoid too much stress."

I wondered how that was possible for a doctor, but said nothing as the door clicked shut. In response to the woman's terse statement, Audrey sat hugging herself in stony silence.

Well, this was probably it. Judging by her look of total dejection, it seemed clear that our time in Morgan's Folly was about to expire. Pangs of disappointment and hunger mingled in my stomach as I rose with a resigned sigh and slipped into a fresh pair of blue jeans. Whitey's special combo plate and the sandwich I'd eaten before bed were long gone and I was starving again. Perhaps it was the higher altitude and cooler temperatures.

"Kendall," she announced so suddenly, I flinched. "I've made my decision. I'm going to meet with Dr. Orcutt."

Considering her confused frame of mind last night, I was surprised, but my spirits lifted immediately. "All right. While you're doing that, I'm going to do a little exploring on my own."

"No. I want you to come with me."

"Are you sure? I mean, most likely he's going to be telling you some very personal and maybe painful things about your family."

She tightened her jaw. "I know. But I *have* to find out what happened eighteen years ago and I'd just feel better if you were there with me. For support."

"Boy, I don't know," I muttered, tucking my shirt into the waistband. "When he finds out I'm a reporter, he may be reluctant to talk in front of me."

In a show of stubbornness I wouldn't have thought possible, she said, "Well, we don't have to tell him."

I shook my head. "He's going to discover it eventually."

She threw back the bedcovers and rose. "Fine, but he doesn't have to find out this morning. I'll tell him you're my friend. That's all he has to know."

I cracked a smile. "Okay. You're the boss."

Enticed by the heavenly aroma of fresh coffee and frying bacon, Audrey and I tromped downstairs and entered the kitchen we'd seen only in shadow the night before. My feelings for the doctor's cold-fish-of-a-wife softened a touch when we learned that she'd left instructions for us to be served breakfast by her smiling maid who directed us to the clinic when we'd finished.

A cheerful chorus of birdsong greeted us as we stepped outside. It was a glorious morning. The sky was a sharp, clear blue and the air was perfumed with the scent of roses from Mrs. Orcutt's well-tended garden.

As we walked uphill to the clinic, dappled sunlight filtering through the lacy overhang of trees, reflected back at us from the puddles of rain water left over from yesterday's storm.

As I reached for the doorknob of the one-story whitewashed building, Audrey's fingers abruptly encircled my wrist. There was a faint gleam of panic in her eyes.

Knowing what I knew now, I understood her misgivings. She'd endured enough bad news to traumatize anyone and there was no telling what awaited her from this point. "There's still time for you to change your mind," I said softly.

She gave her head a vehement shake and took several measured breaths. "It's okay. I just needed a minute. I'm ready now."

Flashing her a smile of encouragement, I gave her

hand a quick squeeze and we stepped into the small waiting area.

"Doctor won't be seeing patients until ten," called a middle-aged Hispanic woman from behind a partially glass-enclosed barrier to our right. "Do you ladies need an appointment?"

"No," I answered, noting that her nametag read: Anna Hernandez. "Dr. Orcutt is expecting us. You can tell him Audrey Morgan is here."

I watched closely to see if Audrey's name sparked recognition, but her expression remained impassive. She spoke quietly into the phone and then directed us down a short hallway to a door marked PRIVATE. Audrey exchanged a final it's-now-or-never-glance with me and rapped on the door.

A gravelly voice called for us to enter and she swung the door open to reveal a gray-haired man of perhaps sixty-five seated behind a large, paper-strewn desk. An inscrutable look passed over his austere features as his gaze flickered past me and settled on Audrey. Slowly, he rose and came around the desk to cradle both her hands in his. "Well, well, well. So you're little Audrey, all grown up. And beautiful, just like your mother." His deep voice conveyed a wistful note, but I detected a trace of anxiety behind his faded blue eyes when they turned on me. "And who might you be?"

"Kendall O'Dell is a friend of mine," Audrey cut in before I could reply. "Anything you have to say is okay for her to hear."

Seemingly unimpressed by my cordial smile, he adjusted his wire-rimmed glasses and proceeded to engage me in one of those relentless eye duels people often do when they're trying to exhibit superiority. He blinked first.

"Please sit down," he said at length, indicating two chairs facing his desk.

While he fiddled with several sets of Venetian blinds, slanting the bright beams of sunlight toward the ceiling, Audrey perched stiffly on the edge of the chair, her efforts to appear serene defeated by the whiteness of her tightly-knotted fingers.

With both of them pre-occupied for a moment, I surreptitiously opened my purse and started my miniature tape recorder as the doctor settled once again behind the desk.

Watching him shuffle through the papers, I got the distinct impression that he was delaying the inevitable and seemed to be gathering his thoughts when Audrey burst out, "I met my cousins last night. They said some horrible things to me."

"If you'd done..."

She kept talking. "Why did you do it? Why did you allow people to think we were dead all this time?"

Dr. Orcutt's lips compressed into a flat line, straining the chords in his neck. "My wife, Fran, told me you'd stopped at the Muleskinner. It's unfortunate that you didn't follow my instructions and come to the house first. I wanted to spare you..."

"Never mind about that now," she snapped, her voice rising shrilly. "Just tell me!" Then, as if regretting her outburst, she softened her tone. "I'm sorry. Please."

His gaze turned chilly and I thought his demeanor curiously unsympathetic for a man of his profession. "It was not my idea," he said quietly. "It was your mother's. She said it was the only way she'd ever feel completely safe from your father. Believe me, not a day has gone by that I haven't questioned the wisdom of what we did, but I made her a promise and I fully intend to keep it."

"She said almost those exact words in her letter," Audrey marveled.

"May I see it?"

She rummaged in her purse and handed him the paper. He read it slowly, his eyes clouding with an emotion difficult to interpret. I did get the impression, however, that he read the last line several times before handing the letter back to her.

"I want you to understand something. I was not in favor of your mother's ninth-inning decision. I knew it would create an emotional upheaval for you and frankly, it has placed me in a rather awkward position, but..." He blew out a heavy sigh before adding, "I could not, in good conscience, deny her final request. Especially since I may have been inadvertently responsible."

Audrey fixed him with a dubious frown. "What do you mean?"

"One day, during a telephone conversation, I mentioned in passing that plans were in the works to re-open the mine. Unfortunately, that fact, coupled with her illness, apparently altered her thinking process. Then, your father's unexpected death forced me to put in motion the sequence of events that brought you here. But," he continued, "be that as it may, the remainder of my promise to her was that certain things about the past never be discussed. You must appreciate the fact that she was not only a loyal employee and cherished friend, but also a patient."

Audrey looked perplexed. "So...what exactly are you saying? "

"It means that I will tell you only what I feel is pertinent and no more. And if you press me, I'll invoke doctor/patient confidentiality," he said flatly.

Audrey's eyes grew round with outrage. "But...but...you can't do that! I came all this way. You can't...I mean, it's not right..." Her words dissolved into tearful babbling, so I laid a gentle hand on her arm while locking eyes with Dr. Orcutt. "This is a small town. She's bound to hear things from other people. In fact, she already has."

He accepted my words with a nod of affirmation. "So be it, Miss O'Dell. I cannot control what other people may say. But she will not hear it from me." His crisp note of finality discouraged further argument. "Now," he said, facing Audrey once more as he folded his hands on the desk, "let me tell you what you came to hear."

Not only did the man's bedside manner need a little sprucing up, but more importantly, he acted suspiciously like a man with something to hide, doctor's oath or not.

"Your mother came to work for me not long after she graduated from nursing school. I believe that was around 1965 and then..."

"I never knew she was a nurse until your wife told me last night," Audrey interjected in a hushed voice.

"She had her reasons, which I will get to. Anyway, she hadn't been with me too many years when her first husband was killed in a mining accident."

"What?" she demanded, looking positively stupefied. "She was married to someone else before my father?"

Dr. Orcutt's uptight expression softened somewhat. "There are probably quite a few things your mother never told you, but you will soon understand why. May I go on?"

She nodded mutely.

"Three years later, she married your father. Besides the significant age difference, I'm afraid it was not a happy match," he said with a sad shake of his head.

"Why?" Audrey asked.

"Because Grady was...well, Grady."

Audrey brandished the letter. "My mother said he was evil. What did she mean by that?"

His eyes grew distant. "Your father was a rather complex individual. It wasn't easy being one of Jeb Morgan's kids. The old man set impossibly high standards to follow when all Grady wanted was to have a good time. As a result he got pretty ornery and as he grew older, his antics garnered quite a reputation around town. He was cocky and rebellious. Just a plain bull-headed fool at times. Unfortunately for everyone those character traits were not the worst of his shortcomings."

"What else?" Audrey asked, recoiling as though she'd rather not hear.

"Alcohol. Most people can handle a couple of drinks with few side effects but some...can turn into monsters." He paused, as if remembering something then went on. "I'm afraid there were times he vented his anger on your mother."

Audrey's face paled. "You...you mean he'd hit her?"

He nodded. "Once in a while he'd go on a binge and...things happened."

"Why on earth would she marry a man like that?" Audrey whispered.

"Because, when he was sober, he could be a charmer too. Your father was one hell of a good-looking man. And he was clever, very clever, but certainly not motivated to work like his father and brother, Oliver."

"I have an uncle too?"

"Not anymore. He was killed in the same accident

as your mother's first husband. It was a tragic, tragic day. The old man, well...losing his oldest son almost killed him too. Oliver was a helluva nice guy. Helluva nice guy."

For a long moment he seemed lost in the past, but then his eyes cleared and he concluded briskly, "But, that's the lot of a miner. It's hard work. It's dirty. And at times, quite dangerous."

"Did my father work down in the mine too?" Audrey asked.

"Your father hated the family business and even when he assumed control after Jeb died, he avoided going down into the mine whenever he could." His eyes lit up like he wanted to add something else, but he didn't voice it. "Let me get back to what I was saying. After you were born, Rita continued to put up with your father's abuse until she came to me one night crying hysterically." He halted momentarily as if to dispel the memory, then continued in a voice thick with emotion. "She'd been...badly beaten, and she was holding you in her arms, unconscious."

"Oh, my God," Audrey gasped, pressing a hand to her throat. "I don't remember any of this."

"You were just a child," he blurted out, his voice suddenly bitter, his eyes ablaze. "And your mother's beautiful face...all bruised...he'd broken her nose...he'd...if only I'd done more to prevent..."

The jangle of the phone terminated his sentence, and I almost winced aloud in frustration when he reached for the receiver. Damn it. There went the first genuine display of emotion he'd shown since we'd sat down. The rest of his story seemed a little too carefully contrived.

"You okay?" I whispered to Audrey. She nodded silently, her lips pinched together so hard they looked as bloodless as the rest of her face.

"If you'll excuse me just a moment," Dr. Orcutt muttered, swiveling his chair to face the window to my right. The unexpected break gave me an opportunity to scrutinize him further.

Dr. Orcutt looked like hell. His sallow, deeply-grooved face was webbed with wrinkles, broken blood vessels were clustered in and around his sunken eyes, and I was shocked to notice an ashtray and partially-smoked pack of cigarettes on the credenza behind him. Apparently he paid little heed to the phrase, Physician, Heal Thyself.

A million questions jockeyed for position in my mind, but I felt certain he'd stonewall me if I broached them. However, that didn't concern me too much. Knowing small towns the way I did, knowing how closely people's lives intertwined, knowing that secrets seemingly buried forever beneath the surface can boil to the top with a vengeance, gave me confidence that I'd be able to plug the missing pieces into this puzzle.

Pretending to hunt for something in my purse, I turned over the tape in my hand-held recorder and settled back in the chair just as he cradled the phone. He apologized for the interruption and continued his narrative.

The catalyst that fateful night eighteen years ago had been Rita announcing her intention to seek a divorce. Grady had gone into a mad rage and grabbed her, vowing that if she tried to leave he would kill her. She'd broken away and made it to the stair landing where he'd caught her again. Her screams awakened Audrey, who'd come onto the scene and, in the melee, been inadvertently knocked down the stairs.

"You had a concussion," Dr. Orcutt stated somberly, "and your mother begged me to help her escape. I argued against it, but she was absolutely terrified of Grady so I finally agreed. I loaned her one of my cars and she left with nothing but some jewelry and the clothes on her back."

Audrey swallowed convulsively. "So, my father really was an evil man."

Dr. Orcutt steepled his hands beneath his nose and stared vacantly a moment before answering. "Let me put it to you this way. Grady could be your best friend and worst enemy at the same instant."

His answer fascinated me, but Audrey looked just plain befuddled.

The rest of the tale played out pretty much as I suspected. Rita had left Arizona that night, never settling long in one place and staying in touch with Dr. Orcutt every few weeks. Now and then he would wire her money.

When he alerted her to the fact that Grady had hired a reputable private detective agency to track her down, she decided to seek a new identity for herself and Audrey. She prevailed upon Miles to convey the news to Grady that they had died in a car crash in Oklahoma, in hopes that it would end his search for her.

"Excuse me, Doctor," I had to ask, "being that you're a medical professional, didn't you feel that was a bit unethical?"

He fired me a look of disdain and snapped, "Considering all that was at stake, Miss O'Dell, it seemed the best course of action at the time." Turning back to Audrey, he added, "I put her in touch with an elderly aunt who lived in the Pittsburgh area so you and your mother finally settled there."

"So, Aunt Nell was *your* aunt?" she croaked, barely above a whisper. "But...why did my mother work as a housekeeper? Why didn't she take a nursing job?"

He shrugged. "She was afraid if she got paid in

anything besides cash, she could be traced through her Social Security number. Everything was going smoothly until she realized she would have to produce a birth certificate when you entered kindergarten. She was so paranoid that somehow Grady would still find you that...well, she persuaded me to help her fashion a new one that altered the place of birth, and as an added precaution, she changed your birthday to April of the following year."

This was just too good. Fantastic copy, I thought happily. I already had enough for a blockbuster series of articles, and I had a feeling that by the time I uncovered what he *wasn't* telling us, I'd have enough to fill a book.

"No wonder my cousin was so hateful," Audrey murmured, "No wonder he thinks I'm an imposter."

The doctor waved away her remark. "I'll call and have another talk with him. Hopefully, he'll have simmered down. I don't know all the details but, while Grady was busy frittering away the family fortune, Haston has done the lion's share of work the past few years. It's understandable that both he and Jesse would be upset by what's happened. And, if I were you, I'd try to work with them to sort out the particulars of how you want things handled from this point forward." He scribbled something on a sheet of paper and handed it to her. "I've listed the name and phone number of both your father's attorney and accountant in Bisbee."

"I'm not sure what to do," she said, faintly. "I don't know anything about running a mine...or a town."

He stared at her thoughtfully. "It may not even be necessary for you to stay here. If you and Haston can work out the financial arrangements, he may be able to act as your agent and you can remain solely in an advisory capacity. But, that's something you'll need to discuss with the attorney and your cousin."

There was a light rap on the door behind us and his nurse stuck her head in. "Doctor, your ten o'clock is here."

"Thank you, Anna." He immediately got to his feet, so we rose also as he said to Audrey, "I have to go."

His curt dismissal left her with a look of wounded surprise as he swept past her towards the door. He paused momentarily with his hand on the knob before turning to face her. "Don't judge your mother too harshly, young lady. She did what she thought was best for everyone."

"Thank you for...being her friend."

His jaw muscles worked overtime. "I'm not so sure you should thank me," he answered softly.

Audrey looked understandably taken aback and he quickly added, "I'll have Anna call D.J. to come and drive you up to the house. If you have any other questions that I can answer freely, please call me."

I jumped in with, "I have a question, Doctor."

He looked slightly perturbed, but answered, "Yes?"

"Why did you instruct your nurse to call Audrey on Sunday night and give her directions to drive into Morgan's Folly on Boneyard Pass?"

Dr. Orcutt's shaggy eyebrows flew to his hairline. "I don't have the slightest idea what you're talking about."

The early morning coolness had vanished by the time we collected our luggage from the doctor's house and carried it to the street to wait for our ride. My quick phone call to Whitey confirmed that he'd spoken to several people about clearing away the toppled tree, and if I could drop by the Muleskinner after the job was complete, he'd drive me back to retrieve my car.

Edging out of the sun into a small patch of shade, I looked impatiently at my watch. Dr. Orcutt had explained that D.J., the handyman employed at the Morgan house, had been summoned and would arrive shortly to pick us up. That had been well over an hour ago.

Since leaving the doctor's office Audrey had fallen back into her pattern of non-communication. No doubt she was still reeling from the disquieting information she'd learned, and I hoped she didn't regret having asked me to bear witness to the emotion-charged scene that had opened up a floodgate of new questions.

Sitting slump-shouldered astride one of the suitcases, her face cupped in her hands, she stared dully across the roofs of the buildings that fronted the main street, and beyond to the scarred hills encircling the town. To coin one of Ginger's favorite phrases, she looked like she'd been 'rode hard and put away wet.'

"So, if his nurse didn't make that call," Audrey said, suddenly voicing her thoughts, "who did? And why?"

"Assuming he's telling the truth, I don't know who. Yet. But the why is much more disturbing."

"What do you mean?"

I hesitated. I didn't have a smidgen of proof, but I was now viewing our harrowing trip down Boneyard Pass in a new light. A sinister light. It seemed more likely now that the rusted pipe had been deliberately deposited in the road to slow the car and place us in the path of the boulder. Was it meant to merely frighten her or was there something more diabolic behind it? Recalling the questionable circumstances surrounding Grady Morgan's death spurred me to plunk myself down beside her.

"Audrey," I began, "I don't want to concern you unduly, but...there may have been more to your father's death than meets the eye."

She shot me a bewildered look. "What?"

I gave her the gist of the article Tally had recounted to me. When I mentioned the housekeeper's claim of overhearing an argument and then witnessing a woman flee the scene, apprehension clouded her eyes.

"It may only be a coincidence," I added hastily.

"And remember, the article was written last May and at that time there was no proof that it was anything other than accidental but..."

"You don't think it was," she threw in.

"I don't know. I plan to check with the sheriff's department and see if there are any new developments, but it's apparent to me from the little we've heard, that as far as the mine re-opening, your father was damned if he did and damned if he didn't."

"We know Jesse hated him," Audrey said slowly. "But why would she...?"

"Tell me something," I said, patting the perspiration from my forehead, "who else besides Dr. Orcutt could have had access to your telephone number?"

That made her mouth sag open, but the sound of a vehicle roaring up the hill drew our attention to a snazzy teal-blue Suburban rounding the corner into view. We got to our feet just as it screeched to a halt in front of us.

Engine still idling noisily, the driver, an anonymous silhouette behind tinted windows, made no move to get out. Instead, he appeared to be studying us intently while we stood baking in the sun. The beginning of a heat headache drummed at my temples and I bristled with impatience. What on earth was he waiting for? Were there two other strangers somewhere in town waiting to be picked up?

I nodded a curt greeting and reached for my suitcase. That got things moving. The engine stopped and the door flew open. A chunky, pony-tailed man clad in soiled tan slacks and an over-sized shirt slid to the ground. He took a final drag from his cigarette and flicked it aside. "Sorry, I'm late," he offered contritely, smoothing his thin mustache with one finger. "I got held up." With no further explanation, he scooped our luggage from the sidewalk and began to pile it in the back of the truck.

I kept my camera case with me and when he'd finished and slammed the rear compartment shut, he rushed back and opened the side door for us. "So, ah, which one of you is Miss Morgan?"

"I am," she replied wearily, climbing inside. "This is my friend Kendall."

"Danny Morrison," he answered with a deferential bob of his head. "But everybody calls me D.J."

As he closed the door behind me, Audrey wrinkled her nose and pinched it shut to indicate her distaste for the stench that permeated the interior. I nodded my agreement. It smelled like stale cigarette smoke and I hoped he wasn't planning to light up again. My asthma had improved leaps and bounds since my arrival in Arizona, but smoke could still send me into coughing spasms.

Back in the driver's seat once more, he re-started the engine and headed downhill. Thankfully, he didn't reach for the pack of cigarettes I'd seen outlined in his shirt pocket, so I settled back and let the air-conditioned breeze flow over me.

In the clear light of day, we got a much better look at Audrey's new inheritance, and it was obvious by her disillusioned expression that she was less than impressed as we drove though the dilapidated business district.

Personally, I found the place rather charming. The weathered brick buildings with their turn-of-the-century facades exhibited an air of faded elegance. But then, I didn't have to think about what it would cost to refurbish them.

As we wound our way up the hill, it was heartening to see a well-tended house here and there nestled among the crumbling shells of once-proud dwellings perched haphazardly on the terraced slopes. I gathered from the profusion of television antennas crisscrossing the roofs that cable had not yet come to this isolated town.

"Is there ever a rush hour around here?" I asked, making eye contact with our driver in the rear-view mirror.

He stared blankly for a second and then grinned. "Not hardly. It's pretty dead. A lot of people drive over to Bisbee and Sierra Vista and even up to Tucson for work now, so there's actually more traffic on weekends."

"So, you've lived here quite a while? I asked.

"About a year."

"What brought you to Morgan's Folly?"

"Oh, I dunno. This 'n' that. I was tired of the rat race and looking for someplace quieter." He paused, braking to avoid a rabbit bounding across the road and concluded, "Guess I found it."

"How far is the house?" Audrey inquired, stifling a yawn.

"A mile or so." He stretched to make eye contact with her. "Will you be staying here permanently, Miss...Morgan?"

His subtle hesitation made me wonder if he, too, doubted her claim as heir to the Morgan throne.

"I don't really know yet." With that, she closed her eyes and leaned back against the headrest.

I inched forward. "So, D.J., Dr. Orcutt tells me you're employed as a handyman at the house?"

His sharp laugh held a trace of bitterness. "I do a lot more than that. You might say I'm one of them jack-of-all trades."

"Really. How so?"

"I keep up the grounds, help Marta when she needs it and I maintain all the cars. When I'm not doing that and a hundred other things, I work part-time as a watchman over at the mine property."

I said, "Sounds like you keep pretty busy. And you've been at the house, how long?"

"Dunno. Eight, nine months."

"I see. So that means that you were there when Grady Morgan had his accident."

Even though his eyes were partially obscured behind the gray photo chromic lenses of his glasses, his expression turned wary. "I was away when he fell. When I got back later that night, the sheriff was already there."

Audrey sat up, her expression sharpening with interest. "What do you mean *when* you got back? Do you live at the house?"

"Not exactly. I stay in the cottage down the hill from the main house. Look up there," he interrupted himself, pointing, "that's the Morgan place."

Craning my neck forward, I caught my breath in wonder. Both Whitey and Dr. Orcutt had referred to it as the 'big house' and they weren't kidding. Palatial would have been more appropriate. Pretentious, certainly.

The three-story, brick house was Victorian in every sense of the word. The steeply gabled roofs, high arched windows and ornate cupola crowning a round tower gave the place a brooding, almost gothic atmosphere. It was a perfect setting for a mystery, I thought, marveling at the sprawl of an additional, more modern wing that seemed strangely at odds with the older main structure. It presented an extraordinary picture, a monument to the past, dominating the hillside and holding court over the tiny town tucked in the valley below.

Audrey gawked. "What a weird-looking house. There must be a hundred rooms."

I glanced back at D.J. and was surprised to find him

watching Audrey in the rear-view mirror. There was an intense light in his eyes that vanished when his gaze slid to mine. "Hey. You know the old adage," he said, giving me a wink. "If you got it, flaunt it."

He seemed to thoroughly enjoy his little joke, but I could have sworn I detected just a hint of envy in his high-pitched laugh. Glancing at the house again, it was easy to see why. A man in his position, even if he worked a lifetime, would have a difficult time ever attaining such a prize. And it had come to Audrey simply by virtue of birth.

"So, how many rooms are there?" I asked D.J. as he downshifted on the steep grade.

"Twenty-six to be exact. I heard the original house is over a hundred years old and the rest of it was kind of added on piecemeal over the years."

As we passed through a wrought iron gate blanketed by thick vines, I noticed him stiffen. "Uh oh. I wonder what's hit the fan now?" he mused softly, pointing ahead.

There were two vehicles parked in the curved driveway. The first was a spanking new green and bronze pick-up, doors standing wide open, and the second was a county sheriff's patrol car.

I perked up immediately. "What's going on?"

"Maybe Marta finally killed Jesse," he chuckled, braking at the foot of a magnificent set of stone steps that climbed steeply to a spacious screened-in porch, flanked on each side by ornate latticework entwined with pink and white roses.

On closer inspection, I decided the architects had done a rather admirable job of connecting the old Victorian to its more contemporary counterpart by way of a delicate archway that spanned a narrow drive leading to an enclosed garage behind the house.

"Jesse's here?" Audrey asked, grimacing.

"Yeah. I've been helping her and Haston move most of their stuff out this morning. I think she was hoping to be gone by the time you got here," he said with a look of sly amusement. He shut off the engine as we pushed the doors open and stepped out.

"And speak of the devil," I murmured, nodding towards an open doorway just as Jesse appeared, her arms loaded with boxes filled to overflowing. When she spotted us, she flung her cargo into the front seat, then swung around, a murderous look blazing in her blood-shot eyes. "You little bitch!" she snarled at Audrey. "You've got a hell of a nerve calling in the middle of the night and ordering us out without so much as a by your leave."

Audrey's mouth gaped open. "I didn't..."

"Don't bother denying it." She cast a furtive look at the old house, growling, "I don't give a good goddamn anyway. This place gives me the creeps."

"Wait a minute," Audrey cried, "I...I never called you."

Jesse leveled a contemptuous look at her before clambering ungracefully into the truck. She slammed the door, gunned the engine and shouted a final warning out the window. "If you try screwing us over like that pig-headed old man of yours, you're gonna regret it."

She peeled out in a plume of blue tire smoke and got only a few yards before she realized the passenger door was open. Practically standing the truck on its grill, she squealed to a stop, stretched to close the door, then shot forward, vanishing through the gate.

From childhood, I'd been accused of possessing my grandmother's red-hot Irish temperament, but my tantrums paled in comparison to Jesse's. Audrey was definitely going to have her hands full. Sober, the woman seemed just as nasty as she'd been drunk. Could she have been blitzed enough to dream up a call from Audrey? If not, someone had played a heartless joke on her. And it had to be someone who would benefit from renewed friction between the two heirs. "Well," I ventured, breaking the silence "at least she doesn't think you're an imposter today."

"No," Audrey answered, thoughtfully. "Today, I'm just a bitch."

"That's probably a step up in her book."

"What in the world was she talking about?"

"I don't know."

She shook her head. "So much for Dr. Orcutt's suggestion that I try to get along. How? She's...she's impossible!"

"Impossible?" echoed an accented voice from behind. "Impossible is a kind word for that vile creature."

We turned to see a short, stocky Hispanic woman of perhaps sixty, standing in the doorway Jesse had exited only moments before. Uncharitably, I thought she was one of the homeliest people I'd ever seen. Her full lips were turned down at the corners and the thick glasses resting atop her blunt nose magnified the scornful gleam in her black eyes. "We can all give thanks to the Virgin Mary that she is gone," the woman continued, moving closer and peering into Audrey's face.

Flinching under the woman's intense scrutiny, she asked, "Are you Marta?"

She grunted affirmatively and inclined her head in my direction. "Who is that?"

"Kendall O'Dell," Audrey answered. "She'll be staying here with me for a while."

Marta returned her attention to Audrey. "Humph!

Jesse Pickrell's eyes must be many times worse than mine. How can she not see that you have the Morgan blood running in your veins?"

She cupped Audrey's face in one hand, turning it right and then left. "You have the same eyebrows, the same hair. I will show you pictures." She started for the door, then turned back to beckon Audrey. "Come into the house. And you too," she tacked on, pointing a finger at me before directing her gaze at D.J, who'd been lounging near the car looking amused. "Put the bags in the kitchen until we decide where everyone will sleep."

He saluted her, squashed his cigarette on the pavement and moved to the rear of the Suburban.

I smiled to myself. It was evident that Marta Nuñez was accustomed to ruling the roost and I could understand why she and Jesse's personalities clashed.

Having finally reached the end of our journey, I was brimming with nervous energy as I followed Audrey and Marta into a small flag-stoned entryway and then along a narrow hall that opened into a spacious living room decorated in rough-hewn southwestern style furniture.

As much as I wanted to hear what Marta had to say, I was curious to find out why someone from the sheriff's department was here. I also needed to check in with Tugg and I was anxious to get back downtown to the Muleskinner to get my car and have another chat with Whitey.

I couldn't be in four places at once I consoled myself, so I'd have to take one step at a time.

"See?" the housekeeper proclaimed, shoving a framed portrait in front of Audrey. "My eyes are not so good anymore but the face is the same, no?"

"Unreal," Audrey murmured. Moving beside her, I

studied the obviously dated photograph of Grady Morgan. Dr. Orcutt was right. He'd been one heck of a good-looking guy and the resemblance to Audrey was unmistakable. So, why had Jesse and Haston insisted she was an imposter with such irrefutable evidence staring them in the face?

"And this is your grandfather, Mr. Jeb," Marta said, pressing a small gilded frame into her hands. Though not nearly as handsome as Grady, the bushy brows were obviously a genetic trait, I thought, staring at the elder Morgan's unsmiling face.

Audrey pointed to another photo. "Who are those people?"

"That is your Aunt Sarah and her husband."

"Haston's parents." I reflected. "Where are they?"

"Dead."

"She was beautiful," Audrey said, tracing the woman's likeness with her finger before her expression turned hopeful. "Are there any old photos of...me? And my mother?"

The woman's heavy features crumpled into pity. "I think maybe no."

"Why not?"

"Soon after I come here, Mr. Morgan is still very, very mad that you and your mother are gone away. Some nights he drinks a lot. He looks at the pictures and cries. Then sometimes when I clean the next day, I see them on the floor torn in many pieces or..." She hesitated and her deepening expression of concern propelled Audrey to ask, "What? What is it?"

"One day he burns them in the fireplace."

Audrey swallowed hard. "All of them?"

She shrugged. "There is a big trunk upstairs full of

many old things. Perhaps you will find more," Marta said, matter-of-factly, replacing the photos on the mantle above the blackened stone fireplace. "But first, you will have lunch now, yes?"

Audrey stared uncomprehending, her hesitation seeming to signify that formulating a decision on that issue was more than she could handle at the moment. Or perhaps it was just plain shock. It was apparent that even though she'd done her best to prepare for this moment, she was still having difficulty accepting the reality of her situation.

Famished as usual, I told Marta, "Lunch would be great." We followed her through an arched doorway and down an L-shaped hallway that led into a large kitchen decorated with cheerful blue and white checked wallpaper. Colorful ceramic chickens of varying sizes apparently were the chosen decor, because they adorned every countertop and windowsill. They also appeared in the form of canisters, salt and peppershakers, oven mitts and refrigerator magnets. Happily accepting frosty glasses of raspberry iced tea, we seated ourselves at the cozy breakfast nook adjacent to a bay window overlooking the narrow slope of lawn leading down to a deep ravine that wound its way behind the house.

A movement at the rear of the old Victorian caught my attention and I noticed a man kneeling there, poking the ground beneath a row of well-trimmed hedges.

Audrey noticed too. "Who's that?"

Marta stopped her sandwich preparation and stared out the kitchen window above the sink. "Is it D.J.?" She narrowed her eyes as if to focus.

"No," I answered. "This guy's older. Gray hair. Wearing a white shirt and tan slacks."

"Oh. That's Orville Kemp from the sheriff's office.

Maybe today he will find something to prove that Mr. Morgan did not..." She aimed a worried glance at Audrey, then said, "I'm sorry. Does anyone talk to you about your father?"

"A little." Her inquiring gaze challenged me to do my job.

I warmed to the task. "So, Marta, we've heard that Mr. Morgan had been drinking heavily the night he fell. What do you think happened?"

Something flickered behind her dark eyes. "I think maybe it is not an accident."

"Why would you say that?" I asked, heeding the troubled look on Audrey's face.

Marta heaved a troubled sigh and pried open a head of lettuce. "Mr. Morgan worries much this past year. Something...how do you say...bothers his mind? Sometimes there are the telephone calls and afterwards his eyes, they are..." she hesitated, apparently searching for words, "filled with torment. His moods grow much worse until the last few weeks before he dies—and then the bottle becomes his mistress, day and night."

"Would you say he was despondent enough to have taken his own life?"

She shrugged, her black eyes reflecting skepticism. "I don't know."

"Was anything else bothering him?" I asked, noting with satisfaction the generous piles of turkey she heaped onto our sandwiches.

"There were many fights with Mr. Haston and his terrible wife," she said, rolling her eyes. "And also with that loco woman, Willow Windsong."

"Willow Windsong?" Audrey echoed.

The two of us exchanged a look of wry amusement,

before I said, "That's a rather unusual name. Where does she fit into this picture?"

Marta scowled. "The foolish woman cries big tears over the birds and squirrels that will be killed if Mr. Morgan opens the mine again."

"Did she ever threaten him?" I asked, swallowing another sip of tea.

Marta stopped her meal preparations and stood for a moment, thinking. "One time she and some of her noisy friends all chain themselves to the gate at the entrance to the mine. Mr. Morgan has them all arrested and she screams at him that he is an abom...abomin..."

"Abomination?" I inserted.

"Yes. Abomination to the earth and all the creatures."

"Was Jesse Pickrell here the day he died?"

Her lips curled in disdain. "Oh, yes. There was a terrible fight. In the late afternoon, Willow comes too. I would not let her in, so she screams at him from the driveway until he orders her away."

"Were either of them here when he fell?"

Another shrug. "That night I visit with my daughter and her family. After dinner, I did not feel too good, so I come home early and go to bed."

"About what time was that?"

Marta pressed the top slice of bread onto the lunchmeat and frowned at Audrey. "Your friend asks many questions."

Audrey flashed the woman an engaging smile that did wonders for her dour expression. "She works for a newspaper. She's an investigative reporter."

"What is investigative?" Marta asked.

"I'm sort of like a detective," I replied, grinning,

"except I get paid a lot less."

Marta tilted her head thoughtfully at me. "You will write about this in your paper?"

"Only with Miss Morgan's permission."

A look of contemplation glistened in the woman's eyes as she set the two gigantic sandwiches in front of us. "This is good. I am happy to know there will be someone to listen with open ears."

After inviting her to join us at the table, I dug into my lunch and urged her to continue her story.

She eagerly recounted how she'd been awakened around ten o'clock when she heard shouts coming from the old wing of the house. Thinking it odd, since Grady Morgan's bedroom was also located in the newer addition, she arose to investigate and, after a cursory search of the house, found him crumpled in the ravine below the balcony at the rear of the mansion. While frantically dialing the sheriff's office from the parlor phone located on the ground floor, she'd looked up in time to see someone run past the window and vanish into the darkness.

"And you're sure it was a woman?" I probed, finishing the last bite of my sandwich.

An emphatic nod. "I think perhaps the sheriff does not believe me, but the moon it is very bright. I can see her hair flying. I can see her long dress." A sudden look of dismay crossed her leathery-brown features and her tone turned reverent. "Mr. Morgan, he lays down there on the rocks," she said, pointing a stubby finger towards the window, "and I think at first he is dead, but when I call his name, his eyes open and they are big with fright."

My heart leaped with anticipation. "Really? Did he say anything to you?"

"Yes. It is difficult to hear him. His voice is very

weak. But I think he says, 'the day is here.'"

Audrey shrugged her puzzlement. "What do you suppose that meant?"

"I don't know. But that is not all. Then I hear him say very clear that she comes to visit him before and now justice is finally done."

"Who came to visit?" asked Audrey in a tense, sharp voice.

Black eyes wide and solemn, she swiftly crossed herself, whispering "The angel of death."

I wasn't quite sure what to make of Marta's story, but as Audrey and I followed her on a tour of the house, I was sure of two things. I didn't believe an angel had been making crank telephone calls to Grady Morgan, nor did I believe for a second that one of the winged creatures had shoved him off the balcony.

Of predominant interest to me was the fact that Grady, Audrey and Jesse had all received calls from an unknown woman. All I had to do now was figure out what linked them.

Audrey declined Marta's suggestion that she stay in Grady's old room, and expressed no interest in the other two Spartanly-furnished bedrooms in the newer wing of the house. She was however, as enchanted as I was with the old Victorian and, much to Marta's consternation, chose a room on the second floor.

We both ooh'd and aah'd over the crystal doorknobs, delicate lace curtains and a carved Early American four-poster bed with matching armoire that would have made an antique dealer drool. Fingering the tiny pink rosebuds on the faded cream wallpaper, Audrey sighed dreamily, "This is the room I want."

"But, there is no air-conditioning on the top floors," Marta protested, grunting as she tugged stubborn windows open to air out the stuffy room. "And this part of the house is not used for many years."

I rather suspected that she did not relish the thought of tackling the steep staircase on a daily basis and, considering her weight and age, I couldn't really blame her.

"It's not all that uncomfortable," Audrey insisted. "A fan will be fine for now."

I'd noticed that the ground floor bedroom boasted a window air-conditioner so I opted for that one.

Realizing she could not dissuade us, Marta shrugged and went away grumbling that she would have to enlist D.J. to help with the cleaning. Audrey announced that she needed a nap and that left me free to undertake the first task on my list.

Using the old-fashioned rotary phone in the ornate sitting room adjacent to my bedroom on the first floor, I put in a call to the paper only to find that Tugg was out to lunch. I gave Ginger the number and told her I'd be available later in the afternoon.

"Oh, hey, sugar. Tally faxed some copy in from Flagstaff a while ago. He's fixin' to come back to town early Thursday morning and said he was gonna stop in here for a short spell before he heads on down to Mexico. You got any messages for him?"

"If he has time, he can call me before he leaves," I told her, feeling a tingle of warmth at the possibility of hearing a final farewell before his trip. "Otherwise you can tell him 'all's quiet on the Western front' for now."

As I replaced the receiver I wished I had time to explore the rest of the house, but since the patrol car was still parked in the driveway, duty called.

I retrieved my camera and hurried down the steps to begin my quest. It would be helpful if Orville Kemp could shed some light on Marta's fanciful tale.

The well-kept grounds were impressive. Apparently D.J. possessed a major green thumb. Tall willow trees dotted a perfectly manicured lawn embroidered with tiny purple and white flowers. The bushes were neatly pruned. The scrub oak and crab apple trees were trimmed to perfection. No sounds, save an occasional birdcall or the intermittent tinkling of wind chimes, disturbed the silence.

My eyes traveled appreciatively over the graceful architecture of the old mansion. Jesse had declared it creepy, but in my opinion the place possessed a distinct air of enchantment.

I snapped a few shots of the house and walked on. Clusters of sunflowers had been artfully planted around the rock outcroppings that bordered a path leading down towards a cozy-looking cottage. I wondered if it was D.J.'s place.

I circled the house searching for Orville Kemp. Strange. Where had he gone? I crossed the ravine and followed the path uphill. Beyond a sagging range fence, almost unnoticeable among the tall chaparral and overgrown mesquite, I discovered what looked like the remains of an old road snaking over the top of the rise.

But still no sign of Orville Kemp. I turned to admire the spectacular view of the San Pedro River Valley spreading out below me. Typical of the summer monsoon, the usual afternoon build-up of thunderheads was in progress. They towered above the distant peaks hovering majestically above the valley floor, their swollen gray bellies already releasing a wispy veil of moisture that didn't quite reach the ground.

"The Indians call that walking rain," said a raspy voice from behind me. Startled, I swung around and stared into the ice-blue eyes of Orville Kemp who had appeared from nowhere. "Sorry," he added, his lips cracking in a wily grin. "Didn't mean to scare you." Head cocked sideways his silver hair glinted in the sun as he appraised me carefully. "You the Morgan girl?"

I told him who I was, where I was from, and why I was there. As I talked, he hitched his hip against a boulder and proceeded to light a pipe. After a moment, he puffed out a cloud of aromatic smoke. "Investigative reporter, huh? You talked to Deputy Brewster yet?"

"Not yet. I was hoping I could get some answers from you first."

One corner of his mouth lifted. "You can try."

By the look of shrewd amusement gathering in his eyes, I suspected that I could ask, but he may not necessarily answer. "For starters, I'm assuming since you're not in uniform, that you're a detective." Homicide, I hoped.

"Yep."

Elation surged through me. Apparently the Morgan case was not yet closed. "Are you still investigating Grady Morgan's death?"

"We've got a few unanswered questions."

"Then, would I be correct in assuming that you've decided that Marta Nuñez's story holds some credibility?"

He didn't answer immediately. Instead, his gaze roamed over the amber hills where the skeletal remains of ancient head frames marked the graves of abandoned mines. "Marta's blind as a bat," he countered lazily, returning his attention to me. "She can't see ten feet in front of her in broad daylight let alone the dead of night."

I studied his craggy face. If he didn't believe she'd seen something, what was he looking for? "Marta says Grady Morgan had altercations with Jesse and another woman the same day he died."

"Yep."

"And, from what little I've heard, they both had strong motives for, shall we say, hastening his demise."

His level stare deepened. I had the impression he was playing cat and mouse with me as he deliberately fiddled with his pipe, tamping it, re-lighting it. "Gotta have proof," he said at length.

"I know. Found anything interesting lately?"

He answered that question with silence, then quietly stated, "I wouldn't get too carried away with Marta's wild tale, Miss O'Dell."

"Oh? What reason would she have to fabricate it?"

With a sigh, he knocked the ashes from his pipe. I thought for a minute he wasn't going to reply but then he said, "No doubt you'll be hightailing it over to Bisbee to get a peek at the DR on Grady, so you may as well know that he filed several theft reports within this last year."

I locked eyes with him, not sure I'd caught his insinuation. "Are you saying he suspected Marta?"

"Pretty much."

"Why? What was taken?"

"Don't remember specifically, but he claimed the stuff was real valuable and the thefts seemed to coincide with her trips across the border to visit her sister in Naco."

"Where's that?"

He squinted over my shoulder. "Little border town over there at the foot of Thunder Peak."

"Why didn't he fire her?"

"Again, Miss O'Dell," he answered succinctly. "Proof."

Buffeted by a sudden gust of wind, we took note of the fast-approaching storm and, without another word, began to move towards the house.

"So," I continued, matching my steps with his. "You think she may have made the whole thing up to cover her activities?"

"Don't know."

"Did Deputy Brewster call you out to investigate the night Grady fell?"

"Yep."

"And, can I assume that the examining physician was Miles Orcutt?"

"Yep."

"Did Grady Morgan say anything to him?"

He slid me a provocative glance. "Don't know."

I sighed inwardly. Getting answers from this man was like pulling impacted molars. But then, I understood. While he was very good at playing the part of the backcountry law officer, I had the feeling that beneath his hick exterior lay the heart of a shrewd detective. I also knew that certain information was public record and the rest he might not be at liberty to divulge. Nevertheless, as we reached the kitchen entrance, I felt like I'd made some headway. Officially, he maintained that Grady Morgan's death was still listed as accidental, but his inference was clear and I now had three female suspects.

Armed with the new information, I looked at Marta through different eyes now as she rushed out the door wiping her hands on a dishcloth. "Whitey Flanigan calls on the phone. He says for you to come downtown now and he will get your car."

"Thanks." I turned to Orville. "Do you think you could give me a lift?"

"Yep."

I grinned and asked if he could wait a moment while I got my car keys. He nodded, bid Marta good-bye and ambled towards his patrol car.

I hurried to my bedroom, snatched up my purse and then took the stairs two at a time to Audrey's room where I found her unpacking suitcases. I was surprised to see that she was not alone. A fuzzy orange cat occupied the center of her bed.

"So, who's your new friend?" I asked, reaching to pet the animal's soft fur. A deep, rumbling purr was my immediate reward.

"I don't know. He...or she was sleeping beside me when I woke up."

"Did you have a nice nap?"

"Oh, yes. It's really peaceful here." Her eyes did look a little brighter and two spots of color graced her high cheekbones. "I'm a little disappointed though," she continued. "I thought when I got here I'd remember something. I mean, if I lived in this house for three years, how come nothing looks familiar?"

"Give it some time. You can never tell what might trigger a memory." I looked out the window and saw that

Orville had backed his car closer to the stone steps. "I'd like to stay and talk but Detective Kemp is waiting to give me a ride downtown."

"So that's where you've been. Did he tell you anything?"

"A little."

"What?"

I edged towards the door. "How about we talk later? I really have to get my car off that road before it rains again."

"Okay," she sighed, pulling a long flowered skirt from her bag, "but I wanted to tell you that I phoned the lawyer and the accountant while you were outside. I've got appointments to see both of them day after tomorrow. Will you be able to drive me to Bisbee?"

"Sure." It would give me a perfect opportunity to drop by the sheriff's office and have a look at the Morgan file. "And you might think about making one more call while I'm gone."

By the look of dread stealing over her face, I knew she was aware of who I meant. "You mean Haston? He's not going to talk to me."

"He has no choice. Find out if we can see them some time tomorrow." She looked decidedly unhappy, but I didn't have two or three weeks to wait while she mustered the courage to face her obnoxious relatives. "You can't put it off forever," I reminded her gently.

"I guess not. When will you be back?"

"Soon as I can," I called over my shoulder just as a rumble of thunder rattled the windowpanes. By the time I reached the patrol car, the wind had whipped my hair into a tangle. "You can drop me a couple of blocks from the Muleskinner," I told Orville, climbing in beside him.

He frowned. "You sure about that?"

"I want to get some pictures," I said, patting my camera. "And I feel the need to walk the streets of Morgan's Folly before I write about it. You know, to try and soak up the atmosphere of the place."

His dubious glance let me know that he thought I was completely nuts. "Guess you don't mind getting good and wet."

I laughed. "After yesterday, I think I can handle it."

He listened intently while I recapped the events of the day before and his frown deepened. "That's mighty strange," was all he said as he eased to a stop beneath a sun-faded sign that would have said Prospector Street if the P hadn't been missing.

I thanked him and stepped out onto the sidewalk fronting the Huddle Cafe, which according to the sign, closed for the afternoon, then re-opened at five for dinner.

"Oh, one more thing, Miss O'Dell," Orville called out.

I turned back and leaned in the window. "Yes?"

"Since it appears that we're going to be partners," he said with an unmistakable twinkle in his eyes, "I reckon you'll keep me posted if anything out of the ordinary happens."

Judging by the events of the last twenty-four hours, nothing in this town seemed even close to being ordinary. I flashed him a conspiratorial smile and signaled a thumbs up. "You can count on it."

I watched his patrol car cruise out of sight thankful that the driving wind had subsided. The clouds were growing darker so the lull in the storm was probably temporary. There were no other cars, no pedestrians, and with the exception of a few birds twittering and the occasional bark of a dog somewhere in the distance, an eerie silence prevailed.

Morgan's Folly emitted an aura of decay and neglect. But as I strolled along the uneven sidewalks, peeking through grimy windows at the sad remains of closed businesses, it was easy to envision what it must have looked like a hundred years ago.

Pausing to admire the intricate stone scrollwork above the arched doorway of one building, I laid one hand against the blackened bricks. Tally would claim it was my over-active imagination, but I felt a distinct sensation, almost a vibration of the rich history of this once-bustling boomtown emanating through my fingers.

I closed my eyes and conjured up the image of these dusty streets alive with the rumble of mule-drawn freight wagons, horses and pedestrians. Beyond the rusted piles of mine tailings, the shriek of the whistle would announce the shift change at the mine. And from the closed, shuttered saloons, I could hear the echo of raucous laughter from bone-tired miners quenching their pent-up thirst. Envisioning the words in my article, I pulled out my notepad and jotted down my observations.

Fortunately, Tally had given me a crash course in Arizona history and I knew that the remains of dozens of ghost towns still littered the state. But, I mused, continuing my stroll and snapping pictures, this was a recent death. The insanity of Grady Morgan's seemingly irresponsible decision to close the mine down struck me again. Of course I knew a little more about his volatile personality since Dr. Orcutt's and Marta's disclosures, but still...

Overcome by curiosity, I picked up my pace, anxious to get the ball rolling on my story. These old buildings couldn't talk but people sure could. And right now my best source of information lay behind the sagging stone walls of the Muleskinner Saloon.

I was only a few feet from the front door when I noticed a late model sedan cruising by. I did a double take when I noticed the driver was none other than Fran Orcutt. She was staring a hole right through me. The unexpected expression of fear and longing reflected in her sunken eyes made me falter.

Puzzled, I lifted my hand and she returned my greeting with the barest glimmer of a smile before accelerating out of sight. What on earth was that all about? I wondered, turning to push open the saloon door.

A sharp clap of thunder mingled with the crack of pool balls as I paused to accustom my eyes to the murky interior. Overhead fans fastened to a burnished copper ceiling whirred softly and from the battered red jukebox, a country singer crooned a sad ballad to the dozen or so people scattered about.

"Hey there, Irish," shouted Whitey from behind the bar. "I'll be damned if you don't clean up real good."

Of course that caused every guy in the place to turn and gawk at me. Slightly disconcerted at being the center of attention again, I slid onto one of the wobbly barstools and grinned at Whitey. "Being dry is a definite plus."

He gave me a friendly wink. "I'd say so. Yesterday you looked like you'd been drug through a knothole ass backwards."

"And I felt like it."

"Howdy do, ma'am," called out another man two stools over. He fingered the grimy bill of his ball cap and I nodded in return, noting that he had three chins, several teeth missing, and the overalls he wore looked as though they hadn't encountered soap in many moons. "I'm Earl.

Me 'n' Buddy 'n' Skeet here," he said, thumbing over his shoulder, "hauled that there tree off the Boneyard for you."

"Well, I'm forever in your debt. I hope you'll let me reimburse all of you for your time and effort."

There was a chivalrous clamor of refusals from the men and Whitey chimed in, "Skeet here's even offered to go and bring your car back, if you like."

I focused on a man Ginger would have dubbed 'a long tall drink of water'. "That's awfully nice of you. Are you sure?"

Reddening, he laid his pool cue down and fixed his eyes on the floor. "I'd be right honored to help you out, ma'am. There ain't no point in you getting yourself all muddied up, what with another storm coming and all."

Touched by his generosity, I was grateful to be in the company of such affable people. It didn't take a genius to figure out that these men were obviously out of work. Why else would they be hanging around a bar at two o'clock on a Tuesday afternoon? I handed him my car keys and he left with a companion in tow.

"What's your pleasure, Irish?" Whitey asked, wiping away a non-existent spill in front of me.

I rarely drank this early and was tempted to refuse, but I had the feeling they were all waiting for my answer. Since I'd entered their world, I surmised that my chances of gaining acceptance would improve if I joined them. "Beer would be great."

Whitey looked pleased. Decked out in a finely-cut, black Western suit with a turquoise bola tie cinched nattily at his throat, I thought him an extraordinarily handsome man, even though he was probably old enough to be my grandfather.

"So then," he began, drawing down the spigot to fill

my mug with foamy brew, "I'm curious to know how it is that you come to be with Miss Morgan? You a family friend?"

As I repeated what I'd told Orville, plus a few pertinent facts from Dr. Orcutt's conversation, his flushed face bore a look of concentrated speculation as he twirled one end of his snowy mustache.

I held my breath. This was usually the time when people who had something to hide closed up tighter than a clam shell, and those who didn't, warmed to the opportunity to become instant celebrities. He didn't disappoint me.

"So, you're a newspaper reporter," he boomed loud enough so everyone in the place could hear. "Castle Valley, huh? That's a real nice little town. You just ask away, Irish, and we'll see if we can't give you some grist for the mill, so to speak."

His expression of *we* seemed an obvious invitation for the other men to throw in their two cents worth. Most of the men quietly abandoned their pool game and drifted nonchalantly towards the bar. Again, I appeared to be providing a diversion from their monotonous routines.

Seizing the moment, I offered to buy drinks for everyone and was rewarded by a sincere chorus of gratitude. I settled myself more comfortably, pulled out my notepad and fired off the first question. "Let's start with the present situation. I'm puzzled as to why Grady Morgan at first accepted Haston's offer of new capital and then changed his mind?"

Whitey shook his head solemnly. "There ain't no one answer to that. The past and present all kind of mesh together into a pretty complicated story."

"How so?"

He sucked in a measured breath. "When Haston

first came back from being down there in Venezuela for eight years, Grady seemed happy as a fox in a hen house."

"What was Haston doing in South America?"

"Had him a good job working for some big company. You did know he's a mining engineer."

"No."

"Yep. Real smart kid," he continued, hitching up his pants. "Anyhow, he was pretty pissed off when he found out Grady had put the mine on caretaker status."

I took a sip of beer. "And what was his reasoning for that?"

"Grady hated running the mine and besides, he was too busy having a grand old time squandering away most everything the family had built-up for three generations."

"I see. So, what did Haston do?"

"Grabbed the bull by the horns and brought in a couple of geologist friends," Whitey replied handing out drinks to the other men. "They pulled the production records and did some studying on the ore reserve and sub surface maps. When they did some test drilling it verified what he suspected. There is one humongous vein of gold down there! Probably a million contained ounces, I hear."

My pulse shot up. Audrey might be a rich woman after all. Very rich. "I'd wager that got Grady's attention."

A bearded man from the end of the bar growled, "Unlessen you get it out of the ground, it don't do nobody no good. And that ol' devil never did give a rat's ass about the mine or us. All he cared about was the cold hard cash."

"If Grady disliked the business so much, why didn't he allow Haston to take over?" I asked Whitey.

"He was all set to do just that till he found out the backer was Duncan Claypool. He was pretty burned up to say the least."

"Burned up?" cackled one old geezer, smacking his hand on the bar. "He 'bout shit a brick."

If the man's rough language was designed to make me flinch it failed. I felt I'd passed the test of being 'one of the guys' as I joined in the appreciative laughter.

I looked back at Whitey. "Okay. Who's Duncan Claypool?"

"I was just about to get to that," he said, grinning. Every man at the bar hunched closer as he launched into a tale that became so engrossing, I forgot to take notes.

Lured by news of gold, silver, and copper strikes in Arizona, Grady's grandfather, Seth Morgan, had left his wife and son behind in New York and headed west to seek his fortune. Because the Copper Queen Mine at Bisbee was producing millions, he was crushed to find that most of the surrounding property had already been snatched up by wealthy speculators. Ever the optimist, he wandered miles beyond the Mule Mountains, convinced that there had to be other rich ore bodies in the vicinity.

"Most folks thought he was a mite touched in the head when he filed claims way out here in this godforsaken spot," offered another man whose deeply grooved face resembled an old work glove.

"Why?" I asked. "I thought there were tons of prospectors in this area?"

"There were," Whitey replied. "But most of 'em weren't as obstinate as Seth. No one else would have stuck it out for ten long, lonesome years with nothing to show for it."

"Wait a minute," I interrupted. "You mean to tell me he left his family stranded back east for ten years?"

"Well, not the whole time," Earl spoke up, grinning. "He must've gone back a couple a times because he and

Hannah managed to rustle up two more kids."

That elicited more hearty laughter from the men and I said, "I admire her patience."

"You got to understand something about the 1872 Mining Act," Earl said. "You can't just stake a claim and set on it forever. You got to file every year. And then, you got to prove you done at least a smidgen of work on it or you lose it altogether."

"Poor Seth was the laughing stock of the whole damn mining district," added the grizzle-faced man, lighting up a cigarette while signaling Whitey for another beer. "But he kept at it. The man had a powerful lot of faith. He told everyone he met that fame and fortune lay just beyond the next shovel full of dirt."

I nodded. "Thus the name Morgan's Folly. But wasn't Seth vindicated in the end?"

"Hold on, you're getting ahead of me," Whitey said. "Seth got word that one of his kids was real sick so he had to skedaddle back home. He wasn't about to just up and abandon the claims, so he contracted with a merchant in Bisbee who'd grubstaked him a couple of times. He asked him to re-register the claims till he could get back. Then he leaned on a buddy of his, a prospector named Henry something-or-other, to witness the agreement. But things didn't work out quite like he planned."

I cracked a wry smile. "Let me guess. The merchant's name was Claypool."

"Jasper T. Claypool to be exact," said Whitey, refilling my beer mug. "Anyway, Claypool hired Henry to work the Morgan claims and didn't pay much attention for a couple of months. Then one day, Henry brought him a chunk of quartz loaded with gold crystals and Jasper's eyeballs about popped out. It was time to re-up the claims, and Seth was still away so..."

"Claypool registered them in his own name," I finished, shaking my head. "But what about Henry? I thought you said he witnessed the agreement?"

Earl piped up. "Jasper was a clever ol' dog. He shipped him off to work in the Alaska gold fields."

Whitey cut in again. "Claypool told everybody he met that Seth had traded him the claims for passage east, plus money to care for his sick kid. Of course no such thing happened and when Seth got back and found out what Jasper had done, that was the beginning of the bad blood between the families. You see, without Henry, Seth had no way to prove his case to the mining district in Santa Fe. So, he got himself a gun and went after Jasper."

Completely caught up in the story, I took a quick gulp of my beer. "Then what?"

"Seth knocked him ass end over tea kettle and pointed the barrel square at his head. But it misfired and that gave Claypool time to dig his piece out and get off the first shot. Unfortunately his aim wasn't so good, and well...it's a damn good thing Seth had already sired him a son."

Whitey's ruddy face was turning a deep shade of crimson as I arched an inquiring brow. "Are you saying...?"

"Yep. Shot the left one clean off."

"Jesus," I whispered, noticing every guy in the place fidgeting squeamishly. "What happened next?"

"He expired," Earl put in, raising his mug in a silent toast.

"But not from the bullet wound," Whitey intoned, a faraway look glistening in his eyes. "Jasper finally hit the vein of gold Seth had known in his gut was there all along. And here's the rub. It wasn't but ten feet from where Seth quit digging. Poor soul died of a broken heart."

I frowned. "But I thought the Morgan family still owned the mine."

Whitey's eyes sparkled with mirth. "Jasper Claypool was a pretty shrewd fellow but he hadn't reckoned on Seth's widow, Hannah. She left the kids with her ma and showed up here to challenge his claim. After some detective work, she found out about Seth's friend Henry and booked passage to Alaska. It took her a whole year moving from camp to camp until she finally located him."

"Pretty gutsy lady," I remarked.

"To say the least. Anyhow, she hauled him back to testify on her behalf and then the lawyers hassled over it for a couple of more years till Claypool finally conceded his claim jumping. Of course by that time, he'd already mined enough copper and gold out of the Defiance to bankroll new claims and go on to become a jillionaire."

"The Defiance?" I inquired, coming back to reality enough to scribble some notes on the still-empty page.

"That's the name of the mine." Whitey's surprised frown indicated he thought I should already know that. Jasper had dubbed it the Devil's Basement, but Hannah renamed it in honor of Seth's bulldogged determination. She managed things till young Jeb was old enough to take over. He finally made the Defiance profitable, but it never achieved the likes of the Claypool Empire."

"Well, the dirty dog," I murmured. "He got away with it."

"Yep," Whitey answered, rubbing the cloth along the bar. "Even after the war when copper prices fell and Jeb was in big trouble, he flatly refused to sell when Jasper's son offered to buy him out. It was Hannah's dying wish that the mine stay in Morgan hands forever."

Everything seemed clear now. The longstanding hatred for the Claypools had obviously ended with Haston who had swallowed the family pride to obtain backing for his venture. I could even understand Jesse's resentment towards Grady who'd stubbornly harbored malice for something that had happened over a century ago. Had her hostility culminated in murder?

Conversation halted briefly when the lights dimmed. Thunder shook the building and we all turned toward the door when Skeet and his companion blew in accompanied by rain-scented wind. "Got 'er out for you just in the nick of time," he announced triumphantly, dangling the car keys in front of me. "Looks like we're gonna get drowned again."

I thanked him profusely, offering to pay for his time and was once again refused. At my insistence, he and his friend finally accepted a beer.

"I noticed you got some pretty sizeable dings in the hood," Skeet remarked. "I could run 'er over to Toomey's if you like."

"What's Toomey's?"

"Only garage left in town. Only place left to get gas and groceries too," he tacked on. "But, anyhow he does real good body work and could probably have 'er fixed for you in a couple a days."

"Thanks, but I think I'll wait till I'm back home. I like having my own wheels."

Whitey leaned on the bar, grinning. "You could drive that brand new Suburban."

I stared at him uncomprehending for a second. "You mean D.J.'s?"

"That ain't his," Earl scoffed. "He can't afford nothing that spiffy. It belonged to Grady. He uses it to run errands and haul Marta around."

"Doesn't she drive?" I asked.

"Naw. Ain't you seen them goggles she wears? They ain't gonna give her no driver's license."

"Even so. I wouldn't dream of taking his car."

Whitey's laugh boomed out. "Irish, you're slipping. Haven't you taken a gander inside that big garage up there behind the house?"

"No."

"There's enough vehicles in there to open a car lot. Good Lord, there's a 1930 Cord, a 1950 Healey and a 1955 Thunderbird as sweet as any you'll ever see. Classics they are, and most of them in mint condition. They're Miss Audrey's now. I'll bet you a dollar to a donut she'd let you pick out any one of them puppies you want."

I opened my mouth to politely decline when Earl cut in again. "Why don't you call Toomey's and get that squirrelly dame, Willow, to set you up an appointment."

My interest level shot up. "Willow Windsong?"

It was Whitey's turn to look surprised. "You know her?"

"Heard of her. What does she do there?"

"She keeps the books, sells groceries 'n' stuff, answers the phones," another old-timer volunteered from the far end of the bar. "She's only there till noon most days. The rest of the time you kin find 'er crashin' around in the brush rescuin' critters or settin' up in a tree on some bird's nest doing her damnedest to hatch eggs." The man's hoarse cackle was so contagious, laughter rippled through the room.

I caught Skeet's eye as I gathered up my things. "Thanks. I may take your suggestion, but right now I'd better head back up the hill before this storm hits. Oh, and thanks to everybody for the history lesson."

There was a returning chorus of gratitude for the beers, but as I slipped off the stool and prepared to go, it struck me. I hadn't asked the one question I needed to. "One more thing. Why was Dr. Orcutt and a man like Grady Morgan such close friends?"

Whitey puckered his lips thoughtfully. "They were an unlikely pair, I'll give you that. The Orcutts didn't have two nickels to rub together, but Miles was a real bright kid and I think Jeb hoped some of his smarts would rub off on Grady. When his pa died, old Jeb paid for the doc's medical schooling. After he and Fran got hitched, it wasn't but a couple months later Grady up and married his second cousin."

I stared blankly. "Wait a minute. I'm lost. Audrey's mother was Dr. Orcutt's cousin?"

"No, no, not Rita. She was Grady's second wife. First time around he married Lydia Crandall."

"I see. Were there any other children?"

Whitey's face clouded. "Yeah. Miss Audrey had an older sister named Dayln. Wild as a March hare, that one."

"More like the Demon's seed, if you ask me," muttered Earl.

A strange pall fell and I glanced sharply around the room, my stomach clenching in anticipation at the uneasy expressions shadowing the men's faces. I looked back at Whitey. "Somebody want to enlighten me?"

Whitey cleared his throat and concentrated on polishing a glass, for once seeming reluctant to talk. "Listen, Irish," he said at last, "there must be a hundred different versions of what really happened. You being a reporter and all and knowing how important it is to get your facts straight...if I was you, I'd haul my tail up Vixen Hill and have me a little chat with the kid's godmother, Ida Fairfield."

I eyed him with skeptical amusement. "Vixen Hill?"

Grinning broadly, he explained that over the years, some of the surrounding slopes had acquired colorful names like Dead Dog, Silver Bird and Devil's Hill.

"That's where the Morgan place sets," Earl offered, adding, "You know why it's called that?"

I looked around at the expectant faces. "No."

"Well, it's cuz of them two big ol' rocks that stick out of the top. When you see 'em from just the right angle, they look just like the horns of old Satan himself."

"I see. By the way, I noticed what looks like the remains of a road behind the house."

Skeet answered, "Oh, that there's the old mine road. Ain't been used much in twenty years, but if you want a nice walk, you'll end up on the mine property."

"Interesting."

Whitey seemed slightly miffed that we'd interrupted his yarn and quickly regained the topic. "Now, then, getting back to how Ida's hill got its name. It seems her ma and several other ladies of the evening once operated the red light district way back when. Yes, sir," he said, arching a downy brow at me, "you can bet your boots the paths leading up and down that hill got used plenty."

I grinned. "No doubt. But I want to backtrack to the subject of Grady's first daughter. Why did Earl call her the Demon's seed?"

"Had a bit of the devil in her, just like her pa. She got into all manner of trouble at school. Hung out with a rough bunch of kids. Anyway, the story goes that when she was about twelve or thirteen Grady accused her of trying to do him in one night with a butcher knife."

I drew back in surprise, searching his face for signs that he might be putting me on. He wasn't. "Why?"

His elongated shrug was combined with an upward eye roll. "Nobody seems to know for sure."

I wondered if Dr. Orcutt knew. "So, what happened next?"

"He sent her ass away," a grim-faced Earl filled in.

"Where? To a juvenile detention center?"

"No," Whitey answered somberly. "To one of those places for the criminally insane."

With great reluctance, I finally tore myself from the friendly gathering at the Muleskinner and stepped outside. The sky was still overcast, but the wind had died down again, leaving the air heavy and oppressive. I was elated with what I'd learned. Bits and pieces of the stories whirled crazily in my head, especially the final one concerning Audrey's half-sister. I'd pressed Whitey for more details, but he'd been adamant that I talk to Ida Fairfield, adding only that Dayln Morgan had died in a mysterious fire over twenty years ago. It seemed unlikely that whatever happened back then had any bearing on the present, but I was itching to find out anyway. And considering how the events of a hundred years ago eerily interconnected with today, anything seemed possible.

The sight of my little blue Volvo parked at the curb brought me a feeling of warm comfort that faded into bewilderment as I drew closer. The car was solidly wedged between two vehicles. An ancient, pea-green Ford Falcon was backed up against the front bumper while a late-model pickup was parked snugly against the rear. There couldn't have been more than an inch to maneuver either way. What kind of a stupid joke was this?

Anger scorching my face, I looked up one side of the street and down the other at first seeing nothing suspicious. But on closer inspection, I spied two men loitering in a doorway and I was pretty sure I'd found my perpetrators. One was short, round and unfamiliar, but the second man was the creep who'd been eyeballing my wet T-shirt yesterday.

I approached them warily, unable to repress a prickle of revulsion at the way the taller man's eyes were boldly undressing me. It was pretty hard to miss the fact that he'd taken pains to spruce up a bit. He'd shaven close enough to nick himself a few times and he sported a clean sleeveless muscle shirt and leather vest.

Before I could utter a word, the chubby one in overalls let out a moronic twitter. "Archie wants to show you his snake."

"Is that so?" I switched my attention to the other man and my skin crawled. Leering, he turned sideways and extended his arm so I could get the full effect of the multi-colored rattlesnake tattoo stretching from wrist to shoulder. Slowly, he bent his elbow and flexed his biceps until the serpent's fangs scissored back and forth.

The notion that he thought his little sideshow would be a turn-on was nothing short of appalling, when in fact, the sight of it actually made me ill. Struggling to maintain composure, I said coolly, "My, my, isn't that impressive. And now, maybe you fellows would like to tell me what's going on."

"Is there a problem?" Archie asked with feigned innocence, running his tongue ever so slowly along his lower lip.

His behavior was irksome enough, but besides the unbridled lust mirrored in his eyes, there was a aura of menace about him that bothered me more. "Why don't you just cut the crap and move your truck."

"Oh, come on now," he coaxed, stepping close enough for me to get a whiff of his musk-scented cologne. "That ain't no way to be. I thought maybe you being a big time reporter and all, you might want to take a ride someplace nice and quiet where we could talk about a couple a things you might find real interesting."

Word traveled fast. It had only been a few hours since I'd revealed my vocation to Marta. I eyed him suspiciously, reluctant to pass up vital information, but if he thought I was going to jump in his truck and be driven God knows where, he definitely had a screw loose.

I pulled the notepad from my purse while forcing a smile. "If you have something to tell me, we can talk right here."

He hesitated. "Well...you sort of have to...you know, see it." His cloying tone was obviously meant to sound enticing and I would have had to be blind to miss the suggestive glint smoldering in his eyes. Suddenly, I was tired of the whole ridiculous game. "All right, Mr...Ah?" I paused expectantly, waiting for him to fill in his name.

"Lawton. Archibald Lawton," he replied smoothly. "But everybody calls me Archie."

"Okay, Archie," I began in a sugary tone, returning the notepad to my purse. "I'll be glad to come with you—as soon as fish need bicycles."

The light of expectation in his eyes darkened to anger when his sidekick brayed with laughter. "Shut up, Toby." He fired a withering glare at me before roughly grabbing his companion's sleeve and shoving him towards the green Falcon.

Then, without warning, Archie lost his footing. He slipped off the curb and had to grab the handle of his truck to avoid falling. That sent Toby into another fit of giggles and it was an effort to stifle my own laughter.

His wounded male ego in shambles, my would-be suitor made a valiant effort to restore his composure by vaulting into the cab. He ground the truck into reverse, backed up onto the curb, and then squealed away in a cloud of dust, much as Jesse had done earlier. I shook my head in wonder. Who were these guys? The two stooges?

It wasn't until I was almost back to the Morgan house that the memory surfaced. Archie drove a white pickup similar to the one I'd seen yesterday speeding toward Boneyard Pass. And his supposed off-hand remarks last night about how brave we'd been now seemed suspiciously coincidental.

But, try as I might, I couldn't figure out the point of this latest encounter. Whatever was going on, I decided, parking my car near the entrance to the big Victorian, Archie Lawton didn't appear to have enough working brain cells to mastermind anything. So the obvious conclusion was that someone had put him up to it. Why, was the question?

I hurried up the stairs, anxious to share my news with Audrey and found her pacing back and forth on the screen porch. "Where have you been?" she snapped, whirling to face me.

I drew back, surprised. "I told you where I was

going. I would have been here sooner except I was waylaid by a couple of scumballs with a rather questionable agenda."

"What do you mean?"

"You remember the nasty-faced guy at the bar last night?"

She blinked. "Which one?"

"Mr. Eyeballs. You know, the horny dude who was staring at my boobs?"

Her lips curled in distaste. "Oh, him."

I outlined my confrontation with the two men and she murmured, "Do you think he really had something important to show you?"

I shrugged and laid my camera and purse on the porch swing. "That I don't know, but I wouldn't be surprised to find that he had something to do with our little adventure with the falling rock yesterday."

She looked suitably stunned, but I could tell by the fearful expression in her eyes that something else besides my lateness was troubling her. "What's wrong? Did something happen while I was gone?"

"Dr. Orcutt was here."

"And?"

"He's real upset."

"About what?"

"You. He knows you're a reporter and why you're here. And he told me that if I allow you to print one word of this and let you go snooping around in the past he said..." She paused, lips trembling. "He said it would go directly against my mother's final wishes and forever tarnish her sacred memory."

It was amazing. In terms of speed, the Morgan's Folly grapevine rivaled the Internet. "Sacred memory, my ass. If you'll recall he admitted to being a reluctant partner to your mother's requests. Think about it, she must have had a deliberate reason for wanting you to come here or she wouldn't have gone to such effort to make sure. If you ask me it's Dr. Orcutt who has something to hide. Did you know that your grandfather paid for his medical schooling?"

Her mouth dropped open. "No. How would I know that?"

"I just found out myself. Remember he said your coming here had placed him in an awkward position? What's that all about? And you want to know something else? He left out quite a few pertinent details during our little chat this morning."

As I repeated what I'd heard at the saloon, a profusion of emotions marched across her guileless face. At first she frowned, sobered by the story of the Morgan/Claypool feud, and then the barest whisper of a smile blossomed during my account of the accidental shooting incident. The knowledge that she was on the brink of becoming a rich woman left her appearing vaguely nonplussed, but the last part, the news about Dayln, triggered a look of utter devastation. "I had a sister," she gasped, clutching her stomach as if in pain. "Oh, my God."

She sat down hard on the glider and stared unseeing into the distance. I kept quiet and the uneasy silence stretched on until she said in a subdued voice, "Kendall, you have a loving family. You can't imagine what it's like to be completely alone. No father, no sisters or brothers..."

"You did have your mother."

"True. But, she was so lost in herself it was...well, sometimes it was like being with nobody. I understand why now," she tacked on quickly, as if I would disagree, "but it still hurts. It hurts so much to know that she deprived me of my family, my real identity and..."

"Audrey, I'm convinced there's a lot more Dr. Orcutt hasn't told us."

"I know. I feel it too. Especially because of the things Mom said in her letter, but you know," she went on in a dreamy voice, "the best part is for the first time in my life, I feel certain that she really loved me and I would never, ever do anything to dishonor her memory."

I leaned my head on the glider back and stared morosely at bursts of violet heat lightning tinting the twilight sky. It was becoming tiresome to have to justify myself at every turn. "What do you want me to do?" I asked after another long empty moment. "I've got the car back. Do you want me to leave?"

She looked disconcerted. "Oh, no. You've been so kind and helpful. Please, I need you to stay. I don't care what Dr. Orcutt says."

I eyed her critically. Boy, she was hard to gauge. Hot one second, cold the next. "Look, Audrey the more I dig into past events, the more dicey things may get so I have to know that you're firmly in my corner. No wavering, no doubts. You think you can handle it?"

Appearing contrite, she compressed rosebud lips. "You're right, Kendall. I've never been much of a fighter, but I guess I have to take a stand sometime. And, you'll be proud of me. I even got up enough courage to call Haston while you were out."

"Well, that *is* progress. And when do we see the divine couple?"

She grinned at my remark. "Tomorrow at ten. He said the office is located about three miles west of here in a mobile home just beyond the main gate to the mine property. And you know what? He was actually fairly cordial to me. I guess Dr. Orcutt must have had another talk with him."

"Let's hope his lovely wife has simmered down," I said, reaching to gather my things. We both rose, but Audrey put a restraining hand on my arm. "By the way, you never told me what you talked about this afternoon with Orville Kemp."

She listened intently and reacted to the information casting suspicion on Marta with a sorrowful shake of her head. "What's been stolen?"

"He didn't say, but I'll know more when I get a look at the reports while we're in Bisbee on Thursday."

"But, Marta told me she's worked here for seventeen years. That means she came only a year after my mother and I left. Why would she suddenly begin to take things, and if she did, and my father caught her..." She turned horrified eyes on me. "So, Detective Kemp thinks Marta may have..."

I put up a hand to interrupt her. "That's nothing more than a theory at this point. Don't forget, he was obviously bombed out of his mind that night and if worst comes to worst we've got several other suspects skulking around besides her."

"I'm hoping his fall was just an accident," she said in a hushed voice. "It's pretty scary to think that someone might have actually...murdered him."

Perhaps it was the unsettling subject matter, or the restless wind rattling the leaves of the sycamore trees. Whatever, it spooked both of us when we heard a faint movement at the front door. "Who's there?" Audrey asked breathlessly, peering into the gloom.

"Sorry, girls," came D.J.'s mellow voice, "didn't mean to scare you, but Marta sent me over to tell Miss O'Dell that a Mr. Tuggs wants her to call him back before ten and that chow's on the table."

Looking relieved, Audrey said, "Thank you."

D.J. held the screen door open for us, reaching behind him to switch on a flowered globe lamp. Rose-colored light cast soft shadows and made the room seem warm and welcoming. He snapped on overhead lights as we followed him along the hall and across the covered walkway that connected the two wings. My intuitively suspicious nature at work, I wondered how long he'd been standing there listening to us.

Explaining that he normally ate in the kitchen, D.J. directed us to the two places already set at the table in the oak-paneled dining room before he pushed through the swinging doors.

Within moments, Marta emerged and served us a sumptuous meal. She had prepared roast duck with all the trimmings in honor of Audrey's first night. Later, as I finished the last bite of homemade pecan pie and set aside my napkin, I decided that this was a life I could easily get accustomed to.

We thanked Marta profusely when she returned to clear the plates. Her face beaming with pleasure, she informed us that D.J. was going to drive her across town to a friend's house for the evening and that tomorrow she would need to consult with Audrey about the week's menu plan. By the look of awe mirrored on Audrey's face as Marta left the room, I think it was finally beginning to dawn on her that she was indeed mistress of this grand house.

Due to the thick cloud layer, another early dusk had fallen when we finally rose from the table. It was my intention to begin compiling notes for the first draft of my article and then return Tugg's call, but Audrey insisted that I accompany her on an exploration of the old wing. "Who knows, maybe I'll discover something that will spark a memory," she implored, grasping my hand with the beguiling enthusiasm of a small child.

Our search of the ground floor revealed an enormous unused kitchen, the entrance to a dank-smelling basement, which she refused to enter and, to our surprise, a genuine relic of bygone days hidden inside one wall in the adjacent pantry.

"It's called a dumbwaiter," I informed her, peering up the shaft after I'd scrupulously checked to make sure there were no spiders lurking nearby. "If my dad hadn't forced me to watch old movies with him I'd have never known what this was."

I explained how the pulley system operated to carry items from one floor to another, but she didn't seem particularly interested so we moved on to the living room where she insisted we set and wind the intricately carved grandfather clock. From there, we roamed from room to room and I sensed her mood of anxious anticipation. Sharing in each new discovery, I began to realize that my role in her life was taking yet another form, evolving ever so subtly from that of guardian into trusted confidante.

After examining every nook and cranny, we headed for the steep stairway. Our footsteps drew squeaks of protest from the ancient wooden stairs and the realization that we were alone seemed to accentuate the deep silence cloaking the old house. At that point, I found it easy to understand why Jesse had proclaimed that the house gave her the creeps.

On the landing Audrey stiffened, her poignant backward glance a clear signal that she was replaying the story of her parents' violent quarrel that fateful night. Did she imagine herself tumbling to the bottom?

"Did you hear something just now?" Audrey whispered, clutching my arm.

I listened intently, but heard nothing. "No. What was it?"

"Kind of a scrunching, squeaking sound."

"Probably mice. Or maybe squirrels. It's hard to tell what might be living in the walls of a place this old."

Instead of putting her at ease, my suggestion seemed to heighten her apprehension. She clung to my arm as we continued our journey along the shadowy corridor, and now that I was cognizant of the Morgan family's capricious history, that same odd sensation of having wandered back in time washed over me again. Somehow, the wavering flame of a candle would have seemed more appropriate than the steady beam of the flashlight we'd borrowed from the kitchen.

"What happened to your little friend," I asked as we passed by her bedroom.

She looked vacant, then smiled. "Oh, you mean the cat? Marta told me her name is Princess. She disappeared before dinner and I haven't seen her since."

"Well, see. That's probably the sound you heard." There were certainly plenty of places for a cat to hide, I thought, turning the knob on the first room. With the exception of Audrey's bedroom, we discovered that only a few of them were fully furnished. Some were either filled with an astounding assortment of clutter while others stood empty, shrouded in hollow dusty silence.

At the threshold of each room, she paused with breathless expectation, her expressive eyes magnifying what I now recognized as not only a burning need to connect with her past, but in addition, her desire to secure a firm foothold on the present.

Thunder was mumbling through the hills as we stepped through modern French doors and outside onto the second floor balcony I'd viewed from below with Orville Kemp only hours ago. Adorned with white wrought-iron furniture and well-tended potted plants, I felt certain that under normal circumstances it would have been a pleasant place to while away some time. But because of the infamous event that had occurred here, Audrey's discomfort was evident as she tentatively approached the low railing.

"That's an awful long way to fall," she said hoarsely, staring into the deep ravine below.

Or be pushed, I reflected, following her gaze. As if she'd read my morbid thoughts, she threw me a look of alarm and scurried back indoors.

On the third floor, we each drew a breath of appreciation when we entered a room that would be an antique dealer's dream. I got the odd impression it should be roped off from the public, so beautifully appointed it was with doily-draped, hand-carved mahogany tables, a graceful turn-of-the-century couch and several high-backed wing chairs upholstered in plush crimson velvet.

Audrey clapped her hands together in delight and crossed to a little alcove in the far corner of the room where the ceiling sloped down to meet an ancient treadle sewing machine. The yellowed material of an unfinished gown draped a dress form close by. "My mom loved to sew," she murmured, running her hand over the old machine. "I'll bet this was her favorite room." Her eyes swept around the room, taking in the delicate pieces of Dresden china scattered about before coming to rest on a large oval portrait hanging on the wall adjacent to a white-marble fireplace. Seemingly mesmerized, she stared at it. "What a pretty lady. Who do you suppose she is?"

I stood on tiptoe to read the name. "Audrey, say hello to your great-grandmother, Hannah Morgan."

While she stared in open-mouthed surprise, I decided that pretty wasn't quite the right word to describe the lady. Striking might be more appropriate. Even with the soft upswept hairstyle, high lace collar and puffed sleeves of her gown, the artist had caught the strong set of the woman's jaw line, the proud thrust of her patrician nose, and most of all the vibrant inner strength that seemed to radiate from her piercing eyes.

"I look a little bit like her, don't I?" Audrey prompted me hopefully, tilting her head from one side to the other as she continued to study the painting.

"A little," I lied, sensing her need for connection, while actually thinking she favored the Morgan's dark-browed looks considerably more. If she had inherited any of this woman's spunk, she hadn't displayed it yet.

Without another word, she left the room and we continued our search of the third floor. Two of the four bathrooms we'd seen so far were a delight, boasting old-fashioned pedestal washbasins and magnificent claw-footed bathtubs that cried out to be filled with steaming water and lavender bubble bath.

"Anything look familiar?" I asked at length after we'd examined the last mothball-scented bedroom.

A protracted sigh revealed her frustration. "Nothing. You'd think I would recognize...*something.*"

"Don't be too hard on yourself. After all, you were just a toddler when you left. Whatever memories you have are still in there," I said, tapping her head softly. "Sometimes it's just difficult to retrieve them."

She made a gallant effort to look enthused, but the sag in her shoulders told me that her resolve was beginning to wane as we climbed the final four steps that would take us to the circular tower room.

The brass knob turned easily, but the door didn't budge. "This area probably doesn't get used much," I muttered, handing her the flashlight before shouldering my full weight against the sturdy wood. After a few tries it finally gave way with a resounding crack.

I groped around in the airless gloom for a light switch and when I flipped it on, the tiny room was bathed in light from an elegant crystal chandelier hanging from the peaked ceiling.

"Ohhh," Audrey marveled in delight, moving past me to turn in a slow circle. "I've never seen a totally round room before. What do you suppose it was used for?"

"Maybe it was a reading room."

Walnut bookshelves filled half the wall space and three tall windows wrapped the remainder. A worn overstuffed chair, end table and floor lamp were the sole furnishings with the exception of a scarred, black steamer trunk that looked as though it had bounced cross-country on a covered wagon. Was this the one containing the additional photographs that Marta had mentioned when we first arrived? My fingers itched to open it, but first I had to have some air.

"It's suffocating in here," I said, crossing the threadbare carpet to tug upward on splintery old windows that ultimately yielded to pressure and allowed the night breeze to waft in. "Whew! That's much better."

The sudden movement of air caused the prisms in the chandelier to tinkle musically and when I turned to remark how pleasant it sounded, I felt a stab of shock at the look of spellbound horror on Audrey's face seconds before she bolted from the room.

Momentarily stunned, I stood frozen, then gathered my wits and charged after her. "Audrey, wait!"

Unheeding, she practically flew down the stairs and didn't stop until she reached my room on the first floor. Heart hammering against my ribs, I rushed over to where she sat on my bed, shaking, her teeth chattering together so hard, I feared they would crack.

"What happened up there?" I demanded, panting for breath. Attempting to follow her unpredictable mood swings was like visiting a veritable amusement park of human foibles.

She looked sheepish. "I'm sorry. You must think I'm completely bonkers."

I'm sure Tally would have pronounced her two tacos shy of a combination plate, but I was careful to say, "No, but obviously something scared you. Did you remember something?"

"It wasn't a memory exactly," she began haltingly. "But...this really awful feeling of...total panic came over me when the crystals jingled. I couldn't think of anything except getting away." She turned bemused eyes on me. "What do you think it means?"

"Well, I'm certainly no psychiatrist, but it's possible that incident is a gateway to unlocking your past."

She chewed a fingernail pensively. "Maybe I shouldn't even be trying. Remember my mother's letter? The secrets of the dead are best buried with them? Well, maybe she just wanted me to get the money and forget everything else," she said, meeting my eyes with fierce intensity. "But that doesn't make sense either. Somehow, way down deep inside, I have the feeling she was trying to tell me something else. What do you think it was?"

"Beats me. But she did say you were entitled to

your inheritance and everything that comes with it."

"Well, what does *that* mean?"

I shook my head. "Audrey, I don't know exactly what your mother had in mind. You said yourself she was very ill when she wrote the letter. We don't know what her thought patterns were at the time. To me, it sounded like she wasn't sure what to tell you and what not to. And remember she didn't expect all this to happen so soon. She had no knowledge that your father would pass away in the same year. Maybe she figured you'd be older and therefore more prepared to handle...whatever."

"Who knows?" Yawning, she rose and headed towards the door. "I'm too tired to think about it anymore tonight."

Would I ever become accustomed to her mercurial temperament? All I could do was go with the flow. "See you in the morning for the meeting," she called over her shoulder.

"I can hardly wait." My dry quip was rewarded with her backward glance of amusement that faded to curiosity when the phone began to jangle in the little parlor adjacent to my room.

She'd still made no move by the fourth ring and it dawned on me that she was probably expecting the housekeeper to answer it. "Do you want me to get it?" I asked. "I don't think Marta's back yet."

"Oh. No, that's okay. I'll see who it is."

She disappeared around the corner and I hauled my suitcase onto the bed to begin unpacking. The book on epilepsy I'd purchased leaped out at me and I withdrew it, making a mental note to browse through it as soon as possible. Perhaps it would reveal some clue to this girl's quicksilver personality.

Some quiet time was definitely in order. I smoothed the wrinkles from my clothing and placed them in the dresser drawers. It was a relief to finally be alone with my thoughts. And there were a number of them spinning around in my head.

I hoped Audrey wouldn't stay on the phone too long, because it was getting late and I wanted to return Tugg's call and bounce some ideas off him.

I shed my clothes and was slipping into a robe when I became aware of those frantic beeps emitted by the phone when it has been left off the hook. Puzzled, I cinched the belt and hurried to the little parlor where I found Audrey standing rigid and white-faced, the phone gripped in her hand.

"Audrey? What's wrong?"

No answer—just a blank stare.

What in the world was happening now? I pried the receiver from her stiff fingers, replaced it, and gently pressed her into a nearby chair. I cradled her icy hands and forced her to meet my eyes. "Who was on the phone?"

Audrey drew a shuddery breath. "It...w...was a woman...."

"And?"

"Well...I'm not sure I heard her right. The line was all...kind of staticky."

"What do you think she said?"

"That I'm an imposter. And if I don't leave this house right away, I might have an accident...just like Grady Morgan."

It took me quite a while to get her settled down and into bed. On the outside chance she had heard correctly, I told her that crank calls were one thing, but death threats were nothing to fool with and that we should contact the sheriff's department immediately.

She vehemently objected, insisting it could wait, that she knew her physical limitations and was too exhausted and stressed-out to be interrogated at this hour.

"Besides," she insisted, "it was probably just Jesse trying to scare me away from the meeting tomorrow."

But I wasn't so sure. What about Jesse's claim that she'd been harassed also? "Did you recognize the voice?" I asked. "Did it sound like Jesse?"

Irritation flared in her eyes. "I don't know. I've never heard her speak in a normal tone of voice, let alone whisper."

That was true. The two times we'd met, Jesse had been shouting at the top of her lungs. "Do you think it was the same woman who claimed to be Dr. Orcutt's nurse?"

"I hate sounding like such a helpless baby. It might have been, but I can't be sure."

"You said there was static on the line. Could it have been long distance?"

Shrugging her answer, she closed her eyes, effectively shutting me out. I stood there for a moment marveling at her amazingly juvenile behavior and decided it would be futile to continue the questioning.

My stomach was churning, as I made my way back downstairs. Her brave assertion earlier that she planned to finally take a stand seemed dubious at best, and I felt more uncertain than ever about my role here. Torn between pity and exasperation, I was beginning to feel less like a companion and more like a nursemaid.

But, I was worried too. Proof or no proof, I was more convinced than ever that Grady Morgan's header off the second floor balcony was no accident. This story was fast developing from purely human interest into something far more menacing. Just exactly what Tally had warned me about, I thought, dialing Tugg's home number from the parlor phone.

"Well, it's about time," his hearty voice boomed over the line. "I was beginning to think you'd forgotten all about us."

One fact was established already. There was no trace of static on this phone, so it had definitely come from the other end. "Hardly," I replied, stifling a yawn. "I've just been up to my eyeballs in one crisis after another till now. Listen, if it's too late, I'll call you tomorrow at the office."

"Sounds like you're the one who's tired."

"I'm okay. How's it going there?"

"I'll tell you, it was good to be back in the saddle again. I didn't get home until almost eight," he said with enthusiasm before confiding, "just between you and me, I think Mary's kind of tickled to have me out of the house."

I smiled to myself, remembering her fervent plea for him to do just that. "Well, I'm glad, Tugg. I've been worried about your health and all..."

"Hey, I'm feeling better than I have for months. In fact, I've been doing some thinking," he added, a sly note entering his voice. "Since you're obviously happier doing what you're doing, and if we can get another reporter on board, maybe you'd be open to discussing a...well, let's say a job sharing arrangement when you get back?"

That made my day. "Yeah," I replied, unable to keep from grinning. "I'd be open to that. But getting back to why you called. What's up?"

We discussed several work-related problems that had developed and after we'd explored solutions, he said, "Tally reminded me of the Morgan piece we ran last May. Looks like you may be jumping into more than you bargained for."

"Things get more complicated by the hour."

His merry chuckle rumbled in my ear. "And knowing you, you're in hog heaven. Got anything for me?"

"Nothing we can print yet. I've got notes and tapes I haven't even had time to go through." I gave him a thumbnail sketch of the last two days and listened to his low whistle of amazement. "So, you think this Dr. Orcutt is the brains behind all these shenanigans?"

"I wish I knew."

"Well, what about the caller tonight? Sounds like it

might be something this Jesse character would do."

"Maybe, but the more I think about it the less sense it makes. She's got an explosive personality, but I can't believe she's stupid enough to threaten Audrey right before such an important meeting. It would be more worthwhile for her and Haston to have Audrey on their side, not to alienate her further."

"Who's your second choice?"

"Could be the lady environmentalist or, it's an awfully interesting coincidence that Marta just happens to be out this evening, and then there is..." I hesitated as another possibility suddenly surfaced.

"What?"

"Well, it's a long shot, but, there's also Dr. Orcutt's wife. I ran into her downtown this afternoon and she gave me a really strange look."

"What kind of strange?"

"Well, it was sort of...melancholy. I got the feeling she was trying to mentally communicate something important to me."

"So, you think she might be the caller?"

"Maybe. She was definitely less than thrilled about Audrey's sudden appearance, but what reason would she have for wanting to chase her away?"

"This whole thing is bizarre as hell. How's the Morgan gal holding up?"

"So-so. She's weathered enough shocks to throw anyone for a loop and frankly, she was ready to turn tail and run, but I convinced her to stay and tough things out."

"You don't sound happy about it."

"Yes and no. I think it's something she needs to do for herself, but at the same time, I don't want to be responsible for placing her in danger."

He was uncharacteristically silent for a moment, then asked in a gruff voice, "What was the reason again for not calling the sheriff after this crank call tonight?"

"She said she was too tired and like you, suspected it was probably just Jesse anyway."

"Hmmmm."

"What does hmmmm mean?"

"Oh, nothing, just that you and I both know that anonymous tips are the life blood of any good reporter, right?"

"What are you getting at, Tugg?"

He apparently caught the tinge of irritation in my voice. "Now, don't get your dander up. Let me play devil's advocate for a minute. How do you know this girl *is* the genuine article?"

"What? Of course she is. I saw the birth certificate myself and..."

"Ah, ah, ah. You told me the doctor devised a fake one for her when she was a kid, right?"

"Yeah?"

"How do you know this one isn't?"

Tuggs unexpected words sent a shock wave through me. "But... but... I'm sure it's valid. The lawyer in Tucson gave it to her personally."

"Did you *see* this guy yourself?"

"Well...no. I didn't actually meet him." My answer sounded lame and I fought the cold uneasiness gathering inside me.

"My point exactly. And how do you know what's-his-face and Jesse aren't correct? Maybe Orcutt and this girl are in cahoots. What do you really know about her other than what you heard from your brother and what she's told you? Hell, she could have lied to him."

I thought of the emotion-filled scene I'd witnessed between her and the doctor. Could it have all been an act for my benefit? "Oh, come on, Tugg. Are you trying to tell me that she and Orcutt and this whole town have cooked up some kind of grand conspiracy to defraud her cousin? What about the old photos I saw? She's a dead ringer for her father, *and* her grandfather."

"Easy enough. The good doctor could have gone out and hired someone who looks enough like the real Morgans to pull it off."

"Give me a break. She'd have to be an Oscar-winning actress to pull off a stunt like this. Listen, I've spent almost every minute of the last forty-eight hours with her. Don't you think I'd notice if there were inconsistencies? No offense, Tugg, but I think you're off the reservation on this one."

My exasperation spawned a sympathetic laugh. "Hey, don't go postal on me. I suppose there's a chance I could be completely off base, but it sounds to me like you're on the verge of losing your objectivity."

"I am not," I fired back uncomfortably aware there was a kernel of truth in what he said. Perhaps it was time to back up and take a careful look at everything. "Okay," I said when he didn't respond, "I'll take what you've said into consideration."

"Good. I have the utmost confidence in you. And remember, you got a hell of a story going here either way."

It took me a few seconds to realize what he was saying and it left me numb. "Gotcha."

After promising to call him again, I replaced the receiver and paced the room with nervous energy, eager to dismiss the damning hypothesis as totally outlandish, but, nonetheless, it weighed on my shoulders like a lead cape.

Was it possible she'd played me for a fool? For a few seconds, I contemplated rushing upstairs to demand the truth, but decided against opening that can of worms at such a late hour.

While washing my face at the pedestal sink in the drafty old bathroom, I stared at my anxious reflection in the wavy mirror. How was I going to find out if Audrey *was* an imposter? It wouldn't be the first time something like this had happened. In the few months since my arrival, I'd learned the sad fact that Arizona was one of the con artist capitals of the United States.

Was I being duped into being an accessory to a diabolical scheme? And what about Tugg's final assertion that even if Audrey was a fraud I'd still have a great story. How did I feel about that?

The roar of a car engine scattered my thoughts like dry leaves, so I ran to the window in time to see Marta climb from the Suburban before it rolled down the hill. Within seconds, lights glowed inside D.J.'s tiny cottage.

As I crawled into bed and piled pillows behind my back, I revisited the notion of Marta as a possible suspect. It seemed logical enough that if she was pilfering items from the house, it would certainly be beneficial for her to have Audrey out of the picture. She knew we'd be here alone tonight. She could have called from anywhere. But for some unknown reason, that theory was as unacceptable to me as Audrey being a fake.

For the next hour, I sifted through my notes and listened to the recording of Dr. Orcutt's conversation before setting everything aside in disgust. I was no further ahead now than before I'd started.

My hand was on the lamp switch when my eyes fell on the epilepsy book. Despite the fact that it was almost eleven o'clock, I began to read and it was close to one before I laid it on the nightstand and turned off the light.

Considering how tired I was, I expected to drift off to sleep immediately. Heaven knows the setting was perfect. Deliciously so. Snuggling into the soft sheets, I listened to the old clock tick a rhythmic lullaby and watched moonlight filter through the gently fluttering lace curtains and dance across the hardwood floor like dew drops. The effect was utterly hypnotic and still, I could not sleep. Instead, I lay there while a profusion of thoughts bumped and rolled around inside my head like balls in a lottery bin, each one generating new questions that spun off in different directions.

Try as I might, I could not banish the sinking sensation Tugg's words had spawned. Had my feelings of compassion for Audrey blinded me? It just didn't seem possible that I could be such a poor judge of human nature. But how could she conceivably be acting? Filled with frustration, I went over in my mind the facts I'd just read.

Apparently there *was* such a thing as an "epileptic personality" which some psychologists described as selfish, emotionally unstable, fawning and irritating. Well, that was Audrey in a nutshell, I concluded, plumping the pillows for the tenth time. And while some professionals claimed these disagreeable traits were a neurological by-product of epilepsy, others blamed the environment of ignorance, prejudice and fear of rejection created by the constant tension of not knowing when a seizure would occur.

Certainly her skittish behavior could dovetail into the fact that the powerful drugs prescribed often generate a myriad of side effects, including hallucinations.

But the paragraph that jumped off the page at me was the one that cited some of the known causes of epilepsy. Besides birth trauma and infectious diseases, it was often attributed to a severe blow to the head. Hadn't Dr. Orcutt said she'd suffered a concussion from her fall? But if everything else was a hoax he could have manufactured that story too.

However, the most damaging evidence of all, was that I'd yet to witness what the book described as a tonic clonic seizure, formerly referred to as grand mal. If Audrey had been coached, she could easily be acting out the absence seizures where the person stares blankly for a few seconds, and then appears disoriented. Had she also faked the incident on the plane?

I stopped the next thought and pressed my hands to my temples. What was I doing? Deliberately driving myself nuts? "Stop it," I said aloud. It took monumental effort, but I finally rendered my mind a total blank and dropped into a sound sleep.

A strange noise woke me sometime later. Senses alert I sat up in bed, my eyes searching for the cause. "Who's there?" I whispered. A sudden movement from the dresser near the doorway made my blood turn cold. A scream rose in my throat as something hurled onto my bed.

It took me a few heart-thumping seconds to realize the dark shape was only Princess. Giddy relief swept over me when she meowed and pushed her nose against my arm.

"You scared the living daylights out of me," I scolded her in a shaky voice, stroking her silky fur until she threw herself down and rolled onto her back. Feeling slightly foolish, I wondered if it was the cat's nocturnal wanderings that had spooked Jesse.

The first faint sounds of bird song surprised me and I turned towards the window. Dawn was already stretching a thin silver thread along the hilltops as the grandfather clock confirmed the time with five resonant bongs.

I moaned softly. Three hours of sleep was hardly sufficient, but positive that I'd be unable to doze off again, I picked up the purring ball of fluff and padded over to kneel by the open window where the cat and I sniffed the sweet morning air.

With the expectation of a fiery showdown looming between Audrey and her cousin, I had little doubt this day would be fraught with emotion. Why not take a moment to savor the unfailing splendor of an Arizona sunrise? I wasn't disappointed. The night sky was quickly eclipsed by a veritable paint palette of pastel pinks and blues, now brushing the eastern horizon. In moments the sun burst over the hill, snuffing out the radiance of Venus, and bathing the surrounding hills in a rosy glow. Was this a good omen for what lay ahead?

Princess had her own ideas of how to welcome daybreak. She vaulted with feline grace from the window-sill and low-crawled through the grass until she came to the base of a crab apple tree. There she paused, still as a statue, waiting for her winged breakfast to appear. It was then that I saw something lying nearby, glinting red in the early morning sunlight.

I had a quick flash of Orville Kemp digging around under the bushes searching for clues to Grady Morgan's death and decided it might be worth while to check it out.

Dressing quickly, I let myself out the front door and scurried across the lawn. The bird Princess had in her sights heard me coming and flapped to freedom leaving the annoyed cat glaring at me in disgust. She rose and sauntered away.

"Sorry, girl." I looked around, but saw nothing. From this angle, I didn't have the benefit of the reflection so

I got down on my hands and knees, trying to gauge the distance from my bedroom window. I combed the area, crawling around in the dewy grass until the knees of my jeans were soaked. I was about to give up when my fingers encountered something hard and smooth. "Bingo." From the thick turf, I withdrew a narrow, gold hair barrette adorned with several colored stones. I turned it over in my hand. It didn't look expensive. In fact, it looked like something one might pick up at a discount store or...perhaps, Mexico?

I rocked back on my heels and turned to study the house. My bedroom window was probably no more than ten or fifteen feet from the front parlor window where Marta claimed she'd seen the silhouette of a woman run past that moonlit night. Cognizant of how poor her eyesight was, I questioned how accurate her description could be.

Was the woman's hair hanging loose because this barrette had been dislodged as she ran? Or...if Marta had fabricated the story, had she herself lost it as she hurried from the scene?

But wait. I rose and shoved the barrette into my pocket. Grady had fallen into a ravine on the north side of the house. If this little bauble had any connection, why had I found it on the south side?

I started back towards the house trying to convince myself that it might have no significance whatsoever. Nevertheless, I made a mental note to show it to the sheriff or Orville Kemp in Bisbee tomorrow.

It was still early, so I decided there was time to enjoy the bubble bath I'd promised myself the night before. The old pipes knocked and whistled as I filled the ancient claw-footed tub. Then, I sank into the lavender-scented water and allowed my mind to drift.

The past two days had been stressful and crisis-filled, but I knew in my heart that being a free-wheeling reporter suited my disposition far better than being chained to a desk and pushing papers around all day. The more I thought about Tugg's idea to job share, the more appealing it became, even if it meant a pay cut.

I couldn't wait to discuss the news with Tally and hoped Ginger had forwarded my request for him to call me before leaving for Mexico to purchase his stallion. It gave me a rather empty feeling to know he'd be out of touch for five days, but I knew we'd have a great time making up for lost time when we were together again. He was definitely one in a million. In spite of our powerful attraction to each other, there were times when our volatile personalities still clashed, but I felt confident we'd overcome whatever obstacles lay ahead.

With reluctance, I abandoned the bath, padded to my room, and chose a short-sleeved, summer suit and low-heeled pumps. Capturing my unruly hair in a matching blue scrunchy, I appraised my reflection thoughtfully. Jeans and a simple T-shirt would have been preferable but it was important that I appear cool and professional.

Audrey had taken pains with her appearance also. As we sat down to breakfast in the sun-drenched kitchen, I thought she looked very pretty in the simple white sundress sprinkled with tiny yellow daisies. But her apprehension was evident. Makeup didn't conceal the charcoal smudges beneath her eyes. She fidgeted with her napkin and picked at the Belgian waffle Marta set before her.

Perhaps she'd slept as poorly as I had, and no doubt she was still troubled by her episode in the tower room last night as well as the crank call that followed. But what if it was more than that?

Tugg's misgivings about her identity resurfaced and I couldn't help but view her in a different light. Was she truly dreading the confrontation or did she fear that Haston and Jesse would expose her carefully concocted scheme?

"Why do you keep staring at me?" she demanded, catching my eye before I could look away.

"I'm sorry. I couldn't help noticing that you look sort of nervous."

She pushed her half-eaten waffle away and rested her elbows on the table. "Can you blame me? I know I promised I'd be strong, but I've never been very good at handling stressful situations. I never had to be. Mom always handled them for me."

"Maybe it won't be as bad as you think. Listen, we have almost an hour to kill," I said, rising from the table. "You want to take a walk before we leave?"

Her face brightened. "Okay. Maybe that will calm me down a little."

Marta stopped us at the kitchen door to ask about lunch and see if it was still all right for her to take her usual Friday off. I felt a smile creep onto my face as Audrey graciously granted permission and then discussed several other household projects including her request for an exterminator.

"Why?" Marta asked, looking puzzled. "He comes only two weeks ago."

"Well, call him again. I keep hearing noises and I don't like the idea of there being mice in my room," she said with a shiver of distaste.

Marta shrugged agreement, and when she hurried off to answer the telephone, I decided that Audrey was beginning to get the hang of being the lady of the manor.

The birds in the desert willow were making a terrific racket as we stepped outside and I suspected Princess was probably skulking nearby still searching for the meal I'd denied her.

"Oh, dear," Audrey exclaimed, shading her eyes from the sun's glare. "Look at all the dents in your car. And the paint is all scratched up. I feel really bad."

"Well, don't. These things happen. Just getting the mud washed off will be an improvement."

She set her jaw. "Kendall, I insist on paying to have it fixed. Isn't there someplace in town we can take it?"

"Actually, there is." I repeated what I'd learned from Whitey and watched her eyes widen in awe when I told her about her father's car collection. "And there's an added bonus," I continued, sidestepping a prickly-pear cactus. "It just so happens that one of our prime suspects, Miss Willow Windsong herself, works right there at Toomey's garage."

"Oh, that reminds me. Marta said she called here yesterday while I was talking to Dr. Orcutt. I never called her back."

"Based on what we've heard, she was probably calling to lobby against re-opening the mine."

"What should I do?"

I grinned. "I think we should go hear what she has to say."

"Well, that settles it then," she said, dusting her hands together. "Let's take a look right now and you can pick out any car you want to drive while yours is being repaired."

We turned and began our hike up the driveway toward the garage just as D.J. roared by and honked a greeting before disappearing through the wrought-iron gate.

"Looks like he's in a bit of a hurry," I said as we reached the massive, wooden structure. "Where do you suppose he's off to so early?"

"Mmmmmm," she answered absently, turning the knob on the side door to no avail. Impressive padlocks adorned each of the four garage doors, so we had to return to the kitchen.

"He keeps all the keys in here," Marta said, ushering us into a small study adjacent to Grady's bedroom and pointing to a roll top desk. From the middle drawer, we chose the key ring marked: GARAGE, and retraced our steps back up the hill. We fiddled with several keys and finally found one that opened the side door.

For a few seconds, we groped around in the shadows until I located a switch and flooded the building with light. Audrey drew in a sharp breath and stared open-mouthed. "Unreal."

Whitey hadn't been exaggerating. A quick count yielded nine magnificent looking cars parked inside the high-ceilinged structure. I remembered Dr. Orcutt's remark about Grady frittering away the family fortune and gathered his penchant for collecting these classic beauties had to be a big part of it.

"They're amazing," she marveled, running her hand over the gleaming yellow paint on the first vintage vehicle.

"And they're all yours. Boy, I'm certainly no expert, but I'd wager there's a fortune tied up in these babies."

We roamed around admiring each one until she finally asked, "Well, which one do you pick?"

I shook my head. "Audrey, I'm not sure I'd feel comfortable driving any of them."

"Oh, piddle, as my Aunt Nellie...or rather Dr.

Orcutt's aunt often said, 'what good are things if you can't use them?'"

We turned to leave when it dawned on me that there was plenty of room where we stood at the far end of the garage for another car. But the space was curiously empty. Perhaps D.J. sometimes parked the Suburban there, I thought, noting the smudged remains of an oil stain. But, that didn't seem logical, since the cars in front would have to be moved in order to drive it out. "I wonder which car belongs here," I remarked, directing her attention to the vacant spot.

She stared at the concrete floor and shrugged. "Maybe nothing belongs there."

I counted the keys on the ring. There were only nine sets, so as we locked the doors and strolled towards my car, I concluded it was just my overactive imagination at work again.

Throughout the drive, Audrey sat in customary silence staring at the caramel-colored hills, many of which still bore deep scars from scores of abandoned mines. It took less than ten minutes for us to arrive at the turnoff and we bounced along a rutted dirt road cratered with mud puddles until we arrived at an open gate marked DEFIANCE MINE. PRIVATE PROPERTY. KEEP OUT. Audrey sucked in a ragged breath at the sight of a second crudely-drawn sign, tacked on below the company name, depicting several dead birds and screaming out, MURDERERS!!

"Oh! Who would do something like that," she cried, clamping one hand over her mouth.

"My guess would be Willow or one of her disciples is sending you a message. I imagine it's coming home to you that you're about to be thrust into the hot seat like your father."

"But how on earth could Willow know I was coming here today?"

I made a cynical face. "The way news travels in this town? She probably knew about this get-together before you did."

She heaved a sigh of resignation, and as we eased to a stop near the door of the mobile home office, it was difficult to miss the candy-apple red Jaguar parked next to Jesse's truck.

After exchanging a quizzical look, we got out and went to stand beside it. I whistled my appreciation. "If this belongs to your cousin, no wonder he's pissed. With you holding the financial reins, he's probably wondering if he'll be able to keep up the payments on this beauty."

Just then, the metal door squeaked open and we turned to see Haston step onto the landing and fasten his gaze on Audrey. His expression of polite interest was cancelled out by resentment smoldering behind his eyes.

Edging closer to my elbow, Audrey croaked out a faint "Hello."

"Good morning," he said crisply. His curt nod in my direction let me know that he knew who I was and his look of displeasure made it clear he wished I hadn't come.

Audrey tensed at the movement behind him in the doorway and I drew back with surprise when, instead of the dreaded Jesse, a young man appeared. And, he was drop-dead gorgeous. Tall, well built, and sporting a thatch of chestnut-brown hair, he flashed us a smile guaranteed to charm any woman under the age of ninety.

"Cousin, Audrey," Haston said, his voice stilted as though it pained him to even mention her name. "I'd like you to meet Duncan Claypool."

Inside the narrow trailer, we seated ourselves on metal chairs in front of Haston's cluttered desk. So far, there'd been no sign of Jesse, and although Audrey seemed visibly more at ease, a palpable climate of strained civility hung in the stuffy room.

Before us, next to Haston, sat the great-grandson of the infamous Jasper T. Claypool, the wily scoundrel who'd cheated Audrey's great-grandfather out of his dream and most certainly hastened his early demise. I imagined she was replaying the story in her mind as I was, and questioned Haston's wisdom of inviting him to this initial meeting, considering the delicate circumstances.

As I suspected, Haston balked at my being there and put up quite a fuss until I convinced him that he could specify that certain remarks be off the record and that I'd already assured Audrey that nothing would be printed without her permission.

Somewhat mollified, he eyed his watch and then leveled a final glare of suspicion at me before turning to Audrey. "Miles Orcutt phoned yesterday to corroborate your authenticity and per his suggestion, I also verified your claim in a discussion with your late mother's attorney in Tucson yesterday afternoon."

His voice was so saturated with indignation, it gave the impression that he might just as easily have been discussing the merits of a pure bred dog having arrived bearing the correct papers. Audrey must have picked up on his tone also, because her dark brows collided in annoyance.

"So, please allow me to extend an apology to you for our reprehensible behavior towards you the other night," he continued in a strained voice. "We both had a little too much to drink and well, I think you can appreciate our reaction to this whole situation which was...totally unexpected, to say the least."

I watched Haston Pickrell with fascination, already formulating adjectives for how to describe him. Hard ass, maybe? There was certainly nothing soft about the man. He seemed all sharp edges and angles. Prickly.

But then *cold fish* seemed equally appropriate. His close-set, colorless eyes were devoid of warmth and coupled with his pointed nose and razor-thin lips, he projected a rather forbidding image.

"It was pretty unexpected for me too," Audrey said. "Until two days ago, I didn't know you existed either. Did Dr. Orcutt explain what happened?"

"Briefly. I can attest to the fact that your father possessed a volcanic temper but, for the doctor to go so far as to fabricate your deaths, well...it seems a bit extreme. But, be that as it may," he added, rolling a pen between his palms. "It's my hope that we can let bygones be bygones and work out a speedy and amicable solution to this predicament, which," he said, gesturing towards Duncan, "is why I asked Mr. Claypool to join us today."

Shirtsleeves rolled casually to his elbows, the young man leaned forward and bestowed another charismatic smile on Audrey. I was elated to see a blaze of color stain her normally pale cheeks. Well, well, this might add an interesting twist. I looked at Haston. Had he noticed the lightning-quick charge of sexual electricity that sizzled between them before she lowered her eyes?

Evidently he had not, for he continued almost in the same breath, "...and because he's unfortunately been caught in the middle of this...this fracas, and that since you are now in the position to make vital decisions concerning the future of this company...of this whole town in fact, I thought it best you two should meet so he can apprise you of where we were in the negotiations at the time of Uncle Grady's unfortunate passing."

"I hope my presence here today has not caused you any distress," Duncan inquired in a pleasant baritone.

"I don't find *you* distressing," she answered, shooting me a playful look.

Oblivious to the underlying sarcasm in her remark that had me struggling to maintain composure, Haston droned on, "And it's my sincere hope that you're not going to continue this ridiculous family vendetta over something that happened a hundred years ago."

Leaning forward, his hands clasped together, Duncan locked eyes with Audrey. "I hope you haven't already formed a poor opinion of me. And just to put you at ease," he said, breaking into an impish grin, "I don't even own a gun."

Audrey, seemingly enchanted by Duncan's disarming personality, returned his smile. "Actually, I haven't had time to form an opinion one way or the other."

"How *did* you become embroiled in all of this, Mr. Claypool?" I asked, secretly rejoicing in their obvious attraction for one another.

Duncan reluctantly withdrew his gaze from Audrey and turned to me. "It was a simple business decision on my part. Haston needed capital for new equipment and developmental costs. After I saw the results of the test drilling, I decided it would be a profitable investment."

"Things were progressing smoothly until Grady discovered who the backer was," Haston cut in, anxiously checking his watch again before glancing out the window. He seemed jumpy.

"If you knew of his deep hatred for the Claypools, why did you contact Duncan in the first place?" I asked.

"I'd heard the stories since I was a kid, but my mother sort of pooh-poohed them. How could I know Uncle Grady was going to behave like a blithering idiot?"

"And you have a lot at stake here."

"That's putting it mildly. By the time I returned from Venezuela, the old fool had already squandered the bulk of the estate. He seemed excited with the results of our studies and gave me his word that if I could bring in the capital, he'd turn over management of the company to me." He plowed a hand through his thinning blonde hair. "Damn him. I've devoted countless hours to this project, not to mention that I've sunk every red cent I own into it. With the metal prices so low and start-up costs so high, I didn't *have* any firm offers other than Duncan's. My back was against the wall...so I cut the deal in secret."

I didn't know a lot about the mining industry, but it

seemed obvious enough to me that if Duncan Claypool put up the lion's share of the money it also meant he would be calling the shots.

"So, you're saying that Grady wouldn't have kicked up a fuss about turning over control of the company to another party. It was just losing to a Claypool that had him in a tizzy."

Haston scowled. "He didn't really care about the mine. Oh, maybe the mystique of three generations of ownership and being top dog in this town, but mostly he just loved the money and prestige that went with it. Heaven help us if he should have actually had to *work* for a living."

"What made you think you could get away with arranging it behind his back?" I asked, noting Audrey's look of rapt attention.

Haston's lips twisted in disgust. "Uncle Grady was in a drunken stupor half the time or ranting nonsensically about one thing or another. I guess I was hoping we'd have operations under way before he got wind of it."

"Who tipped him off?"

"I don't know. Even before he found out about Duncan, he was waffling because that Windsong woman and her bunch of wackos were haranguing him about us destroying animals and birds with toxic waste or some such ridiculous notion. Uncle Grady was back and forth, up and down. Hot one day, cold the next."

Fascinating, I thought, scribbling notes as fast as I could. Audrey's constantly shifting moods had prompted me to have the very same thoughts. Could this eccentric temperament be a family trait?

"What was Jesse's part in this?" Audrey asked softly.

For the first time, Haston had the grace to look

chastened. "I was strapped for cash, so she loaned me the bulk of her mother's inheritance. We both stand to lose a great deal if you don't sign off on this deal."

"So, that's why she was so angry with my father."

"Yes, she was angry. We both were. And don't think we haven't heard the petty whisperings around town that she might have played some role in his accident. But I'll tell you the same thing I told the sheriff. She was home in bed with me that night."

I studied his face carefully. Was he lying? With so much at stake, the motive for Grady's untimely death certainly existed. But like Orville Kemp had said, there was no hard evidence. Yet. I thought again about the gaudy little barrette and decided it just might be something Jesse would wear.

Curious to gauge Audrey's reaction to his alibi, I felt cold shock rip through me when I noticed her eyes were fixed and glazed, her newly-acquired rosy complexion was fading to blue. Before I could react, she toppled to the floor and began to jerk and twitch while saliva bubbled from her mouth.

"Jesus Christ!" Haston shouted, leaping to his feet. "What's wrong with her?"

Duncan's eyes widened in alarm and he gasped, "My God!" as her eyes rolled back and her teeth ground together. Even though she'd warned me, I was hardly prepared for the unnerving and rather grotesque spectacle unfolding before us.

For a few seconds we all stood by helplessly watching until I remembered her instructions to do nothing except keep her head away from hard objects. Gathering my wits, I reached out and scooted the metal chair away.

"What should we do? What should we do?" Haston

screamed hysterically, his eyes bulging in horror.

Duncan lunged for the phone. "I'll call the doctor!"

They both froze in place when I shouted, "No! We do nothing."

I could sympathize with their dual expressions of open-mouthed incredulity and added with deliberate calm, "There's no need to panic. Audrey is having an epileptic seizure."

Haston threw his arms wide. "Oh, great. Just great. First a crazy old man, and now we'll have an invalid running the show."

I fired him a look of complete disgust. If compassion was the milk of human kindness, Haston had only two percent running through his veins. "Try and get a grip," I said. "She'll be just fine in a little while."

Within minutes, she had stopped convulsing and lay motionless, having fallen into the deep sleep that followed a seizure of this type. I sent up a silent prayer of thanks that I'd taken the time to read the epilepsy book last night. And I felt something else too. Relief. This was no act. The uncertainty I felt regarding her true identity all but evaporated.

"Here," Duncan said quietly, handing me his handkerchief and motioning towards the saliva pooling on the floor beneath Audrey's lips.

His simple gesture warmed my heart and bumped him to the top of my 'preferred people' list as I knelt to dry her mouth and pull down the hem of her dress that was hiked up on her thighs.

I rose to my feet and turned to Haston. In an apparent attempt to camouflage his distaste, he began to wring his hands. "How very...um...unfortunate for my poor little cousin." His synthetic attempt to sound concerned fell flat. No doubt he'd noticed Duncan's thoughtfulness and decided that perhaps he'd best say something to diminish his image as a total jackass. He turned his piggish little eyes on me. "Are you sure she's going to be all right?"

"Yes." I was about to suggest we step outside to give her some privacy when I noticed her eyelids flutter and then open wide. At first, she had the same disoriented look on her face as when I'd first seen her on the plane two days ago, but when her eyes focused on Duncan they clouded with humiliation.

Remembering the story of her first, short-lived love interest, I could imagine what she was thinking. She darted me a glance filled with despair and pushed herself to a sitting position. Before I could move to assist, Duncan had rushed to kneel by her side. "May I help you up?"

The look of adoration shining in her huge eyes, combined with my sudden vision of the prince in Cinderella kneeling to tenderly slide the glass slipper onto her foot, made it hard to swallow past the lump in my throat. Now this would definitely make great copy, I thought, mentally framing the scene.

"Thank you," she murmured. "But, I'm still a little fuzzy. I think maybe I'll just sit here on the floor for a few more minutes."

"Sure, whatever. And if you feel up to it Haston and I thought you might like to take a tour of the mine property."

Her eyes remained anchored on him. "I'd like that. If...if I could just have a drink of water and rest a little longer, I'll be ready."

"Of course." Duncan signaled the request to Haston who moved swiftly into the narrow adjoining kitchen and pulled open a smudged, dented refrigerator that looked like it hadn't seen soap and water in decades. The room apparently served more as an extension of the office than an eating facility since the table, counters, and most of the floor space were piled high with boxes and folders.

Returning seconds later with a paper cup, he stared out the front window and his steps faltered at the sound of an approaching vehicle. He whispered, "Shit!"

I followed his gaze and felt a mild twinge of surprise to see D.J. pull up in the Suburban with Jesse seated next to him. When her gaze fell on my car the usual scowl on her face deepened to outrage and she turned her wrath on D.J. Eyes bulging, she cocked her finger beneath his chin like a switchblade. I wished to heavens, I could hear what she was saying.

One thing for certain, D.J. appeared to be one cool dude. Seemingly unaffected by her tongue-lashing, he fixed her with a devious smile and shrugged his innocence.

When she threw open the door, her parting shot of, "I ought to fire your ass!" rang out as she slid to the ground and stomped towards the trailer, her red face distorted, her ample bosom heaving with indignation.

As D.J. drove away, I looked back at Haston in time to see a look of subterfuge ricochet between him and Duncan. Well, well, I thought with amusement. So that's why the loveable Jesse had not been present. Apparently her sly-dog of a husband had managed to outfox her. Until now.

Hastily handing off the cup to Audrey, he managed to put the desk between himself and Jesse before she stormed through the door and slammed a folder down so hard that papers flew. "You lying sonuvabitch! You didn't really need this report, did you?"

"Now, sweetie..." he began only to have her snarl,

"And D.J. was in on this, wasn't he? Car trouble, my ass. You were trying to keep me away."

"That's not true," he sniveled, melting under her flinty glare. "We did wait for you, but...but my cousin isn't feeling well, so we're wrapping it up early."

Jesse's thick-jawed face flattened into puzzlement as she spotted Audrey on the floor, and I couldn't stop myself from fixating on the enormous, brown mole protruding from her upper lip.

I almost felt sorry for her at that moment. Nature had not been kind in the looks department, and to make matters worse, she possessed the sartorial taste of Bozo the clown. Her orange polka dotted, lime-green blouse clashed stunningly with her overly-tight pink stretch pants, which did nothing except call attention to the unsightly bulges rumpling her thighs. Bleached blond hair, piled high in a dated beehive, added to her overpowering height, and emphasized more than ever the contrast between her and her scrawny husband. "What the hell's the matter with her?" Jesse asked, pointing a long, blood red fingernail at Audrey.

Haston cleared his throat. "Nothing much, really. She just had a...little...seizure."

"A *little* seizure?" she mimicked, casting a critical eye at first me and then Duncan before returning her gaze to Audrey.

"All right then," he said, his almost non-existent lips expanding in a conciliatory sigh. "It seems that our cousin suffers from epilepsy."

Jesse clapped her hands together and barked out a scornful laugh. "Oh, this is rich! Another mental defective in your family."

"That remark was completely uncalled for," Duncan

said, eyeing her with disdain before slanting Haston a look that challenged him to do something.

Audrey looked wounded but refused to shrink under the woman's withering gaze. It cheered me to think that her heightened confidence level was a result of her new station in life, or perhaps it was Duncan's firm presence beside her

"Shut up, Jesse," Haston said, finally taking a stand. "Mr. Claypool and I we're just about to show the ladies around the property. If you promise to behave yourself, you can come along."

"Screw all of you." She stalked into the kitchen, withdrew a bottle of beer from the refrigerator and pressed it to her mouth. After taking a long swig, she evil-eyed her husband. "How can you allow yourself to be played for such a sucker?"

He glared a warning at her. "That's enough."

"You spineless coward. I can't believe you're gonna just hand over everything we've slaved for this past year. What about the woman who called to tell us about her? Have you forgotten that already?"

Haston's face grew scarlet and he seemed to be calling upon a higher power to grant him patience as he slowly cracked his knuckles one by one.

It all made for fine drama, but I was baffled. Haston actually seemed to possess a modicum of intelligence and for the life of me I couldn't fathom why he had married such a shrew. I could only hazard that she must be dynamite in bed, because to me she didn't appear to have a single redeeming feature.

"You heard Dr. Orcutt say he'd vouch for her validity," Haston insisted. "Whoever made that phone call was obviously trying to stir things up again. Look, we're going to have to play the cards we've been dealt, so you may as well cooperate."

The mole rose higher as her lips curled with contempt. "This whole thing stinks to high heaven. Thank God I don't have shit for brains like you." She slid her hapless mate one final glare before returning her attention to the beer.

In a swift exchange of glances, we read the 'let's-get-the-hell-out-of-here' message blazing in Duncan's eyes as he sharply inclined his head towards the door. Nodding in silent unison we all filed outside.

With Audrey's mysterious phone call from last night still uppermost in my mind, what I really wanted to do was query Jesse about hers. The fact that there was really only room in the truck's cab for three provided a convenient excuse. "Listen, I need to put some film in my camera and then I'll follow along in a few minutes."

They agreed and Haston directed me to meet them at the mine entrance that he indicated was only half a mile further up the road.

After they drove out, I returned to my car to retrieve the camera. I probably lingered there longer than necessary, but it also gave me a few minutes to gather my thoughts and decide how I was going to approach the nefarious Jesse.

I hadn't really formulated a specific plan by the time I trudged back to the trailer, but decided the worst that could happen would be she'd throw me out on my head.

Opening the door warily, I got the surprise of my life when I found her hunched behind the desk, a cigarette burning in one hand, a beer in the other and a trickle of mascara-blackened tears streaming down her cheeks. The expression of unadulterated misery reflected in her eyes caused me to reconsider my firm belief that this blustery woman had no heart.

"What do *you* want?" she asked, dabbing her face with the heel of one hand.

"I just wanted to ask you a couple of questions."

"Go away."

Her command seemed to lack real conviction so,

ignoring her request, I closed the door behind me, hoping her unexpected vulnerability would allow me to puncture her brittle exterior.

"I can understand how you feel. It was really unkind of Haston to leave you out of such an important meeting."

She eyed me skeptically for a few seconds, took a swallow of beer, then rolled the bottle between her hands. "He's a bastard."

I sat down near the desk, trying not to breathe in the cigarette fumes. "Listen, Jesse, maybe you can help me out."

"I doubt it."

I ignored her remark. "What makes you so positive Audrey Morgan is an imposter? The family resemblance is unmistakable."

Her sidelong glare still held suspicion. "I don't know why I should tell you anything. You're on her side."

"I'm not on anyone's side. I'm simply here to report a story as objectively as I can. If you have proof to refute her claim, I'd like to see it and I'm sure the authorities would too."

"I don't have any actual proof." She took a deep drag on the cigarette before smashing it out in the ashtray.

"Just to clarify things. When did Dr. Orcutt first tell you Haston had a cousin?"

Her top teeth clamped over her lower lip for a few seconds before she answered. "I dunno. About two weeks ago, I guess. Right after the old man kicked the bucket. Orcutt showed up here and parked his butt right where you're sitting now."

It was obvious there was no love lost there. "What exactly did he tell you?"

"That he knew Grady's will specified that the closest

living relative inherit the estate, and he was honor-bound to disclose this Angela Martin's real identity."

"But neither of you believed him."

"Why should we? Why should we just roll over and accept his word that some strange girl, who he himself told everyone was dead as a doornail, mind you, suddenly came back to life?"

"Didn't he offer any background information on why Rita Morgan left town?"

"Yeah, yeah. I can buy the part about Grady beating the shit out of her but the rest of it, man-oh-man." She rolled her eyes, tipped the bottle to her mouth again and then croaked out an unladylike belch.

She was a real class act. Careful not to show my disgust, I asked, "What did you do then?"

Her grin was sardonic. "Called him a goddamn liar, of course."

"I heard."

"Yep, he said if we didn't believe him, we could call the girl ourselves."

I raised a brow. "Dr. Orcutt gave you her phone number?"

"Uh huh. He said that was all the proof he could give us until she got here with her so-called credentials, and that we'd just have to take his word for it."

"Did you try to contact her?"

"Nope."

"Why not?"

She rocked the chair back on two legs. "Haston planned to but the next day we got that real strange phone call."

"Really? From whom?"

"Don't know. Some woman. She swore up and

down she knew Rita Morgan from years back and that there was no way in hell the girl who would be coming to town could possibly be her kid."

"Based on what?"

"She said, 'don't be fooled. Ask the doctor. He knows the truth.'"

"Did you?"

"What?"

"Question him about the phone call?"

"Yeah."

"And?"

"He got real uptight, asking us over and over if we knew who it was. We told him no and then he just acted pissed off and said someone out there was just trying to stir up trouble."

I repeated what I'd told Tugg about seeing the birth certificate and how Dr. Orcutt had admitted he altered the name and date. "And if anyone in the world can substantiate her real identity," I went on, "it has to be him. He ought to remember whether he delivered her or not, don't you think?"

"Maybe he did, but that don't prove a shittin' thing. What makes you think the whole goddamn thing isn't bogus?"

She'd hit on the same theory as Tugg and pinpricks of doubt made me hesitate for an instant before saying, "Well...because, he'd have to be an idiot to think that I, or anyone else for that matter, couldn't easily check it out."

Her lopsided smile radiated scorn. "And just how would you do that?"

"Easy enough. If Audrey was five years old when he altered her birth certificate, the real one will be on file."

"Well, good luck trying to find it."

"What do you mean?"

"The old court house burned down fifteen years ago."

"Were all the records destroyed?" I asked hoarsely, trying to ignore the hollow chill invading my stomach.

"You got it, Sherlock. And the doc knows that."

Her inference was damning and took me off guard for a few seconds. "Jesse, the person who phoned you at the Morgan place the other night. Was it the same woman who called the first time?"

"I don't know. It was the middle of the god damned night and it was kind of hard to hear what she was saying anyway."

"Why?"

"Because the connection was all fuzzy."

My heart jumped with excitement. "You mean static?"

A careless shrug. "I guess you could say that."

Bingo! I finally had something concrete to link her and Audrey's anonymous calls. My excitement level rose further when it occurred to me that it might be the same woman who'd been tormenting Grady Morgan. "What did she say to you?"

"Something like, get the hell out of this house. It doesn't belong to you."

For a moment, I chewed on her information, then said, "I've heard from several sources that Grady had been getting crank calls months before his accident. Did he ever talk about them to you or Haston?"

A look of cunning crept into her eyes. "Not directly."

"Did Marta mention the calls?"

She took a sudden interest in reading the label on

the beer bottle. "I can't remember."

Somehow her answer didn't ring true, so I acted on a hunch. "Tell me something, Jesse," I asked, maintaining a pleasant, even tone. "When you were giving D.J. the business a little while ago, I heard you threaten to fire him. Does that mean he wasn't hired by Grady?"

Her attempt to look guileless was so pathetically transparent she finally gave me an unapologetic shrug. "We needed someone to be our eyes and ears."

I couldn't mask my surprise. "He was spying for you?"

The chair lurched forward with a bang. "Listen, O'Donnell..."

"O'Dell."

"Um...yeah, well, you don't know how weird the old man was acting those last months. I mean, he seemed open to Haston's ideas when we first came to him but, after a few weeks he started acting real bizarre. I'm telling you, the man needed a keeper."

The image of D.J. standing silently in the darkened parlor last evening flickered through my mind. Was he still spying for Jesse? "So, it was part of D.J.'s job to keep an eye on things and report back to you?"

"It was for the old fart's own good. He'd get so shit faced D.J. would have to hide the car keys. And a couple a times he had to put the old man to bed after he'd passed out on the floor." Her smile was mocking as she twirled a finger around her temple. "Talk about a loonytoon. D.J. told us sometimes he'd be roaming around the old part of the house at all hours of the night talking to ghosts, for crissake."

She eyed the rim of the empty bottle and heaved a sigh. "Haston hates it when I drink before noon. He says

I'm going to end up a raving alcoholic like Grady. But he's full of it." As if to contradict herself, she rose and crossed to pull another cold brew from the refrigerator. "I can stop anytime I want to. I just...don't want to. She took a long drink and stared foggy-eyed at a faded watercolor hanging askew near the kitchen window.

More important than her own admission was her reference to Grady's erratic behavior that segued into my next question. "I understand you and Grady didn't get along too well."

"That sure as hell wasn't my fault. He was a waste of skin. One day he'd promise to sign the papers, we'd get our hopes all jacked up and the next day he'd shit on the deal."

"And time was running out for you and Haston, wasn't it?"

Her hand curled into a fist. "He knew how important this was to us. He knew damn well."

"Did he refuse again that last afternoon before he died?"

"He wouldn't listen to reason. I could've wrung his scrawny neck..." She paused and glared red-hot daggers at me. "So that's what you've been up to this whole time. Guess you think you're pretty clever don't you, Miss Hot-Shot-Reporter?"

I managed a thin smile. "Well, you and Willow Windsong were the last people to see him alive."

"So what?" She advanced towards me and slammed the bottle down on the desk with such force the liquid rocketed upward. "Did the sheriff put you up to this? The sonuvabitch is still trying to pin this thing on me, isn't he?"

The murderous gleam in her eyes propelled me towards the safety of the door. Crap! My habit of asking one too many questions had caught up with me again.

"Get the hell out of here! And you can tell that skinny little fraud I'm going to haul her ass into court and have her declared mentally incompetent. You hear me? I'm not turning this place over to some retard!"

I needed no further prompting and hotfooted it outside while she peppered the air behind me with a maze of profanity that would have impressed a Marine. "Why don't you go do your job and question that nut-case, Willow Windsong. She's the one who oughta be locked up. That weirdo's been a thorn in my side since we got here." She shut the door so hard, the mobile home rocked on its foundation.

I reached my car in record time and jammed the key into the ignition. As the engine roared to life, I thought that if Grady Morgan was considered a loonytoon, Jesse Pickrell certainly couldn't be far behind. It wasn't difficult to envision her shoving the poor old sot off the balcony.

All along the final stretch of rough road leading to the mine entrance, my thoughts tumbled over one another. If one assumed Jesse was telling the truth, then who was this mysterious woman who'd suddenly surfaced claiming to have known Rita Morgan a long time ago and what did she stand to gain by denouncing Audrey as an imposter? Was she the same person who'd harassed Grady and now Audrey?

But what if Jesse was lying? It was interesting to know that Dr. Orcutt had given the Pickrells Audrey's phone number and it would have been simple enough for Jesse to call and masquerade as Dr. Orcutt's nurse. She'd made no bones about her resentment and could have easily arranged for our near-accident. But what about the static on the phone line? That was an unexplained coincidence.

Dodging a series of mammoth potholes in the poorly maintained road, I decided that one thing about Jesse was consistent. At least she'd stayed in character. I didn't know what to make of Haston's performance. When one considered his enraged state of mind just two nights ago, he'd seemed suspiciously conciliatory today, almost too willing to release the reins of the company to his cousin. My gut feeling told me that if Audrey's plans included signing any kind of partnership agreement with him, she'd best read the fine print with care.

It was a relief when the teeth-jarring road leveled out into a wide parking area, but I was puzzled to see Haston seated behind the wheel of his truck, and the smashingly-gorgeous Duncan Claypool holding the passenger door for Audrey.

I rolled up beside them, cranked the window down and stopped. "You're not leaving already?"

"Sorry, Kendall," Audrey said in a faint voice as I stepped out. "I'm just too tired to walk anymore after...well, you know. Haston says he has to meet someone, so Duncan is going to drive me back to the house," she added shyly, her wan face coloring slightly.

Oh? So it was Duncan already. Skepticism gnawed at me as I watched him help her into the cab. Was he genuinely interested in her or just feathering his own nest? "I'd like to stay and snap a few pictures and then I'm going to stop by Toomey's garage before I come back."

"Oh, that's right. What if you need to leave your car there? How will you get back?"

I grinned. "If push comes to shove, I'll walk. It's not that far."

Haston put the truck in gear, then leaned out the window as I removed my jacket and shouldered the camera.

"If you follow this road around the other side of the hill, you'll come to another gate. There's enough room to walk around it and maybe a quarter of a mile further, you'll see the original entrance to the Defiance. Beyond that, you'll find the Destiny and Pipe dream shafts."

"Thanks.

He started to pull away again, then braked and backed up. "By the way, Harmon Stubbs won't be here for another thirty minutes, so you'll be on your own."

"Who?"

"The watchman."

I frowned. "I thought D.J. was the watchman."

"Well, he can't be here twenty-four hours a day," he snapped in a tone of peevish condescension. "They trade off on night shift, of course."

Of course. That way you can have D.J. spy on us while he's not on duty here, I mused cynically, forcing a smile. "I'll be fine, see you later."

After the roar of his truck faded in the distance, I turned to study my surroundings. So, this was it. The famed Defiance Mine. A sad air of neglect permeated the whole place and except for the soft chattering of birds and the faint whistling of the wind through the giant head frame spiring into the cobalt sky, no sound disturbed the solitude.

Great atmosphere. A little spooky, but great. And an excellent picture, I thought, leaning back against the car while aiming the camera lens at my target. The fact that the towering structure now served as a perch for a flock of mourning doves seemed ironic as I remembered the unsettling sign someone had posted at the gate earlier.

Calling upon the little information I'd had time to garner from the mining book and combining that with Whitey's colorful stories of the past, I could only imagine what it must have been like to work a claim on this lonesome windswept hilltop.

Defiance. Destiny. Pipe Dream. Romantic names that conjured up visions of long ago. I had to hand it to Seth Morgan. It must have taken some kind of spunk to stake out this barren tract of land and persevere during all those years of backbreaking isolation.

For a while, I wandered among the empty sun-faded hoist shacks and deserted boarded up buildings, stopping to peer through a weed-choked chain-link fence at rows of giant trucks and other pieces of mining equipment standing idle. I tried to imagine the place in its heyday. What should have been a noisy, bustling enterprise, filled with grimy-faced men valiantly braving danger to extract precious metals from the bowels of the earth, now lingered in silent ghostly remembrance.

Given the circumstances surrounding the origins of the town, I thought how bizarre it was that Grady Morgan's foolhardy decision had only served to reemphasize the word folly. Was his daughter strong enough to shoulder the magnitude of obstacles and restore the Defiance to its former glory? Only time would tell. Facing the savage glare of the afternoon sun, I swatted at a cloud of pesky gnats that followed me like a second shadow and set out along the road climbing the hill. Even though my street shoes were comfortable, negotiating the sharp stones and slippery gravel proved daunting. I wished I'd had the foresight to throw a pair of sneakers in the car.

I had to clamber over a boulder to bypass the second gate, warning in bold black: TRESPASSERS WILL BE PROSECUTED! And, after hiking for fifteen minutes, I stopped to catch my breath and take in the panoramic view below. Away to the south, gray clouds were gathering like a fleet of battleships around the summit of Thunder Peak, standing in silent vigil over the hazy San Pedro Valley. The warm wind lifted the hair back from my face and I wondered if the rain would make it across the parched desert floor. Most likely we'd experience another of what I had dubbed, "fake-out" storms that came rushing in with the enthusiasm of a used car salesman, all wind and bluster, and then, like yesterday, fizzle to nothing, leaving one with vague feelings of discontent.

I snapped a few more photos, zeroing in on the piles of rusty mine tailings and discarded heaps of machinery resting beside leach ponds covered with a scummy yellow slime.

Even though Mother Nature had done her best to soften the man-made scars by dusting the treeless hills with brilliant patches of yellow and purple wildflowers, I could understand how the blemished landscape would provide the ammunition sought by the environmentalists who held the mine responsible for permanent destruction of the area.

Rounding the bend I drew in an awed breath when I came face to face with the black mouth of the old mine yawning before me. Signs, posted prominently against aging timbers read, DANGEROUS CONDITIONS KEEP OUT! No need to worry I thought with a grim shudder, as the childhood memory of my brother Patrick locking me in the tiny airless closet leaped to mind. To this day, I had not forgotten the gut-chilling terror. The struggle to free myself from the wool coats that seemed to close around my face. Suffocating me. The subsequent case of claustrophobia it had engendered, made the chances of me ever wanting to venture into that black void slim to none.

Totally absorbed in fiddling with the shutter speed, F stop, and finding the right angle for my picture, I didn't pay too much attention to the rustling sound coming from the bushes behind me, but I came close to dropping the camera when a low chuckle reached my ears. I whirled around staring wide-eyed into the thick foliage while a parade of goose bumps skated down my spine. A second chuckle prompted me to quaver, "Is someone there?"

Nerve-wracking seconds passed. When no one answered, a horrifying succession of possibilities flitted though my mind. Kidnap. Rape. Murder!

Panic grabbed me. Frantically, I looked around for some kind of weapon. Seizing a sharp rock, I was poised to do battle when a ground squirrel suddenly skittered from the underbrush, skipped across the road and dove into a nearby hole.

When my thundering heartbeat finally tapered off, the giddy rush of relief left my legs feeling boneless. After willing my paralyzed lungs to inhale, I gave into an idiotic desire to giggle. "A squirrel, for heaven's sake."

Heatedly, I admonished myself for overreacting, but was nonetheless acutely aware of how vulnerable I was—a woman alone in the middle of nowhere. And I couldn't stop myself from dredging up the discomfiting image of Archie Lawton's leering face. And what if that chuckling sound hadn't been the squirrel? That sobering thought propelled my inert legs into action and I quickly retraced my steps.

I was just beginning to relax when the uneasiness returned full force. Above the hilltop, a flock of vultures circled liked an ominous black wreath. Uh oh. These crafty scavengers came on duty for only one reason.

Two of them suddenly broke ranks and spiraled towards the clearing where I'd left the car. A tangible sense of fear clawed at me as I broke into a run. When I rounded the corner, the pair of giant birds flapped away from my car and then I noticed the indefinable lump. "What the hell..."

With each step my apprehension expanded to horror as the gruesome sight materialized before me. Splayed out and gutted, the carcass of a large gray jackrabbit adorned the hood.

"How sick," I cried aloud in disgust, my stomach rolling with nausea. But even worse, was the ominous message ENDANGERED SPECIES! scrawled across my windshield in the dead animal's blood.

Anger replaced my disgust and I was trying to decide how to deal with the hideous mess when a battered pickup—a stranger to paint and sputtering as if it were on its last sparkplug, rattled through the gate and shuddered to a stop near one of the ramshackle buildings.

A fiftyish, sinewy-looking man, whom I assumed was Harmon Stubbs, stepped out, all the while keeping me locked in his quizzical gaze. Slapping his thigh, he whistled to the fuzzy black and white dog hopping around in the truck bed, and then approached me warily. "You mind tellin' me..."

But the words faltered and his eyes practically bugged out when he spotted my ghastly hood ornament. "Shitfire! What in blazes is going on here, lady?"

I started to explain but got no further than Haston's name when, with blinding speed, the dog rushed past him, leaped up, snatched the remains of the rabbit in his teeth and bounded away.

"Jigger, stop it. Give!" he shouted, gesturing wildly with his tattered hat to no avail as the dog ran in circles, refusing to surrender his prize. The man finally grabbed a stick and hurled it at the poor beast, bellowing, "Stupid-assed dog."

"Let him have the thing," I said. "I certainly don't want it."

He heaved a sigh of annoyance. "I don't guess it will hurt him none. It didn't smell putrid or nothing, so it must be a fresh kill."

"That's comforting."

While Jigger retired to a bush to gnaw on his catch, I confirmed the man's identity, explained who I was and why I was there. "Mr. Stubbs, did you notice anyone on the mine road as you came in? Any other vehicles?"

"Nope. Can't say as I did," he mused, rubbing the back of his neck with one gnarled hand as he squinted at the message on the windshield. "But it appears you must've riled somebody up pretty good for 'em to pull a stunt like this."

"I don't think the message is intended for me. It was meant to intimidate Miss Morgan."

Nodding sagely, Harmon Stubbs fished a pack of cigarettes from his shirt pocket, pounded one out and lit it. The relentless wind grabbed the smoke and blew it back in his eyes. "If I was a betting man, I'd wager most likely it was the same person that hung that sign on the gate. And I'll tell you something else. I've about had it up to here with these meddlesome tree huggers. You know who the endangered species are around these parts?" He poked a thumb against his chest. "We are. People. Not birds, not red squirrels, not mountain lions.

Because of their pea-brained shenanigans, I lost my house and had to put my ol' lady to work just to make ends meet. And I'm not the only one. I can't count the number of folks who've had to pack up their families and leave their homes to look for jobs someplace else. If those troublemakers would just leave well enough alone, this town just might have a fighting chance to get back to normal."

His impassioned plea echoed the sentiments of all the men I'd met at the Muleskinner yesterday. "I sympathize with your plight, Mr. Stubbs, but right now, as you can see, I've got a bit of a problem too. You wouldn't happen to have some rags or something I could use to clean my windshield?"

"Yep. Got some stuff in the truck." He pulled a pair of grimy work gloves from his back pocket, slid them on, and when he pulled something that looked suspiciously like an eyeball from beneath one wiper blade and flung it behind him, my stomach rose in revolt again. I had to swallow hard and breathe deeply before saying, "It's hard to believe anyone who claims to love and respect animals could do such a cruel thing."

"Who else around these parts would be harping about such nonsense? You tell Miss Morgan to hang in there and not let these people bully her."

I agreed to convey his sentiments and while he trotted back to his truck to get the cleaning materials, I visualized Audrey's reaction to this gruesome scene. She would have been hysterical. Exactly what the perpetrator wanted. And yet I would have to tell her.

Taken collectively, the bizarre sequence of events that had transpired since our arrival left little doubt that

Grady's tormentor had Audrey in her sights. Mentally, I added this latest incident to the list of other things I intended to discuss with the deputy sheriff tomorrow.

"Good thing D.J. ain't here today," Harmon remarked a moment later, grimacing slightly as he poured water from a jug onto a handful of paper towels and began to sop up the bloody mess.

"Why is that?"

"Most likely he's gonna be between a sharp rock and that hard place, seeing how he's working for Miss Morgan and at the same time, making goo-goo eyes at Bitsy Bigelow."

"Who's she?"

He paused and used his forearm to wipe perspiration from his brow. "Nice gal. Waits tables down at the Huddle Cafe."

"I don't get the connection."

"Ever since coming back to town last spring, she's been working hand in hand with Willow and her bunch."

"Really? In what capacity?"

"Oh, you know," he replied, wadding up a clump of soggy towels, "helping 'em make up fliers and signs, going to them protest marches and such. Kind of being her right hand man...or woman, so to speak."

Well, that was interesting. Apparently D.J. was making a career of playing both ends against the middle. Underneath his mellow demeanor lurked a man of subterfuge. "So, doesn't that cause a little friction between them? I mean, to Bitsy, isn't that like he's working for the enemy?"

"Oh, that ain't the only thing that gets her goat," he added with a raspy chuckle. "Her no-account husband was a drunken skunk, so she ain't too wild about D.J. hanging around the Mule."

"Really? Does he have a drinking problem?"

He dismissed my question with a hasty wave. "Oh, hell. He hoists a few brews just like the rest of us. If you ask me, I'd say the real drawback is she don't like him consorting with the likes of Archie and his ex-con buddies."

An alarm bell sounded in my head. "Archie Lawton?"

His face registered mild surprise. "Yeah. You know him?"

"Oh, yes. Charming gentleman. And wonderful tattoos."

Harmon's slack-jawed look of disbelief made it hard to keep a straight face and when it finally dawned on him that I was kidding he let out a braying guffaw. "You had me going there for a minute."

I grinned in return, trying to ignore the sound of Jigger's teeth crunching the rabbit bones while I tried to think of a reasonable scenario for D.J. to align himself with a disreputable character like Archie. Somehow I didn't think Audrey would care for this new information any more than I did, and she might want to re-evaluate the need to have him in her employ. "So, what kind of a guy would you say he is?"

"Who?"

"D.J.."

"Seems nice enough."

"So, why do you think he associates with a low-life like Archie Lawton?"

He arched one salt and pepper eyebrow at me. "Couldn't tell you for sure, but one thing's certain. At least them two being buds pretty much stopped all them crazy rumors about him."

"What rumors?" My mind whipsawed with possibilities and I thought Harmon Stubbs looked decidedly uncomfortable as he squashed the butt of the cigarette beneath the toe of his boot before answering. "I got to admit, the first couple of times he come into the Mule, some of us had our doubts about him."

"What do you mean?"

I could tell he was making a concentrated effort to avoid eye contact with me.

"We ah...pondered the notion that he might be...kind of a twinkie."

"A what?"

His crinkled face reddened. "You know, a little bit swishy."

I gawked. "You think D.J. is gay?"

"Naw, not no more. For one thing, Archie and his gang sure as hell wouldn't hang around with no fruit and now that he's dating Bitsy, well, he seems real different."

"In what way?"

He hesitated, apparently searching for the right words. "Well, he spruced himself up, lost some weight, and just looks...well, a lot tougher."

"Tougher. You mean like he's working out?"

His shrug was noncommittal. "He ought to lose that ponytail. It makes him look like one of them damn hippies."

After refusing my half-hearted offer to help him clean up the remains of the rabbit, saying a 'classy lady like myself shouldn't have to fuss with such a durn mess' he returned to his truck for more paper towels.

At least it was a nice afternoon to be stranded, I thought, eyeing the row of vultures perched on the head frame, still hoping for a meal. While a silken breeze softened the sting of harsh sunlight, I stood there slapping at bugs and trying to sort through everything I'd learned.

So far, everyone else I'd met in this polarized community appeared to be firmly rooted in separate camps. So how was it D.J. had managed to pull off such a unique balancing act, working for Grady, spying for Jesse and Haston and yet, linked to Willow Windsong because of his ties to Bitsy?

Harmon's boots crunched through the gravel as he walked up and laid more wet towels on the hood, muttering under his breath, "Stupid-assed people," while he resumed wiping away the sinister message.

"Tell me a little more about Bitsy. You said she'd come back recently. When did she live here before?"

"She was born right here."

"Really? And how long ago did she leave?"

He lifted the battered cap from his head and scratched thoughtfully. "Oh, quite a while. Fifteen years, maybe?"

"So, you've been here a long time yourself?"

"Oh, hell, yes." He pointed to the ground and flashed me a tobacco-stained grin. "Worked down in the hole since I could crawl."

"I see. What can you tell me about Bitsy?"

He stared at me with memory-fogged eyes. "Not much, really. She was a real sweet little kid and my daughter and her was friends, but when they got to junior high, Doreen, that's my wife, well, she didn't want her coming around no more."

"Why?"

"I ain't too clear on the details," he mused, "but it seems like she got real mouthy and rebellious. I think she's the one...no wait, maybe that was the Wickert girl...well, anyhow, one of 'em used to pal around with the Morgan kid until..."

"Dayln?" I asked sharply.

His quick glance held appreciation. "Looks like you been doing your homework."

"Whitey Flanigan told me she was bad news. Did you know her too?"

"I'd see her around town. You gotta remember something...Miss O'Dell, was it?"

I nodded.

"I was just the hired help. Didn't really mingle much with the big shots at the mine. Or their families. So, most of what I know is gossip, pure and simple."

"I'll take gossip."

The conspiratorial glint in his eyes matched his grin. "Okee dokee. From all I heard, Dayln Morgan was smart as a whip, but didn't get no real discipline."

"Why?"

"Some say it's 'cause she was just a hell-raiser like her pa, but other folks think it was because her ma was so sickly. The poor lady spent most of her time in hospitals or home in bed."

"Oh, yes, the first wife, Lydia. What was wrong with her?"

A faraway look settled in his eyes again as he absently scratched his chin. "I ain't sure, but she was ailing a good long time, and wasn't up to keeping a watchful eye on the kid. Next thing you know Dayln got herself mixed up with a rambunctious bunch of boys and there weren't no controlling the girl. I heard she was in trouble for vandalism, shoplifting, starting fires and all manner of devilment."

"And where was Grady in this equation?

A look of irritation crossed his face. "He didn't win

no prize for father-of-the-year, or husband neither that's for sure. Too busy pleasing himself on the side, if you get my drift."

"Lots of lady friends?"

"Lots."

So, I could now add infidelity to the man's growing list of shortcomings. "How old was Dayln when her mother died?"

He pursed his lips for a few seconds. "Eight, nine maybe."

"I see. And did you know Grady's second wife, Rita?"

His face softened. "The doc's nurse? Sure did. She was a real sweet lady," he murmured, looking wistful. "But, getting back to Bitsy, it wasn't but a year or two after the Morgan girl died that she run off and married some cowboy who come through with the rodeo. Didn't even finish high school."

"So, what brought her back here after so many years?"

"Doreen says she finally got up enough nerve to dump the no-good rotten sonuvabitch."

I must have looked expectant because he filled in my unasked question. "I heard he busted her up pretty bad. Last time, he damn near killed her. Doreen says them scars on her face are from cigarette burns and that she looks like a whole different person since she got her broken nose and jaw fixed."

"I'm assuming she's finally divorced the scumbag."

"Yep. Cooling his heels in jail right now."

"Good. So, does she have family left in town?"

"Just her Aunt Edna. Waitressing don't pay much, so I guess she's bunking with the ol' lady till she gets on her feet."

I mulled over everything he'd told me and then pointed to the car. "Does she seem like the type of person who could do something like this?"

He frowned and sprayed a blue liquid on the glass. "No, she don't."

"Does Willow, pardon the pun, have the guts?"

He cackled merrily. "To get her point across? Man, I wouldn't put nothing past that one. I guess she means well trying to help save them critters and such, but I wish to blazes they'd all simmer down. The rest of us need Miss Morgan to get this place up and running again, so we can get our lives back."

We chatted a few more minutes and I expressed my sincere thanks for his efforts. I left him there still trying to coax Jigger out from under the bush. The poor animal probably still feared punishment for his deed, but I for one was grateful that the dog's antics had helped diffuse this latest piece of mischief.

But as I turned onto the highway, I was deeply troubled nonetheless. While the rabbit prank itself had proved harmless enough, the underlying message was ominous. If it was the militant environmentalists, to what lengths were these people prepared to go should Audrey choose sides with Haston?

By the time I located Toomey's Garage at the end of Carbide Street, adjacent to the remains of several gutted brick buildings splashed with peace symbols interspersed with X-rated graffiti, I was burning to confront Willow Windsong.

But the interview would have to be earned, I thought with a sigh, turning into the driveway. Judging by the number of bored-looking men who took immediate interest in my arrival, like the Muleskinner Saloon, this too was apparently a popular daytime hangout.

The crumbling remains of a concrete foundation, now served as a handy card table for one foursome, while several other groups of men lounged against a stone retaining wall, drinking and smoking. They looked to be a younger, rougher crowd of guys than I'd met at the Muleskinner yesterday.

The good news was that meant gossip would flow like beer at a frat party. The bad news was I had to get out of the car and enter this testosterone-charged den of male humanity. Wishing more than ever I'd worn jeans instead of the short, tight skirt, I shrugged on the suit jacket and braced myself to endure the gauntlet course of ogling that was sure to come.

Doing my best to appear nonchalant, I got out and walked swiftly towards the entrance. I didn't have to wait long for the first comment.

"Hey, Red," came the expected shout from one lecherous-looking dude whose grizzled face hadn't encountered a razor blade in days, "if you're having trouble keeping your engine running, you jest let me know and I'll be glad to slide in under your hood and oil all the parts."

Raucous laughter erupted and a chorus of wolf whistles followed along with several other ribald remarks including one cat call I'd never heard before. "Whooee! Get a load of the hitch in her git-a-long."

"Thanks, fellas," I shouted back good-naturedly, never missing a step and not daring to turn around for fear my face would be as scarlet as it felt. I hurried inside the garage and spotted a stout man sporting a sandy crew haircut. He pulled a cloth from the pocket of his paint-smeared overalls and asked, "You looking for somebody special, young lady?"

"Lamar Toomey."

"You found him."

"Oh, hi. My name is Kendall O'Dell. How are you today?"

"Fine as frog's hair," he commented, transferring a wad of gum from one cheek to the other. "And most folks just call me Toomey." He stopped a few feet from me, wiping his hands on the cloth while looking me over with interest. Unlike the lustful scrutiny of the other men, his eyes held only curious appreciation.

I told him about the damage to my car, that he'd come highly recommended by the patrons of the Muleskinner, and was there any way possible he could repair it in a few days? When I noticed several other cars reposing in various stages of restoration, I added apologetically, "I meant to call first for an appointment, but..."

He beamed me a friendly smile. "That's okay. "I've been expecting you."

I wasn't surprised. "Of course you were."

He edged a look behind me. "Looks like you got the boys all hot 'n' bothered, Miss O'Dell."

"They act like they've never seen a woman before."

He smiled and shook his head slowly. "Not like you." He strode to the doorway. "Hey! You boys best behave yourselves. I can't afford to have you aggravating my customers, you hear?"

Like Whitey Flanigan, he seemed to command respect. Several of the men shrugged sheepishly while others leveled me glares of resentment before returning to their card games or sauntering away.

What these able-bodied men needed was a good

day's labor. I remembered my grandmother's wisdom about idle hands being the Devil's workshop and decided that Morgan's Folly was a perfect example.

Toomey grabbed a clipboard from a hook on the wall and accompanied me out to my car. This time there were no whistles or catcalls.

As he slowly circled my Volvo, jotting notes, I mentioned that I'd seen Grady's classic car collection and how much I admired the restoration work he'd done. "That must have kept you busy for a few hours."

"Just a couple."

"You must have gotten to know Grady Morgan pretty well then," I remarked smoothly, watching his tawny brows pinch together as he ran a finger across one deep gash in the paint.

His eyes sparkled with amusement. "I was wondering when you were going to put your reporter's hat on."

I acknowledged his remark with a gracious nod and waited for his answer, which came after a moment of contemplation. "He wasn't an easy man to know. Grady was kind of like a whole bunch of folks all wrapped up in one."

His reply gave me pause. It struck the same chord as Dr. Orcutt's remark. "Are you saying he had multiple personalities?"

"I don't know as I'd go that far, but people did tend to walk on tiptoe around him."

"Did he appear to be mentally unstable to you?"

He rubbed his chin thoughtfully. "The Morgan's were all sort of high strung. Grady just happened to have a powerful temper that he could cut loose if you looked at him cross-eyed. Yep," he mused, backing up a few feet to view the car from a distance, then scribbling on the paper, "sometimes I'd get real flusterated trying to deal with his moodiness."

Flusterated? That was a new one on me. "And the last few months before his accident, did he seem to be more stressed than usual? Preoccupied?"

"Didn't see him that much. Oh, he'd call and we'd talk about this and that he wanted done on the cars, but most times he'd send D.J. down with a list."

"Oh, yes, the loyal handyman. I understand he took pretty good care of the old man."

Toomey squinted at my front fender and remarked dryly, "I'm not so sure about that."

"Oh?"

"If you ask me, D.J. didn't help matters much."

"In what way?"

"Guess you already know he goes down to Naco every couple of weeks."

"Yes, with Marta Nuñez. So?"

"Hell, he was supplying the poison that was killing Grady."

I frowned disbelief. "D.J. was bringing back liquor from Mexico? Who told you this?"

"Some of the fellas," he said, inclining his head toward the small group of men still playing cards.

While Toomey assessed the damage, I pondered this strange new information. Not only did D.J. hang out with Archie Lawton & company but while playing nursemaid to the old man, as well as spying for Jesse, it appeared that his inappropriate actions could have very well hastened Grady's death. Had the devious Jesse put him up to that too?

Moments later, when Toomey handed me the clipboard and told me the work could probably be completed before noon on Friday, I had a strong suspicion he was bumping me ahead of other jobs.

"That would be fantastic." While signing off on the estimate, I eyed a smudged door marked OFFICE and casually asked, "Is Willow Windsong working today?

"You just missed her. She only works mornings."

"I wonder if you could tell me where she lives."

His sea-green eyes gleamed with curiosity, but all he did was point to a series of what looked like a thousand stone steps scaling the hill behind the garage. "Up there."

My jaw dropped. "I think I'd rather drive to her place."

"You can't. Copper Canyon Bridge got washed out in a big storm last month. Good thing it happened while she was here at work," he said, motioning towards an ancient VW bus embellished with brightly painted birds and flowers, its dented bumper attached to the frame with duct tape. "You could park over near the creek, but it's actually shorter to go this way."

I let my eyes rove upward once more. "How far is her place once I get to the top?"

"When the stairs end, follow the footpath for about half a mile."

"Is there a specific address?"

His broad grin matched the impish light in his eyes. "You'll know it when you get there, but if you don't mind my saying so, those shoes you're wearing are a little bit fancy for hiking, don't you think?"

I stared ruefully at my already scuffed pumps. It would be more practical to go back to the house first and change clothes, but then I'd feel bound to tell Audrey about today's episode. Then she'd want to come with me and the inevitable clash between the two would vaporize my chances of questioning Willow in a calm setting. Plus that, I rationalized, because of Audrey's earlier attack, it was unlikely she'd be up to such an arduous climb at any rate. I flashed him an optimistic grin. "I've already hiked the mine road in them, so I guess they'll do."

He stuck his hand out. "I'll take your car keys and get started right away."

I handed them to him, got my camera and purse, accepted his offer of a cold 'sody pop,' and had my foot on the first step when guilt set in. This initial meeting with Willow might prove significant and Audrey had a right to be in on it. After wrestling with indecision a moment longer, I decided that perhaps I'd better call and see if she wanted to come along. And in addition to that, I needed to arrange for a ride back to the house.

I spied a pay phone around the side of the building, looked up the number in my notebook and dialed. Marta answered on the second ring. "Morgan residence."

"Marta, this is Kendall O'Dell. Is Audrey around?"

"What?"

We had a very poor connection so I said in a loud voice, "Is Audrey available to talk?"

Hiss. Pop. Crackle. "I think she is still sleeping."

The revelation dawned on me slowly, prickling my scalp. I had found the staticky phone.

In the wake of my inadvertent discovery, I was still wavering somewhere between elation and shock by the time I set foot on step number sixty-eight. Of course there could be other telephones around in the same condition, but its close proximity to one of Grady's most ardent adversaries seemed to point the finger of guilt firmly in Willow's direction.

Not wanting to box myself into one theory, however, I had to consider the other suspects. Grady wasn't alive to confirm what time of day he'd received the bulk of his crank calls, but in any case, why would Jesse use this particular phone in the dead of night or any other time? Why would Marta for that matter?

I couldn't discount the likelihood that it was none of these women. The caller's cryptic admission to Jesse that she'd known Rita Morgan a long time ago opened up a score of other possibilities. What about Fran Orcutt? She certainly fit into the category of mysterious and she had been closely acquainted with Audrey's mother.

My feet burned, my legs ached, and I was beginning to regret my decision as I stared up at the seemingly insurmountable column still waiting. Willow must be in some kind of great shape, I mused ruefully, glad that I wasn't trying to tackle this back home in Castle Valley's 110 degree heat. At least the light breeze and the higher altitude afforded somewhat cooler temperatures, and all things considered, it still beat being stuck behind a desk.

My breath was coming in wheezy gasps when I collapsed onto a wide landing at what I hoped, was the half-way point. A few months ago my asthma would have made a climb like this impossible and I was still rather awed by my newfound stamina.

I slipped off my shoes and massaged my aching toes while surveying the view. From this lofty perch, I could take in the whole canyon, from the barely visible ribbon of road that was Boneyard Pass to the east, past the stubby pockmarked mounds hunching over Morgan's Folly, to the pointed gables of Audrey's house perched regally on Devil's Hill to the west.

I'm sure to the casual eye, it would appear idyllic, but every instinct I possessed warned me that underneath the sleepy facade of this dying town lay a morbid secret someone did not want unearthed. And considering everything I knew now, combined with the disturbing events of the last few days, Whitey's hypothesis that the past and present could not be separated, seemed not only plausible, but a certainty. And I was determined to ferret out the connection.

Acting on Whitey's suggestion to contact Ida

Fairfield, I flipped open my notebook and jotted a reminder to call her. I also wanted to question D.J.'s lady friend, Bitsy Bigelow, as well as make another attempt to get Dr. Orcutt to divulge more of what he'd stubbornly sworn not to. That would probably take some doing. And while I was at it, perhaps a discussion with the doctor's elusive wife might prove fruitful.

But right now, I needed to get on with the business at hand. Wincing slightly, I squeezed my shoes over the blisters forming on my heels and rose to my feet, dusting off the back of my skirt.

The stairs took a sharp turn to the right and drove upward at an even steeper angle. At this point, the shifting earth and constant erosion had pushed several of the upper steps over the lower ones, reducing the foothold to mere inches.

My heart racing with exertion, I clung to the wobbly handrail and edged a wary glance down the craggy bluff to the valley below. Sheltered in the overhang of lush foliage, I could see where the raging creek had carved a new path and splintered the wooden planks of the bridge, rendering the road impassable except for vehicles with four-wheel drive. And even that might prove daunting. I decided either restoration of the bridge was dead last on the highway department's list or the road was private and there were no funds available for repair.

The treacherous stairs finally ended and I tramped along a narrow, winding footpath. Ahead, I could make out fragmented portions of perhaps a half a dozen houses, tucked away in the deep folds of the hills.

Several minutes later, the sad remains of a dwelling loomed large before me. Gutted by fire, the house, having slid about ten feet off its foundation, now clung tenaciously to the slope, mirroring the devastation of this tiny community. Like the old Defiance mine, an air of ghostly melancholy prevailed and suddenly the gaping windows looked more like empty eye sockets. "My, my, aren't we getting fanciful," I reproached myself, hurrying down the path, unable to resist a backward glance every so often.

I didn't usually mind being alone. At home in Castle Valley, my house in the desert was miles from town and I never felt threatened but today... It may have been the perception of utter isolation, but most likely I was still jumpy as a result of this morning's sick prank.

I'd only gone a few hundred yards further when I froze in my tracks and gawked at the most bizarre looking fence I'd ever seen. It appeared to be made up entirely of old, rusted headboards, some tall, some short, some arched, some squared. The whole silly conglomerate was fused together with chicken wire and artistically embellished with an assortment of old tools, kitchen utensils and a cracked wooden toilet seat. Well, this was different. I stopped and snapped pictures from several angles.

Two railroad-crossing markers flanked a dilapidated metal gate, where a sun-faded plaque informed me that I had reached the JUST DUCKY RANCH. Other signs sprinkled along the fence proclaimed SAVE THE ANIMALS! VEGETARIANS DON'T LET FRIENDS EAT MEAT. PEACE, JUSTICE, EQUALITY - SUPPORT THE EVERGREEN PARTY.

I smiled to myself. Clearly, this was Willow's place. Scaling a final set of steps made from old truck tires and bordered by pink, plastic lawn flamingos wading knee-deep among spiky, purple Irises, I peered across a yard tangled with weeds and cluttered with crude wire pens, rabbit hutches, several tumbledown sheds, and assorted piles of junk. Barely visible amid a thick stand of trees and untamed shrubbery, I could just make out the weathered shingles of a house.

No sooner had I pushed open the squeaky gate than a cacophony of sounds erupted. Flinching, I drew back when at least a dozen ducks, obviously surprised by my sudden appearance, appeared from beneath overgrown bushes and began to waddle and flap in my direction. Several hens hurried to join the procession along with a curious goat and a nubby cream-colored sheep.

They all gathered around, sniffing, grunting, clucking, and I was actually rather captivated by my animal fan club as they followed me towards a tiny, unpainted cottage that was really little more than a steeply-pitched tin-roofed shanty. Above the barnyard clamor, I could hear the tinkle of New Age music wafting out the front door.

This was too good to pass up. I attached the wide angle lens so the photo would encompass not only the petunia-filled wringer washer and crumbling bird bath, but the astounding assortment of cats lounging on junked appliances and frayed, upholstered couches clustered beneath the sagging porch. If houses reflected the character of their owners, I could hardly wait to meet Willow. "Hello?" I called. "Is anyone home?"

The response was instantaneous and my heart plummeted when three dogs burst out the door. Their furious barks turned my insides to jello and I was contemplating a dash back towards the gate when a female voice shouted from inside, "Just stand still and let 'em sniff you!"

The ducks and hens scattered in a flurry of feathers as the dogs bounded off the porch and began their investigation, which included one of them ramming a damp snout into my crotch.

"Crystal Moon! Don't be rude."

I pushed the dog away and looked up to see a short, sturdy-looking woman shouldering open a battered screen door. "Come here, girls," she bellowed. The dogs immediately abandoned their exploration of me and romped to her side, tails wagging. She patted each of them on the head before shooing the pack inside. "Sorry about that. Haven't had many visitors up here as of late."

"No harm done," I said, swiping moisture from my skirt. "Are you Willow Windsong?"

"Yeah?" There was an unmistakable undertone of suspicion punctuating her tone as she retreated behind the screen door. "If you're from the loan company, you can tell Mr. Bosco I'll get a check to him next week."

So. Willow was having financial problems. "I'm not from the loan company," I assured her with a friendly smile, moving onto the porch.

"Then who are you?" she asked, edging the door open once more.

As I ran through my credentials for the umpteenth time, I scrutinized the woman's distinctive appearance. While some of the townspeople had characterized her as merely weird or squirrelly, others labeled her a raving environmentalist wacko whose contentious activities had single handedly bankrupted Morgan's Folly.

But as first impressions go, she appeared totally non-threatening. More like a middle-aged hippie, although it was difficult to guess her age because her plain unlined face bore not a trace of make-up. She could have been thirty or even forty. Her 1970's frayed bell-bottomed jeans and wide-collared blouse looked as though they'd come from a thrift shop while the dark roots of her disheveled silver-blonde hair cried out for a touch up.

But it was her eyes that captured my attention. They were two distinct colors and I couldn't decide whether to look at the brown one or the aqua-blue one. "Ah...if you have a few minutes, I'd like to get your perspective concerning the ongoing environmental debate about the possible re-opening of the mine."

"I don't really have time today. I'm trying to get things ready for a rally this weekend."

I stood firm. After conquering those stairs, I had no intention of going away empty-handed. I assumed my most innocent expression. "Just a few questions. It won't take long. I promise."

She rested a forefinger alongside her broad nose and studied me reflectively. "The last reporter I talked to twisted everything around something god-awful. He ended up making me look like some kind of a...a...paranoid idiot."

With an inward sigh, I reiterated that I had taken no stance and it was my job to listen to both sides of an issue and write an objective piece.

She looked unconvinced. "I'm sure the Pickrell's and most everyone else in town have already filled your head with propaganda about me. And anyway, it's the Morgan girl I should be talking to. I called her yesterday. Why isn't she here?"

I started to tell her, but then remembered my promise not to divulge details of Audrey's condition. Although with Haston and Jesse having witnessed the seizure I doubted, with the exception of Willow, that there was a person left in town who didn't know by now.

Without going into detail, I explained that she was under the weather. "But as soon as she's feeling better, I'm certain she plans to give you a fair hearing before making any decision. And besides," I continued before she could voice further protest, "as long as I'm here it might be helpful to your cause if you can illustrate why you consider it so important that the mine stay closed permanently."

She seemed to be assessing my words carefully and the hard light of skepticism in her extraordinary eyes began to ebb. "I want to show you something." She led me around the side of the house to a junk-littered, wooden deck that hung precariously over a rocky precipice. Mounted on a tripod near the railing, a telescope stood pointing towards a grove of sun-capped cottonwood trees bordering the creek below. She fiddled with the focus for a few minutes before excitedly waving for me to take her place. "Take a look. See for yourself what will be destroyed if the Morgan girl doesn't listen to reason."

Curious, I peered into the eyepiece, but saw nothing but the magnified image of pearl gray branches. "What am I looking for?"

"Don't you see it?"

"It's a fine looking tree, if that's what you mean."

With an impatient snort, she waved me away, refocused, and then motioned me back, prompting "You see that little bird?"

I looked closer. "You mean the brownish-olive one with the yellow throat?"

"Yes! That's the Southwestern Willow Flycatcher. Isn't he magnificent?"

I thought magnificent a bit overblown, but said, "Well, yes, it's pretty, but..."

"They're very rare, you know," she informed me in a tone edging towards reverence. "These beautiful creatures are helpless against the evil encroachment of man into their kingdom. They desperately need our help to survive and sometimes...sometimes it requires drastic action to protect them."

Convinced of her sincerity, I had a quick flash of the bloody message scrawled on my windshield. "Are you suggesting they're an endangered species?" I challenged her, lifting my gaze in time to gauge her reaction.

"Absolutely. Did you know there are only a handful of them left in North America?" Her blue eye glittered with passion while the brown one seemed to smolder.

"And the connection to the Defiance would be?"

She shot me a look that verified my ignorance. "The most important thing to a bird, to any animal for that matter, is their food supply." Her words were unmistakably spiced with scorn. "Food! Food! Food! If the Morgan girl permits the mine to re-open their critical habitat will be destroyed forever."

"I don't understand why? It's a couple of miles from here, isn't it?"

"Have you been out there yet?"

"Yes, we were just there this morning."

"Then you saw the devastation. The waste ponds full of toxic acid like cyanide, that can seep down and contaminate the ground water. But that's not all," she added with wide-eyed drama. "There will be drilling and blasting and dust pollution. All of these things contribute to the destruction of nesting areas." Breathless with indignation, she began to pace. "And on top of that, it won't be underground mining like before. No. Now it will be open-pit."

"I'm not sure I'm following you. Can't the birds go live somewhere else?"

She gaped at me as if I was truly mentally deficient. "You really don't understand, do you?" she said, shaking her head.

"I make no claims to be an expert on the environment. That's why I'm here talking to you."

"Well then, you need to be educated." Beckoning me to follow, she trotted to the back door. "You'll have to excuse the mess. As I told you, I'm preparing for a demonstration so things are a little disorganized today."

The rank smell hit me the minute I stepped inside. Was it garbage or animal urine? Probably both. Whatever, I could hardly catch my breath as I surveyed what I assumed was the living room. Disorganized, she'd said. That had to be the understatement of the century. Placards of every shape and size lay strewn about the floor. Stacks of brochures and pamphlets blanketed every stick of furniture, including the wood stove. In the adjacent kitchen, fliers were scattered over the countertops, refrigerator and table. Through a doorway beyond that, I could see file folders heaped on an unmade bed.

She shut off the music and ordered, "Stay," when the dogs shot to attention and lunged towards me. I hung back while she got them under control and then flinched violently when a gray dove came zooming down from the rafters and used my head for a landing strip.

"Don't worry. That's just Lovey Dovey," she reassured me with a giggle, swiping piles of folded laundry from a chair, then indicating that I should sit. "The poor little thing was almost dead when I found her a few months ago. I nursed her back to complete health."

"That's commendable," I remarked, feeling warmth as the bird hunkered down in my hair. "But, what is she doing?"

"Looking for a place to lay her eggs," she muttered absently, flitting around the room, whipping up a storm of papers as she gathered up handfuls of literature.

I was aghast. Willow's love for all nature's creatures seemed indisputable and perhaps she accepted these activities as commonplace, but I wasn't too keen on the idea of becoming a nest or a bathroom for Lovey Dovey. "If you don't mind," I began, endeavoring to be tactful, "I'd rather she'd do that somewhere else."

"What? Oh, yes, sure." She untangled the bird's feet from my hair, set it on her own head and resumed compiling material, her eyes glazed with preoccupation.

I eased onto the chair and tried to decide whether Willow was really as ditsy as she appeared, or was this all a clever ruse?

"Where did that article go?" she mumbled, fingering through a bookcase stuffed with magazines.

With Willow fully absorbed in her quest, it gave me an opportunity to examine her living quarters. It struck me almost at once that while the walls were hung with photos, plates and paintings of animals and birds, and the window sills crammed with colorful glass miniatures of dolphins, there wasn't one single photograph of a person.

"So, Willow," I began, pulling out my pen and notepad, "are there any other family members involved in the animal rights movement with you?"

"What?"

"Is there a Mr. Windsong or any little Windsongs?"

"No." Her multicolored eyes were beacons of apprehension.

"Isn't it an interesting coincidence that your name is so perfectly suited to the type of activities you're involved in?"

"Mmmmm, yes." The dove's wings flared out for balance as Willow bent over a battered desk and began rifling around in a drawer.

"What nationality is it exactly?"

Her movements stilled completely and when she turned, her crestfallen expression spoke volumes. "Okay, Ms. O'Dell," she said softly. "I'm sure you're gonna be snooping around, so I may as well tell you now."

My pulse rate shot up a notch. "That you're name isn't really Willow Windsong?"

I must have looked expectant because she let out a caustic laugh. "If you're holding out the hope that I'm some kind of crazy fugitive who's been on America's Most Wanted or something, you're barking up the wrong tree."

"So, why *did* you change it?"

Her smile was sheepish. "When I joined the Evergreen Party my family sort of disowned me."

"Why?"

"I'd wager if your name was Mrs. Spaulding Canisaw, you'd change your name too."

"Spaulding Canisaw," I murmured, searching my memory banks before firing her an incredulous look. "As in Canisaw Chemical Company?"

"My ex-husband."

I was dumbfounded. The giant corporation was known worldwide and it taxed my imagination to capacity when I tried to picture this rather eccentric woman hobnobbing with the high society set. Yet, she'd apparently given up a life of wealth and luxury to pursue her commitment. And although such a move appeared foolhardy on the surface, I couldn't suppress a flare of grudging admiration.

I was no less surprised to hear that not only had she left her husband, but also her two teenage sons. "Before you pass judgement," she cautioned, holding up a finger.

"You need to know that I was traveling around a lot and I felt the kids were better off with their father."

"How do they like your new name?"

"They don't. But it was an embarrassment for me to even be associated with my old one, considering those people are to blame for plundering the earth by dumping their toxic waste all over creation and polluting our rivers and oceans." She slammed a drawer shut and began piling brochures into my lap. "You tell Miss Morgan to read everything. Then she'll understand why I, and lots of other people in this town, will never allow the mine to reopen."

I remembered the bitter expressions on the miner's faces when they'd relayed the pain and adversity suffered at the hands of this woman and, her casual use of the word 'allow' compelled me to question her unblinking effrontery.

"I gather you don't consider your activities just a tad extreme?"

The upward flight of charcoal eyebrows revealed her surprise. "Not in the least."

"What about the other point of view? The miners feel that your actions are largely responsible for destroying their livelihood. As far as they're concerned, *they* are the endangered species."

"What a load of crap! If we don't do everything we can to protect these birds and other species, they'll be gone. Extinct means forever."

"I understand. But what about the fact that the mine property is private. That means the owner should be able to use it however he or she wishes, doesn't it?"

"No! The land should be donated as a preserve."

"Are you suggesting the property be confiscated?"

"If necessary."

I stared in surprise, thinking that her answer defied

logic, but feeling certain that to her it made perfect sense. "But, Willow, do you think it's fair to punish these men and their families? What about the human cost?"

"That's their problem. These men and their greedy ancestors have been raping the earth for centuries. Let them get retrained to do something else."

It was easy to see how her incendiary rhetoric could have spawned the aggravation leading to Grady's fateful decision, as well as the impasse that now pitted the citizens of Morgan's Folly against each other.

Several deliberate breaths seemed to restore her composure and she finished in a reasonable tone. "The birds and animals were here first. Remember, it's man who has ruined the environment, it's man who should leave and allow God's creatures to live in peace."

I could tell she was dead serious. But unlike some of the townsfolk, I didn't believe she had a screw loose. This was a woman with deep convictions willing to wage a valiant fight for her crusade. But would she kill for it? "Willow, tell me truthfully, do you actually believe those little birds are more important than a human being?"

The guarded expression on her face confirmed that she'd caught my implication. "That's a trick question, isn't it? Listen, lady, you're a day late and a dollar short. I've already been questioned up the wazoo about what happened last May. And if there was any proof that I'd done away with the old bastard I'd be in jail, wouldn't I?"

"Something's still not clear to me. Since your efforts had already succeeded in keeping the mine closed for four years and, apparently everyone in town knew Grady was resisting Haston's proposal to reopen it, what was the problem between you two? I would have thought you and Grady would be on the same team, for different reasons, of course."

"Don't believe everything you hear. That depended on when you talked to him, or if he was sober. One day he'd swear that it would stay closed forever and the next he'd deliberately taunt me, saying he'd changed his mind. Make no mistake. He was using the situation to get even. To torture me."

I frowned. "That's odd. He used the same seesaw strategy on the Pickrells. Why?"

"Because, that's the kind of person Grady Morgan was. It was a game with him. It made him feel superior. God-like. I'm not sorry that horrible man is gone. I only hope his daughter, or whoever she is, doesn't waffle on her promises the way he did."

So, she doubted Audrey's authenticity as well. "What promises?"

An expression of profound misery clouded her plain features as she reached up to extract Lovey Dovey from her hair and set the bird tenderly on the back of a kitchen chair. "He vowed that if an agreement was ever reached he would set aside several acres of the property for a riparian preserve."

"He put that in writing?"

She nodded her reply.

"And he reneged on it?"

"He was laughing..." Her voice cracked and she swallowed hard. "I pleaded with him not to, but he was cackling like a mad man and tore up the agreement right in front of me."

"When?"

Her unusual eyes glowed with distress. "That same afternoon."

Her admission was stunning. "So, besides Marta

Nuñez, you were the last person to see him alive."

"I'm not stupid. And I'm also well aware of how incriminating this all looks, but I'm not so sure I was the last one."

"What do you mean?"

She moved aside a stack of papers from one end of the sagging couch and sat down with a tired grunt as the dogs gathered around her feet, panting, and pawing her legs for attention. "I was so mad afterwards, I just got in my car and started driving."

"Where?"

"I don't know. Out past the mine road. I was crying and yelling and pounding the steering wheel and well, it was getting dark when I finally got back to town and..."

"About what time was that?"

"Eight-thirty, maybe."

"Go on."

"When I passed the road leading up to the house, guess whose truck I saw turning into the drive?"

Since pickups seemed to be the vehicle of choice for this hilly community, my mind raced with possibilities. "You tell me."

There was a shrewd gleam in her eyes. "Jesse Pickrell's."

That set me back. "You're sure of that?"

"Absolutely."

"But. Marta claims Jesse was there before you came."

"Maybe she was."

"And you told this to the deputy?"

"Yes."

I digested the information for a few seconds. "The windows on her truck are pretty heavily tinted. How can you be sure it was Jesse driving?"

"I can't, but like I said, it was almost dark."

"You're positive the truck went up the driveway?"

"As far as I know."

"I see." I remembered Marta's account of how she'd come home early and gone to sleep. If she was telling the truth, she couldn't have known Jesse had returned. And if Jesse had done the deed, why hadn't Marta seen the truck or at least heard it leaving the scene? But what if it had been parked down the hill out of sight? That would explain how she'd escaped after Marta had seen her running past the window.

And then again, I reminded myself, this could also be an elaborate lie. One thing was certain though. Willow undeniably had the motive and opportunity.

Preoccupied with my thoughts, I was a little disconcerted when she suddenly jumped to her feet. "Look, I've got a deadline to get this stuff done, so if that's all the questions you have, I've got a lot to finish up."

She accepted my thanks for her time with an impatient nod and shooed me towards the door. Outside on the porch, I bundled the papers under my arm and squinted at the hazy afternoon sunlight pouring through the trees.

While pleased with the fact that I'd gained valuable insight on her activist mentality, as well as the intriguing information entailing Jesse's second trip to the Morgan house that day, a measure of frustration permeated my psyche. I'd wanted to grill her about the threatening sign posted on the mine gate, as well as the slain rabbit, but most importantly I was disappointed that I had failed to come up with one ounce of proof to buttress my suspicion that Willow was the phantom caller.

Feigning forgetfulness, I snapped my fingers and

whirled around just as the screen door closed behind me. "You probably don't have a phone up here, do you?"

"Sure I do. You need to use it?"

That shot my theory all to hell. "No. Thanks."

"You won't forget to give that stuff to Miss Morgan, will you?"

I patted the sheaf of papers. "Got 'em right here." Thoroughly disheartened, I started towards the gate, then acting purely on impulse, I swung back to fire one last question. "By the way, I don't suppose there's an outside chance that you were ever acquainted with Rita Morgan?"

She hesitated a few seconds before answering. "As a matter of fact, I was."

Willow's closing remark took me completely by surprise and I threatened to camp out on her doorstep until she agreed to divulge more information.

In a nutshell, she'd met and become friends with Rita while attending high school in Tucson. They'd continued to write to each other even after her family had moved to Chicago during her junior year. But the letters stopped after the death of Rita's first husband and Willow had lost track of her in the midst of her own personal problems and the messy divorce from the chemical giant. Enmeshed in her various causes, Willow's vagabond lifestyle had carried her to the far corners of the earth before she'd returned to Arizona years later to tackle the timber and mining industries.

Thankfully negotiating the last few steps leading down to Toomey's garage, I mulled over the evidence. Willow appeared to meet all the criteria necessary for her to qualify as the villain. She'd known Rita in the past, she'd made no secret of her unavowed hatred for Grady Morgan, and lastly, she certainly possessed a strong justification for discrediting Audrey, even to the point of labeling her an imposter. And what about her apparent money woes? Were they severe enough for her to risk stealing from Grady? Even though her profound zeal regarding the animal rights movement could no doubt justify her motives, somehow, I could no more picture her skulking about the Morgan house pilfering items for her cause than I could imagine her issuing death threats.

But one thing I was sure of. Willow could not have slaughtered the rabbit. Although, I had to consider the disquieting possibility that she might have arranged for someone else to do it.

It worked to my advantage that I'd stayed later than expected at Willow's because Toomey was just closing the garage and offered me a ride. It had been a terribly long day and by the time he dropped me off, I felt physically and emotionally drained. I was anxious to share all my news with Audrey but the small amount of sleep coupled with the unexpected exercise had taken its toll to the point where I could barely clamber up the front stairs to my room.

In record time, I'd stripped, bathed, and changed into shorts and a T-shirt before allowing myself the luxury of flopping onto the bed. The downy mattress seemed to fold around me and with a grateful sigh I closed my eyes, reveling in the notion that except for the phone call to Ida Fairfield, my agenda for the remainder of the evening included little more than a large dose of peace and quiet. The crowning touch would be another of Marta's scrumptious meals followed by a good night's sleep.

But I'd barely completed the thought when a faint sound at the doorway caused me to look up just in time to see Audrey hurl something at me. Instinctively, I raised a hand and deflected the book before it crashed into my cheek. Caught somewhere between stunned amazement and outrage, it took me a few seconds to get my bearings before scrambling to my feet. "What the *hell* are you doing?"

Her eyes flashed fire. "Admit it! You think I'm crazy too."

I groaned inwardly. Not another tantrum? At that particular moment I came close to conceding the possibility, and had to marshal what little patience I had to keep from reaching out and shaking her. "Jesus, Audrey. What's bugging you now? I thought you'd be in a great mood considering the way Duncan Claypool fawned over you all morning."

"Oh sure, like I believe him. He's just being nice because of all the money at stake."

"You're not making much sense."

"Of course I'm not. I'm a mental defective, remember?"

"Oh, please. Get a grip, will you?"

"But what if it's true? What if Jesse's right?"

"Oh, I get it. You've been lying around all afternoon worrying about that stupid remark. Well, forget it. No one thinks that."

"You do."

I met her glare of accusation with disbelief. "What are you talking about?"

She pointed a trembling finger. "That."

Puzzled, I reached over and picked up the book she'd thrown. It was mine—the one on epilepsy I'd been reading the night before. I shot her a look of irritation. "Why were you snooping around in my room?"

"I wasn't snooping. I found it by accident."

"By accident? I left it on the night stand."

"It was on the floor. Right here," she said, pointing to the doorway.

I must have looked skeptical because she burst out, "I thought you were going to be my friend?"

"You don't make it easy."

Angry tears jumped to her eyes. "I saw the page you marked. I read the part about the epileptic personality," she said, placing special emphasis on the word epileptic. "I know exactly what's going to happen now. I've seen it before. You're going to treat me like I'm some kind of a freak like everyone else does when they find out."

I gritted my teeth. "No, I'm not. I bought this last week to educate myself about something I know very little about, so stop trying to read something sinister into it."

Apparently stung by my rebuke, she looked chastened. "I'm sorry, Kendall. I guess I was...I thought maybe you'd be afraid to be around me anymore."

"That's not true."

Her despondent sigh filled the room. "Can you believe my shitty timing? Of all the places on earth, why did I have to have an attack in front of Jesse and Haston and...Duncan."

Oh. So that's what was really bothering her.

"When he left this afternoon, he promised to call, but I know he won't." She hugged her elbows and leaned into the doorjamb, whimpering, "And it's my own fault."

"Don't be silly. You can't control the seizures." I expected her to agree, but instead she stood in stony silence, looking guilty. "Audrey, what is it?"

She fiddled and picked at the material on her long skirt before answering. "Sometimes, I don't take my medicine."

"What? Why not?"

"Because a lot of times it makes me feel sick."

"What are you taking?"

"Dilantin."

"And how long have you been on it?"

She gave a slight shrug. "I don't know. Years."

"Well, for heaven's sake. Why didn't you say something to your doctor?"

"I told you. Mom told me not to discuss it, so I just... didn't."

I thought her explanation both lame and irresponsible, but somehow right in character. I rose and pressed the book firmly into her hand. "Here. Apparently, you need this worse than I do. And I think you should go see Dr. Orcutt about a change of medication right away."

"I don't want to."

The abject panic in her eyes puzzled me. "Why not?"

"What if it does run in the family?"

"You mean epilepsy?"

"No," she said through trembling lips. "Insanity."

The sight of tears streaming down her grief-stricken face evaporated my exasperation. With an inward sigh, I put my arms around her, once again, holding her while she wept. Try as I might, I couldn't banish the vision of her radiant expression this morning as she'd basked in the warmth of Duncan's attention. Poor kid. Was she right? Had it all been a ploy? A craven scheme cooked up between Haston and him to break down any resistance she might have for their plans?

I swallowed the sour taste of resentment gathering in my throat, preferring to believe that his actions were genuine and he was not some jerk bent on romancing this vulnerable young woman for his own selfish purposes.

But my own reaction presented another uncomfortable dilemma. I was dangerously close to losing my objectivity. Teetering on the edge. And that wasn't good.

From my first day on the job four years ago at my dad's little newspaper back home in Spring Hill, I'd carried with me his sage advice. "Go ahead and get emotionally involved with the subject matter of your story. It makes for passionate writing. But steer clear of emotional attachments to the people. It skews the facts and eventually obscures the truth."

I patted her on the back as she pulled away and delicately blew her nose on a tissue. "Listen, Audrey, you're not crazy, so you can chalk that off your worry list."

"What about my father? He talked to ghosts, you know," she said, fluttering her fingers through the air. "And what about my sister? She died in an asylum, remember?"

"Why dwell on them? Look at the bright side. From what we've learned, you also have relatives like your great-grandmother, Hannah, who were intelligent, courageous, hard-working people. But if it will put your mind at ease, why don't you ask Dr. Orcutt about your sister's condition when you see him?"

She looked doubtful. "What if that's one of the things he promised my mother he wouldn't tell me?"

"Then we'll go around him and talk to the other people who knew her." Her continuing expression of uncertainty prompted me to add, "I promise you, we're going to find out what happened, but right now, I think it's just as important that we keep our eyes on the ball and deal with the present situation first. Tomorrow's going to be a big day for you, and maybe when you know where you stand legally and financially, you'll feel more in control."

She wiped her eyes, looking no less miserable. Maybe."

I sat down on the bed and motioned for her to join me. "I have a lot of things to tell you. Do you feel up to talking?"

"I suppose." The material of her long skirt flared out around her like a field of wildflowers as she plumped down cross-legged at the foot of my bed. "Oh my," she gasped, clapping a hand over her mouth. "What happened to your feet?"

I followed her line of sight to the red welts covering my heels. "Poor planning. The next time I go hiking, remind me to wear the proper shoes."

Tiny frown lines etched her smooth forehead. "Why were you hiking?"

"I'll get to that in a minute. But right now I want to tell you what I learned from Jesse." As I repeated the conversation, her expression grew so bleak that, for sake of maintaining what was probably a tenuous calm, I decided to skip over the rabbit incident and concentrate on the other things I'd learned.

When I concluded, she sat blinking in confusion. "Oh, wow. They both sound totally weird. So, which one do you think it is? Jesse or Willow?"

"Good question. Let's go over the facts one at a time starting with Jesse, and let's assume for the time being that she is telling the truth."

Audrey drew a big breath as if to steel herself. "Okay."

"We know that your father, Jesse, and now you, have all been contacted by a woman who claims to have known your mother from a long time ago. From the list of people that we know of, that could be Marta, Willow, Fran Orcutt, and from what Harmon Stubbs tells me, D.J. is dating a woman named Bitsy who may have been friends with your sister, Dayln."

Audrey's eyes were huge as she sat listening intently, alternately bunching then smoothing the material on her skirt. "So, that means she knew my mother too."

"I would imagine so. And it's certainly one of the questions I intend to ask her as soon as I can. But that brings us back to square one. Who, besides Jesse, has anything to gain by challenging your identity?"

She shrugged.

"Okay, how about this? Suppose Jesse isn't telling the truth and that she was the one tormenting your father with crank calls because of his refusal to sanction Claypool's involvement. Now we know from Marta that she was here that last day arguing with him, and from what Willow just told me, it appears she was here after Marta left for the evening."

Audrey's mouth sagged open. "She came back?"

I held up a hand. "So Willow claims. Although she can't swear Jesse was driving. But let's say she was. Let's say she and your father had another big blow up, she loses it and dumps him into the ravine."

"Well, she's definitely mean enough to have done it," Audrey commented dryly. "But, what about Haston? You think he knew about it?"

"Who knows? But, picture this scene. The coast is

now clear to sign on the dotted line with Duncan, move into the mansion and assume control. Then, out of nowhere, here comes Dr. Orcutt with his questionable disclosure about you. Couple that with the fact that he gives them your phone number which could have prompted Jesse's first call to you."

I could see the realization dawning in her eyes. "Oh! So you think because D.J. was really working for her, that he and his scummy friend Archie had something to do with what happened on Boneyard Pass?"

"Sounds logical to me. And if Jesse can convince everybody that you and Dr. Orcutt hatched this whole scheme, she could tie things up in court for a long time."

Audrey finished chewing what was left of her thumbnail and dropped her hand into her lap. "How? I have my birth certificate now."

"She'll probably contest it."

"How can she?"

"Because, she told me the original documents were destroyed when the courthouse burned down. She could contend that the birth certificate you picked up in Tucson is as phony as the one claiming you were Angela Martin."

"But I *am* telling the truth. Why would my mother lie about such a thing? Why would Dr. Orcutt? And besides, everyone says I look just like my father."

It was amazing how she'd come from not even knowing who she was two days ago to passionately defending her new identity. For an inkling the lingering doubt spawned by Tugg's assertion surfaced again, but I expelled it just as quickly. For my own sanity I simply had to proceed on the notion that she was who she claimed to be. "It's too bad your father is dead. A simple blood test would prove paternity."

"But what if Jesse isn't lying?" Audrey mused. "Who else could it be?" Before I could reply, she cast a furtive glance at the doorway and lowered her voice to a whisper. "What about Marta? Remember what Detective Kemp said? Maybe she scared Jesse away and hopes I'll go too so she can keep stealing stuff from the house."

"I suppose it's possible. I don't know about all of them, but it appears likely that at least some of the calls were made from the pay phone at Toomey's."

I told her about the static and watched her eyes bug out. "So, it is Willow."

"Not so fast. Let's stay with Marta for a minute. Unless there's a second phone line here at the house we don't know about, logically, she'd have to go someplace else if she was making the calls to Grady, right?"

"Yeah. But why a pay phone?"

While pondering the answer, I listened to the shrill, dinnertime bird chatter outside. "For one thing, it's fairly close. She could walk, if necessary. In your case, there'd be no record of who made that long distance call to Pennsylvania and the same reason she had to leave the house to call Grady would apply when Jesse lived here, and now you."

Her forehead crinkled with doubt. "But wouldn't someone have seen her?"

"Maybe. For the daytime calls it's worth checking on, but it's unlikely anyone was around there at night."

"But...I still don't understand why she would want to..." pausing, she silently mouthed the words, 'kill him.'

"What if he confronted her with evidence of her thievery and threatened to turn her in? She could have made up that whole story about seeing another woman running away to cover her own tracks. And that reminds me." I rose, pulled my purse from where I'd left it on the marble-topped rosewood dresser and motioned toward the window. "I found this in the grass over there by that tree."

Audrey's look of skepticism remained as I placed the hair barrette in her hand. "You think this fell out of Marta's hair that night?"

"It fell out of someone's hair, but whether it's related to that night, I don't know."

Unexpectedly, a look of sly excitement sparkled in her eyes. "Maybe we can question her again and somehow find out if it's hers."

"I guess we could," I said, amused that she was finally getting into the spirit of the hunt.

She brightened perceptibly. "Okay, but what about Willow? She works right there at the garage. It would be easy for her to do it..." She paused, blinking. "But, wait. How could she have made that first call to me when only Dr. Orcutt and the Pickrell's had my number?"

"Ah, but how do we know that? It's no secret that Willow's been organizing demonstrations at the mine. Remember Whitey told us that she and a bunch of other people got arrested one day for chaining themselves to the gate?"

"Yeah."

"And, it's a good bet Willow was in on posting that warning sign we saw this morning."

"Okay, but I don't understand the connection to the phone call."

"Let me finish. Let's say the Pickrells left your number laying on the desk at the office or, if she was there the day Dr. Orcutt came, it's possible she may have overheard what he told them."

Audrey frowned. "It sounds kind of far-fetched,

huh?"

Another headache was lurking and I rubbed a hand over my forehead. I needed to eat and get some sleep. "Yeah, I guess it does."

"But then again, from what you've said, she had every reason to hate my father...and now me if I don't give her what she wants. Right?"

Our eyes locked in silent agreement and I knew there would be no better time to tell her about the rabbit. I braced for her reaction and recounted the event.

Her face turned white as parchment. "Oh, gross. That is so totally disgusting!"

"I'll say."

"So, you think she..." The sudden jangle of the phone displaced her revulsion with a look of fear. I knew what she was thinking. Another threatening call.

But, by the third ring, hope flared in her brown eyes. "Maybe it's Duncan." She was off the bed in a flash, almost tripping on her skirt as she sprinted for the parlor. I was right behind her.

She scooped up the phone and gasped out, "Hello?" Almost at once disappointment overshadowed her flush of anticipation. "What? Oh, yes, of course. We'll be there in a few minutes." She replaced the receiver and slumped into the chair. "I knew he wouldn't call."

"Who were you talking to?"

"Marta."

"Marta? Where was she calling from?"

"From here," Audrey snapped. "We picked up the phone at the same time. It was for her anyway and she said we should come to dinner now."

Even if my tired brain had been too busy to monitor the time, at the mention of food, my stomach rumbled a reminder that I'd never had lunch. "Dinner sounds like an excellent idea to me."

Her response to my enthusiasm was to shrink deeper into the chair. All the air seemed to have gone out of her as well as her fleeting zest for adventure.

"Hey, cheer up. The day's not over yet. He may still call. Plus that, I thought you were anxious to try your skill as an investigative reporter?"

After throwing out the challenge, I was positive she was going to wimp out on me then retire to sulk in her room. She surprised me by pushing to her feet. "You're right," she said, linking arms with me. "Let's go eat and afterwards we'll see if we can pry the truth from Marta."

"That's the spirit."

We were halfway across the breezeway when I realized I was still barefoot. "I'm going to run back and get my sandals."

"I don't care if you have shoes."

"I need my notebook anyway," I said, grinning. "I'll be along in a few minutes."

"Okay."

I retraced my steps to the parlor and had reached the door to my room when I heard a floorboard creak in the direction of the stairway. I stopped and whirled around. No one was there and except for the muffled ticking of the clock, the house was steeped in silence.

Oh, well. These old places were always shifting and settling. While retrieving my sandals from the rug near the bed, I noticed that in her haste to get to the phone, Audrey had forgotten to take the book on epilepsy.

I picked it up and fanned the pages thoughtfully. Her violent over-reaction to my having it still puzzled me. And if she hadn't been in my room as she claimed, how had the book gotten from my nightstand onto the floor? I fingered the tasseled bookmark and thought back to the surprise visit from Princess early this morning. The silky thread would make a wonderful cat toy and it certainly seemed a plausible explanation—assuming that Audrey was telling the truth. But what if she wasn't? What reason would she have to be in my room?

A quick peek into the closet and chest of drawers revealed nothing out of order, but as I toed into the sandals, the shadow of doubt still hung over me.

Even though my intuitive feeling told me she was genuine, tomorrow I would phone my brother to see if he or Margie could shed any more light on her sketchy background—just to put Tugg's mind at ease, I assured myself. I replaced the book on the night stand with a reminder to return it to Audrey later along with Willow's brochures.

I paused momentarily by the window to watch the evening shadows steal across the valley. The amber hills turned a deep coral and mourning doves warbled a mellow farewell to the blistering sun now cradled between the jagged rocks on top of Devil's Hill. The effect was mesmerizing.

Having had almost no contact with the outside world for three days, I had the oddest sensation that I had journeyed backward to a different time zone. Indeed, apart from my call to Tugg, I hadn't seen a paper, listened to the news or watched television for three days.

I snapped on the little table lamp and, filled with eager anticipation at the thought of another tasty dinner, started out the door. Another creak, this time from the floor above held me frozen. Was someone in Audrey's room?

While my mind fleetingly touched on the irrational concept of ghosts, I shrugged away the sudden twinge of uneasiness. Marta and Audrey were in the other wing, so if it wasn't the cat, more than likely it was D.J. Instant irritation blossomed when it occurred to me that he'd probably overheard our entire conversation and would now scurry like the loyal spy he was to report back to Jesse and Haston. The jerk.

Half of me was willing to forget it, but when I turned toward the breezeway my impetuous half intervened. How would he feel if the tables were turned?

I slipped off my sandals and tiptoed up the stairs, creeping towards Audrey's bedroom, which stood empty. A quick search of the other rooms on the second floor yielded no answers. Had I imagined the noise? I was beginning to doubt my own ears, when I noticed a scrub bucket and mop on the third floor landing. I crept up the stairway and was rewarded to see dim lamplight streaming through a doorway at the end of the hall. Careful to stay on the carpet, I made a stealthy approach and peeked around the doorframe.

Just as I thought. D.J. was in the ornate drawing room Audrey and I had explored last night. Whistling tunelessly to himself, he bent over to plug in an upright vacuum cleaner then whipped a cloth from the back pocket of his jeans and began to dust the furniture.

I stifled a sigh of disappointment and gave myself a mental kick. Great detective work, O'Dell. Pretty exciting stuff. As the aroma of lemon-oil wafted towards me, I stood motionless, the minutes passing slowly. When a cramp flamed in my right foot, I wrestled with pangs of uncertainty. What if he hadn't been spying on us? What if he was just simply cleaning house as it appeared?

I turned to look down the empty hallway thinking I'd best get out of there. If he discovered me, no doubt he'd be annoyed and who could blame him? But worse, it might ruin my chances of cooperation when it came time to get his version of the night Grady Morgan died.

I shifted my weight back, all set to retreat when he suddenly abandoned the dusting chore and crossed to the corner of the room where he began to circle the satin and lace-clad dress form with fluid grace. Moving to an unheard melody, it seemed as if he were performing some bizarre dance routine. He did this several times, then stopped directly behind it. For a few seconds, he stood motionless and then, his expression turning dreamy, he slid his hands around the form's slim waist.

I recoiled in breathless shock. Whoa! When his fingers began to glide ever so slowly upward to fondle the breasts, my face grew so hot it could have melted butter. Propriety dictated that I should leave immediately. What right did I have to intrude on this man's private fantasies? But curiosity glued my feet to the floor.

Both fascinated and repelled, I continued to watch until he ended his sensual massage. Then, he kissed one finger and tenderly planted it on the face of his imaginary woman before moving across the faded Persian rug to stand beneath the portrait of Hannah Morgan.

I strained forward as far as I dared and it was a lucky thing for me that he stood opposite the mirror above the mantle piece or I wouldn't have seen the shrewd smile dawning as he fingered his mustache.

Silently I cursed the fact that he wore those damned tinted lenses. The smoky-gray color all but obscured the emotion in his eyes.

In much the same manner as Audrey had done last

night, he stared transfixed at the portrait and then reached up to slide one finger along the gilded frame. "Thy will be done, my lady," he murmured, "Thy will be done."

I was happy to see Audrey's spirits revived as she chattered amiably over Marta's savory lasagna dinner. The accompanying Caesar salad and crisp garlic toast would have normally had me in ecstasy, but the whole weird episode with D.J. had put a damper on my appetite.

His kinky sexual habits were certainly none of my business, but the episode haunted me nonetheless. One thing for sure, his amorous exhibition had certainly served to squelch any suspicions that he might be gay, but I wondered what Bitsy Bigelow would think of his on-going relationship with the dress form? I'd probably never know, but even more intriguing was his apparent fixation with the portrait of a young Hannah Morgan. His final words rampaged through my mind but I had no clue as to what he meant. Thank heavens the roar of the vacuum cleaner had masked my hasty exit from the third floor. I couldn't even imagine what I'd have said to him had I been caught.

I was burning to share my findings with Audrey, but I couldn't take a chance on being overheard as Marta banged in and out of the kitchen door, delivering each course. Plus that, D.J. could walk in at any moment.

"Don't you like the peach cobbler?" Audrey asked.

Her sudden question sent my thoughts stampeding. "What? Oh, yes, indeed. I love it." I dug my fork into the flaky, cream-soaked crust and forced down another bite while she eyed me dubiously.

"You told me you were starving, but you didn't even finish the lasagna."

"I guess I'm too busy thinking about questions for Marta," I whispered, hoping that response would do for now.

Her eyes blazed with excitement. "How do we start?" she asked, keeping her voice low. "I mean, how do you get her onto the subject you want?"

I grinned. "Most of the time, I just let people do what they like best."

"What's that?"

"Talk about themselves. All I have to do then is guide the questions in a specific direction."

"Well, let's get to work," she said, giving me a conspiratorial wink as we left the table and pushed through the swinging doors. The kitchen, still warm, and permeated with the pungent aroma of onion and garlic, stood empty, but we soon found Marta outside the back door seated on a weathered rocker. She was busily snapping the ends off fresh green beans.

"You like Marta's supper?" she asked hopefully, glancing up at us through Coke-bottle lenses.

Audrey grinned and patted her flat, almost concave,

abdomen. "I'm totally stuffed. Thank you."

"It was beyond wonderful," I agreed, pulling up a lawn chair and motioning with my head for Audrey to sit also. "You really should think about opening a restaurant."

Her thick lips stretched wide, revealing crooked, discolored teeth. "This is something I have done already."

"No kidding? When was that?"

"Oh, many years ago. My husband Emilio and me, we have a little place in Nogales. But when he dies, I come to be near my daughter because her husband works in the mine. Soon I take the job here with Mr. Morgan."

It was amazing how a simple question like that could open the door. "I'm glad you mentioned that," I said, meeting Audrey's eyes briefly. "If you have time, I wonder if I could ask you a few more questions about the night Mr. Morgan died."

She snapped a long fat bean and dropped it into the colander in her lap. "If Miss Morgan does not mind if the dishes wait."

"Don't worry about that," Audrey said with an impatient wave. "This is more important."

With the lavender sky swiftly fading to deep orchid, I squinted momentarily at my notes before beginning. "Now, you said D.J. brought you home early."

She popped a bean into her mouth and crunched it. "Yes."

"And you went right to bed."

"Yes. My stomach does not feel so good."

"I'm a little confused about something. When I spoke to D.J., he claims he wasn't here until around midnight."

The harsh light from the outdoor fixture above her head accentuated her surprised frown. "You mistake his words. He is here when I call him to bring me home. He says that Mr. Morgan drinks very much and he puts him in his bed. He tells me he will go now to the Muleskinner and see his friends."

"But, you don't know when?"

She shook her head.

"Okay. When you have dinner at your daughter's place, what time do you normally get home?"

She chewed the remainder of the bean and swallowed. "Most times D.J. will come around eleven or eleven-thirty."

Audrey piped up, "That's kind of late, isn't it?"

"Friday is my day off. It's a nice thing to sleep in sometimes."

Wide-eyed, Audrey turned to me. "Oh, I get it. Whoever came here that night didn't expect Marta to be home yet."

The old housekeeper responded to her statement with a canny nod. "The woman does not think I will see her."

"Tell me something, Marta," I said, swatting at one of the army of insects now swarming around the light, "Willow Windsong swears she saw someone driving Jesse's truck up here about eight-thirty or nine. Did you hear anything?"

"That night it was very hot, so I have the air-conditioner on and the windows closed."

"So, how is it you heard Mr. Morgan shouting?"

The barest hint of annoyance glimmered in her eyes. "That comes from inside the house. And it is very loud. Loud enough to wake the dead," she intoned ominously, fingering the cross at her throat.

"Could you make out what he was saying?

"His voice, it was not clear."

"Did it sound like he was arguing with someone?"

"The sheriff asks me this too, but I'm not so sure."

"Did he make a habit of talking to himself when he was drinking?"

"I told you, the drink it makes him loco sometimes."

So, she could not really verify anyone had been there when he fell. Realizing I'd come full circle and still had no answers left me vaguely frustrated. "Okay, so you got up, checked Mr. Morgan's room and he wasn't there, right?"

An affirmative grunt.

"But, you determined the noise was coming from the old part of the house and you crossed the breezeway?"

"Yes. Anymore I don't move so good but I go as fast as I can, all the time calling Mr. Morgan's name. But," she added in the same breath, "I hear no answer from him."

"Were there any lights on in that part of the house?"

"No. I turn on the lamps, but there is no one. Then I go up to the second floor."

"Was that dark too?"

A slow nod. "The lights in the hall I turn on and I look inside each room, but there is nothing. Then I go up to the next floor and that is the strange part."

"What?" Audrey was leaning forward so far I thought she might tumble off the chair.

Obviously relishing her moment in the spotlight, Marta slowly raised a stubby finger and pointed with theatrical flair. "In that little room, the light is on."

Following her gaze, I stared up at the round turret outlined against the twilight sky and a delicious thrill shot through me. As horrifying as the possibility was that Grady had been murdered, I couldn't help but appreciate the spooky setting. But when I turned to judge Audrey's reaction, it was apparent she didn't share my zeal. Ashen-faced, she quavered, "Why do you think he was up there?"

Marta hunched her broad shoulders. "There are many books. Maybe he is reading, maybe not. There is no explaining Mr. Morgan. Sometimes he wanders through the house and cries. Sometimes he falls down. It makes for much worry and many times D.J. helps me put him to bed."

I angled my notebook towards the light, flipping to the next page. "You told us he kept old photographs in a trunk. Do you mean the big one in the tower room?"

"Oh, yes. There are many old things inside. And there are more boxes also in his bedroom."

"So, it's possible he was up there looking through the trunk. Was it open or shut?"

She stared unseeing for a moment before mumbling, "I...don't remember."

Searching the old trunk suddenly jumped to the top of my list of important things and I realized my original plan of a restful evening and early bedtime was fading as fast as the crimson remains of daylight hugging the horizon. Stars were visible now, twinkling brightly, and a soft breeze sifted through the low-hanging branches of the chestnut tree as I continued my questioning. "Okay then, so when you couldn't find Mr. Morgan, what prompted you to look behind the house in the ravine?"

"When I come back downstairs, the doors to the balcony are open, so I go out and I see something down there."

"Were the doors open when you passed them the first time?"

A look of confusion fanned out across her blunt features. "I...I am not sure."

"Did you hear anything or see anyone on your way

down to the first floor?"

"No. Well, there is the cat. When I am on the telephone, she runs very fast from the old kitchen. Her eyes are very big and she spits like maybe there is something making her afraid."

Audrey exchanged a calculating look with me and I knew we were thinking the same thing. Could Princess be the sole witness to Grady's nocturnal visitor?

"Did you tell the deputy that?"

"I think so."

"Now, when you spotted this mysterious woman, which direction was she running?"

She paused briefly, her age-spotted face crumpling into a thoughtful frown. "East, I think."

"Towards D.J.'s cottage?"

"I don't know. Maybe." Her look of speculation fueled my suspicion that the mysterious phantom was most likely Jesse. Armed with sufficient motive, and being a frequent visitor here, she had to be familiar with the house and grounds. And the fact that D.J. was secretly in her employ reinforced the notion that they may have been working together. But Marta's account had the woman wearing a long flowing dress. From what I'd seen, that didn't fit in with Jesse's wardrobe at all. But what if she was playing the part of a phantom to terrorize Grady Morgan? It could have been prearranged that she'd use the cottage to hide or change clothes afterward.

The crickets had begun their nightly chorus as I scribbled more notes. "Marta, do you know Lamar Toomey?"

One silvery brow edged above the frame of her glasses. "Everyone in this town knows him."

"He said something curious about D.J., and I

thought maybe you could clear it up for me."

"I will try."

"I understand you visit relatives in Naco every couple of weeks."

"Yes. It's good that D.J. must go there so often. He's very kind to let me sometimes go with him."

It took a few seconds for her statement to fully sink in. "Wait a minute. Are you saying that D.J. initiates the trips and you just go along for the ride?"

"Yes."

Well, wasn't that fascinating. "I heard he frequently brought back booze for the old man. Is that true?"

"Sometimes. But, you must not think bad of D.J.," she added quickly. "Mr. Morgan orders him to buy it."

"I see. But, Lamar says D.J. still goes down there every few weeks like clockwork. Why? Mr. Morgan's been out of the picture for three months now."

She made a great pretense of avoiding my eyes and for a few seconds the sizzling hiss of moths hurling themselves against the hot light bulb resonated above the crickets. "D.J. does much good for my family. When I visit my sister's house, he goes to the Farmacia..."

"What's that?" Audrey interrupted, tapping my arm.

"Pharmacy," I answered her. "You know, drugstore. Go ahead, Marta. Why does he go there?"

"He brings medicine for my grandson," she replied, looking downcast.

"What's wrong with your grandson?"

Marta cracked the ends off the last bean, threw them in a bag near her feet, and settled deeper into the chair. "His kidneys are very bad. D.J. also brings the pills to make my daughter sleep better."

"But why drive all the way down there?" Audrey

inquired.

Marta's ample bosom rose in a sigh. "Just like the grocery store and many other places in this town, the Farmacia closes two years ago. There is one in Bisbee, but you must understand that the special medicine costs much money in this country."

"I've heard a lot of people go to Mexico because a doctor's prescription isn't always required," I said, watching her shift around in her chair while she unnecessarily smoothed the hem of her checkered apron.

"This might be true," she said finally.

I would bet a million dollars she didn't declare her purchases at the border, but beyond that a wild theory began to germinate. What if D.J. was using Marta as a cover to smuggle illegal drugs into the country? If he needed a distribution network that would certainly go a long way in explaining his peculiar association with the likes of Archie Lawton. And what a perfect place to carry on such an illicit business. Who would suspect anything like that going on in this forgotten little town tucked away in the middle of nowhere? "I'm sorry to hear about your grandson," I said. "His illness must place a terrible financial burden on your family."

"Oh, yes. With the mine closed, my son-in-law does not always find steady work. For them it is very hard."

"And sometimes it's probably necessary for you to do whatever you can to help them out, isn't it, Marta?" I asked, carefully gauging her reaction.

"Yes. Sometimes."

I edged a see that's-how-it's-done look at Audrey and watched the realization blossom in her eyes. We now had a motive for theft. Altruistic perhaps, but a strong motive nonetheless. I turned back to Marta. "You say that

D.J. often goes to the Farmacia. Why? Is he sick too?"

"He takes something for allergies."

"What kind of allergies?"

She shrugged. "He also must take a special medicine to make him feel more strong."

That sounded odd. "Vitamins, or do you mean steroids?"

Again the shrug.

"Does Miles Orcutt prescribe these drugs?"

"I don't know."

Audrey, apparently bored with my line of questioning, blurted out, "Ask her about the barrette, Kendall. Tell her..."

My sidelong glance of reproach silenced her next words and I looked back at Marta in time to see something flicker behind her eyes, then vanish.

A deep breath kept my irritation at bay. Nothing like having the element of surprise blown by giving the possible suspect time to think of an alibi. I dug the hair clip from my pocket and held it out in my palm. "Do you know who this belongs to?"

She stared at the cut glass jewels, glowing a dull ruby red in the lamplight. "Where did you find this?"

"In the grass outside my bedroom window."

The jingle of the phone brought Marta to her feet with a grunt and she shuffled stiffly towards the screen door. When she was safely out of earshot, Audrey whispered, "I'm sorry. I guess I wouldn't make a very good reporter."

Inwardly, I agreed, but kept my opinion under wraps. "Don't worry about it. There are some instances where in-your-face journalism works, but there are also times where subtlety is better. Sometimes a person's initial reaction can tell you more than the words that come out of their mouths."

"I don't know why I said anything."

"Consider it a learning experience. You'll notice I didn't come right out and ask her if she'd been stealing from your father but we got the desired results anyway, didn't we?"

"Mmmmm. I see. Yes. Uh huh..."

Judging by Audrey's fixed, glassy-eyed stare and the way her words trailed off, I thought at first she was having one of her absence seizures, but I soon realized she'd abandoned any pretense of listening to me. Instead, she was focused on Marta who finally laid down the receiver and approached the screen door. The look of yearning on Audrey's face intensified as she half-rose from the chair and said in a barely audible voice, "Who is it?"

"It is Mr. Claypool."

She let out a strangled squeal and practically squashed Marta against the doorframe as she dashed inside. "She flies without wings," the older woman muttered with a shake of her head.

Grinning, I asked, "Have you ever seen Duncan Claypool?"

Humor sparked her ebony eyes. "His smile makes a woman's heart light as the air, yes?"

"Apparently so."

But her mood changed abruptly when she extended the barrette to me. "I know you try hard to find the truth of that terrible night, Miss O'Dell, but I don't think this will help you very much."

"Why not?"

She tapped the barrette now lying in my upturned palm. "Many women wear them. They're very common and can be bought for next to nothing in my country."

"Have you ever seen Jesse or Willow wearing anything like this?"

Her level stare held pity. "When D.J. goes to Naco last Christmas, he brings back gifts for everyone."

"This exact type of jewelry?"

"Oh, yes. He gives one to my daughter and for my granddaughters, he brings pretty bracelets with such stones. For me, he brings a pin to wear here," she said, patting the flowered material near her heart.

"And your granddaughters come here to visit you?"

"Yes."

"I see." Disappointment charged through me as the relevance of the clue fizzled. I should have known that was too easy. While it was still possible the hair clip could have been dropped by Jesse, Willow, or even Marta, the more likely scenario was that one of her granddaughters may have lost it. No doubt Detective Kemp would reach the same conclusion.

My next question, poised on the tip of my tongue, went unasked when Marta re-entered the kitchen, insisting that she had to finish the dishes and pack food for D.J. before he left for his night shift at the mine.

Scratching a profusion of bug bites dotting my bare arms, I followed her inside just as Audrey hung up the wall phone and whirled around. Her cheeks burned with color and her eyes were twin beacons of excitement. "Duncan is flying to Los Angeles tomorrow on business but guess what? He wants to pick me up Friday afternoon around two and show me some of his mine properties near Tucson and after that he's taking me to dinner."

I couldn't help grinning. "Hey, what did I tell you?"

"Can you even believe it? He actually called me. I

didn't think he would. Not in a million trillion years. But he did. He really did. Wheeee!"

When she began to twirl madly around the room, Marta and I traded amused glances. While Audrey's childish antics were certainly uplifting, a sliver of doubt persisted. What if she was reading too much into his simple dinner invitation? She could be setting herself up for a heart-aching fall.

After several minutes of excited cavorting, she grabbed my arm, insisting we go upstairs immediately so I could help her choose something to wear.

"Okay. But, remember, I still have to see if we can set up a time to visit with Ida Fairfield."

"Oh, right, I forgot."

We thanked Marta again for dinner and while I reminded her that we'd be leaving for Bisbee late the following morning, Audrey, who was already pushing through the louvered doors, cried out in pain when they suddenly swung inward.

"Hey, I'm really sorry," D.J. said, his hands darting out to steady her. "You're not hurt, are you, Miss...um...Morgan?"

Was I mistaken or had I detected that same deliberate hesitation, that same provocative note of mocking insinuation he'd used when he first addressed her on Monday?

Audrey, appearing shaken but unhurt, pulled from his grasp and rubbed the spot on her forehead that had collided with the door. "I'm fine."

"Boy, that's a relief and a half."

I don't know why, but for some reason, his ingratiating behavior hit a sour note with me.

"I'm glad you're here, D.J.," I said, moving beside

Audrey. "I want to talk to you about Grady Morgan."

Something unreadable behind those shaded eyes streaked by like a shooting star and then was gone. "Can't right now. I'm already late for my shift."

"When then?"

"How about tomorrow afternoon?"

Why did I suddenly suspect that he'd been standing on the other side of those doors the whole time, listening? If that was true, it meant he'd clobbered Audrey on purpose. But why would he harbor any malice towards her? "Unfortunately, we won't be here," I replied. "How about first thing in the morning?"

"I'm not gonna get back here till after nine. I gotta catch me some Z's sometime."

"Five minutes."

"I don't think I can tell you anything you don't know already," he said, dismissing me with a flippant shrug. "But, sure. Whatever." He turned his back to me, sauntered over to the sink where Marta stood loading the dishwasher and lightly smacked her behind. "Hey, old woman. Hope you're happy I did all your work. You got my food ready?"

She giggled and playfully slapped his hand away. I watched them with interest and it occurred to me that D.J. occupied a uniquely neutral position in this whole affair. Considering the fact Marta's contempt for Jesse was no secret, these two appeared to share a close camaraderie nonetheless. It was also interesting to note that his relationship with Bitsy inadvertently aligned him with Willow. I would have liked to stay and observe their actions further, but Audrey's fierce whisper invaded my concentration. "Come on, Kendall, I want to go."

When she grabbed my hand I had little choice but to

follow her as she pulled me along the breezeway, babbling something about Jesse and Haston dropping by in the morning before we left to bring a final proposal from Duncan that he'd instructed her to present to the lawyer.

When we reached her room, she raced to the tall wooden armoire and began holding up various outfits in front of the wavy old mirror before settling on a rose-colored dress. "What do you think of this one?"

"It's nice, but listen, Audrey, I really need to talk to you about D.J. for a minute."

"No," she said, reverting to her petulant mode. "I don't want to talk about him." She turned sideways to study her reflection. "Do you think this one will make me look fat?"

"Are you kidding?"

"Mmmmm. What about shoes?" she continued in a distracted tone. "The white ones go best, but the beige ones might be more practical if we do a lot of walking."

I shrugged my opinion and when the sound of the Suburban's engine drew me to the window, I watched until the taillights vanished around the bend. Why did I have such a distinct feeling of relief knowing D.J. was gone from the house? Was it because I knew we could talk without being overheard? Or did it spring from a growing discomfort stemming from his unorthodox behavior? It was the perfect time to share the incident with Audrey, but she was off in la-la land talking a hundred miles an hour about Duncan. Oh, well, we'd be alone in the car tomorrow, I'd tell her then.

"What about jewelry?" Audrey prattled on, rummaging through a small quilted case. "I have a little gold locket, these beads, or I could wear the pearls my mother left me."

"Nix on the pearls," I advised her. "Too old. Look, Audrey, it's almost nine o'clock. I've got to make that call and then I'm going to look through that trunk upstairs. You want to come with me?"

Her movements stilled and I met her apprehensive gaze in the mirror. "I don't feel like going up there right now. But, if you find any photos, you can bring them down here."

Considering her stark terror last night, I wasn't all that surprised that she declined. "Will do."

Downstairs in the cozy parlor, I phoned Ida Fairfield. The voice at the other end of the line was thin and quavery, indicating she must be quite old. After initial confusion on her part, I patiently explained the purpose of our visit and asked if we could see her Friday morning.

"Can't do it, honey," she informed me, "got to drag these old bones over to Sierra Vista to see my doctor, but I should be home before noon. Why don't the two of you come for lunch?"

That would only give us a couple of hours until Audrey's forthcoming rendezvous with Duncan. "That sounds great." I wondered why she didn't avail herself of Dr. Orcutt's services as I jotted down directions to her house and hung up. That resolved I climbed to the third floor and re-entered the little circular room, slightly out of breath after scaling the steep stairs. For a moment, I stood still, listening to the sound of my own rapid heartbeat, and wondering again what had caused Audrey to flee in terror. But nothing untoward struck me, nothing disturbed the utter silence.

As anxious as I was to explore the old trunk, I dallied for a while to examine a few of the books lining the floor-to-ceiling shelves.

Their covers tattered, the bindings cracked, some appeared to be quite old. Sure enough, when I selected one threadbare volume and opened it, a musty smell wafted out. The copyright date confirmed that it had been published over a hundred years ago, so I shelved it with care, cognizant that many of the books might possess great value.

It was interesting to note that, interspersed among the scores of mining journals, historical works, and technical manuals, someone in Audrey's family had been a fan of the Zane Grey Western series. It wasn't difficult to imagine generations of Morgan children thumbing through the frayed pages.

Someone, D.J. no doubt, had closed the window since our visit, so after jostling it open a second time to allow fresh air to permeate the stuffiness, I dropped to my knees in front of the old trunk. It didn't open easily, but when I gave the latch a final tug, the lid creaked upward. The sharp scent of mothballs stung my eyes and nose as I began to sift through the assortment of private family keepsakes. There were a few masculine items, including a chipped shaving cup with stiffened brush, and a heavy gold pocket watch. But everything else was distinctly feminine, from the dainty satin and lace undergarments to the pewter brush and mirror set. Delicate wooden embroidery hoops, still fastened firmly around yellowed doilies, a few of them with threaded needles still pinned to the unfinished floral designs, gave me the wistful impression that they'd been set aside temporarily with plans to finish them the next day.

I picked up one hoop and admired the exquisite pattern of tiny pink and blue flowers. It was fun to imagine that it had belonged to Hannah Morgan, but perhaps that was too fanciful. It could have just as easily belonged to Grady's first wife or even Audrey's mother. But how would we ever know with all of her relatives, with the exception of Haston, now deceased?

After unloading almost everything in the trunk, I finally found what I was looking for. Photo albums. The spine of the first one, its maroon and gold cover appearing positively ancient, almost crumbled away in my hands when I picked it up.

Settling onto the floor cross-legged, I began to turn the pages with care. Faded pictures, filled with the faces of strangers dressed in the fashions of a bygone era, stared solemnly back at me. At the bottom of each one, the dates had been diligently recorded in a stilted hand. 1892. 1895. 1901. 1909. But it was disappointing to find that no one had bothered to record any names. Lucky for me, because of the photos Marta had shown us when we first arrived, I recognized a younger Jeb and most likely a very old Hannah Morgan. In fact, I was sure of it. Age had erased her striking beauty, but the embers of her legendary spirit still burned in her eyes.

By the clothing and the make and model of the cars, I figured the first album took me up to about the early 1950's. I set it aside and pulled out a thick brown album in much better condition.

This one contained newer photos, some in color and some in black and white. One blurry picture showed a robust Grady Morgan standing near the mine entrance flanked by a prim-faced young woman with short-cropped hair holding a small child whose face was in shadow. I wondered who they were. It dawned on me then that I'd never seen a picture of Rita Morgan, so I couldn't identify her. But of course Audrey would know.

I turned the page. Then another. Now this was odd. Places where photographs had once been were strangely blank. Well, well. Perhaps Marta's tale, recounting Grady's maniacal desire to erase all traces of Audrey's mother from his life was really true.

At first, as I continued to leaf through the pages, I felt only a tinge of sadness. But, little by little, a distinct sense of unease emerged.

Something wasn't right. Somehow, this cruel act of expulsion didn't seem to portray the reckless actions of a person ripping out photos in a frenzied, drunken rage. Instead, it appeared that someone had taken great pains to methodically remove them.

Fierce sunlight and the shrill reveille of birdcalls woke me at half past seven the following morning. I'd slept far longer than I intended, and even though it would have been nice to stay and savor the soft comfort I jumped out of bed.

Among the many things I needed to accomplish today was to have a heart-to-heart with Audrey concerning the missing photos. My opportunity last night had never materialized because when I'd returned to her room, she was stretched out across her bed fully clothed and sound asleep.

After dressing in jeans and a comfortable cotton blouse, I took a few minutes to page through the book on southern Arizona Tally had given me and try to absorb as many facts about the Bisbee area as I could. Then I gathered together Willow's brochures, the epilepsy book, and picture albums before checking to see if Audrey was up. She wasn't. Sometime during the night she must have wakened, because she was buried under the covers with Princess nestled close beside her.

I shook her gently. "Hey, sleepy head, it's almost eight o'clock. What time are Haston and Jesse coming?"

She moaned and squinted at me in confusion before answering. "I don't know, nine or ten, I think."

"Okay. Well, listen, while you're getting ready, I'm going to eat because I need to buttonhole D.J. and make a couple of phone calls before we leave."

Tousled and yawning, she sat up absentmindedly stroking the cat before her eyes cleared. "Oh? Now I remember. I went to sleep before you came down last night. Did you find any pictures?"

I patted the albums. "Yep. But, before you look through them, could you show me a photo of your mother?"

She threw me a look of bemusement, clambered out of bed and pulled a wallet from her purse. "I have a lot better ones at home. This was taken two years ago right after she got sick."

I made note of the sad eyes and vague smile on the careworn face of Rita Barnes Morgan, confident now that she was not the woman I'd seen pictured with Grady. Was she wife number one, perhaps?

One thing struck me though. Dr. Orcutt had referred to Audrey's mother as beautiful and while there lingered in her fine-boned features the faded remains, time, stress and disease had certainly taken a terrible toll. To me, it seemed as if Audrey's dark beauty came from her father's side, because she bore little resemblance to this wispy-haired woman.

"Let me see the albums now," she demanded, plopping back onto the bed.

As she thumbed through the pages, her expression of animated curiosity dwindled to dismay when I pointed out the blank spots. "So, Marta was right," she said. "He took out all the pictures of my mother."

"Maybe so, but that isn't what's bothering me."

Her sharp glance held resentment. "Well, it bothers me."

"No, no. That's not what I meant. Look how painstakingly they were removed. Does that look like the work of someone enraged or half in the bag to you?"

Her somber voice matched her expression. "No. It looks like he meant to do it. He must have really hated her...and me too."

I had no idea, but said quickly, "What reason would he have to hate an innocent three year old?"

"But, he must have. There are no pictures of me either."

Good point. "Well, that's probably because you were in the photos with her."

She looked only slightly mollified, so I reminded her of Marta's claim that there were more boxes of pictures in her father's room.

Hopeful determination filled her eyes as she jumped to her feet. "I'm going to go look right now."

"Fine. And when Haston gets here, you might want to show him the albums and see if he can identify some of these people." I set the book and brochures on her night-stand and when I informed her of our appointment with Ida Fairfield, her interest level seemed to edge up a few more notches.

Downstairs, I phoned my brother and was disappointed to learn that he was out of town again. I left a message with Margie for him to call me when he got in, then followed the aroma of fresh-baked muffins to the kitchen.

Breakfast was a mouth-watering delight and I'd no sooner finished my second helping of salsa-smothered Southwestern quiche accompanied by warm, homemade tortillas than I saw the Suburban flash past the window followed by a battered red Pinto.

Well now, who was this?

I grabbed up my notebook, hollered a thank you to Marta who was outside in the back yard hanging clothes on the line, and headed down the flower-lined path, stopping for a minute to pet Princess who was spying on a fat gray dove.

"Still trying to round up breakfast, huh, girl?" At my touch, she stretched and purred with delight. I echoed her sentiments. It was a glorious morning. Above the almond-colored hills, the dazzling sun dominated a sapphire sky and, thankfully, there was just enough of a breeze to mitigate the rising heat.

Last night's sound sleep had done wonders for my spirits, but I decided it was more than that. Not only was I looking forward to the adventure of being on the road again, the prospect of talking to Tally once more before his departure, made my heart feel considerably lighter.

The well-worn path veered sharply left and intersected with the gravel driveway. I followed it down the incline toward the cottage, arriving just in time to see a slender woman clad in a black skirt and white blouse, helping D.J. load an assortment of placards proclaiming WE LOVE ANIMALS! KEEP THE MINE CLOSED and

DEFY THE DEFIANCE! into the rear of the red car. Obviously unaware of my approach, he leaned in and planted a tender kiss on the nape of her neck before disappearing into a small shed nearby.

At the sound of footsteps crunching on the stones, the woman turned towards me. My immediate impression of her age was early thirties and most likely, the color of her ultra-brassy, auburn hair, pulled loosely into a ponytail, had come from a bottle. "Hi, you must be Bitsy Bigelow."

"Who are you?" she asked in a none-too-friendly manner.

While giving her a brief rundown, I studied her with interest, deciding that her over-sized, wrap-around sunglasses not only shielded her eyes from the sun's glare, they also covered a good portion of her face. But even at that, she hadn't quite managed to conceal the jagged scar etching one cheek. The sight of puckered flesh along her upper lip sent a rush of sympathy through me and gave credence to Harmon Stubb's contention that she'd suffered burn wounds at the hands of her sadistic ex-husband. Vaguely, I wondered what her now thinly sculpted nose had looked like before plastic surgery.

"If you have a few minutes," I said, moving closer, "I'd like to ask you some questions."

A long hesitation. "About what?"

"For openers, Audrey Morgan's sister."

Her chin sagged. "Dayln? My God, I haven't thought about her in years. What's she got to do with anything?"

"Well, nothing really, except with both of Audrey's folks gone, we're having a little trouble piecing together some recent family history."

"To do what with?" she said, her voice rising shrilly.

"Print in the paper?"

I thought her tone surprisingly caustic for such an innocuous question. "Perhaps, but since you were her friend..."

"You're wrong! We weren't friends. Not at the end anyway. Not after she..."

"Leave her alone!"

I turned sharply and assessed D.J.'s irate expression as he brushed past me and deposited two cans of paint into the trunk of her car.

Had the mild-mannered, supposedly unflappable D.J. finally lost his air of cool detachment? When he slipped a protective arm around her waist, I tried to dismiss the memory of him fondling the dress form, reminding myself again that his sexual proclivities had no bearing on Audrey's story. "This has nothing to do with you, D.J.," I put in mildly.

"The hell it doesn't." His lips were drawn tightly against his teeth. "Stop bugging her and lay off."

The hostility in his voice puzzled me. "Chill out, will you? I didn't plan to...."

"And anyway," Bitsy interrupted, her confidence level apparently buoyed by his presence, "I don't see how bringing all that stuff up after such a long time is going to help anybody."

"Well, we were hoping you could tell us..."

The remainder of my question was terminated by Bitsy's terrified scream when Princess suddenly bounded from the field of knee-high, Black-eyed Susans and landed on her foot.

"Get it away from me," she screeched, clutching D.J., who unceremoniously dropkicked the cat about five feet. Fur puffed, back arched high, Princess hissed and vanished into the heavy underbrush.

Disturbed by D.J.'s surprisingly aggressive behavior, I felt a full measure of guilt knowing the cat must have followed me and when I turned back to them, I couldn't resist saying, "Well, it's certainly heartwarming to see how much you both love animals."

Shame-faced, Bitsy disengaged herself from D.J.'s grasp. "I can't help it. Cats scare me. Their eyes look evil."

"Don't sweat it. She ain't hurt," D.J. grumbled, as if that excused his actions. "That stupid cat's always sneaking around getting into things."

With great effort, I kept my face impassive and swallowed back a biting retort. "Bitsy, if I could just ask you a few more questions..."

"No! I don't have time. I have to go back to work." She landed a quick peck on D.J.'s cheek and when she turned to jerk the car door open, shock zapped me like an electrical charge. A jeweled barrette in her hair, almost identical to the one I'd found in the yard, glinted in the morning sunlight

Stunned by the implication and intrigued by her evasive, panicky behavior, new doubts plagued me. "How about later," I called after her, finally propelling myself into action. "I could come by tomorrow..."

"Give it a rest, will you?" D.J. cut in, eyeing me with displeasure. "Can't you see she don't want to talk no more?" He reached in and gave her shoulder a gentle squeeze. "I'll call you later, babe."

I got one last apprehensive frown from Bitsy before she gunned the car up the hill. Wow. The mere mention of Audrey's sister seemed to really set people on edge.

More eager than ever to meet with Ida Fairfield, I felt a hard knot of tension settle in my stomach as Rita

Morgan's cryptic words about the secrets of the dead being buried with them, reverberated in my head once again.

When I swung my attention back to D.J., his placid expression had returned. "Don't feel too bad," he said, pulling a cigarette from his shirt pocket and scraping the match to flame with his thumbnail. "She doesn't like to talk much about the past. Even with me."

"I heard about her nasty ex-husband and I didn't plan to get into that."

"Tell you one thing," he said, clicking his tongue for emphasis, "all I'd need is a couple minutes alone with that bastard and he'd never lay a hand on another woman."

His half-joking words were spoken lightly, but I sensed menace behind them. And it was enlightening to note that from what I'd observed to this point, none of the emotional situations he'd been involved in had cracked his calm veneer. Until now.

"When you talk to Bitsy later, tell her I'll keep the subject matter confined to Dayln Morgan. That's it."

"It's ancient history, but sure."

"So, you know the story?"

"Bits and pieces."

"Such as?"

"I heard she tried to do in the old man with a butcher knife and then bit the big one in a fire at that nut house he shipped her off to."

I cocked my head with interest. So, that explained where she died, but it didn't explain Whitey Flanigan's assertion that there'd been mysterious circumstances surrounding the blaze. "That's all?"

Yawning, he massaged the back of his neck. "I don't really give a crap. Whatever happened back then doesn't concern me."

"But it may concern Miss Morgan."

"Whatever. Hey, listen, Marta gave me the word you needed a car, so I've got one sitting outside the garage all gassed up and ready to go."

"Thank you."

"Yeah, now, you want to get with the program 'cause I'm gonna crash in about ten minutes."

I had a feeling he knew more than he was telling but recent history took a front seat to the past, so I rattled off my questions.

His version of that night last May differed very little from what Marta had told me. Yes, he'd overheard Grady arguing with Jesse and Willow and he also confirmed the fact that Grady had been drinking heavily that day. After helping the old man to bed, he'd gone to pick up Marta, dropped her off, then stopped by his place to change clothes before going to meet friends at the Muleskinner. When he'd arrived home close to midnight, Grady was dead.

"I wasn't all that surprised," he concluded, "the guy drank like a friggin' fish."

"And he'd suffered falls before, correct?"

"Oh, sure. It's pretty hard to walk straight after you've guzzled a quart of Jim Beam."

Which you provided him, I thought, glancing at my notes. "Tell me something. If he was so hammered you had to tuck him in bed, how do you suppose he ended up on the second floor balcony in a pitch black house?"

He hitched his shoulders. "Who the hell knows? He must've slept a few hours and got up later to scout out more booze."

Smooth answer. Logical and smooth. "Seems like Grady Morgan was uniformly disliked by most people. What about you? Did you like him?"

He flicked an ash from the cigarette. "He wasn't all that bad when he was sober. Kind of pathetic, really. Lonely, I think. Man, he'd talk your head off if you looked half-way interested."

"Really? About anything in particular?"

"Oh, I dunno. This and that. He was always ranting and raving about one thing or another."

I thought his answer conveniently vague. "But, he didn't know you were a paid informant for Jesse, did he?"

I was hoping to get a rise out of him but he remained stoic. "Look, I did my job just like I was paid to. So I picked up a couple of extra bucks now and then for passing on a few tidbits of information, so what?"

"What did Jesse want to know?"

"Who he talked to. What he was saying about her and Haston, but mostly she wanted to know what he said about what's-his-name, Claypool. No real harm done."

I thought about our close call on Boneyard Pass. "You're sure of that?"

One corner of his mouth tilted sardonically. "You're wasting your time trying to pin this thing on Jesse, and if you got some dumb idea that I'm covering her ass, you're blowing smoke."

"Am I?"

His movements stilled. "I don't know squat about what happened that night, and to tell you the truth, I don't really give a rat's ass as long as somebody signs my paycheck."

I found his cavalier attitude disturbing. "Yeah? Well, you may have to choose sides. Miss Morgan is less than happy about your alliance with the people claiming that she's an imposter." Audrey had made no such statement, of course, but I decided to take a little journalistic license to see if it would provoke him. It didn't.

He inhaled deeply and the rising wind sailed the smoke over his head. "Well, I can't do anything about that now. I guess Miss Morgan will do whatever she has to. And so will I."

The words sounded benign, but was there some underlying significance? "Meaning what?"

"Meaning if she doesn't want me here I'll get work someplace else," he replied mildly, yawning again. "You done yet?"

"Almost. What do you make of Marta's story?"

"You mean the one about somebody sneaking into the house, knocking the old fart off the balcony and then flying away on a broomstick into the night?"

"You don't believe her."

"I believe she thinks she saw something. Come on. Marta's a cool old gal, but let's face it, she's blind as a newborn pup."

"What about Mr. Morgan? She's sure she heard him talking to someone."

He studied me in silence for a few seconds. "For a reporter, you don't listen so good. He was a drunk. Most likely, he was having an argument with one of those ghosts only *he* could see and ended up scaring himself shitless."

I was unable to curb my sarcasm. "What about the crank calls he reported to the sheriff. Do you think ghosts were placing them?"

D.J. polished off the cigarette and ground the butt under his boot. "Look, lady, we're talking about a guy who'd be so totally blitzed, he'd wet himself. If you ask me, the old coot imagined the calls too. The booze pickled his brain cells, get it?"

"What about..."

He eyed his watch and held up a hand. "You want to talk more, catch me later. Right now, I gotta get some shut eye." With that, he turned and swaggered towards the cottage. Before he disappeared inside, I couldn't help but wonder again why he chose to wear such unattractive, baggy clothes.

Piqued by his curt dismissal, I flipped my notebook shut and started back up the driveway while unanswered questions swirled inside my head like a horde of pesky gnats. Not only did I believe D.J. knew a lot more than he was telling, as far as I was concerned, Bitsy Bigelow's erratic behavior and possession of the jeweled hair barrette had thrust her on stage as a major player in this puzzle. But just how did she fit into all this? Was her reappearance only weeks before Grady Morgan's demise coincidental, or was there more to it? And why the panic when I'd mentioned Audrey's sister? I was becoming more convinced by the second that there was some connection, but what it could be eluded me completely.

'Gotta have proof,' Orville Kemp had said. "And you gotta have a motive," I muttered to myself, pondering her link to Willow Windsong. Based on the older woman's vociferous stance concerning the Defiance, it seemed entirely plausible that the two of them had conspired to do away with the old man.

The guttural roar of a car engine from the direction of the main house derailed my train of thought. I glanced at my watch. The ever-charming duo of Haston and Jesse had no doubt arrived. In no particular hurry to share their company, I paused to savor the rush of wind through the sycamore trees. Once again I was captivated by the stark beauty of Audrey's little kingdom sequestered within the oddly domed hills that tumbled away into the valley like golden gumdrops.

A soft *thunk* nearby drew my attention to a small shed adjacent to D.J.'s cottage. Princess, apparently recovered from her run-in with him, had dumped over a can and was busily clawing and chewing her way into a plastic garbage bag. Increasing wind gusts rolled aluminum cans across the narrow clearing and captured bits of paper, pinning them against the tall gamma grass. Ordinarily I would have kept going, but a sudden pang of apprehension jabbed me. The cat was in full view of the open cottage windows and judging from D.J.'s recent display of cruelty, who could tell what kind of punishment he would mete out if he caught the unsuspecting animal?

"Princess," I whispered, gesturing fiercely, "get away from there." Either she didn't hear me, or chose to ignore my pleas as she snagged something from inside the bag.

A strong rush of wind tumbled several sheets of paper along the driveway and I tried to grab them, but they spiraled away into the air like white kites. At this rate, D.J.'s personal correspondence was going to blow all over creation.

What to do? I wrestled with the dilemma for another moment and after convincing myself that my motivation stemmed solely from a strong desire to rescue the cat from possible harm, I darted towards the shed.

Quickly righting the can, I stuffed one of the bags back inside it. Princess, now only a few feet from me, continued to tear at the bony remains of what looked like chicken parts, seemingly oblivious to any hint of danger.

"Come on, girl, get away from there," I coaxed in a soft voice while it suddenly occurred to me that even if I did get Princess safely away, the evidence of her mischief would remain.

Well, that could be remedied. I knelt and began to gather up some of the papers and other items before drawing back in surprise. What was this? There were several syringes scattered about along with a small glass ampoule. I reached for it, then hesitated. Should I invade D.J.'s privacy by sifting through his personal belongings like some rag picker? I looked towards the cottage and after seeing no sign of him, grabbed up the vial and studied the label.

Unfortunately, it was so smudged with an oily compound, much of it was unreadable. The name, D.J. Morrison and the date 6-22 were legible, along with the dosage of 1 ML. every two weeks. But when it came to the substance, all I could decipher were the letters d-e-c-a-d---- My eyes were almost crossed. Was that an R or a U? The remainder was hopelessly blurred with the exception of the store's origin. Farmacia Naco. I looked up thoughtfully. So this much of Marta's story was true. He really was going to Mexico for drugs. But, if his allergies were actually so severe that he required injections instead of pills, how come I'd seen no obvious symptoms? Suddenly a whole host of questions clamored for answers. What did anyone really know about this man? Where had he lived and what had he done before coming to Morgan's Folly?

After shoving the little vial into one pocket, I began to gather up more papers when the return name on one envelope caught my eye. B-r something, something - c-h-e Society, P.O. Box 262, Trinidad, Colorado. The postmark read July 5th. Trinidad. Now why did the name of the town ring a bell? I must have read or heard something about it recently. But other than the common knowledge that it had once been a prosperous mining town much like

Morgan's Folly, I could not think of what it was.

It would be interesting to find out what a background check on this guy would unearth. I stuffed the envelope into my back pocket and rose to my feet thinking that collecting clues was a little like eating hors d'oeuvres. They usually came in small pieces, were tantalizing, and one hoped they would eventually lead to the main course.

The sound of an approaching vehicle snagged my attention and I drew back at the sight of Archie Lawton's white pickup roaring down the steep driveway. Oh no! He was going to catch me red-handed rooting around in D.J.'s garbage. Not a pretty thought. I ducked into the shadows beside the shed only seconds before he flashed by. A cautious peek around the corner gave me another start. D.J. was standing at his front door. So much for him being asleep. The liar. I wondered what else had he lied about?

Archie slid from the driver's seat with a wily grin pasted on his face. "Hey, man, how're they hangin'?"

D.J. stepped off the porch. "You stupid son-of-a-bitch!"

Archie and I both flinched in surprise and he took a little hop backwards as D.J. advanced on him, face contorted in rage. "You were supposed to be here last night. Where is it?"

"I...I tried, but I couldn't get hold of him..."

D.J. looked unconvinced. "Shut up. I've waited long enough for you to get your shit together. Now, listen to me real careful," he said, altering his tone ominously. "If you try and stiff me on this deal, your ass is grass."

It was enlightening and a bit unnerving to witness yet another quicksilver evolution of D.J.'s easy-going personality.

"Awe, come on, you know me better than that,"

Archie simpered, sounding like a whipped dog.

"Do I? Then what the hell's taking so long?"

"This ain't so easy to unload as the other stuff. If you want top dollar, you gotta give me time to make the right connections. Can't you wait until this weekend?"

"I want the goddamned cash today. Not tomorrow. Not next week. Today."

Archie swerved away as D.J.'s fist crashed into the truck only inches from his head. "Hey, man, t...take it easy. You're gonna get it. I...I promise."

His placating words seemed to pacify D.J. somewhat and when he spoke again, his tone was more moderated. "Look, things aren't going too swift here. Time's running out and I can't risk doing anything like that again. You better come through like you promised."

Archie rubbed his chin, still eyeing him nervously.

"Okay. Okay. I'll see if I can arrange to get with this dude today. If we can cut a deal, I ought to have the dough by tonight."

Expectation kicked my pulse into high gear while questions rampaged through my brain like a herd of stampeding cattle. Arrange to get with whom about what deal? D.J.'s curious comments about time and risk coupled with the knowledge that he was headed for Mexico tomorrow coincided with my ripening suspicion that he and Archie were running drugs.

"I'm counting on you, buddy," D.J. said, lighting up another cigarette and flicking the match away.

Apparently satisfied that D.J. had cooled off, the guileless expression on Archie's angular face turned shrewd. "Ah...I guess you realize this is gonna take a bit of doing on my part and well I was thinking maybe...maybe we ought to talk about upping my percentage."

"What for?"

"I always get the job done, don't I?"

D.J.'s sharp laugh held scorn. "What about Tuesday? You blew that big time."

Archie's face fell. "That was different. If you'd just give me..."

"Yeah, yeah, save the sniveling. Tell you what. If things don't go my way in the next few days, you'll get a chance to redeem yourself. And if you don't screw this up I might be in the mood to talk about it. Wait here a minute." When he re-entered the cottage, Archie's self-satisfied grin stretched all the way to his wide pork-chop sideburns and lasted until his cohort's return seconds later.

"Get what you can for this," D.J. said, shoving a box at Archie who issued him a sharp salute before he jumped back into the truck and accelerated up the hill.

For another minute, D.J. stood staring intently after the truck and I wished I could read his mind. My left foot was now sound asleep and when he finally went inside again, I scrambled up and stamped the ground until it tingled back to life.

Now, all I had to do was get out of here without being seen, without him realizing that I'd eavesdropped on their entire exchange. I could only hope that this time D.J. had truly gone to bed because my options for exiting the area undetected appeared nonexistent with the possible exception of crawling up the mesquite and chaparral-covered hillside.

I abandoned that idea and began to make my way back through the field toward the driveway. Pent-up excitement made it difficult, but I forced myself to walk slowly and even pause to pick a few flowers in the hope that if he did happen to spot me, it would appear that I was merely out for a peaceful morning stroll.

By the time I reached the house, a whole new set of suspicions were incubating and I was burning to know what had been in the box D.J. had given Archie. One way or the other, I intended to get to the bottom of this puzzle

I'd guessed right. The Pickrell's snazzy pickup was parked near the new wing so most likely they were closeted in the kitchen with Audrey. As tempting as it was to jog over to see how she was handling herself with the gruesome twosome today, time was short so I headed straight for the parlor phone, anxious to share my information with Tugg.

"You just missed him, sugar pie," chirped Ginger. "He's headed up to Yarnell Hill. A big tanker truck crashed through the guard rail and went down the embankment."

"Sounds bad. Do you know when he'll be back?"

"Nope."

"Crap." Frustration immobilized my thoughts momentarily and then I asked, "Well, what about Jim? Is he around?"

"Afraid not. Being so shorthanded and all, he's been

as busy as a one-armed paper hanger...hold on a minute, darlin'." Her voice trailed off and I could hear muffled conversation in the background. "You picked a perfect time to be gone," she informed me, seconds later. "There are electricians swarming all over the place doing that re-wiring for the new computers."

"At least that's good news."

"Easy for you to say. You ain't sitting here with no air-conditioning sweating like a pig in a wool suit."

I laughed aloud, then said with genuine sympathy, "Sorry about that. Say, I don't suppose Tally's back from Flagstaff yet?"

"Come and gone. Dropped off his final copy before the chickens were up."

"Oh?" Disappointment left a dull ache in my heart. "Too bad he didn't have time to call and say goodbye," I said matter-of-factly.

Ginger giggled at my transparent effort to sound blasé. "He said he'd phone you later on from the ranch."

I noted the time. "We're going to be on the road within the hour, so I'll have to call him."

"You need to get one of them mobile phones."

"Tell me about it." I'd already promised myself that if there was any money left over after the renovations, new press and in-house computers, a cell phone and notebook computer for me were number one on my list.

"Should I leave a message for Tugg?"

"No, I really wanted to talk to him right now."

"Sorry, sugar, I guess this just ain't your day."

Unwilling to admit defeat and propelled by an inexplicable feeling of urgency, I said, "Ginger, I need somebody to do some leg work for me. How would you like to be my research assistant today?"

"Me?" Her shriek of delight was deafening. "Okay, but you know I'm sort of chained to this here phone until five o'clock."

"You can do this after work."

"Okay. What do you need?"

I dug the tiny glass bottle from my pocket and read off the letters to her in between interruptions while she answered other calls. "I know it's not a lot to go on, but if you call Phil over at Crandall's Drugs he might be able to figure out what kind of medication this is, what it's normally prescribed for, and, oh yes, tell him the prescription was filled at a Mexican pharmacy."

"Anything else?"

I thought about the return address on the envelope I'd found. It was probably nothing, but then again..."Yeah. This one will probably take a little more time. You can start at the library and if you bomb out there have your little brother get on the Internet and see if he can find anything."

I read her the fragmentary information on the envelope and she let out a squeal of frustration. "What in the Sam Hill is that? B somethin' R somethin', c-h-e somethin' Society?"

"That's all I've got. I know it's going to take some work, but I don't have time to research it right now, so I'm counting on you to help me out."

Ginger promised to tackle the assignment in two shakes of a dog's tail and call me as soon as she found anything. More upbeat now, I thanked her then pressed the switch hook and dialed the Starfire Ranch. Tally's sister, Ronda, answered and told me to hang on while she ran outside to get him. Moments later, he was on the line.

"Well, well. Isn't this a nice surprise?"

The sound of his pleasant baritone made me smile.

"Hey there, Talverson, you can't get away from me that easily."

"Getting away from you was never my intention, and if you'd waited two minutes, I planned to call you."

"I couldn't wait."

"That does wonders for my ego." His voice was warmly suggestive. "Wish I had time to come and see you before I head south."

"Me too." For a few seconds I daydreamed about the appealing possibility, but then reality intruded. "Lovely idea, but listen, I called to tell you that I have to drive Audrey to Bisbee shortly. I don't know what time we'll be back."

"What's in Bisbee?"

"Her lawyer and accountant. And by the way, how did you manage to file your story so early? I thought you were going to stay through this morning's practice session."

"Couldn't. It got cancelled."

"Why?"

"Didn't you hear about the big storm last night? We damn near got washed off the mountain."

"No, but then, I'm not surprised. This place is kind of like being in a time warp. I haven't read a paper, listened to the radio or watched TV since I left Castle Valley. Honest to gosh, it's like being thrown back into the horse and buggy era."

"Sounds peaceful. Say, Tugg filled me in on his idea of you two job sharing."

"Oh, pooh. I wanted to surprise you with that news myself."

"I'm not surprised," he said with an undertone of resignation, "and from what he tells me, it sounds like you're diving into something much bigger than you first thought."

"A lot of things have happened since Tuesday. It gets better." When I told him about the gutted rabbit, his voice grew somber. "I don't like the sound of this one bit, and I sure don't like the idea of you tramping around alone at that old mine. You're not planning to explore any open shafts, I hope."

"Are you kidding? With my claustrophobia, that's the last thing I'd do. But let me tell you the rest." After I relayed my suspicions about Jesse, Willow, Marta and Bitsy, he let out a long, low whistle. "But, as of now, you don't really have anything tangible to link one of them to old man Morgan's death?"

"Nothing that's confirmed yet, but I'm working on it. Lucky for me I've got a new partner helping me sniff out clues."

"Who? The Morgan girl?"

"No, a cat."

"What?"

He chuckled at my inadvertent discovery of the barrette, but when I mentioned the disturbing scene upstairs with D.J., and the strange happenstance surrounding my most recent eavesdropping episode between him and Archie Lawton, his next words were spiced with exasperation.

"Oh, this is choice. And right up your alley. Not only is it looking more and more like the old guy may have been murdered by one of these ditsy dames, on top of that you're mixed up with some kind of a drugged-out, convict-loving pervert."

"Yeah. Pretty intriguing, huh?"

"For you, maybe. I think weird is a better word. And what the hell's the matter with the Morgan girl? Considering everything you've told me, I would have fired this guy's ass at the get-go."

"I haven't actually had an opportunity to tell her about the last two incidents with D.J. just yet, but I'm going to today. After that, it's my bet he'll be gone."

He met my admittedly lame explanation with silence, then said, "Listen, Kendall, I know you. You're happiest when you're elbow deep in something preferably dangerous and even better, life-threatening."

"You say that like it's a bad thing."

"Kendall, I'm serious. Does your bedroom door have a lock on it?"

"I'm not sure."

"If it doesn't, get one. Today."

"Tally, don't get all jazzed about this. Granted, I got myself into a little trouble last time..."

"A *little* trouble? You damn near got yourself killed."

"Okay, okay. You're right. Look, I'm on my way to Bisbee right now. I'm going to tell the investigating detective everything I've told you. Does that make you feel better?"

No answer.

"Tally?"

"Not really. Not unless he's going to stand guard outside your door."

"I can ask him."

"Right."

It was evident by his skeptical attitude that he was not a happy camper and knowing his determined nature, I doubted he would give me his blessing. "Tally, you're a sweetheart to worry about me but, really, what's the worst that could happen?"

He let out a groan. "I don't even want to

speculate."

"Oh, come on. Think about it. If I do manage to stumble onto something in the next few days that would tie one of these women to Grady Morgan's death, there's going to be an arrest and I'm going to have..."

"I know, I know," he relented gruffly, "one hell of an ending to your story."

I could tell the conversation was going to go downhill from there so I said sweetly, "I've got to go. Have a wonderful trip and I'll see you next week."

"Yep, you too."

At the same instant I cradled the receiver Willow Windsong's garishly painted VW bus lurched around the bend and slowly ground uphill, pinging and sputtering. Well, this ought to be fun. Jesse plus Willow would no doubt equal fireworks.

Eager to be in on the action, I started for the door, but paused when I heard a strange scraping sound coming from the direction of the old kitchen.

I listened intently, hearing nothing but the rhythmic ticking of the old clock and my own heartbeat drumming in my temples. Most likely it was Princess, or perhaps it was the mice Audrey had mentioned. Just to satisfy my curiosity, I tiptoed across the frayed carpeting and peeked around the corner. Ancient kitchen appliances stood at attention in the shadowy gloom broken only by a few patches of bright sunlight stealing through the shuttered windows. The room was empty and everything appeared to be in order.

Oh, well. Must have been my imagination. Turning away, I hurried outside, down the stairs and trotted along the driveway towards the flowered bus. Willow was so busy scooping piles of papers from the interior that she failed to notice my approach until I called out a greeting, the same instant Jesse threw open the side door.

Dressed in another simply awful pantsuit embellished with purple and yellow swirls and wearing her ever-present scowl, she confronted Willow. "What the hell do you want?" she snarled, her fleeting glare of contempt in my direction dismissing me as an unimportant player.

Burdened by an armload of pamphlets, the petite activist firmly planted moccasined feet and faced her nemesis. "I'm here to see the Morgan girl."

Animosity smoldered in Jesse's pale, close-set eyes and the unsightly mole crowning her tightly drawn lips appeared to pulsate as she pulled the door shut behind her. "You can't. She's busy doing important things."

Apparently unaffected by the woman's sarcasm, Willow waved a piece of paper between two fingers and said mildly, "You aren't queen of the hill anymore and you can't stop me from seeing her. What I have to show her is a thousand times more important than any thought that might accidentally form in that vacuum you call a brain."

Jesse's complexion grew pink. "Oh, really? Well, get this you...you cockeyed hippie freak. You're too late. She's already agreed to re-open the mine."

Willow's wide-eyed stare of disbelief mirrored my own suspicion that Jesse was bluffing. "You're a liar."

"Suit yourself. But, if I was you, I'd take that shit load of propaganda and haul my ass out of here 'cause we're not gonna stand by and let you browbeat her like you did the old man."

"You're a fine one to talk," Willow said with a snort of derision. "If anyone's to blame for what happened, it's you."

"Oh, no you don't." Nostrils flaring, Jesse seemed

momentarily at a loss for words, then said, "Okay, okay, so we had a little blow up that day. You pissed him off more than I did and everybody knows you were here after I left."

"But you and I know better, don't we?"

Jesse's whole face twitched and reddened to the point that I thought she was going to have a stroke. "Are you still peddling that asinine story about me coming back here that night?"

"I saw your truck."

"That wasn't me, you moron. Haston came over to talk to D.J. about changing his schedule at the mine."

Undaunted by the fact that Jesse was at least a foot taller and probably outweighed her by fifty pounds, Willow absorbed her insult without blinking and took a step closer. "Get out of my way, Jesse Pickrell."

"Make me."

As the two women eyed one another with equal malice, I stood quietly on the sidelines trying not to giggle at their childish antics when, without warning, Willow lowered her head and charged, butting Jesse squarely in the solar plexus. Air whooshed from her lungs in a strangled honk and transformed her mottled-red complexion to chalk white. Glassy-eyed, she staggered backwards, gasping. "You...you...stupid bitch."

"Murdering fat, greedy pig!"

The words had barely cleared Willow's lips when Jesse lunged and grabbed a handful of her hair. There was a blur of arms and legs. Screams. Pamphlets flew in all directions. There was little I could do but watch and wait in stunned silence as they clawed at each other and tumbled to the ground.

Well, I was definitely getting the fireworks I'd expected and it was hugely entertaining, but when Jesse pinned Willow beneath her and the smaller woman began to howl in genuine pain, I decided this was enough foolishness. Should I jump in and try to stop them? Did I really want to get in the middle of these two brawling females? I eyed the garden hose. It worked for dogfights so...

I ran over and scooped it up just as Haston burst out the door followed by Audrey and Marta. For a split-second, they all stood there open-mouthed before Haston shouted, "What the hell is going on?"

I said, "They're having a little disagreement."

"Somebody stop them," Audrey cried.

Haston grabbed Jesse by the shoulders. Like an animal intent on killing her prey, she slapped him away and reached for Willow's throat. Haston, spineless wimp that he was, withdrew and began to dance around the two, helplessly waving his arms like a referee at a prizefight and pleading to no avail.

Enough was enough. I reached for the spigot only to find that Marta had gotten there before me. We exchanged a conspiratorial grin before she gleefully twisted the handle. Water shot out and their screams of pain and anger instantly changed to confusion.

I kept it full force on Jesse until she loosened her grip enough so that Haston could pry her away from the hapless Willow. Unfortunately, there was no way to avoid drenching all of them, so when the skirmish finally came to a standstill and I turned the water off, it was all I could do to keep from exploding with laughter at the pathetic sight.

Stringy-haired and chest heaving, Willow slowly rose to her feet while Haston fought to restrain his hotheaded wife who was still peppering the air with obscenities. When it dawned on her who had administered the unexpected shower, she trained a look of hatred on me that would have melted lead. I think she was toying with the idea of coming after me, but when I put a tentative hand on the handle again and Marta brandished a broom, she faltered and seemed to deflate before our eyes.

"Will somebody please tell me what's going on here?" Audrey pleaded, dividing a stricken look between the two disheveled women.

Crafty as ever, Jesse pointed a trembling finger. "Why don't you ask her? She started it."

Audrey's gaze swung back. "Who are you?"

"Willow Windsong."

"So...what's this all about?"

Willow's face crumpled in distress as she surveyed the torn, soggy pamphlets strewn about and then panic lit her remarkable dual-colored eyes. "Oh, my Lord. Look what she's done. Everything's ruined. Ruined! And where's my agreement?"

"What agreement?" Audrey asked, looking more puzzled than ever when Willow dropped to her knees and began rifling through the remains.

"It's identical to the contract your father destroyed," she said in a choked voice. "I brought a new one for you to sign..." She stopped and aimed a look of accusation at me. "Didn't you tell her about it?"

I met the profound bewilderment in Audrey's eyes and quickly reminded her of Willow's demand that Grady set aside sections of the mine property to create a riparian preserve. That set Jesse off again.

"You cretin! She'll sign it over my dead body."

"Shut up," Haston roared, digging his fingers into Jesse's arm before turning to Willow. "Bring another copy by and we'll consult with the company attorney."

I suspected his words were designed solely to

diffuse the situation, but I kept my own counsel as Willow accepted his offer, brushed herself off and with as much dignity as she could muster returned to her bus. She yanked the door open, climbed in and fired up the ignition before leaning her head out the window. "If you really are Grady Morgan's daughter, I hope you're not as wrong-headed as he was," she shouted over the rattling engine, "because if you are, it will be on your conscience if one more innocent creature dies. And mark my words, I'll do whatever it takes to keep that from happening."

Spewing blue smoke, Willow's dented clunker sputtered away and I turned back to assess the effect of her parting words. Haston's face was a colorful mosaic of anger and frustration, Marta wore a wide-toothed grin, Audrey looked just plain bewildered and Jesse was still pissed.

"What a total asshole. For all I care, she and the rest of her animal-worshiping ilk can go to hell."

"Your displeasure has been duly noted," Haston said wearily. "Let's go."

But Jesse wasn't through. She pinned Audrey with her piggish little eyes. "You better arrange to buy, steal or rent some balls, missy, or she's gonna walk all over..."

Haston gripped Jesse's arm. "For God's sake, haven't you done enough damage for one day?"

Over her continuing protests, he managed to hustle her to the pickup and as they drove off I wondered for the umpteenth time what he could possibly find attractive about this odious woman. But that aside, the impromptu scuffle reaffirmed my suspicion that both women were passionately opinionated and undeniably capable of violence. And how interesting that it had been Haston who'd visited the Morgan estate that fateful night. By my count, I now had about ten thousand questions to ask Orville Kemp and I was eager to get going.

"Could things possibly get any more weird?" Audrey marveled with a slow shake of her head.

I leveled a lopsided grin at her. "With this cast of characters? Absolutely."

After reminding her that she'd be late for her appointments if we didn't get cracking soon, she scurried into the kitchen to retrieve the legal documents Duncan had sent with Haston.

Marta handed us an ice-stuffed water jug for our trip and offered to make lunch. Audrey declined, saying she was too nervous to eat, but I, having no such problem, downed an apple and a handful of cookies while she left to get her purse and the big key ring from Grady's desk.

When she returned, I told her that D.J. already had a car ready for us, so we trudged up the hill to the big garage.

A swell of pleasure warmed me at the sight of the spiffy red Corvette poised in the driveway, but Audrey had other ideas. After rushing around inside the big building like a kid in a toy store, excitedly bouncing in and out of each car, she finally settled on an elegant cream-colored Packard convertible sporting huge curving fenders and wide white-wall tires.

"I've never been riding in a car with the top down before," she announced with a look of wonder.

I had a hunch it was worth major bucks and felt uneasy at the thought of inflicting so much as a scratch on the custom paint job. "Audrey, are you sure about this? The Corvette's a convertible too and I have a feeling this one is outrageously expensive."

"You said whichever one I wanted," she reminded me, plumping onto the passenger seat and running her hand over the polished walnut dashboard. "Look at this thing. It's awesome."

"Okay, it's your call." After a last wistful glance at the gleaming Corvette, I took a few minutes to familiarize myself with the controls and felt a mild twinge of dismay when I noticed there was no air-conditioning. It would be at least ten to fifteen degrees warmer when we dropped altitude.

"My mom would have called this one of life's big ironies."

"What?" I answered absent-mindedly, fiddling with knobs and dials.

"That I own all these cars and I'm not allowed to drive."

"She would have been right."

Audrey fell silent, then offered coyly, "I can, you know."

"You can what?"

"Drive."

"Really?" Having claimed to lead such a sheltered life, the girl had more surprises than an unopened piñata. "I'm amazed your mother would allow such an activity."

Her smile was secretive. "She never knew. My friend Robin used to take me out on a deserted country lane after school."

I wanted to remind her that with her particular disability, that might not have been wise, but instead I shrugged it off with a tolerant smile. "Well, as long as no one got hurt..."

"No one did," she said rather smugly, settling back into the plush upholstery.

I finished my inspection, turned the key and the engine purred softly to life. Using extra care, I eased the big car down the drive. "Just to be safe, let's stop by Toomey's garage and gas up. We can also find out if this thing is road worthy and make sure we take the right route." We attracted more than a little attention as we cruised along the downtown streets. The few people we saw froze in their tracks, gawking openly at Audrey who smiled and waved regally as if she were a member of the royal family. I suspected her giddy mood had more to do with her impending date with Duncan than anything else, but nevertheless, it was so contagious we were both laughing hilariously when we pulled up to the pump in front of Toomey's place. Our arrival caused a similar stir among the small cluster of men sitting idle, still hunched over cards or dice as if they'd never moved from yesterday.

"Maybe we should have chosen something a little less conspicuous," I said under my breath.

"No way," Audrey whispered back. "This is way too much fun."

Just then, Lamar Toomey emerged from the garage, wiping his hands on a rag and strolled up to us. "You two gals look like you're up to no good," he said with an ear to ear grin that accented his ruddy cheeks.

"Always," I answered lightly before introducing him to Audrey.

He touched the brim of his grease-smudged cap. "How do, Miss Morgan. I see you got good taste, just like your pa." His face glowed with reverent pride as he ran the cloth along the gleaming hood. "You picked the nicest one of the bunch."

I winked at Audrey. "We decided to travel in style."

"I don't really know much about these old cars," she said with a shy smile, "but I guess they're kind of valuable."

"Yeah, kind of."

I was puzzled by his solemn tone and hooded look of consternation.

"Kendall says you did a lot of work for my father."

"Yep, I did most of the restoration on this baby and I know for a fact it's pretty near impossible to get hold of a '36 Packard in this condition."

"It's that old? How much would you say it's worth?" Audrey asked with youthful candor.

Toomey shrugged. "In the neighborhood of a hundred thousand or so."

Audrey and I exchanged a look of awe. "That's a very nice neighborhood," I said at length. "I told you we should have taken the Corvette."

"I did most of the work on that little beauty too," Toomey announced with a proud smile.

"But I like this one better," Audrey said. "And anyway, what could happen? We're not going to take Boneyard Pass this time, right Kendall?"

"That goes without saying."

We would have saved a lot of time if we'd taken the car D.J. had already prepped for us. Besides gas and water, the old Packard needed air in all four tires and just as a precaution, Toomey instructed us on how to secure the canvas top in case of rain.

"And rest easy, I'll have your Volvo ready bright and early Friday morning," he assured me as I started the engine once more.

"Make sure you bill me for all the damage," Audrey shouted to him as he waved good-bye.

Armed this time with a clearly marked map we headed up the steep narrow highway. For the first few miles the stress of driving such a grand, not to mention unbelievably pricey piece of machinery, weighed heavily on me as I white-knuckled it around the dizzying curves. But as the road plunged steadily downward and I grew more familiar with the feel of the car I was seized by an intoxicating thrill of adventure when the broad sun-splashed vista of the San Pedro valley opened up before us. When we finally rolled onto level ground and turned onto the state highway that shimmered away into the distance like a long silver ribbon, Audrey's heightened spirits seemed to mirror my own as she excitedly urged me to greater speed. The drop of two thousand feet jacked up the afternoon temperature, but at least riding in the open car somewhat tempered the furnace-like wind that whipped our hair into a mass of tangles and painted a rosy glow on Audrey's normally waxy cheeks.

"This is so cool," she shrieked, holding her hands high in the air as we sped past the turn-off to Tombstone and glided toward the Huachuca Mountains towering above the dusty basin like a gigantic blue tidal wave.

Mindful of Audrey's euphoric mood, I was reluctant to bring up the subject of D.J., but she had to know and I couldn't put it off any longer. I slowed the car until the noise of the wind diminished. "Before we get to the lawyer's office there are a few things I need to tell you."

As I relayed the story of D.J.'s rendezvous with the dress form and his mysterious conversation with Hannah Morgan's portrait, Audrey's expression of puzzled interest dissolved to shock. "Oh, wow. That's so creepy. Do you think he's some kind of a psycho?"

"I don't know but the next chapter is even more disturbing." By the time I'd run through my encounter with Bitsy, sketched out the scene with Archie and tacked on evidence of possible drug use, she looked positively grim. "What do you think I should do?"

I shrugged. "D.J.'s kinky parlor games may be harmless, but this business with Archie Lawton could be another story."

She started in on her remaining fingernails. "So, what should I do? Get rid of him?"

"That will have to be your decision."

Her shoulders drooped and she fell silent for a few minutes, staring ahead vacant-eyed at the mound of clouds floating like fluffy meringue above Thunder Peak. The silence stretched so long, I was beginning to think she was having one of her absence seizures when she finally turned back to me. "What if you're wrong?"

"About what?"

"About D.J. and Archie. You don't have proof that they're doing anything illegal."

My brief glance at her revealed dark eyes brimming with uncertainty. "But what about the bottle and all the syringes I found at his place?"

"Maybe he has allergies just like Marta said."

Her underlying note of childish optimism made me suspect that she was taking her usual route to avoid making a decision, but her reservations did cast a shadow of doubt on my theory. She was right, of course. I didn't have a speck of evidence and had to grudgingly admit that I was relying solely on reporter's intuition. While the subject of drug running was an interesting side issue, I had to face the unpleasant truth that I may have built it up in my mind because it would add additional drama to her story. Was Tally right? Was I looking for intrigue where there was none?

"I've got a gal at my office checking with a pharmacist right now," I informed her. "And let's say she comes back with the fact that he's taking a perfectly legal substance. What about that odd exchange with Archie? And wait, something else just occurred to me. Remember I told you D.J. handed him a box? Well, what if he and Marta are in league together? They seem awfully cozy with each other."

"What do you mean?"

"What if they're both stealing things from the house?"

Audrey seemed to melt into the cushions. "Oh, no. What am I gonna do? Jesse and Willow already hate me, and if I fire D.J. then Marta and Bitsy will too."

"That's a chance you may have to take."

"And what about this woman, Bitsy, anyway?" she said with a sudden flare of passion. "Why wouldn't she tell you anything about my mother?"

"I never got to ask. The minute I mentioned your sister's name she freaked out."

"I wonder why?"

"I don't know," I said, braking to avoid a scrawny coyote loping across the road, "but Bitsy is not alone. When your sister's name came up at the Muleskinner the other day, every guy in the place acted positively weird. By the way, I learned something new."

Her face turned a shade whiter as I repeated D.J.'s assertion that her sister's death by fire had occurred at the institution. "And speaking of weird, did you have a chance to ask Haston about those missing pictures in the photo albums?"

"No. I was just about to when all the commotion started outside."

"We'll definitely take them with us tomorrow to show Ida Fairfield. If Whitey's right, we may finally get the scoop on what really happened all those years ago and maybe she'll be able to give us some clue as to why Dr. Orcutt didn't bother to mention your sister either."

"It's probably one of the things he promised my mother he'd never tell."

Her disheartened tone was disturbing. "But, you do want to find out, don't you?"

She shrugged. "Do I really want to know that my sister tried to kill my father? What if she really was crazy?"

"What if she wasn't? Don't forget the reason your mother left him. He could have very well been beating the crap out of your sister too."

"If that's true, where was my mother while all this stuff was supposedly happening?"

"Good question. I'm hoping we'll find the answer."

"It must be horrible," she said, rubbing her arms as if she was suddenly cold. "So horrible no one will tell us. And you know, at this point I'm not sure how much more I can stand to hear."

The ring of finality underscoring her words was disquieting enough but as she leaned back and closed her eyes I knew that if she retreated into her sheltered cocoon I'd never learn the end of this story.

More accustomed to her mood shifts now, I relinquished a long sigh and centered my concentration on the road. As we left the tawny grasslands behind and climbed into the smooth contours of the Mule Mountains, I wondered if she was once again pondering the cryptic warning contained in her mother's letter.

Unique. Quaint. Enchanting. All worthy adjectives but none of them could even begin to describe my first view of Bisbee, folded snugly between topaz hills blanketed with lush green vegetation that magically transformed it into a desert oasis.

Piloting the big car down into the shady depths of Tombstone Canyon, I couldn't help but gawk at the remarkable mishmash of houses, shacks, and dilapidated buildings lining the twisty labyrinth of narrow streets and then straggling upward to perch haphazardly against the steep slopes. The whole fascinating architectural stew was interconnected by tributaries of crumbling stone steps that appeared to number in the thousands.

While some dwellings had been lovingly restored, the abandoned remains of others, propped behind multicolored rock retaining walls, brought into sharp relief some of what I'd read this morning about this once-thriving community.

I looked over and smiled at the dreamy expression masking Audrey's face. Apparently she'd fallen prey to Bisbee's charm as I had. "It kind of reminds me of Morgan's Folly," she sighed. "Except it seems more...alive."

"It has some other interesting parallels besides the fact that the surrounding hills all have names like Quality, Laundry and Youngblood."

"Those are strange," she murmured, listening intently as I relayed the story of a lonely prospector, much like her grandfather, who'd drunkenly gambled away his claims to what would become the ore-rich Copper Queen Mine. And how the valiant citizens of this century-old town had doggedly survived both floods and fires only to have the coffin lid sealed when the mine closed in 1974.

For a while, it seemed that Bisbee would suffer the same tragic fate as Morgan's Folly, but then a strange and wonderful resurrection began when the influx of artists, craftsmen and retired people reached an uneasy truce with the older mining families. That spawned restoration of the elegant European-style buildings where new shops and restaurants now flourished.

Some of the gracious homes once owned by company officials had blossomed into a profusion of bed and breakfasts and daily tours of the old Copper Queen Mine and Bisbee's close proximity to the Mexican border also helped breathe new life into the dying town.

"What a totally cool place," Audrey said, pointing to one three-story Victorian house boasting pots of bright red geraniums. "Why couldn't Morgan's Folly be like this?"

"Anything's possible," I said as we entered the

cluttered downtown business area where we, or rather the car, collected a host of admiring stares and a few enthusiastic thumbs up.

After several wrong turns, I finally pulled up to the curb in front of a blackened brick building in Brewery Gulch bearing the address of both her attorney and accountant. "This is the place. What time shall I pick you up?"

"Wait a minute, aren't you coming with me?"

"No. I'm going to the sheriff's office, remember?"

Every speck of color drained from her face. "But...but you have to. What if I don't understand what he says? I don't know anything about legal stuff or mining. I don't know much about...anything." Her complexion was now pale blue and she was breathing so hard I thought she was going to hyperventilate. "And what if I have a seizure? They're going to think I'm a retard."

"No, they won't. You have your medic alert bracelet, or better yet, you can just tell them at the outset."

"What if they don't believe I'm really Audrey Morgan? What will I do then?"

It was amazing. She was like a toddler. Everything was a first for this shut-in woman-child, protected and coddled by her mother until she'd been rendered helpless to survive in the real world. She'd done Audrey no favor and while I wouldn't have phrased it as crudely as Jesse, it was definitely time she started developing a little hide. "Take it easy. You have the will and a copy of your mother's letter, and you're not going to have a seizure because you took your medicine this morning, right?"

She fidgeted with her purse strap and didn't answer.

"Audrey," I said, unable to suppress a weary tone. "Why didn't you take it?"

"I told you it makes me feel sick, so I thought I'd

wait and take it after the meeting." She curled her fingers around my arm. "Please, Kendall, I can't do it. I can't go in there all alone."

Inwardly, I was eager to hear every little detail, but I put my hand over her ice-cold one and maintained a reassuring tone. "I know it's difficult but this is one thing you have to do on your own. Both of these men are going to be discussing very private, very personal family and financial matters that are none of my business. And besides, don't you think it's more important for me to see if I can learn more about what might have really happened to your father?"

Her colorless lips trembled. "I suppose so."

I gave her an encouraging smile. "Let's make a deal. I'll tell you everything Detective Kemp says and you can decide what information you want to make public." I edged a look at my watch. "It's two o'clock now. If you get finished before me you can call the sheriff's office and I'll come and get you. Otherwise I'll wait for you out here."

I could tell by her stiff posture and pinched expression that she was waging a fierce inner battle. "You'll be fine, and plus that when you see Duncan tomorrow I'm sure he'll be interested to know what you've decided."

The mention of his name seemed to bolster her self-assurance. "You're right as usual. I have to keep reminding myself that I'm not poor little Angela Martin anymore." She shouldered her purse and stepped out on the curb smoothing the wrinkles from her red and black print skirt. "I have a big responsibility to all those people."

"Just one word of advice," I said, handing her the folder. "If there's anything in here written by Haston, I'd read the fine print with a jumbo magnifying glass before signing it."

The impish smile sneaking onto her face relieved the tense lines around her mouth and as she turned and entered the building I felt confident she'd be all right.

With another crisis resolved, I followed the winding road south through town past a deep chasm called the Lavender Pit Mine and arrived at the turn-off in less than five minutes.

As I guided the stately car up the curving drive into a crowded parking area, a ripple of surprise swept through me. Unlike most of the crumbling structures I'd seen, the Cochise County Sheriff's Office was housed in a spanking new pink and coral stucco building wedged between a gigantic waste dump and the sharp incline of the Mule Mountains. The only somber note detracting from the cheery scene was the ominous glint of razor wire looped atop the formidable fence surrounding the nearby narrow-windowed jail.

Heavy glass doors opened into a spacious foyer packed with an assortment of people milling about. Passing by a door marked Justice Court, I was thankful I wasn't among the glum-looking men huddled on long benches awaiting judgment or the cluster of tired-faced women struggling to control energetic toddlers and fussing babies.

On the other side of the room I presented myself to a middle-aged clerk whose remarkably featureless face would make it difficult for me to recognize if I met her an hour later. "Is Detective Kemp in?" I asked, speaking through the wire cage spanning the chest-high front counter.

He was. She directed me through double doors past the lively dispatch area. After negotiating a series of short hallways, I finally reached a tiny office halved by two cramped cubicles at the far end of the building where Orville

Kemp sat hunched in deep concentration over a small desk piled high with papers.

I rapped on the doorframe. "Hi, there. Got a few minutes?"

Orville Kemp's blue-eyed gaze above the rim of his reading glasses pinned me with a look of keen speculation. "Been expecting you," he said, motioning for me to sit opposite a partially open file cabinet stuffed so full it leaned toward him at a precarious angle. "I guess you'll be wanting to see what we got on the Morgan case."

"If it's not too much trouble," I replied, sliding onto the metal chair as he swung around and yanked open a drawer. He rifled through it and handed me a thick manila folder before settling back in his seat.

"So, Ms. O'Dell, now that you've had a couple of days to do some snooping, what's your take on the fair citizens of Morgan's Folly?"

I had a feeling he already knew the answer but I accommodated him. "Well, most of them seem as warm and fuzzy as a comfortable old slipper, some I would definitely place in the space cadet category and, as I'm sure you've discovered, a few of them appear to be less than forthcoming."

Eyes narrowed, he viewed me with quiet appraisal for a few seconds. "Seeing how we agreed on being partners and all, I'm kind of surprised I haven't heard from you till now."

"I probably should have called you sooner." I watched his deeply lined face gather in a critical frown as I relayed the sickening incident with the rabbit.

"Thought you were going to let me know right away if anything out of the ordinary happened."

"I probably should have but because of the bloody

bird sign already tacked on the front gate I thought it was another prank initiated by the animal rights people. Now I'm not so sure." I also filled him in on the disturbing call to Audrey along with my theory of the staticky pay phone at Toomey's garage.

His eyes were mere slits now. "And your reason for not reporting that was..."

His tone of mild disapproval was unsettling and I was sure my excuse would sound lame. "It was late and Miss Morgan didn't want to cause a stir because she thinks it was Jesse trying to scare her."

"What do you think?"

"I've got a couple of theories cooking that I'd like to discuss with you, but first I wanted to find out what you know about those crank calls to Grady Morgan."

He pulled a pipe from his shirt pocket and fingered it longingly. "Damn new county rules say I can't smoke in here anymore," he grumbled, peering into his empty coffee cup and then rising to his feet. "Tell you what. I'm gonna step outside a couple of minutes. In the meantime, you can take a gander at that." He pointed to the file in my lap. "We'll talk after."

It seemed like a reasonable suggestion, so as soon as he vanished around the corner I opened the folder.

The first complaint dated back almost a year, and after that, there'd been three more formal reports of threatening calls. It bothered me though that when quizzed, Grady Morgan refused to be specific as to the nature of the threats. That, coupled with his vague, unsubstantiated accounts of a mysterious intruder that no one else had ever seen, came across as little more than the demented ranting of a drunken old man.

I set the first group of papers aside and picked up

the theft reports, hopeful that perhaps these would contain some juicy new tidbit, some incriminating piece of evidence.

Over the course of several months, Grady had charged that small amounts of household cash were missing from a desk drawer in his office. Several valuable paintings stored in one of the unused rooms had also vanished, as had a lock box containing personal family items such as photos, jewelry and collector coins. Various other art pieces, including a Hummel collection and several hand-painted vases, also could not be accounted for.

Interesting. All easy items to hock. And once again, it seemed to point the ugly finger of blame at Marta, especially now that I was aware of her ailing grandson and the family's constant need for infusions of cash. And when I thought about the affectionate display in the kitchen last night between her and D.J., it brought forth a troubling scenario that sent my stomach plunging in a downward spiral.

What if they'd been working together with a wink and a nod quietly looting the place right under Grady's nose each for their own separate gain? If one of them had been caught in the act, would they cover for each other? But then, where did the harassing phone calls fit in? Were they connected to the suspected thefts?

I set the second group of reports aside and sifted through the desk report on Grady's fall plus the medical report issued by Dr. Orcutt. It was dry, factual, and there was nothing to indicate that it had been anything other than an unfortunate accident. It was enlightening to note that his blood-alcohol level, which was high enough to kill a horse, appeared to confirm D.J.'s assertion that the old man had indeed been drinking heavily that night.

To date, the only clue to go on was the rambling

statement by Marta who was considered to be an unreliable witness due to her eyesight. Nevertheless, all the entrances to the house had been dusted for fingerprints. There were no conclusive results.

As far as alibis went, Willow Windsong swore up and down she was at home arranging placards for another protest, Haston vouched for Jesse's company and D.J. maintained he'd been at the Muleskinner. Again, that left only poor Marta without an alibi. But there was one intriguing side note. Several patrons at the saloon remembered that D.J. had gone outside for awhile to work on Archie Lawton's truck. Some witnesses reported that he'd been gone less than half an hour, others insisted it was closer to one hour. But all agreed that he'd been there the bulk of the evening.

My high expectations began to fizzle. The witness statements accounted for all my suspects with the exception of Bitsy Bigelow. Where had she been that night?

I heard footsteps in the hallway and looked up as Orville strode through the doorway accompanied by the aromatic scent of pipe smoke. "You want coffee?" he asked, thumbing over his shoulder.

"No thanks."

He set his replenished cup on his desk and sank back into his chair with a satisfied sigh. "So. You still got questions?"

I looked him right in the eye. "Why don't you have this listed as a homicide?"

During the protracted moment of reflection, it wasn't difficult to interpret his look of pained resignation. *'Who does this young upstart reporter think she is breezing in here from out of town to dispute a career law man who'd been solving cases since before she was born?'*

He cocked his head to one side. "I guess that would suit you a lot better."

"Suit me?"

"Yep. A murder would sell more papers than just a chance fall, wouldn't it?"

"Granted. But that's not why I'm asking. Considering the players and acrimonious atmosphere surrounding this case, are you really convinced that it was just an accident?"

"It doesn't matter what I think. Right now, I don't have any hard evidence to the contrary. Got some thoughts?"

"I have a couple of hunches."

"Me too, but that's not enough to get an arrest warrant. You found out something else I ought to know about?"

I took the challenge. "Maybe."

His probing gaze deepened and then looked at the wall clock. "I've got about twenty minutes before the staff meeting. Convince me that Grady Morgan's death wasn't accidental."

"All right. Starting with the crank calls. Don't you think it's rather odd that he would lodge a complaint and then be unable to remember anything this mysterious woman said to him or even offer a clue as to who it might be?"

"He sounded pretty irrational both times I talked to him."

"So I've heard. But what if he really did know? Audrey understood the woman perfectly and if Jesse Pickrell's telling the truth, it might be the very same person who claims to have known Audrey's mother from way back when. I think this is key since Morgan's Folly seems to be saturated with people who've suddenly shown up out of the blue the past few years."

"Go on."

"Okay. What do you know about Bitsy Bigelow?"

"Who?"

"D.J. Morrison's girl friend."

"I don't know anything about her. Why?"

I hunched forward in the chair. "Remember Marta Nuñez's story about someone running by the window that night? Well, it's possible it may have been this woman."

His silver eyebrows edged a little higher. "Based on...?"

"This." I dug the barrette from my purse and dropped it in his outstretched hand. "I found it in the front yard of the Morgan place yesterday and when I met Bitsy this morning she had one just like it in her hair."

"Do tell."

Of course I was bound to divulge the fact that D.J. had purchased more than one of them as gifts and given them to several people. But I drove home the point of Bitsy's recent and coincidental reappearance in town as well as the fact that she'd apparently been acquainted with the Morgan family in the past.

Lips pursed in thought, he turned it over in his hand a few times. "Mind if I hold onto this for a bit?"

"Keep it."

He set the barrette down and drummed his fingers on the desk. "Got a motive?"

He had me there. "No, I don't, except for the fact that she's linked to Willow Windsong who certainly had a compelling motive for murder. And she's also tied to Jesse Pickrell through D.J. who's buddy-buddy with Marta who just happens to be in dire need of cash to cover medical bills for her grandson."

"It's pretty complicated all right," he acknowledged with a rueful grin. "I'll see what I can find out about this woman."

"Thanks, and before I forget, what do you make of Grady Morgan's last words to Marta? Something about the angel of death?"

Skepticism seeped back into his eyes. "Oh, yes, the visiting spook," he muttered, thumbing through pages until he found what he wanted. "Okay. She claims the old man was mumbling incoherently, but she thinks he said something to the effect of "the day is here. Justice is done."

We stared at the question marks in each other's eyes for a few seconds before I said, "If we accept the fact that Marta quoted him correctly, it sounds to me like he believed that his impending death would somehow atone for a past injustice."

"Could be."

"I have another idea, too." I ventured my theory about D.J. and Archie Lawton fencing stolen goods to buy drugs and smuggle them across the border. "What can you tell me about D.J. Morrison?"

"Not a whole lot, I'm afraid. We ran a check on him but can't find any criminal record."

"What about Archie Lawton? What was he in prison for?"

His lips twisted in disdain. "Which time? He's got a rap sheet as long as my left leg."

"No kidding?"

"Yep. Archie and his older brother Vincent followed along in their old man's footsteps. He spent most of his life in and out of the pen and poor Mrs. Lawton couldn't control those two boys. They've been in trouble since they were in diapers. Started with petty thefts and shoplifting and went on from there to burglary and attempted murder."

"Wonderful. And the family's always lived there in Morgan's Folly?"

"Yep."

"What was Archie sent up for last time?"

He turned to the file drawer again, and pulled out a thick folder. The wall clock ticked softly as he thumbed through it and finally chose a sheet of paper. "Auto theft."

Hold the presses! I sat bolt upright as the memory of my first visit to Grady's garage pushed to the front of my mind. "Did Mr. Morgan ever report having one of his cars stolen?"

"Not technically."

"What does that mean?"

He pulled yet another folder from the cabinet. "It says here that a red Mercedes-Benz Coupe was reported stolen about a month later while Grady was still in the coma."

"Why isn't that in his file?"

"Because it wasn't stolen from the Morgan place. The car was locked up at Toomey's shop being restored. He's the one who reported it missing."

Well, well. That affirmed my suspicion that there should have been a tenth car sitting in the vacant spot in Grady's garage and why there were only nine sets of keys on the ring. Now I understood Toomey's forlorn expression this morning. "Have you been able to connect Archie Lawton with the theft?"

"Not yet."

My pulse accelerated. This added an interesting new dimension to my hypothesis. D.J. would certainly have known the car was at Toomey's and with Grady safely tucked away in a Phoenix hospital, it would have been easy enough to spirit it across the border.

"Hey, Orville," came a female voice from behind me, "if I have to sit through this boring meeting, you do too."

He rose to his feet. "Keep your britches on, Greta."

I turned to see a petite, blonde woman in uniform return his smile of easy familiarity.

"Sorry, Ms. O'Dell. It appears my esteemed presence is required."

"That's okay," I said, rising to follow him out the door. "I appreciate the time and the information."

I'd only gotten a few steps away when he hailed me. Pausing, I appraised his shrewd expression. "I expect you'll try a little harder to keep me informed this time, right, partner?"

I grinned and nodded. "I'll do my best."

On the drive into town, I tried to coalesce my topsy-turvy thoughts into some semblance of order, but the endless possibilities lined up before me like mathematical equations.

The villains in this deadly soap opera could possibly be Jesse and D.J. It could also be Marta and D.J., or it might be Bitsy and Willow. What about a combination of Archie, D.J. and Bitsy? Or...

A new thought hit me in the stomach like a closed fist. Where was Duncan Claypool in this crazy mix? The hatred between the two families was well documented and who else stood to gain more? Being aware of the Pickrell's financial plight, he could have easily masterminded the plot to drive the old man over the edge—maybe in more ways than one.

Audrey's unexpected appearance may have thrown a

monkey wrench into his plans and made it necessary to initiate the imposter rumor designed to discredit her. Had the near miss on Boneyard Pass been devised merely to frighten us or had something more sinister been planned? And since that and the threatening call had apparently failed to send her scurrying out of town, would he still attain his goal of ownership by romancing this guileless young woman?

This new hypothesis sounded so frightening logical it gave me one of those full body shivers. What should I do now? Wait until I could unearth some good solid evidence, or broach the subject with Audrey based solely on unfounded suspicions prompted by my wild imagination?

That would probably be a mistake. Knowing how she felt about him, she'd surely reject it out-of-hand as preposterous. No. For the time being, I would keep it to myself.

When I didn't see Audrey waiting outside the building entrance I parked the car under a shade tree a few doors down. I was in the process of scribbling some notes when I realized a small throng of people had gathered around, abuzz in open admiration for the Packard, of course.

One elderly man engaged me in conversation, saying he'd once owned a car just like it, and as the minutes stretched on, I also learned more about modern-day Bisbee, especially the burgeoning crime problem associated with drug running and 'border bandits'.

"These people are pretty darn slick," he said, hooking his fingers through red suspenders. "A bunch of them broke into old Miss Tinsdale's house last week—in broad daylight, no less—tied her up and snatched everything that wasn't nailed down. They were back across the border in about six minutes flat."

Several other residents chimed in with their own stories and by the time Audrey finally emerged from the building, the late afternoon sun had dipped behind the rusty, cone-shaped hills, leaving Bisbee to bask in the reflective amber glow of early dusk.

She waved a friendly greeting and I could tell immediately that something was different. A bold spring in her step had replaced her usual slump-shouldered posture and as she drew closer, her eyes glittered with a look of contained excitement I'd never seen before.

Clutching a bulky accordion file, she slid into the seat next to me while the small crowd of car enthusiasts began to disperse. "I hope you didn't have to wait too long," she said with a slight catch in her voice.

"Not very."

"Did you find out anything new from Detective Kemp?"

I turned the ignition key. "A little. But let's hear your news first. I gather things went well?"

Instead of answering, she stared straight ahead, her lips compressed in a cagey little smile. I was puzzled by her silence and when we pulled away from the curb, I'm sure she caught my inquisitive glances as we rolled along a narrow street lined with neat shops. Curiosity was burning a hole in my tongue when she finally burst out, "Kendall, you're not gonna believe how rich I am. I still can't quite believe it myself."

"So your father didn't squander the family fortune after all?"

"Well, he did. Sort of. The accountant said he went through a ton of it. But there's still a lot more stuff. I mean, there aren't piles of just plain cash sitting around in banks, but listen to this..."

"Wait a minute," I cautioned her. "I can't wait to hear everything, but can all this be on the record?"

"I guess so." Her words tumbled over each other as she breathlessly reeled off a list of assets that included all but a few pieces of real estate in Morgan's Folly, the mine property, equipment and all mineral rights. On top of that, there was an impressive portfolio of utility stocks and Treasury bonds Grady's father Jeb had wisely tucked away in an interest-bearing trust so that his errant son couldn't get his hands on the principal. "I think that's everything," she concluded in a trembling voice.

"Don't forget the car collection," I reminded her, patting the steering wheel. "And what about the house and all the furnishings?"

"That too. Oh, Kendall, this is all so unreal. I mean, I'm like...a real millionaire."

While I was very happy for her, the news validating her substantial wealth left me vaguely uneasy. Three days ago it appeared she was to be mistress of a dying town, but the reality that she was literally sitting on top of a gold mine reinforced just how much was at stake. It's no mystery that people will do strange things for money. Especially when there's a lot of it. Little wonder that Audrey's untimely arrival had generated such discord.

I grinned. "Now see, you were all in a tizzy over nothing and I'll lay odds your lawyer didn't doubt your identity for a minute."

"He didn't. In fact, he told me I looked like a clone of my father."

"So what do you want to do now?" I asked, slowing to allow a group of camera-laden Japanese tourists to cross the street. "Head home?"

Her hand flew to her middle. "I can't face that twisty road on an empty stomach. I have to eat something first."

I looked at my watch. "It's not quite four-thirty. You want to go someplace for an early dinner?"

"You bet. And it's my treat," she announced benevolently. "Let's find the best place in town."

"According to the old guy I was talking with a few minutes ago, that would be the Copper Queen Hotel." I pointed to a gracious four-story building overlooking us from the street above.

We parked the car nearby, strolled past several young couples sharing early drinks on the narrow veranda, and were soon seated next to an impressive burled-wood sideboard in the spacious but nearly empty dining room.

"This place is really ancient, huh?" Audrey remarked, her appreciative gaze sweeping over the robin's egg-blue walls edged with dark crown molding and finally coming to rest on the lace-curtained windows.

"According to my book, almost a hundred years."

"Wow."

A neatly attired Hispanic boy, bearing ice water and menus beamed a bright smile and, in halting English, informed us that the waiter would come shortly. I opened the leather-bound menu and perused it with interest. "What looks good to you?" I asked Audrey who was staring dreamy-eyed out the window.

After a moment's review, she proclaimed, "Everything."

I raised a brow. "Everything?"

The impish grin dimpled her cheeks. "Suddenly, I'm totally starved. Let's order prime rib. It costs the most."

I studied her animated expression, marveling at the sudden change in her. Was this the same girl who was usually ambivalent about eating at all?

When the friendly waiter arrived, she surprised me further by boldly ordering appetizers and a sinfully expensive bottle of champagne. Fascinating. In the space of a few hours, she'd progressed from timid young girl to poised woman-of-means. There was no doubt her display of self-confidence was the direct result of her new station in life.

In breathless fragmented sentences, Audrey chattered on about her good fortune until the champagne arrived. After the cork had been popped and the bubbly golden liquid poured, she proposed a toast. "To my mother," she said, misty-eyed. "How I wish she was here to share this super-wonderful incredible day with me."

"Here, here," I concurred, touching the rim of my glass to hers.

"Mmmmm," she sighed after the first sip. "It tastes as cool as it looks."

"So...you've never had any before?"

Her smile was demure. "No, but my friend Robin used to sneak us beer once in a while."

"Well, I'd go easy if I were you. Champagne has a way of sneaking up on you."

We polished off the smoked oysters and marinated artichoke hearts in short order and when I reminded her again about taking her medication, she dug a bottle from her purse, extracted a white tablet and downed it with a gulp of her drink.

"So, it's okay to mix alcohol with your pills?" I

asked, eyeing her flushed complexion.

She gave an indifferent shrug and giggled. "I don't know."

Her jubilant mood, probably heightened by the champagne, continued throughout dinner. She likened her unexpected situation to that of someone winning the lottery and jabbered non-stop, regaling me with fanciful daydreams that included traveling to far away places and buying enough clothes, shoes and jewelry to sink a cruise ship.

I shared her joy, but also realized that at some point soon she'd have to face reality. Hating to burst her bubble, I nevertheless gently nudged her with, "So, what are your plans for Morgan's Folly?"

She looked momentarily nonplussed and pushed her plate away. "Please don't make me think about that now. It will ruin the very best afternoon of my whole life."

Instead of saying, 'Fine. Bury your head in the sand,' I said nothing and finished my meal to the soft clink of silverware and subdued conversation from the other patrons in the packed dining room.

"Okay. Okay," she blurted out in a tone of impatient exasperation. "What do you think I should do?"

I looked up and studied her petulant expression. Apparently she must have interpreted my silence as censure. I laid my fork down and leaned back. "I couldn't tell you, but let's look at your options. You could always follow up on Dr. Orcutt's suggestion and take the easy way out by signing control over to your cousin, Haston. Then, all you have to do is agree on a suitable income and return to your old life in Pittsburgh with no worries."

Her expression hardened. "No way. I don't trust that little weasel any further than I could throw him."

"Okay. Option two. You could sell off the bulk of

family assets to fund the mine opening, retain Haston to run the show, but stick around to keep an eye on him and the venerable Jesse."

She wrinkled her nose at that suggestion, so I said, "Or, you could accept Duncan Claypool's offer of majority ownership and pay Haston and Jesse to get out of the picture."

She brightened perceptibly. "Now, that sounds a whole lot better."

"But remember, if you do that you'll be going directly against your great-grandmother's wishes that the Defiance Mine remain in the family. Also, there's Willow Windsong. Are you prepared to take the heat she and her group are bound to dish out?"

Her deep sigh held resignation. "If it's the best thing for most of the people in town to re-open the mine again, what choice do I have? Either way, I'm toast."

"You've got some real tough decisions to make all right." Another uneasy silence fell between us until I ended it. "Aren't you at all curious to hear what I learned at the sheriff's office?"

"Do we have to talk about it right now?" She pressed a hand to her forehead. "I was feeling so good. Thinking about all this stuff is making my head spin."

"It's probably the champagne." She looked annoyed so I said, "Okay, just one more question and I'll shut up. What did your lawyer advise you to do?"

"He read through Duncan's proposal and said it's a very generous offer."

"And?"

"He said if he were me, he'd give it serious consideration."

I clamped my mouth shut, determined not to allow

my misgivings about him to dampen her hopeful expectations. She insisted on ordering an enormous slice of Black Forest cake for dessert and by the time we returned to the car it was nearly six-thirty.

Bathed in twilight, its quaint streets cloaked in an aura of hushed tranquility that denoted a community that had come to terms with its own destiny, Bisbee's distinctive allure captured a special place in my heart. Audrey must have felt the magic too because she seemed reluctant to leave, and suggested we take another leisurely jaunt through town before heading back to Morgan's Folly.

Conscious of her propensity toward carsickness, I took my time on the curves and by the time we descended out of the flower-sprinkled hills and reached the valley floor again, I felt relieved the desert heat had relinquished its harsh grip.

As we cruised along the vast empty expanse of cactus-dotted grasslands on a highway almost devoid of traffic, Audrey sat in thoughtful silence wearing a long, somber expression.

I tried, but couldn't ignore the guilt gnawing at my insides. Look what I'd done—gone and spoiled her euphoric mood by forcing her to confront the cold hard facts of life. Mentally, I kicked myself for not leaving her alone to enjoy her moment of glory. Worse yet, I couldn't think of anything witty to say or do to make it up to her.

But, then an idea struck me. Oh, boy. Dumb. If Tally were here, he'd label it just plain idiotic. And, my dad would accuse me of acting in my usual impulsive manner but...what the hell. I searched the distance and when I slowed and swung onto a deserted ranch road, Audrey turned to me looking mystified.

"What are you doing?" she asked as I brought the

car to a stop and turned in her direction.

"How would you like to drive your own car?"

Her mouth dropped open. "For real?"

"For real." I shifted into neutral, slid out and trotted around to the passenger side where she sat unmoving. "It's okay, Audrey," I said, laying a comforting hand on her shoulder. "I'll be right beside you."

Tears misted her eyes. "Kendall, you're the best. I don't know how I would have managed things without you."

Grinning, I pulled the door open. "Scoot over."

She had a little difficulty mastering the clutch and gears, but after a few false starts, she got the hang of it. And with me practically in her lap, ready to grab the wheel at the slightest sign of trouble, we bumped along the narrow road, never getting much above thirty miles an hour. But it didn't appear to matter. Her delighted squeals and expression of total ecstasy seemed worth any qualms I had resulting from my snap decision. When the road suddenly dipped lower and dissolved into a rutted, weed-choked track near the sandy riverbed, I said, "Whoa. This isn't a jeep. Better stop or we might get stuck."

She braked and the car skidded a little when she brought it to a neck-snapping halt. "That was the most fun ever," she cried out, clapping her hands together. "Now it really has been the best day of my life."

When she threw her arms around my neck, my heart melted. She really did have some endearing qualities, but I cautioned myself again about staying impartial. I told her she was very welcome and we switched places again. It was no easy task turning the big car around in the narrow space, but I finally succeeded. When we reached the top of the rise, she let out a gasp and we both stared transfixed at the western skyline, ablaze in brilliant shades of cinnamon and tangerine.

"Wow," Audrey breathed. "That is so awesome."

I echoed her sentiments wholeheartedly but she looked a little dubious. "Oh, come on. You probably take something like this for granted, huh?"

"Hardly. Remember I've been here barely four months myself so I'm still a relative newcomer. I'll tell you what though, as far as the spectacular sunset category goes, Arizona's definitely got the market cornered."

And then, as if to illustrate my words, fiery shafts of sunlight cut a swath through gold-rimmed clouds and spread the evening shadows over the surrounding hills like dark icing.

"Look at that," she marveled. "It looks like God is about to speak. Maybe it's a good omen."

"Let's hope so."

By the time we reached the highway, I decided that if the picture-perfect sunset was a harbinger of better times ahead for Audrey, the menacing black clouds gathering in the direction of Morgan's Folly were not. I switched on the headlights and gave her a sidelong glance, anxious to share what I'd learned at the sheriff's office, but yet reluctant to tarnish her mellow mood. "So, you want to know what I found out this afternoon?"

"Do you think we're going to get caught in another thunderstorm?" she asked, frowning into the distance, adeptly sidestepping my question. "Maybe we should stop and put the top up."

"Let's wait a few minutes. Those clouds are still pretty far north and could drift away like they often do."

Silence prevailed again, so I let it linger on a few more minutes, before saying, "You sure you don't want to hear?"

She flung me a pained look. "Oh, I guess so."

With the miles falling away behind us in the fading crimson light, I filled her in on the few new things I'd discovered. She appeared puzzled as to why her father would refuse to divulge the contents of the threatening calls and reacted with stunned bewilderment when I told her about the car stolen from Toomey's place. "Do they think there's any connection between that and the other things taken from the house?"

"I don't know, but Archie's shady background certainly puts an interesting spin on that theory."

"So, you're pretty sure it's him and D.J.?"

I gunned the engine as we climbed into the mountains once more. "It's all speculation at this point, but it could very well be a combination of him and well, any of them, including Bitsy Bigelow."

"I guess I'd better get rid of him tomorrow."

"Um...it can't hurt to wait a couple of days."

She looked thunderstruck. "Why? I thought you were so hot on me firing him."

"Look, I'm ninety-nine percent sure he's up to his eyeballs in all this, but Detective Kemp is right. We need hard evidence. Why don't you wait until I hear back from my office? Plus that, if he doesn't suspect that we're on to him, he's more liable to get careless and make a mistake. And anyway, he won't be around tomorrow because it's his day off and he's supposed to drive Marta to Naco, remember?"

"That's right, I forgot." She seemed relieved to have the decision postponed and within minutes was fast asleep.

The clouds continued to darken and savage flashes

of lightning illuminated the indigo sky, but other than the incessant grumble of thunder and a few scattered raindrops, the impending storm threat appeared to have subsided.

We arrived back at the house by nine o'clock and were surprised to find Marta in the kitchen. She explained that her daughter had unexpected company, so she'd opted to skip her usual Thursday night dinner routine and stay in. "I would be just one more mouth to feed," she said with a shrug. "But, it's good I am home because that loco Windsong woman comes banging on my door."

"She was here again?" Audrey asked.

"Less than twenty minutes ago. That woman's mouth goes a thousand miles an hour," Marta said with a wry smile, indicating the massive piles of brochures cluttering the kitchen table. "She says you must read all of them and she will bring more important papers tomorrow."

Audrey's only response was a glassy-eyed stare. Fearing the worst, I braced myself for another full-blown seizure, but within seconds, she blinked and mumbled in a dazed voice, "What?"

Marta frowned and repeated her statement. I said nothing, but once again questioned the wisdom of Audrey's decision to keep her illness a secret.

"Also," Marta continued, "the exterminator comes today. He is here a long time and says he looks everywhere but does not find the signs of mice or squirrels."

Audrey looked puzzled. "What else could those weird squeaking noises be?"

"Sometimes when the wind blows, the old house makes many strange sounds," Marta said and then fished a slip of paper from her apron pocket and extended it to me. "A woman from your office called."

Anticipation flared inside me as we thanked Marta

once more and beat a hasty path across the breezeway to the little parlor where I quickly dialed Ginger's home number. "Hey, there. It's Kendall. You got something good for me?"

"Sure do," she crowed. "I talked with Phil Gross over at the pharmacy and he showed me this big ol' book and you wouldn't believe how many different types of drugs..."

"Ginger," I interrupted gently. "Did he have any idea what it might be?"

"He didn't have a whole lot to go on, but he's thinks it might be Decadron."

"What is that?"

"A steroid kind of like cortisone."

"What's it used for?"

"All kinds of allergies for one. Some folks take it for arthritis and some people use it for asthma like you got."

"Hmmm."

"Hmmm, what?" she asked with a giggle.

"Did you mention that the prescription was filled in Mexico?"

"Sure did. And it's just like you thought. Most kinds of drugs are a darn sight cheaper and sometimes folks don't need a doctor's prescription at all."

"Oh." My high hopes for getting the goods on D.J. went sliding down the tubes. "What about the second project?"

"I'm going to the library on my lunch hour tomorrow and Brian's promised to do some surfing on the Net when he gets home from class."

"Thanks, Ginger. Oh, one more thing. Call Phil back and ask him for a list of any other drugs that begin with those same letters."

"I'm on the case, sugar."

Wishing I could share in her elation, I cradled the phone and turned to Audrey. "D.J.'s taking a steroid just like he told Marta."

Her small rosebud lips formed a perfect O. "So, he and Archie aren't mixed up in illegal drugs like you thought?"

"Maybe, maybe not. I'm not throwing in the towel just yet. Let's wait and see if Ginger comes up with anything new tomorrow."

Audrey tried to suppress a yawn and lost the battle. "I wanted to show you some of the stuff the lawyer gave me but I don't think I can stay awake much longer."

"That's okay," I said, suspecting her introduction to champagne combined with the recent absence seizure was adding to her lethargy. "Go on to bed. I'll look at it in the morning."

It wasn't quite nine-thirty yet, so I spread out my notes on the bed and began to compile all the data in chronological order. I finished writing a rough draft of my article and it was well past midnight when I finally gathered everything together and set it aside.

In retrospect, it was a mistake to have my mind engaged so close to bedtime, because it produced fractured sleep saturated with frenzied, work-related nightmares filled with missed deadlines and broken print presses.

During those restless hours, I was vaguely aware of the rising wind and before long the storm I'd pronounced 'dead on arrival' punched through the hills with the force of a freight train and bore down on us carrying a full cargo of lightning and thunder.

Still half-asleep, my tired brain was unable to identify the sudden clatter filling the room. I fought my way to consciousness and sat up. Hailstones were pouring through the open window, bouncing like miniature ping pong balls on the hardwood floor.

I grabbed my bathrobe and hurried to the window, wincing as my bare feet encountered the pea-sized ice pellets. At first, the humidity-swollen frame wouldn't budge and I had to endure a barrage of hail stinging my face until I finally slammed it shut. Breathing hard, I rested my weight against the wide sill. It was time for Audrey to invest in some window screens.

As quickly as it had come, the volley of ice vanished and was replaced by huge drops that splattered against the glass with such force I thought it might shatter. The wind rose to an eerie wail and lashed nearby trees into a wild frenzy.

I hugged my robe tighter and watched Mother Nature's dazzling fireworks display illuminate the rain-soaked landscape in garish blue flashes. One spectacular bolt exploded with such force against the ground, it knocked me back on my heels, leaving me temporarily stunned as the thunderous aftermath shook the old house to its foundations.

It was only when the deep rumbling began to subside that I heard the scream. It was ear shattering, horror-filled and sent an icy river of fear skimming down my spine. "Audrey?" I shouted. Seconds passed. There was no answer. I scrambled to my feet and fumbled for the table lamp. Snap. Snap. Nothing. Damn. My flashlight was in the car downtown at Toomey's place.

"No!" came another scream. "Get away." A loud crash from upstairs galvanized me into action. Dry-mouthed, I stumbled towards the doorway and groped my way across the shadowy living room amid strobe-like bursts of ferocious lightning.

"Audrey," I hollered again over the rolling thunder, "What's wrong?"

The absence of a response had my mind inventing all manners of unspeakable horrors. Faster! Faster! I'm sure I was running, but it seemed more like slow motion. Precious seconds passed until I finally reached the stairway but my mushy legs refused to perform. Come on. You can do it. Right foot up. Now left. Now right. Good. Halfway up, my toe caught on my robe and sent me sprawling forward. My chin smashed into a wooden step and pain exploded in my head. Dizzy and disoriented, I forced myself to crawl the rest of the way to the landing, where I struggled to my feet and then froze when a brilliant flicker of light revealed ugly shards of broken glass that would have sliced my feet to ribbons.

"Audrey, where are you?" Dread twisted my insides and I gripped the banister tighter when I heard footsteps pounding towards me from the blackness beyond. "Is that you?" At first I saw nothing, but then, amid the sporadic electrical bursts, I saw her race from the shadows, arms outstretched, eyes huge with terror. "Don't let her get you," she screamed. "Run!"

"Watch out for the glass," I warned, watching in stunned disbelief as she barreled unheeding towards the staircase. What was wrong with her? "Audrey, stop!" I grabbed for her, missed, grabbed again, and then she swerved and lunged at me, shoving hard. Panic tore through me and I desperately clawed the air for a handhold before catching the sleeve of her nightgown. Screaming, we both pitched headlong into the darkness.

We landed at the bottom of the stairs in a tangled heap of arms and legs. For some time, I lay in numbed confusion trying to remember exactly what had happened.

My chin ached and my head felt like it was filled with cobwebs. Piece by piece, I reconstructed the scene. Was I mistaken, or had Audrey deliberately knocked me down the stairs? The memory evoked sudden anger and the adrenaline charge helped revive me. But when I tried to rise, a blinding pain pierced my left shoulder. Oh no. Rotating it slowly convinced me that it wasn't broken but I feared it might be dislocated.

With care, I disengaged myself from Audrey's limp frame and rolled to my knees, fearing the worst when she made no sound. "Are you all right?" Met with stony silence, I fought down a surge of panic and laid my ear against her chest, gratified to hear steady beating. Thank heavens. Probably knocked cold, but how badly was she injured?

Something soft bumped against my ankle and I stiffened in horror. It was only when another blaze of lightning reflected the glow of iridescent-gold eyes that my galloping pulse tapered off. "Sorry, girl," I said in a shaky voice, gathering Princess tightly against me. "Did I scare you?" Her rumbling purr joined the grumble of thunder as the diminishing storm blew away leaving the room submerged in shadows.

My number one priority was getting help for Audrey so I pushed to my feet, set the cat aside and started to feel my way towards the parlor, fervently praying that the phone lines weren't out again. I'd only moved a few feet when I heard Audrey stir and moan softly. Retracing my steps, I knelt beside her. "Thank God! Tell me where you're hurt."

"My head...and my right foot stings."

I slid my hand down her leg and it came away wet and sticky. "You must have stepped on some broken glass. You'd better not move until I can get hold of the doctor."

"No wait. I think I'm okay." I gritted my teeth against the pain in my shoulder and helped her to a sitting position. She leaned back against the wall, muttering, "What happened?"

"I was about to ask you the same question. Why did you push me down the stairs?"

The faint remains of lightning disclosed her look of total shock. "I didn't push you. I was trying to save you."

Her answer was so preposterous I could hear Tugg's words of doubt about her echoing in my mind again. "Save me? From what?"

"You won't believe it."

"Try me."

"I saw the ghost."

"Come on, Audrey. Get real."

"She was there on the stairs, right behind you."

She sounded so earnest, for a split second I was inclined to believe her before common sense prevailed. "There are no such things, Audrey."

"Something was there."

"Maybe you mistook those lace curtains at the window. They were whipping around me in the wind and that's probably what knocked the bowl and pitcher off that little table."

"I knew it," she said with an indignant catch in her voice. "You think I'm crazy, just like my father and sister."

"Don't put words in my mouth."

"I know you think I'm hallucinating. And it's all because of your stupid epilepsy book."

"You know it's one of the possible side effects of your medicine. And maybe with the addition of the champagne..."

"No! I saw her long, white dress and her face was real spooky—all chalky looking like a dead person and her eyes were all rimmed in black."

My stomach jumped. "A white dress? That was no ghost. It's got to be the same woman who was harassing your father. That's it," I announced, pushing to my feet again. "No fooling around this time. I'm calling the sheriff right now."

She gripped my leg. "Please don't go. I know this is going to sound totally off the wall, but I don't see how it could have been a real person."

My patience was dwindling. "Why not?"

"Because she was in my room, and by the time I ran down the hall and got to the landing, like...like magic, she was already behind you on the stairs. How could anyone move that fast?"

It certainly didn't seem humanly possible, but if what she said was true, it reinforced my suspicions that there were at least two people involved in this latest bit of chicanery. The only other explanation had to be that in her state of hysteria, she'd mistaken my white terry-cloth bathrobe and the blowing lace curtains for the mysterious specter.

Still pondering her words, it slowly dawned on me that dim light was spreading throughout the room. I turned to the window, surprised to realize it was daybreak, and within minutes there was enough light to make out a dark pool of blood on the floor beneath the cut on Audrey's foot. The disquieting knowledge that she'd injured herself in a vain attempt to save me from who-knows-what, sent me on another guilt trip.

I stripped the belt from my robe and she cried out when I wrapped it tightly around her foot. "Sorry," I said, trying to ignore the throbbing pain in my shoulder. "Don't move. I'm going to find out if Dr. Orcutt can come here."

"He's gonna be mad if you wake him this early," she stated, matter-of-factly, pulling Princess onto her lap.

"I don't care if he is. You need medical attention right now and anyway, being a country doctor, he's probably used to emergency calls at all hours." I hurried to the parlor phone and almost screamed with frustration to find it as dead as I'd feared. Damn. So much for that and alerting the sheriff. I returned to Audrey's side. "The lines are out again so I'm taking you to his house. Sit tight while I get Marta."

"I don't want to stay here alone."

"Look, I don't think you should put any weight on

that foot and I'm going to need help getting you to the car."

"But what if the woman comes back?"

"I sincerely doubt she's going to take a chance on us seeing her in the light of day, but if you hear or see anything unusual, anything at all, scream your head off. I'll be back in two minutes flat."

"Okay." She gathered the cat closer, still looking uncertain. Her ashen complexion worried me, but I had no choice except to leave her there huddled on the floor while I dashed across the breezeway propelled by growing fury. This current scare had been carefully engineered, just like Boneyard Pass and the dead rabbit and the threatening calls.

Positive that one of the women on my suspect list had been prowling around the house with the deliberate purpose of terrorizing Audrey had cold fingers of apprehension tracing the back of my neck. Was it Jesse or Bitsy? Or Willow? Marta said she'd been here last night before our arrival. Whoever it was appeared to have unobstructed access to the house whenever she chose, and logic dictated that the woman's conspirator was most likely D.J. Morrison.

The intuitive belief that things were swiftly coming to a head induced an overwhelming sense of foreboding. The answer had to be right in front of me. Why couldn't I see it?

Marta was already in the kitchen brewing coffee on the gas stove and because she was still on my suspect list I tried to gauge her reaction as I breathlessly relayed our nocturnal adventure. Her expression of surprise appeared real, but why the flicker of skepticism in her eyes?

She rummaged around in a drawer until she located a first-aid kit and from a second, she removed two flashlights. "These you will keep in your rooms," she said, pressing them into my hands. Then, as fast as she could move her bulky frame, we hurried back to the old part of the house. Along the way, she sheepishly admitted that she'd taken to wearing earplugs at night and hadn't even heard the storm.

Leaving Audrey in her care, I hurried to my room and, using mostly one hand, finally managed to pull on jeans and a T-shirt. Ten minutes later, I had the big Packard parked out front with the motor running. Thank goodness I'd injured my left shoulder or shifting gears would have been agony.

By the time I returned Marta had Audrey's foot encased in a mountain of gauze. We helped her to stand and, flanked by the two of us, she hopped toward the waiting car all the while firmly overruling Marta's generous offer to forego her day off to stay home and play nurse.

"Okay," the older woman finally relented, "but I will ask D.J. to bring me back early from Naco."

"Thanks, Marta," I said as we negotiated the last step, "and by the way, where is D.J.?"

"I think he is probably still with his lady friend," she grunted, laboring for breath.

Had he and Bitsy been together all night? How convenient.

"And I hope she makes him feel much better," she continued with a wily grin as we assisted Audrey into the passenger seat, "because he's very unhappy with you when he wakes up yesterday afternoon."

"Oh, yeah? Why is that?"

"He says he goes to great trouble to prepare for you the red car and then you choose another."

"That was my decision," Audrey spoke up and then winced. "Oh! My foot aches with every heartbeat."

Marta hastily waved us on our way and we sped downtown through rain-freshened air into the blinding glare of the rising sun. The sky, now a brilliant cloudless blue, shone in stark contrast to the dark violence of the storm just hours ago. But the evidence was everywhere, from fallen trees and scattered debris to washed out mud-streaked roads. By the time we arrived at the spacious, two-story house, I was hopeful this chance visit would provide an opportunity to pose some pointed questions to the evasive doctor.

As expected, when we presented ourselves at the front door just shy of five-thirty, Fran Orcutt's dour expression broadcast her annoyance at being rousted out of bed by us for the second time in a week. But after I'd explained why we couldn't call, she eyed Audrey's bandaged foot, ushered us into a small sitting room and instructed us to wait while she awakened her husband.

Moments later, a disheveled Dr. Orcutt shuffled into the room buttoning his shirt over rumpled trousers. He knelt down, and with swift professional movements, peeled off the wad of bandages and examined Audrey's foot with practiced hands. "You need stitches," he announced tersely, rising to his feet. "We'll have to go to the clinic because I don't have the proper supplies here at the house."

After bundling Audrey into his car, I followed him two short blocks and parked the big Packard beneath a gnarled sycamore tree towering behind the building. Amid the cheerful racket of birds from the overhanging branches, he let us in the back door. While we sat in the shuttered waiting room, he solved the dilemma of no electricity by activating a generator, and then with the overhead lights wavering, he helped me assist Audrey down the hallway into a cubicle and onto one of the examining tables.

When Dr. Orcutt snapped on latex gloves and began to swab the gash with a strong-smelling, orange disinfectant, Audrey sucked in a sharp breath. "Ouch, that hurts."

He said, "I'm sorry," and pulled a syringe from the cupboard and began filling it. "This is going to sting a little, but I have to deaden the area first."

Audrey threw me a beseeching look, so I took her hand and gave it a comforting squeeze. She gritted her teeth and hung on until he'd completed his task, then lay back on the pillow while he checked her blood pressure, determined that she should have a tetanus shot, examined the lump on her forehead, and then inquired about her medication. It was only then that he asked what happened and as he listened intently to what now sounded totally inconceivable with radiant sunlight pouring into the room, his craggy face crumpled into a pensive scowl. "I'd better examine your shoulder, Miss O'Dell."

Much to my relief, he declared it to be only a bad sprain but added the caveat that I should not overtax myself for the next few days. "As for you, young lady," he said, returning his attention to Audrey, "in the future, I would strongly suggest that you avoid mixing alcohol with your seizure medications. That's probably what caused you to hallucinate."

Audrey's uncertain gaze locked with my skeptical one and she pushed to a sitting position, saying softly, "Kendall doesn't think I was."

"What complete nonsense. More likely it was the thunderstorm combined with the power of suggestion." He fired a look in my direction. "Remember, it's to Miss O'Dell's advantage to have you believe in such fanciful tales because it will help her sell newspapers."

The stubborn set of Audrey's chin told me that his attempt to sow seeds of doubt had failed so I said, "I think the woman she saw is not only quite real, but probably the same one who was scaring the crap out of her father." Remembering my interview with Jesse induced me to tack on, "I don't suppose you have any idea who it might be?"

He did a masterful job of ignoring my remark and addressed Audrey instead. "Considering your ongoing problems with Dilantin, I'm going to recommend that you experiment with a different drug." He rifled around in the cabinet and handed her some sample packages. "Depakene is a relatively new anticonvulsant, but be warned that it can produce its own set of side effects."

"And while we're on that subject, Dr. Orcutt," I ventured smoothly, "did any other member of the Morgan family suffer from epilepsy?"

"Not that I'm aware of."

"How about mental illness?"

He divided a suspicious glance between us. "I don't know what you're getting at."

I darted a meaningful look at Audrey who caught my silent message and pinned him with an accusatory glare.

"Why didn't you tell me I had a sister? Did you think you could you keep something that important a secret forever?"

It may have been the florescent lighting, but it seemed as if his already sallow complexion turned green. "No. I knew you would hear eventually, but..." He paused for a few seconds and his next words sounded carefully arranged, "your inquiries place me in a difficult position."

"Why?"

"I already explained that I made your mother certain promises..."

Audrey flung him a look of pure frustration. "Okay. Fine. We'll just get our answers from Ida Fairfield."

His momentary look of surprise was replaced with a deprecating smile. "I wouldn't put much stock in anything she has to say. The woman is almost ninety years old. Her memory is probably as faulty as her hearing and eyesight."

His acid remark seemed surprisingly unprofessional for a physician, not to mention callous, but nevertheless it spawned a tremor of doubt. Whitey had seemed confident we'd get the straight skinny from her, but how much faith could I place in the memory capacity of someone of such advanced age?

"I don't understand," Audrey said. "You're the one who brought me here in the first place. Why won't you answer my questions?"

Dr. Orcutt absorbed the indictment in her eyes with grim silence before snapping off his gloves and throwing them into the sink. "I'll tell you this much. It's probably to your benefit that you never knew your sister. She was a very difficult, very troubled girl who suffered from...well, some acute emotional problems."

I chimed in, "Such as?"

"I can't go into them."

"Can't or won't?" My persistence earned me a glare of granite-jawed hostility.

"Both, Miss O'Dell. Dayln Morgan was a patient and I'm not at liberty to discuss the specifics of her case. Especially with you." He turned to Audrey and assumed a placating tone. "Take my advice and send this woman packing right now. It's obvious she has no genuine concern for your welfare. Her sole purpose is to dig up dirt and splatter your private family business all over the headlines. You must not allow that to happen."

Audrey looked momentarily bewildered. "But, Kendall's my friend. She's only trying to help me."

"Trust me. It can serve no purpose to dredge all this up again. What's done is done. For your sake, for your dear mother's sake, I hope you'll leave it alone."

"Or is it for your sake, Dr. Orcutt?" I cut in softly.

His eyes turned frosty and he slammed his stethoscope onto the counter. "This conversation is over."

"Please," Audrey pleaded, grasping his arm. "I know you don't have to tell me, but I have to know this much. Was my sister...insane?"

For a long moment he stared at her stricken face, not seeming to breathe at all before saying in a hollow voice, "In my professional opinion, I believe what she did could only be interpreted as an act of insanity."

I thought his answer vague at best.

"Then it's true." Audrey said. "She really did try to kill my father."

"I'm afraid so."

"Why?"

"She would never say."

She pressed a hand to her lips, murmuring, "Oh, my God."

It was easy to tell that he was still hiding something. "You're not a psychiatrist," I said matter-of-factly, "whose decision was it to have her committed?"

His wintry expression turned positively glacial. "I consulted with a very reputable man who concurred with both her father and me."

"Really. What's his name?"

"I'm afraid he passed away some years ago." I didn't miss the glimmer of triumph in his eyes before he turned back to Audrey. "Believe me, I did what I thought was best for your sister and for everyone else involved."

In a barely audible voice, she said, "But it wasn't the best thing, was it? At least tell me how old she was when she died?"

Just when I thought the man was made of stone, a genuine look of guilt-edged regret marched across his face. "Fourteen."

She swallowed hard. "We heard there was a fire. What happened?"

He cleared his throat and seemed to be pondering how to answer. "It started late one night in one of the dorm rooms. It was very hot and windy. The facility was quite old and unfortunately had no sprinkler system. All of the children were lost."

Audrey gasped, "How terrible."

"There were no survivors?" I asked sharply.

"The adult staff members managed to escape but not before several of them were badly burned in a rescue attempt before authorities arrived."

"How many kids died?"

"Twenty-eight."

Visualizing such horror left me speechless for a few seconds. "Were all the bodies positively identified?"

"No. The flames were so intense some were burned beyond recognition. And remember," he said, as if anticipating my next question, "that was prior to DNA testing that we have now. But, twenty-eight bodies were accounted for. End of story."

His brusque tone conveyed a note of finality, but the fleeting shadow behind his eyes convinced me there might be more. "What's behind the allegation that Dayln Morgan died under mysterious circumstances?"

Looking like a trapped cat, his gaze shifted around

the room before settling on Audrey. "A lot of rumors circulated afterwards. It could never be proved, but one of the surviving aides claimed it was deliberately set...by your sister."

Horrified tears jumped to Audrey's eyes. "You mean she might have been responsible for killing all those other kids?"

"Do you understand now why your mother wanted to spare you this unpleasant news?" He patted her shoulder while firing me a self-righteous scowl that clearly said, 'see what you forced me to do?'

I ignored him. "And where is this place?"

He hesitated then said, "Located in a small town called Coolidge. It was called the Children's Colony, but if you're thinking of snooping around over there you'd be wasting your time."

"Why?"

"The entire structure was incinerated."

"Along with all the medical and dental records, of course."

"Unfortunately, yes."

My suspicions about him intensified. First a fire at the courthouse and then the asylum. It was just too convenient.

Just then a faint noise in the hallway caught our attention. "Who's out there?" he called. At first only the silence of the empty building met our ears, but when Fran Orcutt suddenly appeared in the doorway, his apprehension was visible. "What are you doing here?" he asked coldly.

"I knew Anna wouldn't be here yet, so I thought maybe... maybe you'd need some help."

He strode over and laid an arm along her thin shoulders. "I'm fine, my dear. In fact, I'm wrapping things up now. You go on back to the house. Thank you for your concern." The sincerity in his voice never reached his eyes and some emotion I couldn't fathom flitted across Fran Orcutt's face before she turned and left without another word.

The brief interlude refreshed the memory of the supplicating look she'd bestowed on me only days ago, but it also allowed Dr. Orcutt the opportunity to resurrect a professional facade. After inquiring to see if we were allergic to any particular medications, he dispensed muscle relaxants and pain pills to me and antibiotics to Audrey along with instructions for changing the dressing on her wound. Then he brought her a pair of crutches, ushered us outside and, after refusing any sort of payment, shut the door firmly in our faces.

"Man, you could drive a truck through the holes in his story," I confided to Audrey in low tones as we started down the flagstone walkway.

Still appearing shell-shocked with the disclosure, Audrey murmured, "I don't know what to do now. Mom said Dr. Orcutt would give me good advice. Maybe I should take it."

I stared at her, aghast. "You didn't buy into that load of horse pucky, did you?"

Her expression ranged somewhere between distress and uncertainty. "Don't you think he was just trying to protect me from the fact that my sister was a...a monster?"

"Baloney. I think he made your mother a death-bed promise he regrets and now he's trying to save his own ass."

"From what?"

"I don't know, but think about it. Last Monday the good doctor talked about your mother, your father, your uncle, your cousins, and even your great-grandparents for heaven's sake, but somehow he forgot to mention you had a sister? Please. Now, I don't know what the connection is to you, but it's becoming more and more apparent that there is one."

Her brows clashed in a thoughtful frown and she was silent as I helped settle her into the car once more. "I was thinking about mom's letter," she said. "What do you suppose she meant when she said she hoped I could find it in my heart to forgive her? For what, Kendall? For what?" She gave me a look filled with such profound sorrow I knelt down beside her.

"Beats me, but like I promised you from the start, I'll stop looking for clues right now if you want me to, even though my gut feeling is your mother really wanted you to find out whatever it is Dr. Orcutt is concealing."

"I wonder," she mused almost to herself. "Can we go now? My foot hurts, my head hurts and I need to eat something and take a nap before I can think about this any more." She turned her head away and closed her eyes.

Damn Dr. Orcutt. All the self-confidence she'd displayed yesterday seemed to have vanished, so rather than press her, I shut my mouth and hoped she'd swing back in the other direction by this afternoon.

I stowed her crutches in the back seat and was heading toward the driver's side when an urgent voice called out, "Psssst! Over here. Come quickly."

I whirled around to find Fran Orcutt beckoning to me from behind a thick stand of mesquite and shoulder-high sunflowers sprouting from the remains of a crumbling foundation. I edged closer, almost jumping out of my skin when her skeletal fingers shot out of the shadows and locked around my wrist like bony handcuffs. "You have to help me, Miss O'Dell. We're both after the same thing."

"And what's that?"

She shot a panic-filled look towards the clinic door, then back to me. "The truth. For twenty years...the not knowing for sure...it's eating me up inside."

Her grip was so tight my hand began to ache. I pried her fingers apart and asked as calmly as possible, "What are you trying to tell me, Mrs. Orcutt?"

For a few seconds, she said nothing, but even in the soft dappled light of her leafy hiding place, the anguish imbedded in her eyes broadcast inner conflict. And pain. Old pain. "I want so desperately to believe my husband and I pray that I'm wrong...you see, I only overheard part of their conversation, but it was enough...Oh, God," Her voice broke, so I asked, "What conversation?"

She swallowed hard. "He forbid me to ever mention it but if *you* should find out..."

As I fought to comprehend her rambling words the intuitive notion that had been hovering on the perimeter of my mind for days began to percolate. "Does this have anything to do with Rita Morgan?"

Bitter tears glittered in her eyes. "He stayed in touch with her all those years. I have to know about the baby..." The remaining words died on her lips as the clinic door squeaked open behind me. "Oh, mercy! He mustn't see me talking to you."

She sprang away as I pleaded a frantic, "Wait a minute! What baby?"

"Go to Weaverville, Miss O'Dell," she whispered fiercely, withdrawing into the shadows, "go to the cemetery and read the dates on the gravestones

Like a specter she vanished from sight, leaving me adrift in a sea of unanswered questions. What had she been talking about and how on earth did a graveyard figure into any of this puzzle?

My heart rate pegged on high, I somehow had the presence of mind to snap off some stalks of sunflowers and when I swiveled around to meet Dr. Orcutt's penetrating eyes, I could only hope the excitement didn't show on my face. "Gorgeous, aren't they?" I said, forcing a cheery smile while laboring to control the tremor in my hands. "Hope you don't mind?"

"Not at all."

But the residue of suspicion lingered in his eyes and I could feel them boring into my back when I turned to pluck a few more flowers while I searched for any sign of his wife. Was she still crouching somewhere in the dense shrubbery or had she managed to slip into the culvert extending beneath the road above?

I wanted nothing more than to stay and grill her further but, fearful of drawing attention to her, I completed my task and returned to the car uncomfortably aware that the doctor was still scrutinizing my actions.

I laid the bouquet across my lap and Audrey's eyes blinked open when I started the engine. She stared blankly at the flowers. "Who were you talking to?" she asked, covering a yawn as I maneuvered the big car along the narrow alley while casting intermittent glances in the rear view mirror.

"Fran Orcutt." I felt relieved when the doctor's car finally appeared behind me and then turned in the direction of his house.

"What did she want?"

I hesitated. What should I tell her? That I now strongly suspected that Fran Orcutt was the mysterious female caller? But why would she insist Audrey was an imposter unless... A feeling of sick dread invaded my heart. What if the relationship between Audrey's mother and Dr. Orcutt had gone beyond mere friendship? Was that the forbidden secret? Did Fran Orcutt fear that Audrey was her husband's child?

Accelerating up Devil's Hill I made a snap decision. Until I had concrete proof, I would relay only parts of the strange conversation to Audrey.

"Read the dates on the gravestones?" she echoed back to me in wide-eyed wonder. "But, how are you supposed to know which one to look for? Why didn't she just tell you?"

I chose my words carefully. "Evidently that's all her conscience will permit her to say. And it's my guess she's convinced herself that if I'm the one to expose this secret Dr. Orcutt is harboring, she'll be absolved of breaking her pledge of silence."

"I'm tired of all the stupid riddles. Let's go back and ask her straight out."

"Fat chance. My guess is she's hotfooting it back to her house before hubby gets back and I doubt she's going to risk getting caught talking to me again."

"So...you're going to run off and poke around this cemetery when you don't even know what you're looking for?"

The eager anticipation of doing just that made me feel like a truckload of cold sand had been dumped in my stomach. "Things are definitely starting to rock and roll and I'm not about to pass up a hot lead like this." I shot a look at her wan face. "But first, let's get you settled."

The power was back on when we reached the house, but as I'd feared the phone lines were still dead. Now what? I hated the sensation of helplessness, of being completely marooned. What if Ginger was trying to get hold of me? My frustration level combined with the dull ache in my shoulder set my nerves on edge. I was tempted to take one of the pain pills Dr. Orcutt had given me and catch a couple of hours sleep but, besides the fact that I'd made a promise to Orville Kemp, I wasn't about to let last night's shenanigans go uninvestigated. Somehow, I had to think of a way to contact the sheriff's office short of driving all the way to Bisbee.

I'd almost convinced myself I was too agitated to eat when the aroma of frying bacon lured me to the kitchen. Perhaps just a little bite of something would improve my spirits.

Audrey reverted to her usual state of morose silence

and listlessly picked at her food while I managed to polish off three slices of bacon, coffee, juice and an impressive stack of blueberry pancakes.

"I can't go with Duncan this afternoon," Audrey announced unexpectedly, pushing her plate away.

I stopped in mid-chew. "Why not?"

"Because, that looks totally gross," she cried, pointing with disgust at her bandaged foot. "He's not going to want to be seen with me. On top of everything else, now I'm a...a cripple."

That figured. Of all the sobering incidents she ought to be concerned about, including the latest one portraying her half-sister as a murderous psychopath, concerning herself with how she appeared to Duncan Claypool apparently topped the list. "Don't be silly," I said, "so you have a few stitches. He wants to take *you* to dinner, not your foot."

For a few seconds, she stared at me blank-faced and then burst into a fit of giggles that became so infectious that Marta and I soon joined in. I was delighted that my glib remark had cheered her, but after Marta and I got her upstairs and tucked in bed, I was again struck by her abrupt mood swings.

After a quick one-handed sponge bath, I returned to my room and stood staring blankly at the closet. What to wear? Blue jeans and a T-shirt seemed too casual for Ida's luncheon, but since I'd be tromping around Weaverville immediately afterwards, a dress wouldn't do. I decided a gaily-flowered blouse would spruce up my plain outfit and, wincing aloud from shoulder pain, I finally tamed my unruly, static-charged curls into some semblance of order.

The finishing touch was a finely tooled leather belt complete with the stunning silver and turquoise buckle Tally had given me for my birthday just two short weeks ago. A tingle of pure pleasure radiated through me as I fastened it around my waist. What a great guy. What a sexy guy.

Entertaining myself with pleasant memories of times spent with him coupled with the giddy anticipation that we'd be together again in a few short days jump-started my spirits as I strolled back to the sunlit kitchen and accepted Marta's offer of more coffee. I was contemplating my next move when something occurred to me. "Marta, does anyone around here have a cellular phone?"

She stopped loading the dishwasher and pushed her thick glasses back against the bridge of her nose. "I think maybe Whitey Flanigan."

"Great." The kitchen clock confirmed that it was barely eight o'clock and I doubted the Muleskinner opened that early. "Where does he live?"

"Behind the bar in the little green house."

I downed the remainder of my coffee and rose. "Can you stick around and keep an eye on Audrey until I get back?"

"Oh, yes. D.J. comes in only a short time ago. He says he will take a shower and change before we will go."

"Thanks." I was back in the car and traveling through downtown streets so deserted I felt like I was starring in one of those old Twilight Zone episodes depicting the last person left alive on earth.

As I suspected, the bar was closed, so I parked the big car in the alley adjacent to it and walked the remaining few yards to a run-down cottage matching Marta's description. I rapped on the front door.

"Hey, Irish," Whitey's voice boomed as he swung the door wide and stepped out onto the porch shrugging a denim vest over a faded checkered shirt. "Ain't seen you around for a couple of days. I figured maybe you got tired of our little wide-spot-in-the-road and flew the coop."

"Not at all. I'm planning to stick around until Monday."

He cast a knowing grin over my shoulder. "Looks like you're traveling in style these days."

"Yeah. She's a lovely lady and I'm going to miss driving her."

"Toomey got yours all gussied up?"

"I plan to run by and get it when I leave here."

"You'll be pleased as punch. He does real good work..." Whitey's little speech trailed off when the unexpected roar of machinery rumbled through the morning stillness.

I turned in the direction of Boneyard Pass and squinted into the blinding-white glare of the sun. "What's going on up there?"

Whitey shaded his eyes and followed my gaze. "Dozers and graders. Well, what do you know? Looks like the highway crew's finally getting around to fixing the road. Good timing. That was some storm last night. Wrath of God type stuff, huh?"

The whole dramatic event was etched in my memory for eternity. "I should say."

"So, you getting all your questions answered," he asked, eyeing me with a shrewd glint.

"No, they keep multiplying like rabbits but listen, Marta tells me you might have a cell phone."

"Yep. My son bought it for me last Christmas."

"I was wondering if I could use it."

He grimaced and pushed a thatch of unruly white hair from his forehead. "You could, except the damn thing's useless till we get cell service in these parts."

My heart fell. "What about a CB? Surely someone has a CB radio."

"Got one in my jeep.

"Thank goodness. Can you get a message to the sheriff's office?"

His silvery brows collided. "What's going on?"

I supplied a thumbnail sketch and watched speculation flare in his cornflower blue eyes. "So, you think that even with Miss Morgan's...er..ailment there might be something to it?"

It took a second for his statement to sink in. Then I understood Marta's dubious reaction to the ghost story. "Let me guess. Jesse Pickrell's been busy blabbing Audrey's condition around town."

"Is it true?"

"Yes, but I don't think she was seeing things."

He fixed me with a look of quiet appraisal. "Okay, I'll get on the horn right now."

I accompanied him along a dirt driveway toward a ramshackle wooden carport behind the house and couldn't help but think that Whitey could have used D.J.'s artistic green thumb on his neglected, weed-infested yard. I particularly liked the ancient pink Edsel set up on blocks with raggedy shrubs sprouting from the broken windshield.

While Whitey fiddled and fussed with the knobs, I stood at the edge of a sizeable mud puddle slapping flies away and listening to the hiss and crackle of his radio until he finally made contact with a trucker pulling into Bisbee.

"That fella's gonna deliver your message personally," he announced stepping out and slamming the door behind him, "but he said it might be awhile before anyone gets here because they got one hellacious bunch of storm damage last night."

"Thanks a lot and before I go can you tell me how to get to Weaverville?"

His freckled forehead crinkled. "Whatcha need to go out there for? Not much left except a few tumbledown buildings and the cemetery."

I grinned. "Got a hot prospect to interview."

He looked suitably perplexed, but after enlightening me with a few historical facts concerning the old ghost town he directed me to proceed eight miles past the mine road. "Watch real close or you'll miss the little wooden sign telling you to turn right. The graveyard's back in the hills about a mile or so."

"How come it's so far out of town?"

"We had one here up until about thirty years ago." Fingering his white mustache, he cocked his head to one side, looking expectant. "So, I guess you haven't heard the story of Otto Pigwell yet?"

I sensed another yarn was about to unfold. "No. I think that's a name I'd remember."

"Well, you're gonna love this one," he said, flashing me one of his amiable grins. "Seems poor old Otto was down in the drift one day, minding his own business, merrily drilling away at the rock face, when all of a sudden the back caved in and guess what came down and conked him smack on the noggin?"

I shrugged. "A rock?"

"Nope. A casket."

I'm sure he relished my look of disbelief. "He was underneath the cemetery?"

"You guessed er Chester. And since they were following a real rich vein, Jeb Morgan wasn't too keen on abandoning it. Instead, he donated a big chunk of land he had setting on a couple of old mining claims he owned and had the whole shebang moved out of town."

"Fascinating.   Oh, and one more thing.   You remember the other day when you suggested I talk to Ida Fairfield about Audrey's sister?"

"Uh huh."

"This morning, Dr. Orcutt implied that she may not have all her faculties about her and even insinuated that I'd be wasting my time talking to her."

He seemed taken aback and picked absently at the stubble on his chin. "That's news to me. I mean, granted the old gal did have stroke a couple a years back, but last time I talked to her she seemed pretty clear headed."

"So, you think her memory is intact?"

"Hey, she forgets little things, we all do, but she doesn't seem to have any trouble remembering stuff from a long time ago."

"I got the feeling there's no love lost between her and the good doctor."

Whitey threw back his head and guffawed. "Most likely he's still itching to get even with her for telling everybody in town he was a quack."

My ears perked up. "Really? Why'd she do that?"

"You recollect the story I told you about Grady's first wife, Lydia, being so sickly 'n' all?"

"Yeah."

"Seems like the doc was treating her all those years for cancer but after the poor lady died it turned out to be some sort of rare blood disease."

"Dr. Orcutt misdiagnosed her?"

"Yep. After that, I mean to tell you Ida was out to fry his eggs. She ended up raising such a ruckus she darn near got his medical license yanked. They've been on the outs ever since."

How enlightening. That explained Dr. Orcutt's disparaging attitude towards the old lady.

I thanked Whitey once more and headed towards Toomey's garage while the tense scene with Fran Orcutt replayed itself in my mind. It rekindled a white-hot fire of expectation inside me. Once again, I wished I could be several places at once. If I didn't feel it was so vital to report last night's incident to the sheriff and if I hadn't already scheduled the long-anticipated meeting with Ida Fairfield, I would have headed for the cemetery right then and there.

Good to his word, Lamar Toomey had the bodywork completed. My car shined like a new penny. "Wow," I exclaimed with unabashed admiration, running my fingertips along the smooth blue paint, "it looks brand new."

He beamed with pleasure and pointed to his grease-caked associate rolling a tire towards the bay. "If you want to take her now I'll drive the Packard up the hill later on and have Buzz here bring me back."

I agreed, thanked him again and, feeling just a shade of regret knowing I'd probably never get the chance to drive such a cool-looking car again, I climbed behind the wheel of my own and had just started the engine when Willow burst out the door shouting, "Wait a minute!"

Oh, boy, what now? As she trotted towards the car, I decided that Lamar Toomey must be a really laid-back boss to tolerate Willow's bohemian, post-hippie appearance. Her ill-fitting tie-dyed blouse was buttoned wrong and the way her hair stuck out at crazy angles gave me the impression she hadn't brushed it since her impromptu shower with the hose yesterday.

"You can save me a trip up the hill if you'll give the Morgan girl this new contract I wrote up last night," she said, shoving an envelope through the car window. "And you can tell her I meant every word I said. If she wants to stop any more trouble, she'd better sign it today."

Her distinctive eyes, burning with the same intense passion she'd exhibited yesterday, left no doubt she intended to continue the battle. Unwilling to embroil myself in a pissing match with her, I accepted the document along with her not-so-subtle threat. How Audrey was going to mediate this impasse to everyone's satisfaction was beyond me.

Cruising along the main street, I spotted the now-familiar white pickup parked in front of the Huddle Cafe. I slowed down and felt a twinge of surprise to see Bitsy Bigelow and the ever-bewitching Archie Lawton standing practically nose to nose, engaged in deep conversation. Suddenly, she tossed her head back, laughed, and then playfully squeezed his arm.

Well, well. More small town intrigue. Did D.J. have a clue that Archie was schmoozing his lady-friend behind his back? I'd bet money he didn't.

As if sensing my scrutiny, Bitsy's gaze fastened on me. Her smile dissolved into a look of fear-laden hostility before she abruptly turned and made a beeline for the door of the cafe. How odd. Her curious behavior toward me made no more sense today than it had yesterday morning.

Archie, however, was a different story. In the nano-second we made eye contact, he fastened such a brazen look of animal lust on me that I shivered with revulsion. Smarmy creep. I stepped on the accelerator and wound up the hill, my mind bouncing back to the strange confrontation at the cottage yesterday between him and D.J. Had he done as ordered last night and carried out D.J.'s questionable demands? Somehow I had to find out what the two of them were up to.

My trip had taken a little longer than expected and it was almost ten o'clock by the time I reached the house. Good to her word, Marta, now dressed for traveling in a long red cotton skirt and loose, white embroidered blouse, met me at the kitchen door, purse in hand. "Miss Morgan is still sleeping."

"Good. Sorry I'm late, and by the way, there's no need to come rushing back from your visit. Miss Morgan will be having dinner with Mr. Claypool and I'm not sure what time I'll get back from Weaverville this afternoon."

Solemnly, she crossed herself. "My aunt is buried there. My cousin too." She cocked her head to the side. "Why will you go there, Miss O'Dell? It is a lonesome place."

I repeated only what I'd told Whitey, took the house key from her outstretched hand and then watched her waddle down the hill towards the cottage before heading to my room. Moments later when the Suburban flashed past the window I couldn't contain a twinge of aggravation.

Too bad D.J. wouldn't be here when the investigator arrived. I'd love to analyze his reaction to questions like: 'Explain your close association with that scumbag Archie Lawton? Is he fencing stolen property for you? Or, where were you at approximately four A.M., Mr. Morrison? And by any chance, does Ms. Bigelow have in her possession a long white dress?'

Well, they'd be something along that order I thought, trying the office number for what seemed the fiftieth time. Unreal. How long was it going to take the phone company to fix the problem?

With a frustrated sigh, I dropped the receiver back on the cradle and rubbed my aching shoulder. If I took one of the pain pills now, hopefully the effects would wear off before I had to drive very far.

I went to the kitchen for water and had barely swallowed the capsule when a fresh-faced Deputy McHenry from the sheriff's department presented himself at the side door, clipboard in hand.

Disappointed to learn that it was Orville Kemp's day off, it took me a few minutes to fill him in on some of the recent events. When I led him to the scene of the "ghost sighting", now absent the blood and broken glass Marta had so efficiently cleared away, he admonished me sternly. "This area should have been left untouched."

"I know, but considering the emergency medical situation I didn't have time to tell the housekeeper to leave things alone."

He appeared unimpressed by my excuse. "I'll need a statement from Miss Morgan."

Audrey, already cranky at being wakened and me forcing her to confess her illness up front, was less than gracious. His expression, impassive and professional at first, slowly disintegrated to skepticism with each subsequent question. "It wasn't the lightning or the champagne," she insisted with tight-jawed conviction, "and I wasn't hallucinating. I don't know how the woman managed to get behind Kendall without me seeing her."

He edged me a doubt-laden glance. "And did you see this alleged intruder?"

"No."

His gaze swung back to Audrey. "Do you know if anything was stolen?"

"No, but then I can't be sure since I've only been here a few days."

Now wooden-faced, the deputy wordlessly scribbled

notes on the investigation report before abruptly rising to his feet. "Thank you for your cooperation. I'll see that Detective Kemp gets a copy of this tomorrow morning."

He did a cursory search of the house and grounds and twenty minutes later Audrey stood next to me at the living room window watching the patrol car disappear beyond the gate. "He didn't believe a single word I said."

"You have to admit, it all sounds pretty bizarre, but considering he wasn't really familiar with the particulars in this case, can you blame him?"

"I guess not."

"Don't worry, when Orville Kemp hears about it I'm positive he'll want to follow up, but right now you'd better get ready so we can get going to Ida's place."

"Are you happy with how your car turned out?" she asked, still staring out the window.

"Very. And by the way," I said, pulling the envelope from my back pocket. "Willow wants you to sign this today."

She looked utterly defeated. "I can't deal with this now. Can you help me upstairs?"

"Sure."

Because of the crutches, our ascent was slow and awkward. When we finally reached her room, she insisted she could bathe without my assistance, so I returned to the landing and sat down on the top step to contemplate the whole fascinating cocktail of events. Princess, doing her usual cat thing, appeared noiselessly from somewhere and bumped against me, mewing for attention.

"Okay, partner," I said, stroking her soft golden fur, "let's reset this table. If we assume the phantom is real then how did she get from Audrey's room to the bottom of the staircase so damn fast? What do you think, girl? How'd she do it?"

Princess fixed her luminous eyes on me and twitched her tail.

"Well, you're no help today," I said, scratching behind her ears. "What about the banister? Do you think she slid down it?"

The mental picture comprising any of the possible suspects attempting this feat, especially Jesse, brought a wry smile to my lips. No, not probable. I would have heard something. As I sat there in deep reflection, inhaling the sweet flower-scented breeze wafting in the window behind me, another thought popped into my head.

Wait just a minute. I rose and peered outside. To my left, a rickety drainpipe snaked down the wall. Could she have gone this way? Nope. It looked too flimsy. I surveyed the sturdy branches of a walnut tree, only yards away. Now that held possibility. Could the woman have climbed down and sneaked in the front door? But wouldn't there have been telltale signs like water or mud?

I don't know how long I stood there sifting through the different compartments of my brain, when all at once an obscure detail from the night of Grady's death jabbed me like a sharp stick. I whirled around to stare at the cat's impassive face. "Marta didn't see anyone in the house that night but you did, didn't you, Princess?"

Thankful that the throbbing pain in my shoulder had subsided, I charged down the steps, scooped up the flashlight I'd left on my dresser and dashed across the living room. If I was right, Marta's contention that she'd seen Princess bolt from the old kitchen hissing in fear, combined with Audrey's claim of persistent noises along with that scraping sound I'd heard yesterday when I was on the parlor phone, might have an explanation.

I pushed through the swinging doors, snapped on the overhead light in the pantry and made a beeline for the dumbwaiter secreted in the wall. "Please, let me be right," I whispered in breathless anticipation, yanking open the waist-high wooden door.

Cool, musty air rushed out at my face as I played the light around the opening and the sudden realization made me gasp. Why hadn't I noticed this the first time I'd looked? There wasn't a spider web anywhere! And if that wasn't a dead giveaway that the old contraption was still in use, what was? But more importantly, the wooden platform looked solid enough to support a person. I reached up and pulled one of the two ropes hanging side by side. The platform rose smoothly. A few tugs on the second rope lowered it again.

I shined the light upward into the gloom, revealing the pulley system situated directly above what appeared to be an opening to the second floor. I knew what I should do, but when I stuck my head in the hole, panic clogged my throat and I jumped back.

As always, I despised myself for succumbing to my nemesis. Yes, it was illogical. Yes, it was irrational. But the thought of becoming trapped in the constricted shaft had my heart hammering like a pneumatic drill. I paced around the room trying to convince myself that I could overcome my foolish fears, but met with no success. I turned back to stare at the dark cavity and stopped in my tracks. Perhaps there was another way.

Retracing my steps, I stopped again on the stair landing and leaned over the banister. The kitchen was below and to the right. I pointed in the approximate direction of the shaft and moved my finger up. Oh, yes indeed. That would put the opening in the room right next to Audrey's. Eager to prove my theory, I rushed to the top of the stairs and almost collided with her as she stepped from the bathroom, enveloped in a haze of gardenia scented steam.

"Oh, my God," she shrieked. "What are you up to now?"

"Sorry," I said, reaching out a hand to steady her, "I didn't mean to scare you but I'm dying to check out a hunch. If I'm right, I think we'll have the answer as to how our lady phantom works her disappearing act."

"How?"

"Follow me."

She stayed close behind as I turned the crystal knob and pushed the squeaky old door open. There was no overhead fixture and in the low light of the shuttered room it was difficult to make out much except for a jumble of furniture and boxes. I snapped on the flashlight and we picked our way among the clutter, following the dust-filled beam.

"What are we looking for?" Audrey asked in a hoarse whisper.

"You'll see." If my calculations were correct the opening should be behind the high-backed chair positioned against the far wall. I dragged it to one side and pointed in triumph. "Ta-dah. There it is."

Audrey stared at the small wooden door. "There is what?"

"The entrance to the dumbwaiter."

She continued to look befuddled so I explained my theory. "Now I want you to go into your room and tell me if this is the noise you've been hearing."

"Okay."

After she turned and hobbled around the corner, I

gave her a minute or so, then opened the door and began pulling on the rope. The wheel on the pulley squeaked softly and sure enough, a gentle scraping sound echoed up the shaft as the platform slowly ascended to the second floor. The experiment concluded, I sped to Audrey's room calling out an expectant, "Well?"

Seated at the dressing table in a modest white slip, she directed a blank stare at me. "Well what?"

"Was that the noise or not?"

"I didn't hear anything."

Doubt tweaked me. "Are you sure?"

"Positive."

"Impossible. You must have heard something."

"I didn't."

I slapped my palm against the doorframe. "Damn it. I don't understand. It's the most sensible explanation to this whole fiasco."

"Well, thanks for trying, Kendall, but this just goes to prove what everyone thinks anyway."

"Which is?"

A self-deprecating smile hovered at the corners of her mouth. "That I imagined the whole thing, of course. That I'm a certifiable nut-ball just like the rest of the Morgans."

I rolled my eyes. "Oh, please. As my grandmother used to say, you might as well get up off the pity pot, it serves no purpose."

"Pity pot?" she repeated, promptly dissolving into a fit of giggles. "I never heard that before." She turned her back on me and began to rummage around in a dresser drawer, mumbling, "What did I do with my white belt?"

Deeply dismayed that my theory had been a complete dud and slightly miffed that Audrey had lost interest, I left the room and got halfway down the stairs when I paused. Holy cow. There was no weight. No weight to strain the ropes on the pulley. I beat a path back to Audrey's room, catching her in the middle of buttoning an ankle-length green dress. She looked up at me. "What?"

"I want to try one more thing, so tell me if you hear anything this time."

"Whatever."

I returned to the vacant bedroom and began piling boxes onto the dumbwaiter. "There," I said, dusting my hands together. "Now, let's do this again."

This time the pulley emitted a series of resonant creaks and groans as the platform descended to the bottom of the shaft. "Bingo," I whispered gleefully, turning to trot down the hall once more. "What about that?" I shouted, poking my head around the doorjamb.

In the center of the room, Audrey stood frozen in a statue-like stance, the anticipated answer to my question clearly evident in her fear-shocked stare.

Perhaps it was just the drama of the moment unfolding, but it seemed as if the sultry wind fluttering the lace curtains suddenly stilled. The lively chorus of birds outside the open window grew silent and, as the full impact of my startling discovery slowly sank in, the fleeting glow of triumph inside me vaporized and left in its wake a coil of cold urgency.

"Jeez Louise," Audrey said in a shaky voice, her already pasty complexion fading to the color of alabaster, "this is pretty heavy-duty, isn't it?"

Fearing she might be poised to have another seizure, I sprinted to her side. "You gonna be okay?" I led her to sit on the bed and she clutched the comforter. Her breathing was shallow and uneven for a few seconds before she finally exhaled a calming breath. "Yeah. I guess that new medicine Dr. Orcutt gave me is working okay."

"At least that's good news," I said, sitting down beside her. "The bad news is someone's got free reign to wander around this house at will."

The realization slowly crystallized in her eyes. "So...that means someone's been watching and listening to everything we've said."

An electric thrill zapped my heart. It now seemed probable the noise I'd heard yesterday coming from the old kitchen was the intruder. If so, that meant whoever it was had overheard every word of my conversation with Tally.

I rose and began to pace the room, frustrated by the logjam of unanswered clues clogging my mind. "If you're positive that was the same sound you've been hearing, then our lady in white was no figment of your imagination and this time she may have left behind a full set of fingerprints."

A weighty silence enveloped the room and I turned back to face her. "Your ghost wasn't wearing gloves, was she?"

There was a glimmer of uncertainty in her eyes. "I...I'm not sure."

"Oh, man. Well, one thing for sure, your father wasn't the mental case everyone said he was. And if you factor in Fran Orcutt's disclosure along with your mother's rambling letter, you have to conclude this whole charade goes far beyond this thing last night. You remember your father's last words about the angel of death and the day of justice finally arriving and all that?"

Her expression of puzzlement deepened. "We still don't know what he meant."

I hesitated for a fraction of a second before saying, "This is probably going to sound way out in the stratosphere but if you add up everything we have so far, doesn't it sound like he was expecting something to happen?"

She stared at me agog. "Are you saying he knew who this woman was all along?"

"Yeah, I am."

"But...but, why wouldn't he tell the sheriff?"

"I don't know, but my gut feeling is that somewhere in this crazy mix of past and present there's a common thread that's going to pull everything together."

Her eyes hardened. "It has to be Jesse. You heard her yesterday. She hates my guts and wants me out of here."

"That's certainly a given, but we still can't prove it. There's still Willow to consider and don't forget the barrette I found could point to Bitsy Bigelow. We can't rule out that Marta might be in on it and if you think about it, it could also be just about anybody in this town."

Her mouth dropped open. "You mean like...Haston? You think it might be him traipsing around this house in a dress?"

That presented such a ludicrous picture I couldn't suppress a rueful smile. But I quickly sobered as another more disturbing thought generated a massive case of the creeps. What if Archie Lawton had been our midnight visitor? Suddenly Tally's request for a lock on my door took on new meaning. "At this point, I'm not ruling anybody out."

"I still think it's Jesse," she insisted with an undertone of hopeful determination.

"Let's hope you're right. If this is just another sick joke like the rabbit thing I think we can deal with that, but if it isn't, if it's the same woman who threatened you on the phone... then I don't think it's a good idea for you to be here alone."

She looked like I'd kicked her and as if to cement

the gravity of my statement, the wind suddenly picked up again and whistled eerily down the chimney. Lost in our own thoughts, the hushed spell held us in strained captivity until the roar of a car below drew us both to the window in time to see Duncan Claypool's bright red Jaguar screech to a halt at the foot of the stone steps.

"Oh, m' God!" Audrey lurched away and pinned me with a look of sheer panic. "What's he doing here now? I haven't fixed my hair or makeup! I can't let him see me like this."

Out of the corner of my eye I watched him emerge from his car. "Audrey, calm down. You finish getting ready and I'll go find out why he's..." I flicked a look at my watch. "Three hours early."

"Okay, okay. But, tell him to wait. I'll hurry as fast as I can." She limped to the dressing table as I headed for the door thinking that at least his arrival had restored a modicum of color to her cheeks and ignited her eyes with an intense longing that pleased and dismayed me at the same instant. If, as he'd so compassionately demonstrated on their first meeting, his attentions towards her were truly genuine, it could be a blessing for this ill-fated young woman. But what if they weren't?

I skipped down the stairs, still wrestling with persistent misgivings. Should I say something to Audrey or keep quiet regarding the possibility that Duncan Claypool might be the head honcho behind this frightening masquerade?

I still hadn't made up my mind as I answered his knock and swung the living room door open. "Miss O'Dell," he began, his eyes lighting with relief before his extraordinarily handsome face gathered in a mask of concern. "Is everything all right here?"

"What makes you think it wouldn't be?" I watched closely for any telltale body language that would reveal any knowledge of last night's adventure.

Instead, he appeared nonplussed by my reproving tone. "Well...the...the storm, of course. There's a ton of damage in some places and so...I've been trying to call from Tucson all morning to find out if things are okay but the phone lines seem to be out. I wanted to tell Audrey that I'd rearranged my schedule so we could get started earlier."

His earnest expression coupled with his candid response bore the ring of truth, so I softened my stance. "Come in and sit down. She'll be down in a few minutes."

A sunny smile lit his face and most importantly, his eyes. "Great. This way we can spend the whole day together."

As he brushed past, I inhaled the spicy scent of his after-shave and couldn't help but notice his form-fitting blue jeans. The guy was definitely buff and for Audrey's sake, I hoped I was wrong about him.

Once he was comfortably seated in the living room on the gold brocade couch, I headed back to Audrey's room where I found her applying lip liner. Our eyes connected in the mirror and after I'd explained the reason for his unexpected arrival, a smile of astonished delight blossomed only to be snuffed out by immediate consternation. "Oh no. What about our appointment with Ida?"

I slouched against the doorframe and folded my arms. "She's expecting us in less than half an hour."

"For lunch?"

"Yep."

"And there's no way for us to cancel with the phones out."

"I don't think it's wise to cancel."

She seemed to deflate before my eyes. Uh oh. Decision time. Should she jump at the chance to enjoy a few extra hours with the very adorable Duncan Claypool or spend the time visiting with a woman more than four times her age? Her disheartened sigh betrayed her dilemma. "What should I do?"

"It's your call."

Her internal conflict lasted only a few more seconds and then she announced in a surprisingly decisive tone, "I think it's more important for me to be with Duncan so we can go over these papers the lawyer gave me and try to settle this problem once and for all."

Well. Well. Apparently the realization that she was now a woman of considerable means and influence had bolstered her flagging courage and fostered a sense of maturity.

I said, "I'm sure Ida will be disappointed but it's fine with me."

She brightened perceptively. "You'll know what to ask better than me anyway. Now, don't forget to take those albums with you. I think I left them in the kitchen."

"With any luck, the old lady will be able to plug the gaps in Dr. Orcutt's selective memory and then I'll see what I can dig up over in Weaverville."

My little pun went unappreciated as she beamed me a look of gratitude. "Kendall, you're the best. I'll make it up to you. I promise."

Humming a cheery little tune to herself, she brushed her hair to a lustrous shine, completely oblivious to the inner discord that had my stomach tied in double knots. Should I mention my fears about Duncan and face her inevitable wrath? I really hated to deep-six her lofty mood, but her safety dictated that I must say something.

"Um, I don't want to worry you needlessly," I began, meeting her questioning gaze, "but let's say for the sake of argument that Jesse and Haston *are* the culprits..." I paused, still struggling with how to phrase my warning and then just blurted it out.

Audrey gawked in astonishment for a few seconds, then slammed her brush onto the dresser. "I refuse to believe he has anything to do with all this stupid stuff. How can you even think such a thing?"

"No need to have a speckled cow. Maybe it's just my suspicious nature, but experience has taught me that sometimes the most innocent-looking people can be guilty as hell."

She wavered for a fraction of a second then her eyes grew flinty. "Well, this time you're wrong. And don't mention anything about last night," she said, rising to balance on one foot. "Having the seizure in front of him was bad enough, I don't want him thinking I'm crazy too."

No doubt about it, she had the ability to plumb the depths of denial better than anyone I'd ever met before. I pointed to her gauze-encased foot. "How are you going to explain that?"

She stuffed the brush and makeup bag into her purse. "We'll just tell him that I stepped on a piece of glass. It's the truth. He doesn't have to know the rest just yet."

I could tell by the obstinate set of her jaw there would be no talking her out of it. "You're the boss, but be careful, okay?"

She dismissed my warning with a careless wave and insisted on making a grand entrance for Duncan, minus the crutches. Wincing under her breath, Audrey grabbed my hand and hid her pain behind a tight-lipped smile as we descended the staircase together.

"What happened?" Duncan exclaimed, vaulting to his feet to assist her down the last few steps.

Haltingly, she repeated her rehearsed story and by the time I'd returned to her room and brought the crutches down, Duncan was standing by the front door with Audrey securely enfolded in his arms.

The look of adulation plastered on her face told me that if he grew fangs at this moment, it would make no difference. I repressed my misgivings and mentally crossed my fingers.

"What time do you figure you'll be back?" I asked Duncan in an offhand manner after he'd maneuvered the crutches into the back seat and then eased behind the wheel. "We want to make sure someone is here when you bring her home all safe and sound."

His concerned gaze focused briefly on Audrey's face, strayed to her injured foot and then to me. "Originally, I'd planned lunch, two mine tours and dinner at my club," he replied tentatively, "but that's a pretty long day and well..."

I filled in his pause with "She might not be up to all that."

Audrey let out a little squeak of outrage and snapped, "Of course I'm up to it." Then, as if regretting her brusque behavior, she beamed Duncan a disarming smile before giving me a look that clearly said, 'don't-you-dare-say-anything-else'.

"In that case we won't see you until about eight o'clock," Duncan said as he turned the ignition key and then answered my farewell wave with a jaunty two-fingered salute.

I swallowed back the words of warning still perched in my throat and watched the sleek car ease around the bend in the hill. It was out of my hands now but I'd make damn good and sure to keep my meeting with Ida brief so I would be back from my excursion to Weaverville well before Audrey's return.

Weaverville. The very notion that the long-kept secret to this convoluted puzzle might await me at the old graveyard sent my stomach plunging with hollow excitement. I hurried up the steps and by the time I reached my room the old clock was chiming eleven-thirty. I was already late for my appointment with Ida and was sorely tempted to skip it and head straight for the cemetery. But as I scooped up my camera and notebook, I hesitated. Ida Fairfield was a living, breathing history of this town whereas the poor souls at Weaverville weren't going anywhere. I'd best opt for the living.

I don't know. Perhaps it was the knowledge that I was completely alone in the old house, or my ever-active imagination was working overtime, but all at once an inexplicable feeling of apprehension gripped me. I cast a quick look behind me to the doorway listening intently, but heard only silence. Not just any silence though. It was one of those deep, penetrating, four-o'clock-in-the-morning type silences that caused the moan of the wind beneath the eaves and the ghostly rustle of leaves in the nearby sycamore trees to sound oddly magnified.

Considering what I now knew it wasn't beyond the realm of possibility to conjure up the disconcerting vision of someone hiding inside the house at this very moment. The thought of being watched by unseen eyes propelled me to the phone. Dead air met my ear.

My apprehension escalated as I replaced the receiver but nevertheless, some part of me, the mulish part Tally would insist, tempted me to throw caution overboard and undertake a thorough search of the house. And what would I do if I did find someone skulking about the shadowy corridors or vacant rooms of the old place? What if I encountered more than one person? I had no weapon, no way to summon help, so I snatched up my things and bolted for the car making it to the middle of town before I realized I'd left the old photo albums behind in the kitchen. "Flapdoodle," I muttered under my breath, wrenching the car in a U-turn.

Chiding my stupidity, I gunned the car back up the road. Maybe it was an accident, maybe it was fate, but if I hadn't forgotten the albums, I wouldn't have arrived at the mouth of the driveway in time to look up and see dazzling flashes of sunlight reflecting back at me from something or someone moving between the wind-chiseled rocks at the summit of Devil's Hill.

Snowy-white thunderheads, whipped into frothy pillars by the late morning wind hovered over the palisade of mountains to the east by the time I located the albums and backtracked downtown. The possibilities of what or who might have been on the abandoned mine road behind the house troubled me. Of course, it could have been something as innocuous as a discarded bottle reflecting the powerful rays of the sun, a hiker out for a stroll, or perhaps kids out four-wheeling.

Nice try, I thought as a grim, but more likely explanation pole-vaulted to the top of the list. Nine times out of ten my intuition served me well. I suspected my inadvertent return to the house may have afforded me the prize of witnessing our pseudo phantom high-tailing it over the hill and—my thoughts ground to a halt and a procession of goose bumps raced up my arms when the full impact hit home. Did that mean the person had been hiding somewhere in the house since last night?

If I remembered correctly, one of the guys at the Muleskinner had said the old road on Devil's Hill was a shortcut to the mine property. That could provide the answer as to how our ghost arrived and departed unseen. What if an off road or four-wheel drive vehicle was parked on the other side of the ridge just out of sight?

The blue Suburban jumped to mind. But how could it be D.J.? He and Marta left for Mexico hours ago. There was Willow of course, but I couldn't picture her dilapidated VW bus making it up the steep slope. Duncan Claypool was off the list. So that left Archie or Bitsy. Or Jesse and Haston. And I certainly could not leave out the possibility of Fran or Dr. Orcutt.

I thumped the steering wheel with my hand. Damn! I was driving myself nuts again. With difficulty, I shoved the whole frustrating mess to the back of my mind and swung the car onto Red Lantern Lane. Apropos, I mused, considering the notorious profession chosen by Ida's mother.

Like the rest of the town the majority of dwellings I passed on Vixen Hill appeared to be unoccupied. So when I reached the crest of the knoll and spotted a neat stone cottage appearing weathered enough to be an extension of the rocky hillside itself, I figured it must be Ida's place.

The name on the mailbox confirmed my guess. I parked the car beneath the low hanging branches of an oak tree, scooped up the albums, and hurried along a shady walkway accompanied by the silvery clamor from what must have been a hundred wind chimes all clanging, dinging and tinkling a melodious, yet slightly off-key concert.

My knock was answered by a dour-faced, gray-haired woman of indeterminate age whose blunt features and reddish skin told me she was from one of the Indian tribes in the area. Probably Pima or Yaqui.

Smiling, I introduced myself and informed her of my appointment. Apparently unimpressed, she said nothing, just ushered me into a small living room and gestured for me to wait before shuffling away.

Slightly nonplussed by her uncommunicative manner, I turned to survey the small room filled with a hodgepodge of frayed silk furniture, antique tables and glass-fronted cabinets stuffed with a lifetime of bric-a-brac. I set the albums on a doily-topped table and wandered about breathing in the musty scent of mothballs that reminded me of my grandmother's attic.

As an ancient cuckoo clock began its whistled proclamation of twelve noon, I stopped to admire Ida's collection of pewter figurines and my eyes fell on a large glass Mason jar that looked like it was filled with...what? I leaned in closer. Cat litter and jelly beans?

"Well, Miss O'Dell, you're certainly a tall one," came a soft voice from behind me.

I swung around and stared down at an incredibly shrunken, unbelievably wrinkled woman bent over an aluminum walker.

"You've met Edgar, I see," she intoned with a high-pitched chuckle, peering up at me through thick lenses.

I lifted an inquiring brow. "Edgar?"

Her smile revealed a row of gold-flecked ivory-colored teeth. "My fourth husband. I put the other three in the ground, but Edgar wanted to be cremated and stay right here in the living room by the window so he could keep an eye on his precious garden."

I edged a look outside at the profusion of flowers

filling a rock-walled enclosure. "I see. And the jelly beans?"

"His last request," she said with a grunt, easing into a frayed armchair. "He said as long as he had to spend eternity in that jar, he might as well enjoy his favorite snack. It dresses things up a bit, wouldn't you say?"

"Very colorful and a definite conversation starter," I replied, answering her mischievous grin with one of my own.

She appeared to be studying me closely and finally said, "I believe you favor my mother. That's a picture of her on the wall behind you."

I turned to examine the faded likeness of the famed Madame of Vixen Hill, feeling flattered at the comparison, but not really seeing much resemblance. Perhaps Dr. Orcutt's assertion that the old lady was partially blind held some merit. "Thank you," I murmured, shifting my gaze back to her, "she was beautiful."

"Take a gander at the girl in that oval frame," she said, pointing a bony finger. "Once upon a time, that was me."

With a twinge of melancholy, I stared at a pretty young face that bore not the slightest similarity to this seasoned citizen. As if to echo my thoughts, she lamented, "Don't ever get old, there's no future in it. Plus that, you end up looking like a well-cooked prune."

"Not at all," I fibbed, taking a seat opposite her.

"Oh, honey, if the Lord loved a liar he'd squeeze you to death," she chided me good-naturedly. "Now, why don't you tell me why you're here and Miss Morgan isn't."

After I explained the reasons for Audrey's absence, she made a long face. "Fiddlesticks. I was looking forward to meeting Rita's little girl all grown up."

"She's anxious to meet you too and," I said, patting

the photo albums on the table next to me, "she's hoping you might be able to identify some of these people so she can start reconstructing her past."

"I heard the poor girl favors her late father, that black-hearted son-of-a-bitch."

I grinned. "Not one of your favorite people either."

"There's an ass for every chair."

I laughed aloud at her salty language, then started with surprise when she grabbed a pearl handled letter opener from the adjacent table and rapped loudly on the aluminum walker. "Minnie!" she called out, "Minnie, come here."

The elderly Indian woman appeared in the doorway with hands on ample hips and glared at Ida. "What?"

"There'll only be two for lunch today instead of three."

She gave a brusque nod and strode away mumbling under her breath.

"A woman of few words," I remarked dryly. "Listen, if this isn't a good time..."

"Pay her no attention," Ida said, waving one withered, age-spotted hand. "Her nose is out of joint because I made her drive me to the doctor over in Sierra Vista." She settled back in the chair. "Now then, young lady, let's get down to brass tacks."

I scanned my notes. "I've got so many names on this list, I'm not sure where to start."

"The beginning is always best," she advised, absently fingering loose folds of skin hanging like a shriveled hammock beneath her chin.

Within minutes, I highlighted most of the pertinent events that had transpired since our arrival in Morgan's Folly, including last night's goblin gig, and was about half way through our frustrating confrontation with Dr. Orcutt when she interrupted with a vociferous, "That drunken old quack. I don't know how he sleeps nights. His stupidity was responsible for my god daughter's death and all the other pain he's caused the Morgan family."

Drunken? Well, well. That helped explain the doctor's dissipated appearance. "So, he and Grady both had problems with booze?"

"Humph. Quite a pair those two. Great drinking buddies. They should have revoked that man's license to practice medicine years ago."

"Whitey told me about your crusade."

Frowning, she said, "And to think he's trying to frighten that poor child. You tell Miss Morgan not to worry. Her father was a ruthless, selfish bastard, but only crazy like a fox."

I edged forward in my chair. "I'm sure she'll be relieved to hear that but frankly, it's the rumors concerning her sister that really have her worried."

"What's that?" she asked, adjusting the hearing aid protruding from one ear beneath a thin halo of hair so white it looked like a dandelion gone to seed.

In a louder voice I repeated what few facts we'd been able to drag out of Dr. Orcutt. "At first he didn't even acknowledge Dayln Morgan existed and now he flatly refuses to discuss her case. My question is, why?"

Her eyes grew distant and she retreated into silence while I sat listening to the clamor of wind chimes wafting through the open window for what seemed like an eternity, before gently prodding her with, "Ida? Are you all right?"

Her foggy-hazel eyes slowly refocused as she came back from wherever her memories had led her. "Oh, yes. I was just remembering that whole unfortunate situation."

There was no point in sugar-coating my question so I asked straight out, "Was Audrey's sister insane?"

The ensuing hesitation accelerated my pulse. "Well," she said at length, "let's just say she was always...different."

"Different? In what way?"

"She was a real moody kid. Kind of withdrawn. Unapproachable a lot of the time and pretty much lived alone in her own little fantasy world."

I chewed on that information a few seconds. "Rita told Dr. Orcutt that Grady's drinking and physical abuse were the reasons she took Audrey and fled. Did he mistreat Dayln too? Could that be what caused her to turn on him with a knife?"

"I don't think we'll ever know." In a halting voice, she explained that she and her third husband had been abroad when the attack had taken place. By the time they'd returned, Dayln had already been committed. "I went to visit her twice at that wretched place."

"Only twice?"

"They didn't make it easy if you weren't a blood relative. But anyway, the first time I went she was all doped up and couldn't seem to remember much of anything. When I finally did get her to talk, I couldn't make head nor tail of what she was saying. The second time she seemed really agitated, all wild-eyed, pacing like a caged tiger and still talking in riddles." Her expression grew distant and I could almost see the parade of memories marching before her eyes. "She kept repeating something about not being who she was supposed to be. Claimed someone else was living inside her head and begging me to help her..." The old woman's bony shoulders sank in defeat. "She did kind of sound...well..."

"Unbalanced?" I said, hating to admit to myself that

Dr. Orcutt may have been telling the truth after all.

"Perhaps so," she said in a hushed voice, "but if you ask me I think the poor child was doomed from the start."

"In what way?"

Ida went on to explain that because of the strict provision in Hannah Morgan's will stipulating the mine's ownership be passed onto the sons, Grady was constantly harangued by his father to abandon his lustful wanderings and settle down to produce the much-desired male heir.

"Grady needed a brood mare, not a wife," Ida said. "Lydia got sick not long after giving birth and when she was told it would be dangerous for her to bear more children, Grady didn't try to hide his displeasure. Not only was he unspeakably cruel to her after that, he pretty much ignored his daughter."

"And that's why Dayln hated him," I murmured, scribbling madly on my notepad.

Ida shook her head sadly. "Far from it. She worshipped the ground the foolish man walked on. Craved his attention so much she'd force herself to go down in the mine with him to prove her worth, even though it scared the bejesus out of her."

I stared in confusion. This version was diametrically opposed to everything I'd surmised and demolished the obvious motive. There had to be some other reason. "How old was she when her father remarried?"

"Eight or nine."

"Was she jealous of Rita?"

"I don't know, but she changed a lot after Lydia died. Got real belligerent, and by the time she was oh, maybe twelve, she'd started hanging around town with that bunch of no good hoodlums."

"That I don't get. Rita was her stepmother. Why

didn't she exercise some control over her."

"I think she tried for a while, but if the truth be known, she didn't really pay much more attention to her than Grady did."

"Why?"

"I think it was mostly because she was so obsessed with trying to have a baby."

"Really? You mean she couldn't conceive?"

"Oh, she managed that just fine. Just couldn't carry the babies to term. She miscarried one right after the other until Audrey finally came along and I guess it was a real miracle that she even managed that."

Catching my puzzled glance, she revealed that after almost losing Audrey twice, Dr. Orcutt had ordered Rita to lie flat on her back the last five months of her pregnancy. "It was quite an ordeal. The poor woman spent the remaining two months at some clinic in Tucson. They kept her pumped full of that stuff that keeps women from going into premature labor and even then, the baby was born way too early. She was hospitalized for a long time before Rita was allowed to bring her home." She paused for a breath, then smiled wistfully. "You tell Audrey she was the apple of her mother's eye. Land sakes, I never saw a woman so thrilled to have a child."

"But Grady wasn't thrilled, was he? He still didn't have his son."

"Very true. I guess it wasn't meant to be."

I could see the whole picture pretty clearly now. Rita found herself trapped in the identical position as the first Mrs. Morgan and decided to opt out. But something was still bothering me. Why not just divorce the creep? Why the elaborate identity switch?

"Ida, do you think the long-standing relationship

between Audrey's mother and Dr. Orcutt could have been based on more than just friendship?"

A calculating gleam sparked her eyes. "There were rumors to that effect, but nothing was ever verified."

"Lunch," Minnie announced from the doorway and my stomach rumbled in anticipation. Breakfast seemed like a long time ago.

"Oh, good," Ida said brightly, pulling herself to a standing position. "Bring those albums along, Miss O'Dell, and Minnie, fetch my magnifying glass."

Surrounded by ornate glass cabinets brimming with blue flowered china patterns, we settled into a small formal dining room. In between the cold asparagus soup and chicken salad sandwiches, Ida's gaze misted with nostalgia as she roamed the pages of the albums, identifying faded faces from the past while regaling me with colorful tales of bygone days. She digressed long enough to disclose that her own mother had been a schoolteacher from Virginia.

"Believe it or not, she came into her profession when she began coming west each summer to earn extra money," she said, responding to my look of surprise with an expectant smile. "After a few years, she realized she could make a better living entertaining lonesome miners than if she taught school for the next two hundred years."

I wished I had time to hear more about what it must have been like growing up as the daughter of the town madam in this once lusty mining town, but I steered the subject back to the Morgan clan. "Tell me more about Audrey's great-grandmother, Hannah. Did you know her?"

Her eyes narrowed to pinpoints. "Not well. She wasn't the type to consort with someone who grew up in the red light district and she died in the late forties, long before I became involved with the family."

"Why do you think she was so intractable in her decision about bequeathing the mine to only a male heir? I mean, you would have thought, considering that she didn't exactly bow to the normal conventions of the day that she'd be more open to having any Morgan child inherit the Defiance regardless of sex."

"Hannah was somewhat of a stickler when it came to blood line. Did you know she was already a Morgan before she married Seth?"

My pen stopped in mid-stroke and I looked up "I'm not following you."

"She was his second cousin twice or three times removed. Kissing cousins, they used to call them, but nevertheless she considered herself a Morgan through and through. Anyway," she continued, patting her wispy white hair, "after poor Seth died and she'd dealt with Jasper Claypool's shenanigans, she got downright obsessed with the idea of never losing control again. And remember, things weren't like they are now as far as women being liberated and all that, so she wasn't about to take a chance on having the Defiance pass out of the family through the marriage of a female heir."

Making notations as fast as I could, my head swam with all the new material. It would create great underpinning and really spruce up my article.

By the time we turned the last page on the second album, she confirmed what I already knew. There wasn't a single picture of Rita or Audrey. I was repeating Marta's story of how Grady had destroyed them in a rage when another thought intruded. "Maybe I missed something, but I don't remember you mentioning any pictures of Audrey's sister either."

Ida looked momentarily befuddled and then leafed

back several pages before pointing a yellowed fingernail at the photo I'd examined a few days ago in the tower room. "That's Grady, that's Lydia, and this is Dayln when she was about a year old."

I strained my eyes and even borrowed the magnifying glass, but the little girl's shadowed face was unidentifiable. Could it be that Grady had tried to destroy all evidence of both children but missed this one? And if so, why? I consulted my list of questions while Minnie cleared away the empty plates and served a fruit tart smothered in lemon yogurt for dessert. "Ida, do you remember a girl named Bitsy Bigelow?"

She blinked a few times and then nodded. "Dayln's friend."

"Right. Best friends, supposedly. You knew she was back in town?"

"Oh, yes. I've seen her around. She looks like a different person since her surgery."

"So I've heard. Listen, I tried to talk to her about Dayln yesterday but she positively came unglued. Any idea why?"

The old lady spooned a strawberry into her mouth and munched pensively before admitting she could only repeat gossip. "The story I heard was that Bitsy was mad as hell and refused to have anything more to do with her after Dayln stole her boyfriend away. And when Grady got wind that his daughter was sneaking around with one of those white-trash Lawton boys..."

I sat up straight. "Lawton? Which one?"

"I don't remember, honey. But anyway, Grady flew into a terrible rage and threatened Dayln within an inch of her life if she so much as looked cross-eyed at the boy again."

My mind skipped back to Orville Kemp's disclosure that Archie's father had spent much of his time in prison. So, the mixture of Dayln's scandalous behavior and Grady's ultimatum could very well have provoked their confrontation. But did Dayln's twenty-year old indiscretion justify Bitsy's extreme reaction to my inquiries? No. There had to be more.

"So, did the girls ever see each other again after Dayln was sent away?"

"I don't know. But according to Edna, that's Bitsy's aunt you know, supposedly Dayln wrote to Bitsy every week pleading for forgiveness and begging her to come and see her."

"Did she?"

"I think Edna told me that she and another girl did go visit her once...but, honey, that was a long time ago and I can't be sure."

The old cuckoo clock warbled one o'clock and I was surprised to realize an hour had passed. Overcome with the urgent need to begin phase two of my sleuthing in Weaverville, I quickly summed up the discussion. When I recounted Fran Orcutt's cryptic disclosure Ida looked blank, but when I repeated the doctor's assertion that Dayln may have deliberately set the fire at the asylum, her face crumpled in dismay. "That was never proven, but I know how that rumor got started."

The hollow tone of her voice caught my interest. "I'm listening."

"Did I already tell you that Minnie's cousin, Rose, worked as an attendant at that place?"

"No."

"Because I didn't trust Miles Orcutt one damn whit, I paid Rose extra to keep an eye on things for me. Right before the fire, she told me Dayln was becoming more uncontrollable by the day and vowing that she was going to escape—one way or the other."

That sounded pretty ominous. "Was Rose on duty the night of the fire?"

Her pained expression conveyed profound sorrow. "She said it was the most terrible experience of her life. All the smoke and flames, the children screaming..." She paused to clear her throat. "Rose was badly burned trying to save some of the kids and barely escaped with her own life. By the time help arrived, well, it was too late. But she did tell the authorities a strange story."

My pulse skyrocketed. "What was that?"

There was a slight hesitation and her dubious expression seemed to disavow her next words. "She claimed one of the children did not die."

It was difficult to control the tremor in my voice. "But how is that possible? I thought the bodies of all the patients were accounted for."

"So they said. But to her last breath, Rose insisted that she saw a girl, her face bloody and blackened, run from the flames and vanish into the night."

Fueled by Ida's astounding revelation, my thoughts hop-scotched all over the map, while a keen sense of certainty permeated down to my bone marrow. This was it. I was about to hit pay dirt. My throat tumbleweed-dry, my insides burning with nervous energy, I stomped on the accelerator and sped towards Weaverville along a nearly deserted road festooned with black-eyed Susans nodding encouragement at me. As I wound through tawny hills crowned with limestone outcroppings and honeycombed with scores of abandoned mine shafts, I concluded that my high-strung state was to blame for making it appear as if the yawning cavities perched above rusty skirts of tailings looked like open mouths waiting to swallow some unsuspecting hiker.

"Settle down," I said aloud, trying to gather my outlandish speculations into some sort of logical order. Who should I believe? Dr. Orcutt insisted there had been twenty-eight patients and twenty-eight bodies. Ida had further qualified her remarks by stating that the authorities explained away Rose's questionable allegation when they discovered another attendant huddled under a bush not far from where she'd seen the figure disappear. But what if the woman's eyes had not been playing tricks on her? Who had she seen running away and if so, how had the body count matched the exact number of patients?

The remarkable premise beginning to emerge from the far regions of my mind made my blood surge with excitement, but at the same time, a feeling of unease dogged me like a second shadow as Rita Morgan's final warning to leave the secrets buried, drummed in my head. And here I was poised to unearth them.

The road plunged downward and flattened out into a shimmering slate ribbon that stretched away to the distant mountains where it finally evaporated into the magnificent isolation of the sun-baked desert. I cranked the air-conditioning higher, slowed the car, and kept my eyes peeled for the turn-off. Whitey was right, if I hadn't been paying close attention I'd have missed the time worn sign directing me to turn right.

I swung onto a dusty, mesquite-shrouded road and climbed back into gentle hills, maneuvering as best I could around deep mud puddles left over from last night's storm. Other than a few hawks lazily riding the thermals and a couple of head of scrawny white-faced cattle camped out by a rusted water tank, there didn't appear to be another living creature in sight.

Rounding a sharp curve, I spotted the roofless, windowless remains of several crumbling adobe structures literally melting into the earth. This had to be Weaverville. I stopped the car, rolled down the window and snapped pictures, thinking how sad it was that these sagging tributes to the past were the final remnants of a once prosperous mining town.

I passed another handful of structures in the process of being reclaimed by the desert before the road abruptly ended at a rusty gate that heralded the entrance to the object of my quest—the old cemetery.

After parking the car in the tentative shade of a scraggly tree, I got out to survey my surroundings. Erratic gusts of wind, most likely a prelude to the approaching storm whispered through knee-high gamma grass and hummed an eerie little tune along the crooked barbed wire fence. I pushed open the squeaky gate and then paused to absorb the somber atmosphere of the silent hills standing guard over the cluster of weed-choked grave markers. Which one would offer up the final piece of this bizarre puzzle?

I couldn't dream up a more superbly spooky setting if I tried. And I could see it in print now. Before the ambiance got away from me, I jotted several thoughts on my notepad and then set out to discover why Fran Orcutt had directed me to this forlorn place. I still didn't have clue one as to what I was supposed to find as I roamed among crumbling concrete slabs and crooked wooden crosses.

With the exception of lovingly tended shrines and flower-draped headstones bearing mostly Hispanic names, many others were neglected—hidden among overgrown mesquite, the hand scrawled testimony of the forgotten souls beneath rendered undecipherable by the inexorable march of time. It was as if they had never existed and it left me with a profound sense of sadness.

After ten or fifteen fruitless minutes of rooting

around and kneeling in the thorn-filled weeds frustration began to rankle me. None of these names meant anything to me. So, what was it? What was I supposed to find?

More puzzled than ever, I rose and my eyes strayed to a jumble of headstones perched on the crest of one grassy knoll. I tramped to the top and came to an area enclosed by a sturdy wrought iron fence. Here the tombstones were larger, the graves well tended. And one of them looked quite fresh. I moved closer, nodding ruefully. Of course. This would be the Morgan family plot. It was not surprising in the least that their remains resided on the prime piece of real estate, lording over the rest of the townsfolk, arrogant even in death.

Confident that I was finally on the right track, I studied the smooth marble headstone that marked the final resting-place for the dastardly Grady Morgan. He'd been dead a mere three weeks. Okay. That told me nothing new. I moved on, reading every name, every date on each stone. They were all here underneath these melancholy monuments to mortality: the hapless Seth, and beside him, the dynamic Hannah who must be executing cartwheels in the grave to know her great-granddaughter was fraternizing with a Claypool. Jeb Morgan's intricately carved headstone was impressive indeed and adjacent to it, a smaller one bore the name of Grady's brother, Oliver, who had died way too young. There were other children, aunts, uncles, cousins, everyone was here—with one glaring exception. Dayln Morgan's grave was not among them. Was this the rationale for Fran Orcutt's ambiguous directive?

For no discernible reason I suddenly felt edgy and slid a wary eye behind me. Nothing. Nothing met my searching eyes except the empty expanse of sand, rock and cactus. But the jumpiness persisted. What was it about graveyards that fired the imagination and yet weighed heavily on the spirit? Was it the sobering knowledge that these bone depositories represented the final destiny for all of us?

Whatever, a distinct sensation of apprehension blanketed me as I resumed my search. I couldn't help but think that if Tally knew I had come to this godforsaken place alone, he'd have a king-sized hissy fit and declare my actions to be bullheaded and foolhardy. And he'd be right. Oh, well, he'd never have to find out, and besides, lots of people knew I was here.

I tramped around for another ten minutes or so before stumbling upon a solitary gravestone tucked away in a desolate corner of the cemetery. Kneeling, I parted the thatch of weeds and inhaled a sharp breath at the name etched on the simple granite marker: Dayln Morgan.

This was a cruel and deliberate act, no doubt ordered by Grady himself. Was it because she had disgraced the family name by first attempting to kill him, or because he suspected she'd set the asylum fire? Those were the obvious reasons, but something told me there had to be more to this than met the eye. What else could this girl have done to deserve the fate of being banished for eternity from the bosom of her family, her memory forever tarnished, desecrated?

At the same time, I could not restrain the staggering possibility that now jumped to the forefront. Call me nuts, but what if Minnie's cousin had been right? What if Dayln Morgan really had escaped death that night? The mere thought gave me one of those anxious little stomach twinges. What if...what if she was Grady's tormentor? And if he'd suspected as much, why had he kept silent? Where had she been all these years and what had compelled her to return home after a twenty-year absence? And, I thought, studying the faded name on the stone, if by some wild stretch of the imagination this was so, then who was buried in her grave?

I rose to my feet still not sure I'd resolved anything. With no clear plan in mind, I began to wander aimlessly among the remaining graves, following intermittent cloud shadows skipping across the ground. I found nothing of significance. Admitting defeat, I hiked back up the hill past the Morgan family gravesites and had just started down the path towards my car when I noticed a smaller wrought-iron enclosure sheltered beneath a stand of wind-tossed willows

I stepped inside and spotted a tiny white marker almost hidden in the weeds. When I leaned down to read it, surprise rushed through me. Baby Morgan. It listed the month and year. A few feet away, I found another marker. Baby Morgan. My breathing accelerated. What a dummy I was! Fran Orcutt hadn't been talking about Audrey. She had meant for me to visit the graves of Rita Morgan's unborn babies. But why?

On my knees now, I plowed through the tangle of dry grass and found a third grave. How tragic. My heart went hollow with pity when I found one last grave marker fallen over and encrusted with dirt, the date of death almost indiscernible. I set it upright, wet one finger and rubbed the plastic nameplate. When the first few letters materialized, a chill prickled the back of my neck. I wiped away the remaining dirt. August. The baby died in August. Wait a minute. How was it possible…?

The distinct crunch of a footfall from behind wrenched my gut with cold horror. Half rising, I spun around in time to catch a brief glimpse of masculine scuffed boots and blue jeans before something coarse, like burlap, dropped over my head. Strong arms encircled my waist and blind panic banished all reason when I was pulled roughly against someone. "Stop! Let go of me," I shouted, barely recognizing my own muffled voice as I struggled against my assailant.

The man's grip tightened painfully and I clawed at the smothering fabric until he pinned my arms to my side. I don't know which was worse. The terror of suffocation or the sickening awareness of my dire predicament when I felt his fingers fumbling at my breasts and heard his menacing chuckle close to my ear. "Well, look who we got here."

At first, I balked at the inevitable, refusing to admit I recognized the voice, but an icy sword of terror slashed through me when Archie Lawton growled, "Guess you're not such hot shit now, are you, Miss smart-ass reporter?"

Jesus H. Christ! I tried to lunge away, but his grip was like iron. I kicked wildly and screamed. If only I could see. If only I could get a full breath. Fighting for air and close to hysteria, I searched the pockets of my brain, trying to remember the rules—any rule from my self-defense class. If your life is threatened, the instructor had warned, don't anger your attacker. Better to relax and submit. No way, Jose. I'd rather die.

Fury and revulsion re-energized me. I stomped one sneaker down hard on his booted instep, but his malicious laugh confirmed my ineffectiveness. Okay, next tactic. I allowed my knees to collapse and then propelled myself upward hoping to land a knock out blow under his chin. I missed, but did manage to unbalance him. We both crashed to the ground in a thrashing tangle of arms and legs. I lashed out and apparently landed a sensitive kick because his slackened grip was accompanied by a howl of pain.

But triumph was fleeting. "You stupid bitch!" He

landed a blow on my cheek with such thundering force, my ears rang and a profusion of stars exploded before my eyes. The searing pain left me stunned and disoriented, my stomach quaking with sudden nausea. I felt him tugging my blouse up and I stiffened with dread at the sensation of sharp metal sliding against my bare midriff.

"You better be nice," Archie panted, "or I'll cut you into a thousand pieces and leave you for the coyotes."

Beyond scared at that point, I felt numb. Powerless. Oddly disconnected from myself. I was doomed. Destined to wind up a sensational headline in my own newspaper.

He rolled me onto my stomach and I could do little but flail weakly as he bound my wrists. When he flipped me over and straddled me, hope faded when I felt the prominent proof of his evil intent. "Oh, baby doll, you don't know how much I've been waiting for this."

Dear God, please don't let this happen.

He was fumbling with my belt buckle when, unbelievably, I heard a harsh voice shouting from some distance away, "Get off her, you dumb shit!"

I held my breath, hope surging through my veins. Was it friend or foe?

Running footsteps, a clatter of stones near my head and a dull thud. "Shithouse mouse!" Archie yelped, his grip loosening abruptly. "I was just having a little fun."

The rising wind rustled the grass beneath my head and snatched away most of the newcomer's reply with the exception of "...has to look like an accident."

My heart convulsed. Definitely not friend.

"Keep her still," came the gruff, muted command.

Why did I have the impression the second man was disguising his voice? I couldn't see to identify him, so why bother?

Fear carved away at my senses when I felt someone's full weight pressing down, immobilizing me. "The sheriff knows I'm here," I gasped through the smothering fabric, "you'll never get away with..."

Something solid and smooth, like the sole of a shoe pressed hard on my throat, choking off my words. I flinched at a sharp sting in my upper arm. What was happening?

"Get the truck," came the curt order and I heard footsteps vanish into the distance.

"Too bad you sided with that bitch imposter," the stranger's taunting voice crooned close to my ear, "she's gonna be next."

Did I recognize that silky tone? Before I could contemplate it further, a tranquil glow spread through me, paralyzing my arms and legs. Oh, God! What had he given me?

He was whispering in my ear, but his voice sounded far away and I could make no sense of what he was saying. Something about me interfering with destiny? Desperately, I tried to fight the overwhelming dizziness but my eyelids fluttered shut and I followed a maze of brightly colored lights spiraling down into blackness.

Heat on my face. A strange scarlet-orange light glowing against my closed eyelids. The brilliance faded to gray. Cooler air now. More comfortable. Now the red color again. More heat. My sluggish brain endeavored to explain the sensation of extreme lethargy anchoring my limbs and yet I was floating, weightless.

Little by little the dreamy haze began to clear and cognizant thoughts nudged at me bringing bits and pieces of disjointed memories. I needed to open my eyes, but my lids were too massive. Perhaps I'd sleep some more.

I drifted again for an indeterminate amount of time, but something, some innate sense of urgency warned me that it was monumentally important that I wake up. All at once, wispy visions of Weaverville emerged from the foggy corridors of my mind. The grave markers. Something about the grave markers. The thought, still indistinct, flitted about like a panicked moth at a window and then vanished. What was it? What was I trying to remember?

Sleepy. Too sleepy to care. I don't know how long I dozed before the tortured nightmare of my blind scuffle with Archie Lawton finally roused me from my stupor enough to recall the arrival of his unidentified accomplice and then...what?

"Screee. Click, click. Screee." A strange sound. And close. Then silence. Penetrating silence. No, there it was again. Louder this time followed by a low raspy hiss. Mild apprehension grazed my semi-conscious mind. A noise like that certainly didn't belong here in my bedroom. And why did it seem as if it was coming from somewhere below me?

I forced my eyelids open only to shut them against the painful assault of sunlight. Oh? So, I wasn't home in bed. I was outside. And I was lying flat on my back. Lying on something hard and very uncomfortable. My mind whipsawed, striving for some logical explanation. Either I was dreaming or this was the mother of all hallucinations complete with a searing headache, chalk-dry mouth and— why did my tongue feel a mile thick?

I cracked my eyes open again and squinted up at a rectangular patch of blue sky framed by wooden slats. I blinked a couple of times and stared at a cloud gliding into the sun's path. Okay, that explained the intermittent visions of light and shadow, but the primary question loomed large. Where was I?

Part of me shouted, who cares? I'm alive! And companion to the relief of having the loathsome bag gone was the thrill of emancipation as I gingerly flexed my unbound hands. So far so good.

I lifted my head and looked around. It appeared that

I was lying at the bottom of a crude circular depression, perhaps five or six feet beneath the opening. Feverishly, I fought to re-establish the chain of events that had brought me to this place. What a total dufus I'd been going alone to the cemetery, strolling blithely into a well-laid trap. Sheer horror radiated through me at the memory of Archie's rough hands on my body. Disgusting predator. I harbored no doubt as to his original intent, so why had the second man aborted his plan? And what had been the point of drugging me?

But when the stranger's sinister words, "...has to look like an accident," echoed inside my head, the truth became chillingly obvious. They'd had no intention of allowing me to survive. So...why wasn't I dead? Why had they made it so easy for me to get up and climb out?

I leaned my head to one side and stared disbelieving at a sheer rock wall. Could the shadowy object attached to the side be a rusted ore bucket? Uh oh.

A pervasive feeling of danger engulfed me. Just as I started to push myself to a sitting position, a sudden whooshing sound arrested my movements. The mind-bending sight of an owl flapping upward past my head—so close we were eyeball to eyeball for a fraction of a second, left my lungs airless. Spellbound, I watched it silhouetted like a dark mirage against the small window of sky before it vanished. That resolved the strange noise. But the presumption that I was lying at the bottom of a shallow hole dissolved with a startling realization. The owl had indeed come from somewhere below me. Below me.

Ragged breath constricted my throat and fear squeezed my heart like vise-grips. My imagination careened wildly in all directions as I eased my palms along the rough surface beneath me. Wood. Splintery planks of wood. I extended my arms out further, perhaps two feet on either side of me until I reached the edges of the boards. Beyond that, my fingertips encountered nothing. Nothing at all.

Cold claws of panic gripped me as the horrifying gravity of my situation began to seep in. I understood the reason for the ore bucket. I wasn't lying at the bottom of a hole. I was suspended above it. Those bastards. They'd left me in an abandoned mineshaft.

And if that weren't bad enough, I could feel my chest burning, seizing up at the onset of an asthma attack. Like spent bellows, my lungs seemed to deliver less and less oxygen with each consecutive breath. Without my inhaler, which I hadn't needed for weeks, the possibility of eventual suffocation threatened. Breathe, damn it, breathe! That's it. Now another. Relax. A little deeper now. Good. Calm down. Calm down. It took every ounce of determination I could muster to finally regain some measure of self-control.

More clear-headed, I forced myself to look down the length of my body. Mere inches beyond my toes the end of the narrow platform was precariously balanced on a thin rock shelf. Every cell in my body screamed, "Get up! Get out!" But, when I shifted my weight, the ominous crack of splintering wood turned my insides to mush. One of the planks beneath my right elbow suddenly wasn't there and it seemed an hour passed before I heard the muffled clatter of it hitting bottom.

Horrified, I reached through the gap where the board had been and ran my hand along the underside of the planks beneath my hips. They were all scored, jagged, poised to break. One false move, perhaps any further movement at all could send me plummeting into the inky void. For agonizing minutes, I lay stiff as a flash-frozen carp, unable or unwilling to confront the inevitability. But as time crawled by, reality sunk in. I was going to die. My throat closed. Tears blurred my vision. Would death come quickly from the force of the fall, or would I lie in a crumpled broken heap, a prisoner of the unending darkness, condemned to slow starvation. Or...perhaps I would be here for days broiling in the noonday sun, wracked with hunger and thirst before my flesh was reduced to the consistency of a charcoal briquette. Buzzards would come and peel away my charred skin. Pick my bones clean. And someday, someone would find my bleached skeleton moldering to dust just like the long-ago victims who'd tumbled from the edge of Boneyard Pass.

For no earthly reason, I was seized by sudden glee. Bitter laughter lodged in my throat, almost choking me. If I hadn't startled the owl, I would probably already be dead, just as they'd planned. How ironic. Saved by an owl. At least temporarily. "Thank you, owl!" I cackled. "Thank you, stupid owl. Thanks for nothing." The eerie wail of my own hysterical shrieks reverberating around the shaft spooked me almost as much my predicament. "Help!" I screamed. "Help me, somebody, please!"

Clammy with icy sweat, my insides quivering uncontrollably, I surrendered to overwhelming terror. It slammed into me, consuming my senses, impaling my intellect. The whole fabric of my being unraveled like a spool of yarn, leaving me a quaking, sobbing mass of incoherent humanity. For what seemed like hours, I wallowed in misery, crushed under the weight of my own sniveling cowardice. I thought about everything. And nothing. I did some heavy-duty praying, striking all sorts of bargains with God, vowing aloud, "Dear Lord, if you could see your way clear to grant me one small miracle, if you could somehow show me a way out of this mess, I promise

I'll make an honest effort to do the right thing from this day forward. And, I swear I'll be a better daughter, a better sister, a better friend, better person. I'll work on my stupid temper and try to be more patient." I screamed for help until my vocal chords gave out. Then, a peculiar thing happened. Apparently, abject terror has a life span because all at once, a soothing numbness permeated my psyche and flowed through my veins like a tranquil stream. I fell silent, my trembling stopped and rational thought gradually returned, allowing me to assess my situation with some semblance of calm.

It pained me no end to admit that Archie and his buddy had outfoxed me. They'd devised a brilliant and flawless plan. It was obvious they had not intended for me to die outright. If and when my body was ever found, nothing would appear abnormal. Whatever drug they'd administered would have had plenty of time to filter through my liver leaving no trace for the medical examiner to find.

I still had my watch. My car keys were nestled in the right front pocket of my jeans. I'd simply wandered away from the cemetery and fallen through the rotted timbers that once sealed the mouth of the mine. Happens all the time. And there did not seem to be any possible way for me to escape alive.

The knowledge that I would never see my family again filled me with profound and agonizing sorrow. And then my thoughts came to rest on Tally...my dearest Tally. Knowing that I would never again feel his arms around me or his lips pressed against mine shredded my heart with shards of anguish.

Maybe I should get it over with. Why lie here and suffer? It would be so easy to just roll off. The urge was unexplainable and overwhelming, but fear glued me to the boards as my mind grappled for a solution. Any solution.

Wait a minute. Wait a minute. By tonight, I would be missed. Audrey would call the sheriff. There would be a search, I would be rescued...then my thoughts foundered. Hundreds of these abandoned mines pockmarked the area. How would they ever find me?

Plunged once more into the depths of despair, I cursed my fate as the relentless sun scorched my skin. With each passing moment I could feel myself dehydrating further. I don't know why it mattered, but suddenly I needed to know what time it was. I lifted my arm very slowly and praying the minuscule shift of weight would not disturb my flimsy platform. Almost five. Good grief. I'd been unconscious over three hours.

The drone of a light plane overhead spiked my pulse, but as it sputtered away into the distance, the heavy silence returned, broken only now and then by the faint whisper of wind rattling the dry timbers above me.

I stared dully at the cheerful patch of blue sky crisscrossed with lacy contrails and decided that it was a mixed blessing when the sun finally moved beyond the lip of the shaft. Cool air wafting up from below soothed my sunburn but the onset of night presented the disturbing picture of lying here alone in the dark.

Call it habit, call it my reporter's mindset, or the simple fact that it was imperative to keep my mind occupied or go mad, but I could not stop myself from slogging through the baffling mishmash of events, beginning with the innocent phone call from my brother last week. Each clue, each incident, each conversation piggy backed upon the next until a startling scenario emerged. Man, oh man. How could I have been so dense? The answer had been in front of me all along, but had made no sense until now.

If one assumed that Ida's story of the asylum fire was true then there could only be one possible explanation. Grady's angel of death and the mysterious female caller had to be one and the same. Who else was familiar enough with the house and grounds to pull off such a clever masquerade? And with D.J. and Archie acting as her willing lieutenants, it would have been easy enough to add a little larceny to the role of vengeful murderess. But, of course, the most damning piece of evidence of all was the jeweled barrette, dropped from her hair the night of Grady's swan dive from the balcony.

No wonder she'd panicked at my persistent questions. They would have eventually revealed the bogus story of abuse inflicted by her cruel ex-husband. And those facial scars—was it any wonder no one in Morgan's Folly recognized her? Plastic surgery had altered her disfigured face—a face ravaged by fire. "Son-of-a-bitch," I marveled aloud, "Bitsy Bigelow is Dayln Morgan."

At the time of her disappearance, Rita Morgan had been unable to successfully carry a child to term, so when Dr. Orcutt dropped his bombshell concerning Audrey, it was little wonder that Dayln concluded that she was a conniving little imposter. So many things seemed clear now. The anonymous phone calls to both Jesse and Audrey and the photos missing from the old albums. But why the complicated ruse? Why not simply come forward and claim her inheritance?

I might never discover the answer to the questions, but the one thing I did know for certain twisted my gut into ten thousand knots. Unless I could perform a miracle and stop her, there was no doubt in my mind that Dayln Morgan intended to kill Audrey.

It was hell. Absolute hell. Just lying there. Helpless. Defeated. Impotent. And roasting like a chicken on a spit, torturing myself with feelings of resentment and despair as life went on without me. Red-tailed hawks sailed the thermals overhead. Wasps buzzed around my face and an astounding array of lizards effortlessly scaled my walled prison. I felt oddly disconnected knowing all this activity would continue after my death.

I dragged my tongue across sandpaper lips. Water. Oh, what I wouldn't give for a tall frosty glass filled with clear luscious cubes of ice and garnished with a tantalizing wedge of succulent lime. A sprig of mint, perhaps. The vision danced crazily before my eyes. No wait. Now it was pink lemonade, a whole pitcher of it, a gallon of it. Stop! Was I becoming delirious? I tried to swallow, but it felt like my throat was stuffed with dry flakes of coconut.

The minutes dragged by and for the hundredth time, I berated myself for supreme stupidity. Was Tally right? Did I possess a stubborn compulsion to seek out life-threatening situations?

I could imagine what a psychologist would say. "Well, Miss O'Dell, most likely you are suffering from the middle child syndrome," or "your fierce sense of competition is most likely manifested in the fact that you spent your childhood trying to emulate your rough and tumble brothers." My father had his own theory. He laughingly claimed I was the reincarnation of my pugnacious, flame-haired grandmother, fiery temperament and all.

But, I think it was far more likely that I felt driven to succeed. My adolescent dream of becoming an award-winning investigative reporter at the *Philadelphia Inquirer* had crashed and burned when I'd contracted a rare form of asthma caused by a stupid almost unpronounceable fungus that grew only in cool, damp climates. A stupid fungus, that had rendered me practically an invalid and precipitated my abrupt move to Arizona.

My mind whisked back four short months to my very first assignment from Tugg after my arrival. I was to go undercover to investigate the unexplained disappearance of my predecessor. My sleuthing had resulted in the horrifying discovery that he'd been murdered and I had ended up almost getting myself killed in the bargain. Afterwards, my articles had made the national news and catapulted me to the lofty role of minor celebrity. But had the story been worth risking my life?

My shoulder was throbbing again and the muscles in my back ached from lying in one position. Ever so carefully, I shifted my weight. Another board under my left shoulder blade broke away. Renewed panic chilled me. No avoiding the inevitable. My time was running out. And so was Audrey's.

That somber thought brought a grinding sensation of guilt, overpowering, heart-shriveling guilt. I and I alone would have to shake hands with the grim reaper knowing that I was responsible for this innocent young woman's death. She would have turned tail and run if I hadn't convinced her to stay in Morgan's Folly. Stay so I could get my all-important story. Stay only to be murdered by her own sister. Damn me. Damn me to hell.

I turned and stared dully at the ore bucket fastened to the wall not five feet away, wondering vaguely how long it had been there. It looked solid, enduring, like it had hung in that spot for a thousand years. It was huge, probably six feet high. Big enough to haul tons of rocks and dirt. Big enough to hold several people...holy smoke. All at once, I envisioned myself leaping up, launching myself toward the rim, catching hold and dragging myself to safety. It was a beguiling image. But why torture myself? Why entertain the impossible? The rickety boards could never withstand the strain of my full weight, let alone the stress of me jettisoning into the air. Or would they?

From somewhere in the far regions of my soul, amid the raw carnage that passed for the remnants of courage, a tiny ember of hope flared. What did I have to lose? If I did nothing I was toast. So, why not take the chance? Why not go for it?

I reached my arm through the newly created crevice and walked my fingertips along the underside of the boards again, this time with great care. The two that ran directly beneath my hips seemed a little thicker than the others, the fissures not quite as deep. Could they withstand the pressure for a least a few seconds? That's all it would take. A few short seconds. But what if I missed? What if the planks gave way before I could jump?

I retreated to indecision. If for once in my life, I practiced patience, instead of rushing headlong into dicey situations in my usual hotheaded fashion, if for once I remained placid, rescue might eventually come. But there was no guarantee the boards would hold until a search party was dispatched. Back and forth I waffled, plumbing the depths of my resolve until I arrived back at square one. I had to do it. I had to do it now. And I would have only one chance.

My heart began to thud erratically. It rattled and knocked against my rib cage like a trapped bird while a surge of adrenaline revitalized my spirits and set my blood racing. I prayed aloud and flexed my stiff arm and leg muscles while my brain screamed, just go for it!

It was decision time. No more time for rational thought. Heart thundering now, a bonfire burning in my belly, I sat up. Boards dropped away with a sickening crack. Hurry! Get up. Get up. I scrambled to my feet and swayed dizzily above the abyss. Don't look down. Don't think. Breathe. Breathe. Snap! Another board gone.

I focused all my energy on the rim of the bucket, threw my hands back and jumped. For an instant, it seemed I was suspended in the air, unmoving, before my body slammed against the smooth metal surface. Screaming, I scrabbled for a handhold until my fingers curled around the lip. Dangling above the blackness, I dared not look down. I tried to pull myself up but the pain in my injured shoulder grew so intense, I felt my grip weakening. "I can't hold on," I sobbed aloud. "I can't do it!" Frantic with terror, my fingers aching with the exertion of supporting my weight, I searched blindly for a toehold. "Help!" I yelled to no one. "Help me." My left hand gave out and slipped off. I lurched away, my body losing contact with the bucket. It's over. Numb with fear, I hung there murmuring a final prayer when all at once, my right foot made contact with something protruding from the side of it. I rested my weight on it to relieve the agonizing pressure on my fingers, but sheer terror had me trembling so hard I was in danger of losing my one-handed grip.

I tried to keep panic at bay and draw a calming breath, but suddenly my lungs constricted. Air. I could not get enough air. Aware on some level that panic had triggered my asthma, I counseled myself not to give into it. Concentrate on each breath. That's it. Breathe in. Breathe out. Breathe in. Breathe out. Calm down. Try to think rationally.

I eyed the rim again. How was I going to pull myself up with one arm? Ignore the pain, my brain advised. But it seemed an impossible feat. Balancing on my precarious perch, I felt as if every last ounce of stamina had drained from my body. "I can't do it," I whimpered in a small voice. "I can't."

In rapid succession, indelible images of everyone I'd ever known flashed before my eyes. The last one was Tally. "I'm disappointed in you, Kendall," his disapproving eyes seemed to say, "I never took you for a quitter. Someone who'd give up. Throw in the towel."

Then, to my horror his face morphed into a laughing, leering Archie Lawton. "Gotcha, babe! There ain't no way in hell you're getting out of this one."

"Oh, yeah?" I screamed at the repulsive vision. "You bastard. I'm not going to let you beat me!" Good. The anger was good. As if pulled by an invisible rope my left arm swung upward and I folded my fingers over the edge of the bucket. Infused with what seemed a supernatural burst of strength, I hauled myself up with such force I tipped headfirst over the rim, plunging into something murky and wet. Stunned and disoriented, my mind spun out of control. It took a few seconds for the situation to penetrate. I was in water.

I splashed to the surface, coughing and choking. Was this the greatest irony or what? Five minutes ago I'd been praying for water and now I was chest-deep in it. Rain water from the monsoons. Unbelievable. Shrieking like a mad woman I cavorted and splashed around like a child in a wading pool. After pausing a few seconds to ponder the consequences of it being either stagnant or contaminated, I threw caution to the wind and dipped my head to drink like a parched horse at a waterhole.

When my thirst was satisfied the next order of business was to get the hell out of there. If I stood on the rim of the bucket I'd still be several feet shy of the entrance. It appeared that my only route to safety was to scale the series of cables attached to the top of the aging head frame still hunched over the mine. Not a happy thought, but what choice did I have?

I grabbed the cables, but could not resist a quick glimpse down to where I'd lain only moments before. The boards were gone. "My God," I whispered in horrified awe. I looked away. No point dwelling on it now. With freedom as my beacon, I hoisted myself up the remaining few feet and crawled out into the late afternoon sunlight. I collapsed on my stomach, wheezing for breath. Self-congratulations appeared to be in order. Not only had I escaped unscathed from the ordeal, I'd managed to survive my first serious asthma attack in over a year without the benefit of either inhaler or medication. The hot Arizona desert was working its magic.

For I don't know how long, I lay there, holding fast to the earth, savoring its dusky-sweet smell, reconnecting my soul to it. Everything appeared starkly beautiful. Rocks. Cactus. Sky. Sun. Even the little speckled beetle crawling over my fingers. I lifted my face, treasuring the wind's warm caress. Never, ever again would I take anything for granted.

It was probably the after effects of the adrenaline boost, but it seemed to take gargantuan effort to push to my feet. My initial elation dwindled as I turned in a slow circle, searching the horizon for recognizable landmarks. Nothing looked familiar. Where was I? Had I crawled out of that damned hole just to die of thirst and exposure? Surely, God could not be that cruel. I looked at my watch. It was almost six o'clock. Duncan could return with Audrey any time now. A pang of urgency jolted me. How on earth was I going to get back in time to warn her if I didn't know if I was north, south, east or west of Morgan's Folly? And how far would I get without water?

Another irony. There was plenty of water in the ore bucket. If I stayed put, chances were I would survive until help arrived, but if I set off across the desert on foot not having a clue which direction to choose...? I left the thought unfinished as I studied the immediate area scattered with shards of broken glass, splintered wood and bent aluminum cans.

With no other options before me, I gathered up some cans, swallowed my fear and descended into the mouth of the mine once again. I filled two of the containers and, after tucking them in my waistband, climbed the cables again to deposit them at the top. I did this several more times until I was wincing with shoulder pain and too overcome by fatigue to dare venture down again. I slumped to the ground, breathing hard. These precious ounces would have to sustain me against the unforgiving miles I would now have to navigate.

I scanned the distance once more seeing no evident signs of civilization save a row of transmission towers. My eyes followed the wires undulating above the arid landscape like giant silver spider webs until they vanished into southern horizon. I had a strong hunch that Archie and his cohort hadn't transported me too far from Weaverville. Otherwise, their strategy to make it appear that I'd simply strolled away and taken a header into the mineshaft would never fly.

The mental picture of my triumphant return to Morgan's Folly coupled with the captivating image of Archie being handcuffed and hauled off to jail gave me the impetus to get to my feet once more. Which direction should I choose?

My gaze settled on a rocky outcropping that resembled a giant brown toad wearing a Mexican sombrero. It didn't seem all that far away and from the top I might be able to get my bearings. With a deep sigh, I gathered up as many cans as I could carry and, relying solely on intuition, set out across the desert.

My good intentions to conserve water quickly wilted as I trudged through knee-high chaparral and desert broom dotted with yucca and prickly pear. The air, heavy with humidity from the unrealized storm, pressed down on me like a hot compress shrink-wrapping my jeans and shirt to my body. The blowtorch winds that accompanied my every step dried my mouth to the consistency of chalk. How was it possible to be so thirsty when it seemed I'd just consumed a lake full of water? And how could the pile of rocks that had looked so close still look miles away?

Squinting under the merciless sun, I grew more lightheaded by the minute. Aware that dehydration was taking its toll, I wrestled with the idea of turning back. Instead, I steeled my resolve and plodded onward in a dreamy daze. By the time I finally reached the base of the outcropping, my energy level was rapidly approaching zero.

Weak with relief, I stumbled into a blessed patch of shade beneath a rocky shelf and, after carefully balancing the two remaining water cans on a flat stone, collapsed in a heap on the ground.

My ears hummed from the sudden head rush while the mountains in the distance seemed to pulsate eerily with each erratic heartbeat. I closed my eyes and after a few minutes my heart palpitations subsided. With a groan, I rolled onto my back and stared upward to assess the climb. In my feeble state the task looked impossible but somehow I had to marshal enough energy to scale this mammoth pile of boulders. "Get up and get your ass in gear," I said aloud, reminding myself of Audrey's peril.

The mental kick got me to my feet and after deciding that my remaining water would be safer left behind, I swallowed a few sips of the now warm, brackish water and began the arduous climb.

Panting, sweating, and sporting three ragged fingernails, I finally dragged myself to the top. The first thing I caught sight of was the familiar mass of Thunder Peak in the distance and relief poured through me.

I hauled myself up the remaining few feet and lay spread-eagled on the hot, uneven surface like a lizard sunning itself. When I finally gathered enough strength to sit up, I perused the landscape. Using the steepled crown of Thunder Peak as a benchmark to pinpoint southwest and the spiny ridge of the Dragoons as north, that meant the approximate distance to Morgan's Folly was at least ten miles. My heart sank. There was no way, no way on earth I could make it that far by sundown. I squelched my disappointment. No time to dwell on negativity.

My eyes roamed over the jumble of honey-colored hills to my left. If my calculations were correct, Weaverville should be directly behind them. It was sheer torture to envision the red and white thermos tucked behind the passenger seat in my car. I could only pray my abductors hadn't decided to ditch the car someplace else. I stared at my watch, hesitating. I had better be right because I'd already wasted half my water and more than an hour walking in the wrong direction.

After clambering to the bottom again, I permitted myself the luxury of resting a few more minutes before setting out across the desert floor again. The knowledge that I was no longer lost buoyed my spirits and gave me a small measure of confidence—at least for a while.

But as the sun forged its fiery path towards the horizon my stamina was in the toilet. The incessant pain from the blisters on my heels made each step an agonizing challenge and I was firmly convinced that if and when I got myself out of this mess every square inch of skin on my wind-scalded face would peel off.

Protectively, I clutched my last can of water and trod onward towards tawny hills, that still looked light-years away. It would have been easy to feel sorry for myself at that point but then I sharply reminded myself of the promises I'd made only hours ago. "I will not give up," I choked through gritted teeth. "I will survive this. I will find my car. And then I'll drive back to the house and stop Dayln Morgan before she can..."

I let the rest of the horrifying thought slide and concentrated on putting one foot in front of the other while trying to ignore my blinding thirst. But, little by little, my thoughts backtracked to the puzzling events of the past week and as before they led me to the last thing I remembered before Archie's attack. I'd been on my knees reading the dates on the graves of Rita Morgan's unborn babies. I'd gotten to the last one and then...nothing. Whatever it was had vanished into the swirling vortex of trauma-induced amnesia. I was certain the memory was significant, but try as I might I could not retrieve it.

Totally absorbed in my own world, I pulled up short and stared in shock at the gaping hole that suddenly yawned before me. Another abandoned unmarked vertical shaft. "Jeeezus," I breathed aloud. There was no fence. No warning signs. With extreme care, I skirted the sandy perimeter and decided I'd better snap out of my stupor and pay closer attention. I had no desire to repeat the horror of this afternoon. Or worse.

By the time I reached the squat hills, long evening shadows reached towards the surrounding mountain ranges. Crowned with clouds mounded like pink cotton candy, the rocky peaks below glistened in brilliant shades of ochre and sienna while the purple shadows tucked themselves into deep crevices to await nightfall.

The exertion of scaling the incline just about did me in but when I finally stumbled over the crest I let out a wheezy holler. Tears flooded my eyes when I spotted my little blue Volvo snuggled beneath the tree right where I'd left it.

I half-ran, half-slid downhill, zigzagging madly among the gravestones. I raced through the gate with a grateful shudder, relieved that I would not be joining these long buried souls. With trembling hands, I dug the keys from my jeans and unlocked the car door. The trapped heat hit my face like a blast furnace, but everything inside looked wonderfully normal. I grabbed the thermos from behind the passenger seat, tipped it up and unceremoniously drank from the spout. Amazingly, the water was fairly cool and I was sure nothing in my life would ever taste that good again. I fell into the seat and revved the engine. The clock on the dashboard told the tale. Twenty minutes until eight. Was I too late?

I gunned the car down the dirt road. Only when I reached the main highway did I falter. Why hadn't I taken the time to revisit the graves? It might have triggered the forgotten memory. Half of me wanted to turn the car around but the sensible half won out. Whatever information lay there would do me little good if Audrey was already in the clutches of her obviously deranged sister.

That thought alone provoked a pang of near panic and I floored the gas pedal, recklessly breaking any number of speed and safety laws as I drove like one possessed back towards Morgan's Folly. For once, I wished that a sheriff's deputy would appear, but the road was devoid of traffic with the exception of one hapless driver who happened along just as I careened around a hairpin curve straddling the center line. The look of horror frozen on the poor man's face as I swerved to the right and rocketed past him sent me into a fit of hysterical giggling. It wasn't really funny but I could not stop myself.

Familiar sights jumped into view and icy fear coiled in my gut when I spotted the steep driveway. Oh, my God. Had I made it in time? I hung a sharp left and blasted the car up the incline just as the sun slid behind the jagged horns of Devil's Hill into a molten butterscotch sky.

I roared into the parking area and skidded to a stop. I threw the door open, sprinted up the walkway and burst into the kitchen, shouting, "Audrey! Audrey! Where are you?"

The spacious room was empty. Still calling her name, I slammed through the swinging doors and bolted across the breezeway to the old section of the house. I took the stairs two at a time and arrived in Audrey's bedroom only to find it deserted and bearing no signs that she'd been there since this morning. With the exception of my tortured breathing and the steady ticking of the antique clock on Audrey's dresser, there wasn't another sound in the house. It was a hair past eight. I couldn't believe it. Either I'd made it back before Duncan, or something was terribly wrong.

I hotfooted it back down the stairs stopping in my bedroom only long enough to peel off my sand-filled sneakers. And peel was the operative word. The pain of disengaging my socks from the raw silver dollar sized blisters on my heels made my eyes water. I toed into a pair of thongs and started for the door when I caught sight of my reflection in the full-length mirror. It stopped me cold. I hardly recognized myself. My clothes were torn and filthy. And my hair—unruly in the best of circumstances, framed my scarlet face like a flame-colored dandelion. I looked like something out of a freak show. The urge to shed my clothes, soak in a foamy tub of bubbles and slather a soothing ointment on my burnt skin was almost overwhelming, but it would have to wait until I determined Audrey's whereabouts. I returned to the kitchen, this time shouting Marta's name. No answer. Where was everyone?

It was my plan to search the grounds, but first things first. I grabbed the water pitcher from the refrigerator and drank until the unexpected jangle of the phone shattered the silence. For a long second I stared dumbfounded as if it were some alien contraption before snatching the receiver from the hook. Please let it be Audrey. "Yes?" I shouted expectantly.

A short pause and then a puzzled, "Ah...I need to talk to Kendall O'Dell."

The familiar voice sent a surge of joy zinging through me. "Ginger! It's me."

"Sugar? Your voice sounds kind of weird."

I coughed and cleared my throat. Where to start? "Let's just say I've had better days."

"What in blazes is going on? I been getting a stupid busy signal for hours."

"The phones got knocked out in the storm last night."

"Oh. Well, any hoot, I talked to Phil over at the pharmacy again, and it turns out you guessed right."

"About what?"

"You know. About suspecting that handyman of yours might be taking something different than the drug I was telling you about last night."

"What is it?"

"Phil says it might be...hmmmm, let's see here. I can't read my own stupid writing. Oh, yeah, now I ain't exactly positive I'm pronouncing it correctly, but he says it could be something called Deca-durabolin."

I drew a total blank. "Okay. What's that?"

She giggled. "Phil said if this guy's taking as high a dose of the stuff as you say, then he's most likely got himself a real serious male potency problem."

Her explanation wasn't registering at all. "Ginger," I said, striving for patience, "tell me what Deca-durabolin is."

"Testosterone."

"Testosterone?" I echoed, incredulous. "Now why in the world..."

A sharp gasp from behind startled me. Marta stood in the doorway gawking at me in open-mouthed astonishment. Keenly aware of my disheveled appearance, I couldn't blame her.

"Miss O'Dell!" she cried, dropping the basket of laundry at her feet. "You come back so soon?" She looked me up and down like she could hardly believe her eyes.

So soon? My mind lurched in a hundred different directions. "I just now got here. Is Audrey back yet?"

Her look of total bewilderment baffled me. "Mr. Duncan brings her only a short time ago, but then she goes out again in a big, big hurry."

"Why?"

"To be with you."

Now it was my turn to stare. "With me? Why would you think that?"

"You did not call for her on the telephone?"

"No, I did not." Ginger was still yapping away in my ear, but I was electrified by Marta's look of anxious intensity.

"But...but...the woman who calls...says she is you. She is in very much trouble and Miss Audrey must hurry to the mine to help..."

Little hammers of fear pounded at my temples. "What mine?"

"The Defiance."

Oh, shit. Oh, shit. "Marta, that wasn't me! What do you mean she left? How did she leave?"

"She drives the big car..."

"What? You know she has epilepsy. Why would you let her do that?"

Marta pressed a finger to trembling lips. "She tells me it is okay...because you teach her."

"Oh, Jesus."

"Kendall! Kendall!" Ginger screeched in my ear. "For pity's sake, what's going on? You ain't been listening to a word I been saying..."

Cold with dread, my mind reeling in total chaos, I cut her short. "Ginger, I've got to go right now."

"Hold your horses for two seconds. You know that second thingamajiggy in Colorado you asked me about? Well, Brian finally found some stuff about it on the Internet. It's called the Berdache Society and well, you just ain't going to believe this but..."

As I listened to her explanation, the fresh winds of truth blew through my tired brain. The stunning revelation triggered the forgotten vision of the infant's gravesite at the Weaversville cemetery. The date on the little cross, jumped into sharp relief. Rita's last baby had died in August. August! "Holy cow," I breathed, absently hanging up on Ginger. I bolted for the door shouting to Marta, "Call the sheriff! Now! Tell him to meet me at the Defiance."

In a flash, I was in my car and speeding down the driveway. "You idiot! You stupid, stupid idiot!" I raged as tears of frustration blurred my eyes. If I hadn't encouraged her, Audrey would never have driven alone to the mine, never have fallen into this carefully laid trap. And it would be my fault. "Goddamn it!" I shrieked, pounding the wheel. "Goddamn me!"

Sick with guilt and fear, my thoughts bouncing around like Ping-Pong balls, I hurled down the highway taking the curves so fast I almost overshot the mine road. Tires squealing, I braked, wrenched the car sharply right and fishtailed into the turn. With the scarlet remains of the sunset flashing between the pines, I skimmed along the uneven road, painfully aware that my carefully constructed theory about Grady's tormentor had been wrong. One hundred percent dead wrong. Why hadn't I caught on earlier? The mellow voice, the sparse facial hair, the baggy clothes, the ever-present photo chromic lenses—the insider's knowledge that Audrey whose birth month was October, could not possibly be Rita Morgan's child. So then, who was this frail young imposter who bore such a strong resemblance to Grady Morgan? Wait a minute. My mind back flipped to the contents of the anonymous phone message made to Haston and Jesse. 'Don't be fooled,' the woman had warned. 'Ask the doctor, he knows the truth.' When I combined that with the menacing whisper in my ear just hours ago insinuating my interference with destiny, the foggy picture suddenly crystallized.

It was an incredible leap of logic, but could there be any other explanation? If I was right, Rita Morgan's cryptic letter, plus her plea for Audrey's forgiveness and Dr. Orcutt's zealous refusal to discuss Dayln Morgan all made sense.

In the thickening dusk, I switched on my headlights and frantically searched for any signs of Audrey's car. I burst into the clearing and saw a dim light burning in the window of the mobile home office. After practically standing my Volvo on its grill, I left the engine running and stormed inside. A frenzied search revealed no one. It wasn't surprising the night watchman wasn't on duty. Of course not. Of course not. Heart lodged in my throat, I rushed back outside and searched the gloomy equipment yard. Nothing.

Cursing aloud, I jumped back in the car and raced up the narrow gravel road that led to the mine. I was on the right track all right. The metal gate, closed and locked on my last trip, stood open. I rounded the final curve and was heading towards the mine entrance when out of the corner of my eye I saw movement at the bottom of the hill. I jammed on the brakes, leapt from the car and raced to the edge of the road.

I could hardly believe my own eyes. Eerily illuminated in the cool blue light of the full moon, I could see the big car lying half-submerged in the leach pond and nearby was the spectacle of two figures struggling in waist-deep water.

"Stop!" I shouted, charging down the rocky hillside. "Don't hurt her." The thongs afforded me zero traction, and I ended up sliding and tumbling down the slippery embankment before landing in a heap at the bottom. A fiery pain shot through my injured shoulder and for long seconds, I lay there dizzy and disoriented until the sounds of thrashing and Audrey's choked pleas for help propelled me to my feet. I plunged into the pond. "Stop it, let her go!"

I fought my way through the stagnant water, arriving on the scene in time to see the murderous expression on D.J.'s face as Audrey's head was pushed beneath the murky surface. Stiff-armed, I lunged forward hard enough to send D.J. toppling backwards with a shout of outrage. "You meddling bitch! This time, you're dead."

I hauled a choking, gagging Audrey to the surface, pulled her next to me and turned to face D.J. once more, gasping out, "You're never going to get away with this."

"Watch me."

I said, "Look, I know why you think Audrey is an imposter but..."

"Shut the hell up," D.J. growled, advancing again, fists clenched, teeth bared.

"Listen to me," I implored. "You might be able to pull off having it look like she had a car accident and then drown but how are you going to explain me? Huh? Think about that."

D.J.'s demonic smile was chilling. "I've come way

too far to let you stop me now."

Whimpering, Audrey shrank close to my side as I fervently prayed that my hypothesis was correct. It had better be or we were both in deep shit. It seemed beyond cruel for Audrey to have to find out the repulsive truth in this way, but what choice did I have? "You're making a terrible mistake. Let's all try to calm down so we can talk..."

"Get the hell out of my way."

I put up a warning hand. "No! No, I won't. I know who you are and if you go through with this...you'll be murdering your own daughter."

All movement came to an abrupt halt and after a few seconds of breathless silence Audrey gasped, "What? You...you're my father?"

"No," I answered quietly, looking across the moon-dappled water at the pinched, white face. "D.J. is your mother."

By late Monday afternoon I decided to delay my scheduled departure for home until the following morning for several reasons, one being that I was totally whipped. It had been one hell of a weekend, but it had been worth the loss of sleep to be front row center during the gut-wrenching confessions of Dayln Morgan, Miles Orcutt and Bitsy Bigelow.

Half-listening to the muted chirping of birds outside, I stood amid the bright shafts of sunlight blanching the hardwood floor and stared in dismay at the flurry of notes spread out on my bed, dresser, and on the floor next to my half-packed suitcase. Having talked to Ginger less than an hour ago, I knew Tugg would most likely be returning my phone call any minute. Somehow I had to get this avalanche of material into some kind of logical sequence and even then, this incredibly convoluted tale was likely to sound more like fiction than fact.

Aside from that, I had no intention of leaving without a conclusion to this remarkable story. In what I suspect had turned into a pivotal meeting at the mine office, Audrey, Duncan, Haston, and Jesse Pickrell had already been sequestered for nearly three hours. Whatever settlement was hashed out would no doubt seal the fate of Morgan's Folly. I was dying to hear the outcome, but then, I couldn't be in two places at once. It had been equally critical for me to meet with Orville Kemp and file formal charges of attempted rape and murder against the now-missing Archie Lawton. He'd probably hotfooted it across the border by now and grim reality set in. Even if he was apprehended a conviction was a long-shot at best and if the case ever got to court I could easily imagine the defense attorney's plea '...and so your Honor, Ms. O'Dell admits she never saw her alleged assailant, so how can she positively identify my client... blah, blah, blah...' And he or she would be right. It would be my word against Archie's.

But, more importantly, there was no way on earth I could leave until I knew how Audrey planned to resolve the extraordinary situation pertaining to the anguished soul who was both her mother and her half-sister. Considering what we now knew concerning the dreadful circumstances surrounding her life, could Audrey find it in her heart to file charges of attempted murder? And if she refused, what should my next move be?

I thanked my lucky stars I wasn't in her unenviable position as I settled myself cross-legged on the floor and picked up my legal pad. Might as well start with last Friday night. It had been high drama at its best.

By the time sheriff's deputies arrived at the mine, Audrey, still reeling from the astonishing turn of events, had made a landmark decision. For the time being, until we'd sorted through the appalling details contained in D.J.'s faltering confession delivered a mere half hour earlier, we would say nothing to the authorities concerning her true identity. Weeping copious tears, Audrey begged me to corroborate her hastily contrived story that she had indeed suffered a seizure and run the car off the road.

Cognizant of her fragile emotional state, I reluctantly agreed. It was not lost on me what a momentous occasion I had just witnessed in the wake of my shocking declaration. The two dripping wet women had confronted one another, surveying each other with equal doses of horror and disbelief before Audrey suddenly lunged forward and began pummeling D.J.'s chest. "What kind of a monster are you?" she screamed. "Why would you want to kill your own child? How could you? How could you?"

Ashen-faced, D.J. stood still as a marble statue offering no defense to Audrey's flailing fists.

"Audrey, stop it." I wrestled the sobbing young woman away as Dayln murmured trance-like, "But, Dr. Orcutt said my baby died. How could I know?"

"How about we take this conversation to dry land," I said, motioning for Dayln to assist me with Audrey whose teeth-chattering, glassy-eyed expression convinced me she might convulse at any second. Once on shore, I hiked back uphill and returned with a car blanket, which I wrapped around her trembling shoulders. Then, as the three of us sat facing each other on the moonlit bank of the leach pond, Dayln began to recount the story of her tragic life, beginning with the sexual abuse by her father at the tender age of six. Cowering under threats that her confession could cause the death of her chronically ill mother, Dayln kept the ugly secret to herself. Adding to her misery was the burgeoning suspicion that there was something else terribly wrong. With each passing day, she became increasingly convinced she was a prisoner of the wrong sex trapped in her female body. The abuse, combined with Grady's thinly-veiled disappointment that she would never be the son he so desperately yearned for, nor the male heir her grandmother Hannah had craved, generated feelings of self-loathing so acute that she contemplated suicide shortly after her mother's death. It wasn't until she was thirteen, and terrified that she was pregnant, did she finally gather the courage to divulge the abuse to her stepmother, Rita Barnes. When confronted by his horrified wife, Grady vehemently denied the charge and instead cited Dayln's wild reputation and propensity for lying. He pointed the finger of paternity to the boy she'd supposedly stolen from Bitsy Bigelow—none other than the totally revolting Archie Lawton.

"When Rita bought his bogus story, I just snapped," Dayln confessed in a hollow voice, admitting that it had been her intention to kill her father and how that act had prompted her subsequent removal to the psychiatric facility in Coolidge. "I remember some things pretty clear in the beginning, but later on they kept me so zonked on drugs, sometimes it's hard for me to remember what was real and what wasn't except for..." she paused, swallowed hard and continued hoarsely, "except the night of the fire."

Two blinking squad cars screeching to a halt on the road above aborted the remainder of her story until we had given the officers our fictional version of the incident. By the time we arrived back at the house, my shoulder was throbbing and I was so exhausted I could barely see straight. But after soaking in the most glorious bath of my life and consuming a sizeable late-night snack, I'd felt revitalized enough to stay awake until the wee hours to hear the continuation of Dayln's unfortunate tale before falling into a restless sleep.

Then, armed with an arsenal of new information, I rose early and made a beeline for the doctor's house. A dispirited-looking Fran Orcutt answered my request to speak with her husband with an obviously lame account of his sudden inability to come to the door. Sure. A likely story. Judging by her look of watchful anxiety, I had a feeling he was standing just of sight. Coward.

She was in the process of executing the door-closing bit when I caught her eye. "I've been to Weaverville," I said softly. "Tell him the secrets of the dead are out of the bag."

With a look of angst flitting across her sallow features, she motioned for me to wait. Less than a minute later an apparently rejuvenated, yet sour-faced Dr. Orcutt appeared in the doorway. "Ms. O'Dell, I told you there'd be no further discussion on..."

"Cool it, Doc. Dayln Morgan is alive."

Mouth agape, his eyes bulged like two bloodshot golf balls. "That's...that's simply not possible."

"Oh, but it is."

My unwavering rejoinder apparently convinced him. He shot a panicked look over his shoulder, signaled for me to remain silent, then hustled me into his study and closed the door.

As I confronted him with the damning details of D.J.'s confession, he collapsed into a chair and appeared to shrink before my eyes. When I concluded, he cast me a beseeching look. "As God is my witness, I never intended to harm anyone. Please don't judge me too harshly until you've heard my side of the story."

"That's why I'm here." I switched on my tape recorder and sat down opposite him. The first surprise came when I learned that the bond connecting him to Grady was not friendship, but fear. One warm summer night in 1966, Grady had chanced upon the doctor and Rita Barnes leaving a Bisbee motel room. Horrified, Dr. Orcutt pleaded with his lifelong friend to safeguard their secret and amazingly he had—until payoff time arrived.

"So Grady threatened to expose your affair if you didn't go along with the commitment scheme which was really just a ploy to hide his daughter's pregnancy."

The last bit of color seeped from his face. "When I arrived at the house late that night, Dayln was hysterical, out of control. I finally sedated her because I felt she might be a danger to Grady or herself."

"So you didn't accept her claim that Grady was the father of her child. Why?"

A tortured sigh. "Frankly, I didn't know which one of them to believe. You have to remember that from childhood, Dayln had a history of concocting odd tales. Now I understand her strange behavior, but at the time, I had no knowledge of her situation. So, just to be on the safe side, I didn't see any harm in placing her temporarily in a protective situation until she could be evaluated."

"Whose idea was it to pass Dayln's baby off as Rita's?"

"It was...mine."

I shook my head in wonder. "As a physician, why on earth would you agree to take part in something so...unethical?"

He bowed his head and great wracking sobs filled the wood-paneled room. At that moment, I couldn't help but feel a bit sorry for this man whose wrong-headed decisions had affected so many lives.

Minutes passed before he regained his composure. Watery-eyed, he reached for a tissue box and blew his nose before continuing. "I fully intended to take this secret to the grave with me. Because of...what I did it seemed to be the best solution for everyone."

He looked like he was going to lose it again, but then he took a few deep breaths before explaining how he and Rita had become lovers only months after her husband's death in the tragic Defiance mining accident. The same accident also claimed Grady's brother, Oliver who had stepped in to take his irresponsible brother's shift that fateful day. Afterwards, consumed with guilt and castigated by his family, Grady had begun a downward spiral into alcoholism and madness.

Dr. Orcutt detailed his panic when Rita confessed to him that she was four months pregnant. "I loved her with all my heart, but I had a wife and children and a reputation to protect, for God's sake, so I...I convinced her to let me terminate the pregnancy."

I did a quick mental calculation. Unreal. Not only had this man aborted his own child, he'd risked having his medical license revoked by performing what was at the time an illegal procedure. I tried to imagine the all-consuming desperation that would have provoked such a decision. "But something went wrong," he said. "Because of my mistake, Rita was never able to carry a child to term."

"So, you made it up to her by giving her Dayln's baby."

Nodding, he stared at me with red-rimmed eyes.

"Dr. Orcutt, your wife suspects the affair with Rita continued even after she married Grady. I think she also believes that Audrey is your child. Don't you think she deserves to know the truth?"

He flashed me a bitter look. "Everyone in the world will know after you leave here today, won't they?"

The tone of censure in his remark exemplified the struggle I was having with my own conscience. I'd damned well earned the right to print this piece, but was acutely aware that its publication would destroy the lives of each person involved. I masked my uneasiness behind another question. "I still don't understand why Rita married a scoundrel like Grady Morgan?"

He studied his fingertips before answering. "Who knows? Spite. Panic. Maybe both. Even though we took precautions, she got pregnant again. She pleaded with me to divorce Fran and marry her and when I refused she vowed she'd find someone to be a father to our child."

"But why him?"

"I told you. When he wasn't drinking, he could charm the spots off a leopard."

But Rita had lost that baby too and the next but was still carrying the one now buried beneath the last tiny marker at the old Weaverville cemetery when the explosive situation with her stepdaughter erupted. After Dayln's two unsuccessful suicide attempts at the asylum, Dr. Orcutt had made the difficult decision to sedate her and take Audrey two months early. The rest was history.

The shock of a cold wet nose on my arm pulled me back to the present and I looked up from my notes to see Princess sitting beside me, gold eyes aglitter. I stroked the cat's soft fur. "Hey, girl, did you come to say goodbye?"

I was beginning to wonder why Tugg hadn't returned my call when the phone jangled. Notebook in hand, I jumped to my feet and hurried to answer the parlor phone. I grabbed up the receiver and listened to Tugg's vociferous complaints of how difficult it was trying to conduct business in the midst of the remodeling chaos. "I can't even find my goddamned desk," he grumbled.

I felt a fleeting twinge of guilt. "Sorry I left you with such a mess, Tugg, but when you hear this I think you'll agree the trip was worthwhile."

During the time it took to fill him in on the events since our last conversation, Tugg whistled surprise, marveling, "Are you shitting me?"

"No."

"So, this D.J. fella, er...whatever, is not only the girl's half-sister and biological mother, but gay too?"

"That's not what I said. Dayln Morgan is a transsexual."

"Oh, man. I thought you said Bitsy was his...her girlfriend. Are you telling me she doesn't know D.J. is a woman? How is that possible?"

I didn't blame him one bit for sounding bewildered. It had taken an hour of explanation by Dr. Orcutt, plus reading several articles he'd given me on the subject of gender dysphoria before I had developed a clearer understanding of Dayln's seemingly bizarre behavior.

"Think of it this way. Since childhood, Dayln has believed she's actually male, so her feelings for Bitsy, while appearing homosexual on the surface, are actually heterosexual. She's been able to avoid sex because she invented a clever story about suffering from a rare physical problem that would soon be corrected with surgery."

"No shit she has a physical problem," Tugg said with a derisive snort. "Hells bells. I've covered a bunch of weird stories in my time, but this one's got to win some kind of prize."

"I've hardly begun," I said, flipping the page over. I

went on to recount Dayln's twenty tortured years of existence after leaving Morgan's Folly, her string of failed relationships, odd jobs, and brushes with the law until she'd connected with a support group called the Berdache Society. She received guidance from sympathetic counselors who assisted her through what is termed as "passing" into "full-time" which is the period of one year when transsexuals have the opportunity to become completely habituated to their role performance, or in other words, live openly in the role of the opposite sex. After conferring with a qualified physician, the transsexual is also required to consult with a psychiatrist who can prescribe large doses of either female or male hormones, which must be taken during the year prior to the sex-change surgery. In Dayln's case, she was taking large doses of testosterone, which shrank her breasts and increased her facial and body hair.

"So, that's why the guys at the bar thought he...or rather she was gay at first," Tugg said. "She'd just started taking the hormones and beefed up as time went by."

"You got it. It also accounted for her wild mood swings and because of the expense and the large amount of drugs required, she paid Archie to fence the goods she took from the house, including the car at Toomey's garage. She then used the trips to Mexico with Marta as a cover to buy the drugs at the pharmacia and save for the sex-change surgery."

"How much does something like that cost?"

"The change from male to female can exceed fifty thousand and conversely, female to male can run substantially higher. That's why the town of Trinidad seemed familiar to me. I'd read an article in a magazine last year about it being the sex change capital of the United

States because the doctor who runs the hospital there does two or three of these surgeries a week."

"Jee-zuss," Tugg muttered. "This is all beginning to click now."

I continued. "With nowhere else to turn for the amount of money she was going to need she returned to the one place in the world she knew she could get it. Dressed in men's clothing and wearing the photo chromic lenses helped hide her identity and allow her to live openly as a guy. She was then free to steal things from her own house, which she justified in her own mind as being rightfully her own stuff. And hey, why not bump off her lecherous old dad to boot."

"Sounds like he certainly deserved it."

"No argument on that from me." Last night, Dayln had admitted taking advantage of Grady's deteriorating condition to dispense her own unique method of justice. She began by making anonymous calls from the pay phone at Toomey's garage then, using her intimate knowledge of the house she was able to carry out her masquerade as the 'angel of death'. Her position as night watchman at the Defiance allowed her to come and go at will using the abandoned mine road on Devil's Hill. That explained the reflection I'd seen last Thursday when I'd returned unexpectedly to get the photo albums, which she had already gone through to remove any remaining pictures that might reveal her identity. I thought it fortunate that she'd inherited her mother's soft features instead of the telltale dark brows of the Morgan family.

"But," I told Tugg, "she swears his death was accidental. With the intent of blackmailing him for the balance of the money she needed, she admits confronting him that night with her true identity. She claims he was backing away from her in disbelief when he toppled over the edge. His final words mean something now. He didn't say 'the day is come', he said, 'Dayln has come. Justice is done.' We can only guess that perhaps he had an attack of conscience in his final moments."

Tugg huffed impatiently. "It was a tad late. I hope he and Satan are spending a lot of quality time together."

I agreed and went on. "After his fall, she panicked and was heading for the back door when she tripped over Princess who ran out and hissed at Marta when she entered the living room seconds later. Dayln barely made it outside and was hiding in the bushes when Marta discovered Grady in the ravine. When Marta went back inside to call the sheriff, Dayln made a dash for her place. That's when Marta caught a glimpse of her in the moonlight and that's when she lost the barrette."

Tugg fell silent again and then asked, "But, why the hell did she wait twenty years to come back to Morgan's Folly?"

"That's the second fascinating part of this story. She couldn't come home because she lived in abject terror that she would be charged in connection with the fire that killed all those kids at the Children's Colony."

"Did she set it?"

"Not directly."

"What does that mean?"

"I'll explain." After leaving Dr. Orcutt's house that morning, I'd cornered Bitsy Bigelow at the coffee shop. Without disclosing D.J.'s true identity, I revealed just enough of the story to convince her that I had proof she'd been at the asylum that night and she tearfully confessed her unwitting role in the tragedy.

"Up until then Bitsy had ignored Dayln's

impassioned letters that she come visit her," I told Tugg, "because she believed Grady's deception that Dayln had been seeing Archie behind her back. But, Dayln persisted and finally convinced her that she and Archie were just good friends and of course, that was the truth. She never had a romantic interest in Archie. Her interest was in Bitsy, which she could not divulge. Anyway, Bitsy finally agreed to come and hear her out. She had a friend drive her out there and she brought along a few personal items Dayln had requested, including cigarettes and matches. Now, because Grady feared the true story might leak out, Dayln was never allowed visitors unless he, Rita or Dr. Orcutt was present. Rebellious as ever, Dayln developed an ongoing friendship with one of the male attendants who was able to sneak Bitsy inside. For his own entertainment that night he also smuggled in his current Hispanic girlfriend who was not only an illegal, but a minor as well. Bitsy said the two of them talked all evening and around ten o'clock Dayln offered to trade her gold charm necklace to the attendant's girlfriend if the two of them would go get some booze. A few of the older kids joined in and I guess it was quite a party during which Dayln confided to Bitsy that she had devised a foolproof plan to escape using whatever means were necessary."

"Like burning the place to the ground?" Tugg's words were laden with disgust.

I cut in, "Don't jump to conclusions. I'm not through yet. Bitsy left around midnight and afterwards Dayln claims she fell into a drunken stupor. Unfortunately, someone fell asleep with a smoldering cigarette. She says she'd drunk so much vodka that night, it was a miracle she survived. The smoke and screaming of the other kids woke her and the only reason she escaped the inferno, was knowing which kitchen door had been left unlocked. That's when the woman Ida Fairfield hired to keep an eye on things saw her running away and that's how the story that she started the fire began."

"Okay, if she didn't start it, who did?"

"No one knows. But get this. To save his own skin, the male attendant never uttered a word about his liaison with the illegal Hispanic girl and because she was never reported missing, that solves the mystery of the correct body count of twenty-eight. No further investigation was considered necessary and because the girl was wearing Dayln's necklace, she's the one buried in Weaverville."

"Man oh man," Tugg said, "so, that's why the Bigelow woman didn't want to talk about the Morgan girl. She thought Dayln had started the fire."

"Yep. And she was scared to death that she'd be implicated."

"There's still something I don't get. Why was D.J. so doggoned positive from the get-go that Audrey wasn't Rita Morgan's kid?"

"Oh, I forgot the most important part. After Dayln's second suicide attempt at the institution..."

"Hold it, hold it. If there wasn't really anything mentally wrong with her, why was she trying to kill herself?"

"According to Dayln, she could not reconcile in her mind that there was a baby growing inside her. How could a man physically have a child? The very thought of it was so repugnant, so alien to her, she went off the deep end."

"Pretty sad, " Tugg sighed. "But anyway, back to my original question."

"Yes. Well, Rita, who had miscarried again, came to visit Dayln at the facility. Apparently, she'd finally consulted with another physician who gave her the unhappy news that she would never be able to bear children. She shared this information with Dayln and begged her to not harm herself for her baby's sake. Dayln remembered that conversation, so two weeks ago when she overheard the phone call between Dr. Orcutt and Haston, she was totally convinced that Audrey was an imposter scheming with Dr. Orcutt to claim her inheritance."

I flipped the page and continued reading from Dayln's confession. Head bowed and choking back tears, she admitted that desperation for money drove her to initiate the attempts on Audrey's and subsequently my life, starting with the phone call to Audrey impersonating Dr. Orcutt's nurse in order to lure us to Boneyard Pass. It was Archie's white truck I'd seen disappearing around the bend in the road ahead. They'd unlocked the gate, removed the warning sign, set the old drainpipe in the road to slow us down and then lay in wait to send the boulder plummeting down on us. When they learned later that I was a reporter, they'd hatched the pathetic ruse to have Archie waylay me that first day outside the Muleskinner.

The day of our planned Bisbee trip, she had been hiding in the old kitchen and overheard me telling Tally about her association with Archie. Fearful that Audrey would then fire her, she tampered with the brakes on the red Corvette she had prepared for us to take on the mountainous road. Of course that plan failed when we chose the Packard instead so she took advantage of the storm that night to frighten Audrey again by masquerading as the ghost. But it wasn't until she'd read the epilepsy book I'd left in my room and overheard Audrey bragging about the driving lesson I'd given her, that she'd conceived the idea to lure the unsuspecting young woman to the mine and stage the accident. My trip to Weaverville fit perfectly into her plans. At the edge of town, she faked engine trouble and arranged for Toby to continue on to Mexico with Marta in his car. The morphine she'd injected in my arm had come from the same pharmacia where she obtained her Deca-durabolin. She claimed that Archie had actually done the dirty work by taking me to the abandoned mine where they'd arranged to have my death look like an unfortunate accident.

Tugg was understandably upset when I laid that news on him. "Promise you won't say anything to Tally about that last part. I'd prefer to explain what happened when I see him in person."

"He's gonna go ballistic."

"I know. And I'll be the first to admit this one was a bit close for comfort."

"Hang on a minute," Tugg said. I heard him conversing with someone and then he came back on the line. "I've got to talk to the electrician, but one more thing before I go. Why, after the elaborate subterfuge about Dayln's baby dying at birth and all that did Rita Morgan give up everything, take Audrey, and run out on Grady in the dead of night three years later?"

"Can't you guess?"

There was a heavy silence and then, "Oh, no, don't tell me."

"Afraid so. It seemed life was finally going right for Rita until one night she happened upon Grady and Audrey in the tower room."

He muttered, "Christ. Does she know?"

"I think she had a glimmer of it last week when we were in there briefly, and even though she may not remember now, Dr. Orcutt suspects she will have to deal with it sooner or later. Of course, Rita knew at that instant that Dayln had been telling the truth all along, not to mention the awful realization that Audrey was actually Grady's own daughter."

Tugg grunted, "What a sicko."

"Yeah. It's no wonder the poor woman suffered from depression all those years. Not only did she live in terror that Grady might somehow track them down, but she also had her own guilt to deal with."

"What do you mean?"

"Remember when I told you that Audrey said Rita would never acknowledge that she knew anything about her epilepsy?"

"Uh huh."

"Dr. Orcutt told me that Rita believed that she was responsible for it because of Audrey's fall down the stairs that night."

"Oh, what a tangled web," Tugg said and then his tone brightened. "Well, my dear, looks like you've got a winner. This piece is going to double our circulation for sure!"

"Yeah." Why wasn't I ecstatic? This was the greatest story of my career. I should have been on top of the world.

"So, when are you coming back?" Tugg asked.

After informing him of my plans to depart in the morning, I thanked him again for his help, returned to the bedroom to finish writing my copy, and pack the remainder of my clothes. It was closing in on seven o'clock and I was growing more and more curious about Audrey's whereabouts. Why hadn't she returned? Then, as if my thoughts had somehow been relayed, I heard the distinctive growl of the red Jaguar. From my window, I watched it glide to a stop near the kitchen door. Duncan jumped out, ran around the front of the car and opened Audrey's door.

In the lengthening shadows of early evening, they stood facing each other, talking in low tones, and then Duncan pulled her into his arms. She leaned into his chest and he tenderly kissed the top of her head. My eyes stung and my heart soared with the delicious realization that I was witnessing the dawn of something wonderful and the demise of the ancient feud between the Claypools and the Morgans.

I waited until Duncan's car had vanished through the gate in a haze of dust before I walked down the steps to join her in the driveway. "So, I gather things are working out to everyone's liking?" I said, flashing her an expectant grin.

Her lips curved in a secretive little smile. "I hope so. After Jesse got over her tantrum, we made some progress. There are a hundred details to work out, but I've decided to allow Haston and Duncan to reopen the mine."

Chills ran up my arms. This was indeed a story made in heaven. "If that happens, I don't think you'll be simply mayor of Morgan's Folly, I'm pretty sure they'll give you a crown and declare you queen for life."

"Queen of Morgan's Folly sounds pretty cool, but like I said, it all depends on whether we can iron out all of the other problems."

Speaking of problems yet to be resolved, I hadn't seen hide or hair of Dayln the entire day and wondered what must be going through her mind. Earlier this afternoon, I'd witnessed Dr. Orcutt's anticipated pilgrimage to her cottage. As he drove past, he'd made fleeting eye contact with me and the expression on his face could only be described as profound dread. But, I was gratified to see Fran seated beside him wearing an air of grim determination.

I said, "No doubt one of your problems will be Willow Windsong. When she gets wind of the mine opening again, she's sure to rally the troops against you."

"I hope not, because I intend to honor the agreement my father didn't. Jesse and Haston had a monster hissy fit but I wouldn't budge. I insisted that part of the property be set aside for a riparian preserve or the mine stays closed."

I nodded approval. She'd turned into quite the little negotiator. But, I detected another subtle difference in her too. It was there in her eyes, a new boldness fortified by self-confidence. "And what about you, Audrey? Are you going to stay here or go back home and let the men handle things?"

A little shrug accompanied her sigh. "I'm still not sure. I think I might stay around for a while. There are a lot of things I like about Arizona. Especially the sunsets," she added, inclining her head towards the blazing horizon.

I grinned. "The sunsets. Of course."

A comfortable silence ensued until I broke it. "Audrey, what are we going to do about..." I gestured towards D.J.'s cottage.

A sudden look of uncertainty superceded her newly acquired confidence. "I don't know. After you went to bed last night, we talked longer and she told me she was the one who snitched to Grady about Duncan's offer to buy the mine. She said that after everything she'd been through, she couldn't stand by and have the mine be sold out from under her. She admits that she relished causing as much trouble as possible, but, she also said that it's been sheer torture not to be able to come forward with the truth."

"Does that mean she intends to challenge the will?"

Audrey's face softened. "She says no, Kendall, and she seems...truly sorry about everything that happened. She claims she'll be happy as long as she can get the money she needs for...well, you know."

"And what about you, Audrey? Are you okay with this...situation?"

She looked heavenward as if the answer lay there. "I don't know, Kendall. The whole thing is still totally mind-boggling. I mean, I can't ever think of her as my mother, and she won't exactly be my sister so...I guess I'll have to settle for having...what? An older brother?"

In thoughtful silence, we both watched the sky behind Devil's Hill ripen from coral into a brilliant sea of cinnamon dotted with islands of gray clouds. Musing aloud, I said, "It's kind of a strange twist of fate, isn't it?"

"What is?"

"Thy will be done," I murmured. "Remember? That was Dayln's promise to her grandmother's portrait. Think about it. Completion of the surgery means she will fulfill the prophesy and become the male heir all the Morgans so desperately craved."

She absorbed my comment and her gaze grew introspective. "The money will be nice, really nice for both of us, but all I really want is to try and have some kind of normal life and now, I guess that sort of depends on you."

I drew back. "Me? How?"

She edged me a look of quiet desperation and turned to stare out over the rooftops nestled in the valley. For long seconds, there was no sound save the muffled cheeping of birds settling into the treetops. When she spoke, her voice quavered. "Kendall, I don't even know how to begin to thank you for all you've done for me and I don't know how I can ever repay..."

"Don't worry about it. Having the story is repayment enough, but as far as Dayln goes, I'm not as willing as you are to just forgive and forget."

"Wait!" she cut in. "I've agonized over this all day and well...I keep thinking of something my Mom used to say. Sometimes we have to do what we think is best even if others might consider it wrong."

Her words punched me in the gut. "Jesus, Audrey. Are you asking me to stand aside and give her a pass? Even though she tried to kill both of us!"

Her eyes pooled. "I can't tell you what to do, but for me...for me...well, I just can't do anything else that will add to her misery. Think of what's she's been through. I don't believe she deliberately killed our father and she swore that she would never have done any of those awful things to me, to us, if she'd known who I was. She deserves some happiness in her life. If we send her to prison...if she doesn't have this surgery...she'll die. She'll find a way to..." She paused for a breath and swiped at the tears on her cheeks. "I know this is going to sound totally off the wall, but I've felt so alone all my life and now, for the first time...I have family, real flesh and blood family, don't you see?"

I guess I must have been shaking my head in wonder, because she pleaded, "Kendall, please. You've earned the right to print every word of this, but when you do, everyone on earth is going to know this dirty, sickening, terrible disgusting story and..." A strangled sob aborted the remainder of her sentence as she turned and bolted through the kitchen door.

I just stood there in the fading twilight feeling helpless. Crap. Double crap! And she didn't know yet what Dr. Orcutt had confided to me. The heavy feeling that had inhabited my stomach all day invaded my heart as I trudged back up the stairs to my room. What should I do?

Spike the story? After all the effort? After everything I'd been through? I knew what my father would do. He would say it was my duty as a journalist to report the story as it happened. But, how was I to balance the public's so-called right to know against my own troubled conscience?

Audrey didn't join me for Marta's baked enchilada dinner and afterwards when I went upstairs, I found her bedroom door closed and locked. When I knocked, she yelled, "I don't want to talk to you anymore." I knew her well enough to know that she was in one of her uncommunicative moods, so I decided to drive downtown to the Muleskinner and say goodbye to Whitey Flanigan. Inside, the usual collection of somber-faced patrons huddled around the bar and I nurtured the profound wish that Audrey's plans would come to fruition. Work was what these idle men needed to cure their hopeless hearts. As I shook hands with Whitey, it was hard to believe that so much had transpired in only one short week. I was half-amused and half-annoyed to hear the 'big' story circulating around town. Did I know that if it hadn't been for D.J.'s quick action Audrey Morgan would have drowned in the leach pond?

"We're sure gonna miss your purty face," Whitey said, flashing me a generous expanse of teeth and gums as I turned to wave a final farewell at the door. "You take care, Irish, and be sure to send along a couple of copies of your story. It might bring in a little business and put us on the map again," he added with a wink.

He had no idea. I gave him a thumbs up and drove slowly back to the house, unable to shake my glum mood. I'd no sooner stepped into the cinnamon roll-scented kitchen than the phone rang. "*Sí,* she is here," Marta said, motioning for me to come.

I pressed the receiver to my ear and when I heard Tally's mellifluous, "Hey, there, boss lady," I suddenly felt a whole lot better.

"Hey, yourself," I replied warmly. "Are you home?"

"Yep."

"And here I thought I'd get back before you. How'd everything go in Mexico? You get your stallion?"

"Uh huh. A few interesting things happened, but according to Tugg, my trip can't even begin to hold a candle to yours."

I bit my lip. Thank goodness I'd extracted Tugg's promise not to mention my close call or Tally would be having a major cow. At the moment, I wasn't up to enduring what was sure to be a lengthy I-told-you-so lecture on my mulish propensity to inject myself into life-threatening situations. Eventually, I'd tell him. Just not right this minute. Keeping a light tone, I said, "Well, it did turn out to be just a little more complicated than I originally thought."

"No kidding. I thought your last case was weird, but this one...well, where do you find these people, anyway?"

"They find me."

"Amazing. So, when are you coming back?"

"Tomorrow."

"Good." Tally wasn't one to waste words. "Mom and Ronda will be away. How about dinner at my place?"

The image of time alone with him sent a warm glow radiating though me. "Mmmm. Sounds wonderful."

"I'll have a fire burning for you," he drawled seductively. Smiling, I played along. "A fire? Don't you think it's a bit hot for that?"

"I wasn't talking about the weather."

I giggled and murmured, "Oh, you wicked man. I can hardly wait to see you."

"Ditto."

After hanging up, I eagerly accepted the fresh-from-the-oven cinnamon roll Marta offered me and then headed for bed. As tired as I was, sleep eluded me. After an aggravating hour spent replaying in my mind the events of the last week, I switched on the lamp and grabbed my notepad. Two hours later, I set it aside and fell into a deep dreamless sleep that lasted until I was awakened by loud purring and the feel of claws kneading my shoulder. I cracked open one eye, surprised to see it was after seven o'clock. I'd planned to be on the road by now. "Hey, girl, you should have wakened me sooner," I said with a yawn, scratching my furry alarm clock behind the ears. I'd never had one of my own before, but the idea of owning a friendly feline companion was suddenly very appealing to me.

I enjoyed every bite of Marta's sumptuous farewell breakfast and afterwards, watery-eyed and murmuring endearments in Spanish I didn't quite catch, she gave me a bear hug that squeezed the air from my lungs. Ignoring my protests, she then bestowed upon me a 'traveling lunch' big enough to feed a family of twelve. I was loading my luggage into the trunk when Audrey came running out the kitchen door wrapped in her fuzzy pink bathrobe.

"Were you going to leave without saying goodbye to me?" she demanded, looking tousled and cross.

"You said you didn't want to talk to me."

Her luminous eyes softened. "I didn't mean it, Kendall. I was...sort of upset."

"That's okay. You have every right."

"I did a lot of thinking last night and instead of being mad at you I owe you my thanks. You've been a true friend to me. If you hadn't urged me to stay I wouldn't have ever known what my mom was trying to tell me in the letter. I would never have realized how much she really loved me and I want you to know that, well...I guess it will be okay for you to print the story."

I stared at her in surprise. "Why the change of heart?"

She straightened her shoulders. "I don't know. As totally weird as this whole situation is, I realized something else really important."

"What's that?"

"I can't just run away from it. Somehow, I have to come to terms with what's happened and you know what else?"

"I'm listening."

"It might sound strange, but I don't feel like I'm drifting anymore." She paused, her gaze sweeping the valley and sharp blue sky. " For better or worse, I know who I am now. This is my home. I finally have some roots and I have someone here who needs all the help and care I can give."

Although I'd seen the barest hint of it last evening, her transformation amazed me. Three days seemed an awfully short amount of time for her to have adjusted to all that had transpired and all the problems still to come. The girl was definitely developing some guts after all. I smiled at her. "I think maybe you have someone here who needs your heart too."

She blushed a becoming pink. "You think so?"

My smile broadened. "Yeah, I think so."

We stood in silence for a moment and then I tapped my watch. "Well, I've got to hit the road."

"Are you sure you can't stay a few more days?"

"You don't need me now and besides, I've got someone waiting for me too."

She swallowed hard. "Can I hug you goodbye?"

I nodded and as her thin arms came around my waist, tears stung my eyes. So much for my objectivity, I thought ruefully, returning her hug.

After wishing her loads of good luck, I climbed into my car and headed for Boneyard Pass thinking how much easier it was to maneuver on the newly repaired road rather than the river of mud it had been on the way in.

When I reached the crest of the hill, I pulled over to the side and got out to shoot the pictures I hadn't been able to get last week in the driving rainstorm. With the wide-angle shots, I tried to capture the essence of this secluded town that time had forgotten, an enchanted hideaway that had captivated my heart and imagination forever. I zoomed in on the Morgan house snugly cradled beneath the craggy horns of Devil's Hill, using up the remainder of the film in my camera. Then, I pulled the two sheaves of paper from my purse.

The large bundle in my right hand contained the entire story replete with each salacious detail, the version that would expose the nightmare of Dayln Morgan for all the world to read, and in my left, I held the shorter, sanitized version I'd written last night. I stood there uncertain for a minute, savoring the lonesome whisper of the warm wind rustling through the mesquite. There were a hundred good reasons not to do this. I had Audrey's permission to run the piece and I felt in my gut, it was the best thing I'd ever written. My journalistic sensibilities screamed for me to be logical, but in the time of reckoning the decision wasn't really that difficult.

I shoved the short version into my purse and with great fanfare, tore the long one into a thousand pieces. The wind caught the scraps of yellow paper and scattered them into the air. They hung there for a few seconds as if to taunt me, then gently fluttered to the bottom of the ravine where they would repose in stately silence alongside the sun-bleached bones of the burros whose fate had bequeathed the name Boneyard Pass.

Feeling curiously at peace, I hopped in my car and headed home, leaving the secrets of Morgan's Folly safely tucked away among the amber hills now slumbering in the bright golden rays of the morning sun.

Sylvia Nobel currently resides in Phoenix, Arizona
with her husband and five cats.
She is a member of Mystery Writers of America and
producer of the feature film, *Deadly Sanctuary*.

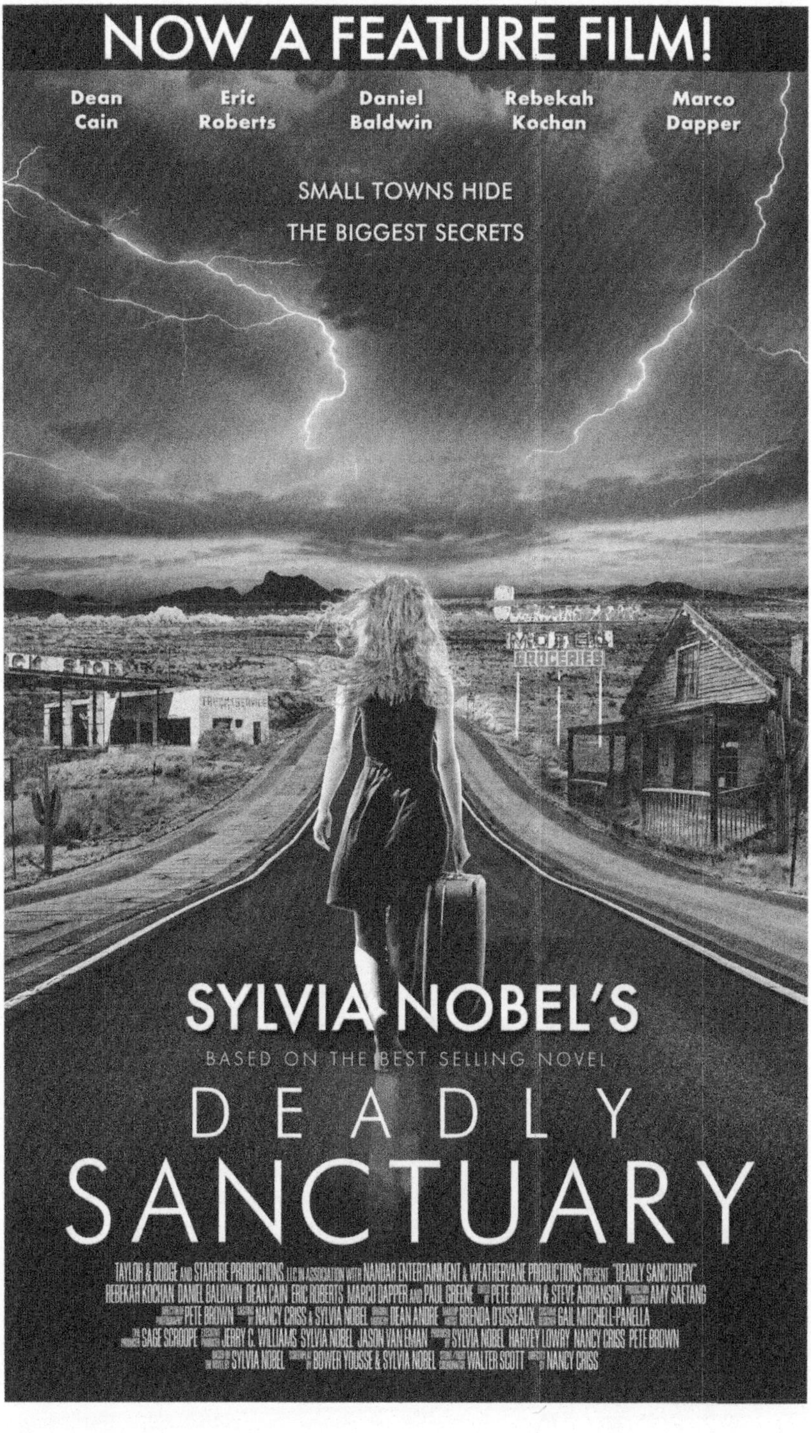
NOW A FEATURE FILM!
Dean Cain
Eric Roberts
Daniel Baldwin
Rebekah Kochan
Marco Dapper
SMALL TOWNS HIDE
THE BIGGEST SECRETS
MOTEL
GROCERIES
SYLVIA NOBEL'S
BASED ON THE BEST SELLING NOVEL
DEADLY
SANCTUARY
TAYLOR & DODGE AND STARFIRE PRODUCTIONS LLC IN ASSOCIATION WITH NANDAR ENTERTAINMENT & WEATHERVANE PRODUCTIONS PRESENT "DEADLY SANCTUARY"
REBEKAH KOCHAN DANIEL BALDWIN DEAN CAIN ERIC ROBERTS MARCO DAPPER AND PAUL GREENE PETE BROWN & STEVE ADRIANSON AMY SAETANG
PETE BROWN NANCY CRISS & SYLVIA NOBEL DEAN ANDRE BRENDA D'USSEAUX GAIL MITCHELL-PANELLA
SAGE SCROOPE JERRY C. WILLIAMS SYLVIA NOBEL JASON VAN EMAN SYLVIA NOBEL HARVEY LOWRY NANCY CRISS PETE BROWN
SYLVIA NOBEL BOWER YOUSSE & SYLVIA NOBEL WALTER SCOTT NANCY CRISS

Made in the USA
Coppell, TX
21 June 2023

18369733R00267